Praise for Ann Harleman's Work

HAPPINESS

"Vibrantly alive....Ann Harleman is a wonderful talent."

—Washington Post Book World

"Harleman's precise and evocative language can depict complex human relationships in a simple scene of chopping wood—or subtly illuminate the peril of romance." *—New York Times Book Review*

"A writer of astonishing clarity and depth. . . . The situations are so real that it sometimes seems as if Harleman has made us her characters. We are right there with them—in their kitchens, their bedrooms, their pasts."

—Boston Globe

"Harleman has a rich, melancholy voice . . . in stories that are poignant and assured." *—Publishers Weekly* (starred review)

BITTER LAKE

"The disappearance of Gort Hutchins, an ethereal presence on whom his family nonetheless pivots, sets off a chaotic search for the truth, not only of what happened to him but of why he holds an almost mystical grip on the hearts of those who love him. . . . Harleman trawls deep, treasure-filled waters in *Bitter Lake.*" *—Boston Globe*

"Thick with family secrets and sadnesses . . . verbal razzle-dazzle . . . mystery . . . Harleman is a dexterous writer."

—New York Times Book Review

"A masterful achievement. . . . Harleman gets it all right: dead-on dialogue, images so apt and original they make you stop and read them again, and suspense so gripping it propels you forward."

—Deborah Tannen, author of *You Just Don't Understand*

THOREAU'S LAUNDRY

"Stellar!"   —*O, The Oprah Magazine*

"Harleman is capable of startling a reader with a perfect descriptive touch. . . . But there's even more pleasure to be had in watching these characters stubbornly continue their march towards love."

—*New York Times Book Review*

"In unfailingly delicate prose, Harleman . . . shows us people confronting the wreckage of their lives—always with compassion on her part, and often with courage on theirs."   —*Boston Globe*

"Brainy, funny, soulful and original." —Meg Wolitzer, author of *The Wife*

THE YEAR SHE DISAPPEARED

"This sophisticated damsel-in-distress tale stars sexy 60-year-old widow Nan Mulholland . . . a perceptive, witty, and self-involved protagonist. Harleman's wry humor and vivid descriptions are in play throughout."

—*Publisher's Weekly*

"A contemporary suspense thriller, complete with kidnapping, chase scenes, changed identities, a high-profile court case, a jailbreak, and a love story. Yet there's nothing typical about any of these elements. . . . The novel's action moves between Nan's present and past, creating a rich portrait of a woman who jettisons her daughter's plan in favor of her own navigational instinct."   —*Boston Globe*

TELL ME, SIGNORA

TELL ME, SIGNORA

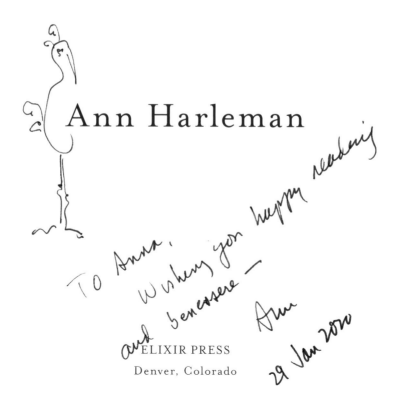

Ann Harleman

To Anna,
Wishing you happy reading—
and benessere—
Ann
29 Jan 2020

ELIXIR PRESS
Denver, Colorado

Book design by Steven Seighman
Cover art: AscentXmedia/iStockPhoto

Library of Congress Cataloging-in-Publication Data

Names: Harleman, Ann, 1945- author.
Title: Tell me, Signora : a novel / by Ann Harleman.
Description: Denver, Colorado : Elixir Press, 2020. | Summary: "Winner of the Elixir Press Fiction Award"-- Provided by publisher.
Identifiers: LCCN 2019025663 | ISBN 9781932418712 (paperback)
Classification: LCC PS3558.A624246 T45 2020 | DDC 813/.54--dc23
LC record available at https://lccn.loc.gov/2019025663

ISBN: 9781932418712

First edition: January 2020

10 9 8 7 6 5 4 3 2 1

For the dream-tenders:
Ethel Margulies
William Howe

Cuore d'altri non e` simile al tuo
The heart of others is not like yours

—Eugenio Montale

Acknowledgments

My heartfelt thanks to Frank Bezner, Mariangela Bruno, Ivana Folle, Laura Giorgi, John Harbison, Nithiphat Hoisangthong, William Howe, Gary Kennedy, Ira Lapidus, Ethel Margulies, Susan Mates, MD, Deborah Michel, Sally Mosher, Joseph Pucci, Virginia Renner, Marina Romani, the late Bruce Rosenberg, Catherine Sama, and the late Janet Hagan Yanos. I owe more than I can say to the members of the deep-hearted Oakland Writers Group (Joanna Biggar, Antoinette Constable, Skot Davis, Grace Feuerverger, Barbara Milman, Claudia Monpere, JoAnne Tobias, and Molly Walker).

Special thanks to Tracy Guzeman, Gail Hochman, Kayla Ponturo, Benjamin Porter, and my beloved Girl Group: Gail Donovan and Elizabeth Searle.

For their generous support, I thank the Rhode Island State Council on the Arts, the Rhode Island School of Design, the American Academy in Rome, Civitella Ranieri, the Bogliasco Foundation, the Rockefeller Foundation, and the Rona Jaffe Foundation.

Parts of this novel have appeared, in a somewhat different form, in *Shenandoah, Southwest Review, Alaska Quarterly Review, Greensboro Review, AARP Magazine, The Georgia Review,* and *O. Henry Prize Stories 2003.*

Readers familiar with the city of Genoa and the life of Sofonisba Anguissola will note that I've taken a few liberties with time and place in order to better serve the story. There is a floor of reality under this book's events and its characters; however, I believe that, as Adam Gopnik puts it, "fiction departs from the truth to intensify it."

Among the many research sources that helped me in the creation of this novel, I am most indebted to Daniela Pizzagalli's *La Signora della Pittura: Vita di Sofonisba Anguissola*, Ilya Sandra Perlingieri's *Sofonisba Anguissola*, Sylvia Ferino-Pagden and Maria Kusche's *Sofonisba Anguissola*, Margaret Barlow's *Women Artists*, Mary D. Garrard's "Here's Looking at Me: Sofonisba Anguissola and the Problem of the Woman Artist," Mina Gregori's *Sofonisba Anguissola e le sue sorelle*, Sally Mosher's *People and Their Contexts: A Chronology of the Sixteenth-Century World*, Kenneth Bartlett's "The Italian Renaissance" (DVD), Virginia Cox's translation of Moderata Fonte's *La valore delle donne*, Wolfram zu Mondfeld's *Historic Ship Models*, Ralph Heymsfeld's "Life at Sea in the Time of Magellan," Larry Larson's "Renaissance Oil Painting Techniques" (DVD), Sr. Lucia Wiley's "The Art of Fresco," William Weaver's "Genoa's Neighborhoods and Palaces," Amanda Adams's *Ladies of the Field*, Bill McMillon's *The Archaeology Handbook*, Jane McIntosh's *Archaeology*, Marilyn Johnson's *Lives in Ruins*, Michael Pollan's "The Intelligent Plant," Beth Kampschror's "Ghosts of Kosovo," Mauro Rizzetto's "Nationalism, Archaeology, and Yugoslavia," the diary of Albana Berisha (online), the Human Rights Watch website, Jillian M. Weise's "Rape as a Strategy of War," Nicholas Schmidle's "Bring Up the Bodies," Enrica Capussotti and Liliana Ellena's "The Way of Oblivion: Refugees in Italy."

The sculpture installation described in Chapter Ten is based on the 2007 art exhibition "Non-Self," by Nithiphat Hoisangthong. This exhibition, at the Rocca di Umbertide Centro par l'Arte Contemporanea in Umbertide, Italy, was sponsored by Civitella Ranieri Center.

SEPTEMBER

Che cosa desidera?

1

Hungry, sleep-deprived, and full of doubt, I tried to let the sparkling sound of Italian buoy me up. Around me other travelers in the Lost Luggage line were chattering and cheerful. I reminded myself how many times the airlines had lost my bags, how they'd always turned up eventually. But on those other trips—all to Tito's Yugoslavia—I'd stood in line with Daniel. Had yawned, ridiculed, complained, cried (once), with Daniel.

Nineteen hours now since I'd closed the door behind me in Providence. Five days past September 11th, Boston's Logan Airport had felt like Belgrade Airport in the '70s. Travelers corralled into a line under the gaze of guards and German shepherds; the terminal, beyond the spotlights beaming down on us, a moat of darkness. Looking up when my passport was demanded, I'd half-expected to see a portrait of Tito on the wall behind the Sabena agent.

Genoa's Cristoforo Colombo Airport—early morning sun streaming through skylights, people juggling coffee and snacks, children running back and forth—was nothing like Logan. I straightened my shoulders and took a deep breath of Italy: espresso and freesias and tobacco and stone dust and—

"Sabena!" said a male voice, behind me. "Stands for Such A Bad Experience—Never Again."

Turning, I saw first the beard—full, curly, graying—then the bearer of it. Tall and a bit heavy, he wore rimless glasses behind which his eyes shone with humor. "You were on the flight out of Boston," he said. "Brave soul." I caught an undertow of Irish in his voice.

His smile was so sympathetic that I found myself saying, "All my stuff is in my luggage. Not just my clothes. My research materials."

"Sure it's only things. Don't they say we're better off in life without baggage?"

My baggage, *c'est moi*, I thought. But I was too tired to argue.

As if he saw this, the man said, "Will I get us each a cappuccino, then?"

He brought back two cups and I drank gratefully, the cinnamon tingling on my tongue. Slowly the line moved forward. A beeping jeep full of elderly passengers cut in front of us, and my companion put a hand under my elbow to steady me. I was aware of something in his stance—a spark. Interest. When he looked at me over the rim of his cup, I felt an answering spark somewhere inside—faint, but there. The very thing I'd made up my mind to avoid.

"Gene O'Casey," he said. He held out his hand, and I shook it. "What brings you to Genoa?" he asked.

"Kate Hagesfeld. I'm—a researcher." If you say "archaeologist" out loud in airports or at border crossings, you're likely to get pulled over and searched.

"Roman history, would it be, then? Or Etruscan?"

"Grave markers, actually," I said. "Tombstone inscriptions. I'm an epigrapher."

"A pig-groper, did you say?" He grinned. "Sure we must have 'em in the old country, though I've not known one personally."

When I didn't laugh—I get a lot of jokes about epigraphy—he looked abashed. "Sorry. My old ma always said, Never tease a stranger."

"It's okay," I said.

Fishing in the pockets of his bomber jacket, he came up with a bright yellow business card and handed it to me. "I build airports."

In my exhausted state, *his* occupation struck *me* as funny. I laughed.

Gene O'Casey smiled. "Fair play. Listen, I'll be back and forth between Boston and Genoa all this autumn. Giving Cristoforo Colombo Airport a facelift. Could we ever meet for a drink or—"

"I don't think so," I said. "I've got barely three months here, and a lot to do."

He stepped back, his smile diminishing. A shaft of sun from the skylight above us turned his glasses into ovals of shine.

I felt ashamed. He'd done nothing to deserve my snub. I put out my hand, about to say, *Wait, I didn't mean—* But a voice shouted "*Prego, Signora! A Lei!*" I moved up to the counter. A sleek young man offered the usual card with photographs of a dozen suitcases. I chose two and gave him the address of the Centro Studi Internazionali in Soccorso, a village just outside the city. When I turned around, the Builder of Airports had disappeared.

At Customs there was an argument going on between a blue-uniformed official and a weary-looking woman with two small boys in tow. "*Zingari!*" I heard someone shout. But these people didn't look like gypsies. The smaller boy broke free of his mother and toddled towards me. Without thinking, I held out my arms. His face broke into a grin, and I felt the impact of his small, warm body. Blue Uniform grabbed him and pulled him out of my arms. "*Clandestini,*" he said to me over his shoulder, with a frown of pain as the child kicked him. Then, at my puzzled look, "*Profughi. Illegali!*" Illegal refugees. The woman and her children were hustled through an unmarked door in the far wall. I stood looking after them, glimpsing a world of misery far darker than my own.

"*Signora!*" A customs official beckoned me over to her counter. I breezed through with, of course, nothing to declare.

Beyond the barrier a woman in an orange coat held up a placard that said, "SIGNORA ROSEN." I stood hesitating under the exit sign. In my jet-lagged state, the substitution of Daniel's surname for mine shook me more than it should have. It seemed like an omen. A warning that what I'd come to Italy to do would be hard, maybe impossible. That I would never escape the shadow of the past twenty years.

———

Anna Maria, the woman with the placard, turned out to be the Centro's onsite director. She led me outside to a black Fiat driven by a small man with very large ears, whom she introduced as Massimo the Gardener. After a heart-stopping half-hour coursing up and down steep streets with blurred green hills beyond, we drew up with a flourish of gravel in a colonnaded courtyard. A loggia ran the length of it on either side; at the end stood a two-story edifice of pale stone. "The Centro's main building, the Villa Baiardo," Anna Maria said. "Seventeenth-century." She'd been brusque from the moment I shook her outstretched hand. I didn't understand why. I'd said nothing offensive, just corrected the error of my name.

Instead of going into the Villa Baiardo we went out through massive iron gates, crossed a narrow highway, and walked up a steep path bordered by shrubs and pines. We passed a structure with windows missing, door boarded up, masonry pitted and crumbling. "The Villa Francesca," Anna Maria threw over her shoulder. "Sixteenth-century. Built by Pope Julius III for his mistress." Keys the size of pocket wrenches unlocked a gate in the wall around it. Entering, we stood just above the back half of the building. This part had been restored, its stuccoed walls gleaming in the morning sun. We crossed a lawn to a set of glass doors.

Inside, Anna Maria strode ahead of me folding back tall clattering shutters, and light poured in through floor-to-ceiling windows. I trailed her through a living room, a kitchenette, a small study, a bedroom with a big brocade-covered bed.

Too much space for one person. Too much *bed* for one person.

"You will have now a small sleep," Anna Maria said. "I will telephone to the airport concerning your luggage and that of Signor Vipavakit. Yours is not the only runaway. Dinner occurs in the loggia, *aperitivi* at seven. You will meet there the other Fellows."

In the doorway she paused, unsmiling. "Welcome to the Centro Studi Internazionali, Signora." She turned and left, the French doors standing open behind her.

———

The clock beside the phone on the bedside table said 10: 30. Four-thirty in the morning in Providence—too early to call Rachel and let her know I'd arrived safely.

I was hungry. The kitchenette's stone floor was cool beneath my bare feet; its cupboards were empty. In the living room I went out through the French doors onto the lawn. A bird made a sound like rainsticks from a large, ancient-looking tree in the center. I went and stood under its branches. A fig dropped at my feet. It was sweet as cream and the seeds crunched satisfyingly between my teeth. I pulled down a branch and picked two more. Breakfast on the plane had been Spartan. I went back inside and lay down on the too-big bed and set my internal alarm, honed during years of hospital vigils.

I woke at sunset in a state that Rachel, back when things were easy between us, would have called sleep-depraved. I dialed her number. A series of trills deposited me on voicemail, as happened so often these days. I left the news of my arrival and the number of the bedside phone, and my love. It did no good to push my daughter; in that, as in so many things, she took after her father.

Through the open window the tolling of church bells mingled with the stuttering of motorbikes. I got up and looked out. The other side of the path was lined with umbrella pines; their pompoms caught the last of the light.

What's your plan? a voice demanded from among their branches.

A part of me had moved out and up when Daniel died. It seemed to regard me from a corner of the ceiling, to hover and advise. I christened it Ceiling-Katherine. *It's all right. You'll be okay*, Ceiling-Katherine said as I moved through the first painful weeks. In the year since, the voice had gone from sympathetic to bracing to testy.

My plan? To go down to the Villa Baiardo and face dinner with people I didn't know, dressed in what Rachel called my "wren wear"—jeans and beige cotton sweater—and none too clean. In the bathroom I splashed water on my face, smoothed my wildly curling hair. The woman in the mirror wore a bruised look. I rummaged in my purse for a lipstick. How could I have forgotten to bring a carry-on? I would've had toiletries and extra clothing and at least some of my research materials. But Daniel had always been the one to do that. Daniel, who loved travel for the same reason I found it hard. When you're on the move, he used to say, anything can happen. There are surprises. Coincidence can find you.

Ceiling-Katherine admonished me from the top of the shower stall, *If you can't be happy, you can at least be brave.*

When I tried to open the villa gate, it gave me an argument. I had a moment of panic: as terrifying to be locked in as to be locked out. Then the lock yielded. I walked downhill and crossed the highway, narrowly missed by a motorbike whose rider turned to shout, "*Cretina*!" I straightened up and threw back my shoulders. This trip was supposed to be the start of my new life.

"—so finally the bartender says, 'You think I asked for a ten-inch *pianist*?'"

The woman to my right shook back hair the length and color of my own and shot me an unamused look that said: *Men*. But up and down the long table laughter rose into the dusk. The joke was a welcome attempt to divert the conversation from 9/11. Outrage and grief and fear had dominated the cocktail hour, followed by gloomy silence as the Fellows took their places at the table in the courtyard. The Centro's brochure, which I'd pored over before I left, said, *Fellows are expected to gather each evening for* aperitivi *followed by dinner, served until the end of September in the pleasant courtyard of the Centro's main building.* Above our heads the sky held onto its last luminous blue. A fountain in the center of the courtyard—Neptune, who else?, with attendant nymphs—made a heartening sound.

I took a sip of my wine. I wasn't used to drinking—Daniel couldn't, so I didn't—and it seemed to motor through my veins. The woman to my right passed me a tray of antipasti. "Laura Sweeney from Connecticut I'm a poet," she said, all in one breath, although we'd already been introduced over *aperitivi*. Young, maybe thirty or so. She could be me, I thought, twenty years ago.

Across the table her husband leaned back, a man whose wife no longer laughed at his jokes. An afro shadowed his brow, and his skin shone almost purple in the candlelight. Hollis—that was his name. By one of Daniel's beloved coincidences, I knew him. We'd met six or seven years ago when he'd come to give a reading at Brown. I remembered none of his poetry, but I remembered his kindness. At the reception after the reading, Daniel tottered and nearly fell. Hollis had caught him discreetly, so that no one noticed. "Good save!" Daniel had murmured.

I looked up and down the table, studying the other inhabitants of the sheltered world where I would spend the next three months. Their faces were dignified by candlelight. Their clothes (*Fellows are expected to dress for dinner, men in jackets and ties, women in dresses, either long or street-length*) ranged from stately—one man wore a heavy-looking black overcoat with curly lamb lapels—to operatic. And here I was, in my airplane-smelling jeans, already not fitting in. I pushed up the sleeves of my sweater and drained my wineglass. Spaghetti with mushrooms and gorgonzola arrived. Conversation—English (the Centro's official *lingua franca*) in various accents, plus shards of Italian, French, even Russian—swirled around me while I ate and drank. Why hadn't I realized how awkward I'd feel in a group of multilingual strangers? I counted ten people, including me and Anna Maria. *Five distinguished scholars, writers, and artists from every part of the globe,* which meant four of the others must be *spouse equivalents.* Despite earlier introductions, in my jetlagged state I'd already forgotten everyone's names.

The man to my left (composer, New York) asked whether any vampire burials had been discovered in Daniel's dig at Vlashnje. He had the sonorous voice of a preacher and heavy reddish-brown eyebrows that met when he frowned, like caterpillars kissing. Beyond him, a severe-faced man (Slavicist, Edinburgh) leaned forward to hear. People always want to know about vampire burials. A young man across the table (sculptor, Bangkok), whose abundant black hair seemed to burst out of his head like the top of some underground vegetable, wondered what kind of pottery had been found at Vlashnje. He must be my fellow luggageless person, I realized. At the foot of the table a petite silver-haired woman kept her eyes on me, listening avidly. The interest in Daniel was natural: his book, *The Past as Prize: Nationalism and Archaeology*—written in the years when he could no longer travel—was a classic. But I was taken aback that everyone here already seemed to know I was his widow.

The only person who asked about my own work was Laura Sweeney. My research, I told her—without mentioning the fact that I'd put it aside for twenty years—involved grave markers. "My project here at the Centro is—"

"Are women's tombstones different from men's? I mean, historically?"

I told her how, on the grave markers of Englishwomen whose husbands had died before them, in the sixteenth and seventeenth centuries, they put, not *Wife* of So-and-So, not *Widow*, but *Relict. Here lies Abigail Chase, Relict of Samuel.*

"Relict?" Laura said.

"It's Latin. It means 'remainder.' But the painter I'm researching here—"

"That's always the way," Laura said.

"—Sofonisba Anguissola, her grave marker is unusual for the seventeenth—"

"Women as possessions," Laura said. "Chattel." Then, "I so admire you for not dressing up for dinner as ordered. It's a great feminist statement."

A little girl appeared suddenly between us, twisting one leg around the other. "Hi," I said. The child looked up at me from under a mass of fine black crinkly hair. Her eyes, an unusual shade of reddish-brown, shone in the candlelight like new pennies.

"Amber!" Laura said. "What're you doing out of bed? Where's Lucia?" Tossing her napkin onto her plate, she got up. "Excuse me," she said to me. "The babysitter seems to have disappeared." She took the little girl's hand and they set off across the lawn and vanished into the loggia.

Across the table Hollis Carmichael watched them go. His eyes fell on me. "Hey," he said, cutting through the monologue of a ferretlike woman (semiotics, Paris) in a red satin jacket. "I remember you." And why not? I thought. It isn't every day someone's two-hundred-pound husband falls on you. We talked about Hollis's visit to Providence, about how my corrupt, crime-ridden city appeared in the poems in his new book. Lines of concern striped his forehead, like the striations on a clamshell. By the time the next course arrived—plump pink scampi on a bed of beans, accompanied by yet another wine—I felt almost at ease.

The petite silver-haired woman at the foot of the table—the one who'd been studying me earlier—came and sat down in Laura's empty chair. "*Buonasera*, Signora Hagesfeld." She had a husky smoker's voice. The candlelight gave her a wise, whiskery look, like a catfish.

"*Buonasera*, Signora…uh," I said, feeling my face grow hot with embarrassment.

But Signora Catfish didn't seem to notice I'd forgotten her name. "I am a psychoanalyst," she announced. Her smile revealed a gold tooth where one of her bicuspids should have been. "What you Americans delight to call a shrink. And you are an archaeologist, Signora Hagesfeld, *vero?*"

I said yes; and we began to talk. Signora Catfish looked to be a generation older than me, in her late sixties. While I told her about my project she leaned toward me, head cocked, intent. The greatest desire of the human heart, my grandmother used to say, is to be heard. The quality of this woman's listening restored me to myself.

Full dark now. A waiter set glasses of dessert wine at everyone's place. Signora Catfish lifted Laura's glass, sniffed, and nodded. "Try!" she urged me. "This will please our fellow passengers. Even the Frenchwoman."

My head already felt dangerously light. I set the glass aside. "Passengers?"

"Do you not think these places"—Signora Catfish's gesture embraced the courtyard, the torches lining the loggia, the star-pocked sky—"are like a long cruise to nowhere? These, what you Americans call, thought tanks."

"Think tanks."

The correction, though automatic, was rude. But Signora Catfish didn't seem to mind. "Or perhaps a long overland journey on foot," she continued, "a pilgrimage, like that of your Chaucer. You know Chaucer, of course?"

I nodded, feeling like a fraud. My high school encounter with the *Canterbury Tales*, having taken place thirty-three years ago, was a blur.

Signora Catfish beamed. "Experience, though noon auctoritee/Were in this world, is right ynogh for me." Mercifully, she decided to translate. "Never mind the authorities. Experience is good enough for me. The Wife of Bath. When I am despaired and nothing works, she comforts me. As you remember, she goes on pilgrimage in memory of her fifth husband. But she is—how do you say?—a cheery widow."

"A merry widow."

"*Esatto*! Why not voyage piously, rather than sit at home and sorrow. And where better to find a sixth husband?"

I laughed.

Signora Catfish said, "Every trip has a secret destination—one the traveler does not know."

After dinner the other Fellows—except for Signora Catfish, who'd disappeared—straggled up the grand staircase to their rooms on the second floor. The Slavicist from Edinburgh offered, in a plummy Sean Connery accent, to escort me back to the Pope's mistress's villa. I declined. This trip was my chance to become self-sufficient, the cat that walks by itself, and what better time to start than now.

But trudging uphill through the fragrant darkness, I wondered whether the others at the Centro saw me as an object of pity rather than a fellow Fellow. Anna Maria had given me a flashlight. Signora Catfish had offered to take me shopping for clothes in Genoa. Laura had returned after dessert to press on me a thick wool cardigan and one of the books she and Hollis had brought from the States. Under my arm I carried Amber's second-best stuffed animal, a green velvet elephant with worn ears. Amber had insisted that "the sad lady needs him." When I reached the Villa Francesca's gate, the heavy keys rang in my hand.

Waking, I grabbed for the phone. My first thought was, *Rachel*. My cell phone wouldn't make transatlantic calls—too expensive—so this was the only number where Rae could reach me. But when I held the receiver to my ear, there was no one.

How many times, in the last year of Daniel's life, had this happened? The certainty that the phone had rung—its clear, peremptory echo in my ear. But there'd be only a dial tone; and when I called the hospital, the night nurse would assure me that, no, nothing had happened, Daniel was sleeping soundly. Report from Planet Morphia, my best friend Janet, who is a doctor, called this. The ringing continued after Daniel died. Finally Janet had persuaded me to see her colleague, a young Israeli neuropsychiatrist who'd explained, with diagrams, about auditory hallucinations and stress. The imaginary phone ringing, she'd said, was a manifestation of PTSD.

From a dark corner of the bedroom, Ceiling-Katherine said, *You're fine! Go back to sleep.*

Sitting up in bed under all the blankets the Pope's mistress's villa had to offer, I pulled Laura's sweater around me. Here in Liguria the autumn night entered one's bones, Anna Maria had warned us at dinner, and Italian law forbade the use of central heating until November. I switched on the lamp (*Fellows will be expected to read in bed on a nightly basis?*) and reached for the book Laura had given me. To my pleased surprise, it turned out to be the poetry of e. e. cummings. I'd been expecting Sylvia Plath. Hollis's name was scribbled on the flyleaf. I settled back into the pillows with Amber's velvet elephant in the crook of my arm. As I read, my eyelids kept sinking. Then came these lines:

> *your homecoming will be my homecoming—*
> *my selves go with you, only I remain;*
> *a shadow phantom effigy or seeming*

And there was Daniel, not-quite-visible beyond the lamplight, a shadow among shadows. I thought of bedtime in the last few years. Hoisting Daniel up and coaxing his limbs together; the weight of him thudding onto my shoulders and traveling down my spine; the separate sigh from each of us when at last he lay, more or less straight, in the bed. I couldn't stretch out alongside him and hold him, because of all the tubes. The

PICC line in his inner arm; the feeding tube in his belly, the permanent catheter in his groin—

Riffling through the book on my lap, hoping for distraction, I read:

Always the beautiful answer
who asks a more beautiful question

The questions at dinner had made me wonder whether I'd gotten this fellowship on the merits of my research proposal, or because I was Daniel's relict. (Was *that* why Anna Maria seemed to resent me?) I'd been surprised but thrilled to get it. The fall semester in Italy with a stipend twice my teaching salary, which—because Daniel's illness made him ineligible for life insurance—I sorely needed. And besides that, my dean at the Rhode Island School of Design had promised me a fulltime position if publishable results came from my research.

But most of all there was Rachel. At twenty-four my intrepid daughter had already logged two years as a fulltime community organizer. I'd often wondered if her activism had developed in response to her father's illness. I knew she thought I'd been overprotective, discouraging her from taking risks, taking none of my own. "You keep us sealed up in our own little world," she'd shouted at me when I wouldn't let her go alone, at fourteen, to Washington for the March for Women's Lives. "We all have to live inside this—this black balloon!" When I'd told her about the Centro fellowship her eyes had lit with new respect. I wanted that respect more than I'd wanted anything since Daniel died.

So, I thought, the Centro had accepted me because I was Daniel's widow? I'd show them I was more than that. Show Rachel—show *myself*—I was more than that. My research materials might be AWOL, but Sofonisba's grave marker was here in Genoa.

"*Domani*," I said out loud to the empty room, and reached up to snap off the light.

2

I pushed through a clot of flower-sellers at the gates to the Cimitero Staglieno. Sofonisba's grave marker was somewhere in this cemetery, set in the floor of a small chapel. She wasn't buried under it; the stone was moved here in the late eighteenth century, when Genoa decided to claim her for its own. Because Staglieno had over 117,000 grave sites, I'd been counting on the visitors' information bureau. It was closed.

Uninformed, I set out into into what looked like a vast sculpture garden. Angels, saints, Virgin Mary's, of course; but also many nearly naked bodies, some voluptuously swooning. Graveyards were one place where I felt at home. Yet here the sense of flesh was so vivid I almost forgot I was in one. I wandered up and down steps and along gravel paths beneath cedars and pines, looking for something that might be a chapel. Each time I thought I'd spotted one, it turned out to be some illustrious family's mauseoleum. Half an hour brought me to the ordinary part of the cemetery, beyond the monuments. Here grass sprouted up through the gravel, and the headstones were grimy and moss-embroidered. Now and then a cat reclining on top of one eyed me with its opaque gaze. Stopping to rest, I watched an old woman in a black headscarf kneel in front of a small stone to lay flowers and light a candle. Like many Italian grave markers, this one held a smiling photograph of the dead person, as if to say, *We choose to remember him happy.*

If only it were that easy.

Sun warmed the top of my head. It could have been a touch—Daniel's touch. It had taken years, back then, to diagnose multiple sclerosis. When the neurologist told us, Daniel had grabbed my hand and squeezed. It felt as if he'd seized my heart. We went home and made love in the middle of the living room in the middle of the afternoon. Afterwards, drops of water sparkled in the hairs on Daniel's chest; till then I hadn't known I was crying. He'd kissed my runny nose and said, with his usual optimism, "We won't let this change our lives."

Here it came. At the very center of me, an incandescent ache, as if my ribs had gone radioactive. If I let it unfold—if I let it yawn and stretch and wake u*p*—

No time for this! Ceiling-Katherine said. *Let's mosey.*

I got to my feet. The woman at the grave crossed herself and rose. I walked over to her. "*Mi dispiace, Signora*," I said. "Can you tell me where the chapel is?" She looked puzzled for a moment, then said, "*Ah—il pan-theon*," and gave me directions back to the center of the cemetery.

The Pantheon was a copy of the one in Rome, circular, with a dome and a Doric portico. Inside, I walked around slowly, scanning the floor. None of the stones was Sofonisba's. Frustrated, tired, and suddenly hungry, I began walking back toward the cemetery entrance. To my right was an overgrown area with a weeping birch in the center. I went over to look. Hidden among tall grass and brambles were a dozen or so flat grave markers—stones set flush with the ground instead of the usual uprights.

I found what I was looking for under the weeping birch. A marble rectangle about four feet by eight feet, with a border of black and red inlay. Scrollwork like ocean waves surrounded a coat of arms and an inscription.

SOPHONISBAE UXORI AB ANGUISSOLAE COMITIBUS DUCENTI
ORIGINEM, PARENTUM NOBILITATE, FORMA EXTRAORDINARIISQUE
NATURAE DOTIBUS IN ILLUSTRES MUNDI MULIERES RELATAE
AC IN EXPRIMENDIS HOMINUM IMAGINIBUS ADEO INSIGNI
UT PAREM AETATIS SUAE NEMINEM HABUISSE SIT AESTIMATA

HORATIUS LOMELLINUS INGENTI AFFECTUS MAERORE DECUS HOC
EXTREMUM ET SI TANTAE MULIERI EXIGUUM MORTALIBUS VERO
MAXIMUM DICAVIT 1632

Like most epigraphers, I studied Latin, the language which epigraphy—a discipline developed in the sixteenth century—cut its teeth on. I translated:

TO HIS WIFE SOFONISBA, OF THE ARISTOCRATIC HOUSE
OF ANGUISSOLA, WHOSE NOBLE LINEAGE, BEAUTY, AND
EXTRAORDINARY NATURAL GIFTS PLACE HER AMONG THE
WORLD'S ILLUSTRIOUS WOMEN, SO FAMOUS FOR PORTRAYING
THE HUMAN IMAGE AS TO BE CONSIDERED PEERLESS AMONG HER
CONTEMPORARIES, HER HUSBAND, OUT OF HIS IMMENSE GRIEF,
HAS DEDICATED THIS LAST MEMORIAL—A TRIFLE FOR SUCH A
WOMAN, BUT THE MOST THE LIVING CAN OFFER

On the hundredth anniversary of Sofonisba's birth, her second husband had had this stone made. Its epitaph, Rae would've said, was dope. I'd loved it from the moment—twenty-five years ago, in a second-year graduate seminar—I first read it. It was so unlike the grave markers of most women. Far from identifying Sofonisba as Orazio Lomellini's spouse, it identified *him* as hers. Her offspring—she died childless—were her paintings.

Being in the presence of the stone was light years away from reading its inscription in a book. I was shaking. I had to sit down in the grass. By now it was mid-afternoon—the *Pausa*, when most people were at their long midday meal—and this part of the cemetery was deserted. I sat with my arms around my knees, the branches of the weeping birch enclosing me and Sofonisba's grave marker in a green world of our own. I didn't understand my reaction. Weirdly, I felt the same premonitory buzz I'd felt just before my first find.

It was on my long-awaited European field placement: the dig at Vlashnje, in southeastern Yugoslavia. Daniel and I had just met, a respected professor of archaeology and a third-year grad student. One foggy morning, after a routine couple of hours excavating yet another neat square hole, my trowel clinked against something. Junior staff were supposed to turn over to a senior member the task of freeing any possible find. But Daniel was the site director, and he was already smitten. He handed me a sable paintbrush and watched me whisk soil away from the rough surface of the ceramic. He was checking, I knew, to make sure the edges of the vessel were dirty. Clean edges would have meant a fresh break, caused by my tools. My breath beat against the bandanna tied over my mouth and nose to keep out dust. Turning the shard over, I saw the maker's thumbprint. I put my own thumb into the faint depression. A shiver struck the nape of my neck and fled down my spine. A millennium later, there it still was: *I made this—I.*

I'd planned to take photographs; but my camera was, of course, in my luggage. Just as well. You only really *see* an object when you draw it, my favorite archaeology professor used to say. Before I caught the bus to the Cimitero Staglieno I'd bought pencils and a drawing pad at a stationer's in the village. The young man waiting on me added a slender cardboard box of oil pastels. He couldn't be persuaded to take them back, so I'd bought them, too. Sitting in the grass, I made a detailed pencil sketch of Sofonisba's grave marker.

Workmanlike, the way I'd been taught to do field drawings, my sketch didn't capture the *feeling* of the object. The nearly speaking stone; the sun-pierced shelter of the birch fronds. Something more was needed. I slid the lid off the tray of pastels. I picked up the apple-green stick and began to draw.

Today she must transfer Margherita, the little housemaid, onto the canvas she stretched and gessoed yesterday. She chooses the best of a dozen red chalk sketch-es. Rolling up the sleeves of her camicia, *she takes a pin and begins to pierce the drawing along all its lines. Wide-set eyes and long neck and sloping shoulders give Margherita the look of a young lamb. This painting will fill the month of Fabrizio's absence, rather than yet another self-portrait—traditional resort of a painter between commissions—in her usual plain male-emulating black, with her usual direct male-emulating gaze. Before his ship set sail for Spain Fabrizio suggested* a cagnolino, *a miniature greyhound or a spaniel, to keep her company. Painting is company, she told him. Not one nobleman—not one man—in a thousand would have understood this. Fabrizio did.*

Done pricking, she fastens the drawing to the canvas with a drop of hot wax at each corner, and props the canvas on her easel. She dips a rag in ground charcoal and begins to tap along the drawing's pin-prick contours. Oh, she thinks—dipping and pressing—I am lucky. I didn't choose my husband; what woman does? But he is an ideal husband in all respects save one. And that one—being a virgin still, in my fifth decade—I know nothing about. Therefore, yearning is foolish.

When the last tiny hole has been blackened, she pulls the paper away from the canvas. And there is the lamblike little maid. Or at least, her char-coal ghost. Will she be able to capture, as Michelangelo taught her, i moti dell'anima—*the movements of the soul? There's plenty of uncertainty ahead. But right now she allows herself to feel complete, the blankness of the canvas vanquished. She arches her back and takes several deep breaths, savoring the mingled smells of linseed oil and mineral pigments and chalk dust.*

My lady! Prego!

Margherita herself stands in the doorway, her face in shadow. Her large hands twist the cloth of her apron.

What is it, Margsherita? Has my pupil come already?

But she knows, before she finishes the question, that it's something else entirely. Something she has feared every day of her marriage.

"Kate!" Laura said. "I was just wishing for some company." She folded her newspaper. "They keep finding more victims. The death toll—"

The café across the road from the cemetery entrance was empty except for the two of us. I slung my bag of sketching materials over the back of a chair and sat down. My head felt cloudy, as if I were coming out of anesthesia. I must have looked more than a little unstrung, but Laura didn't ask why. I liked that.

A photo of the Twin Towers dissolving into a black cloud lay on the table between us. "It's terrible," I said, inadequately. "Did you know anyone?"

Laura shook her head.

"Me, neither," I said.

We shared a moment of silent gratitude.

"Been shopping?" Laura eyed my bag, glad to change the subject. "Isn't this city wild?"

"I did my shopping in the village, then took a bus straight here. It looped around the outskirts of the city. So I haven't really seen it."

"Wait till you do! Genoa's the oldest town center in Europe, unchanged since the year 1000. It's a warren of alleys and tunnels and staircases. You get lost in a heartbeat." She gestured down at her place, which held a snifter with a golden puddle in the bottom. "Want some? You look sort of wan."

Brandy? It was three in the afternoon. I started to shake my head, when Laura added, "I'm going to have an espresso and a *panino*. Can I get you anything?" Cooking smells filled the air: garlic; hot olive oil; something delicious I couldn't identify. Hunger yawned and stretched itself.

I nodded. "The same, please."

While Laura was at the counter I picked up her newspaper. The *Corriere della Sera*, bless her hardworking heart. The front page was divided between the antics of Berlusconi and the aftermath of 9/11—comedy and tragedy side by side. I struggled through a piece about the Victim Compensation Fund. How removed I felt, in this calm and beautiful place, from the terrible grief of my own country.

Laura came back, juggling two espressos and a plate of sandwiches. My fingers curled around my cup, its warmth a comfort.

The first sip felt like a jolt of electricity. "What's *in* this?" I said.

"They call it a *corretto*. The *grappa* corrects the espresso."

I laughed out loud. Laura leaned back in her chair, looking pleased.

While the alcohol detonated softly in my stomach, I tore into a sandwich. I hadn't eaten since breakfast. "Why do ordinary things—cheese, tomato, bread—taste so much better in Italy?"

"Everything is better in Italy," Laura said. "*E` cosi`*." That's just how it is. "Hey, I saw you back there, drawing. Great place, isn't it? I got a poem out of it today. The mausoleums made me think of Horn & Hardart's Automat— you know, all those rows of little glass doors with food behind them?"

For a second I wanted to say, *I just had the strangest experience myself.* But I didn't know this woman well enough. Possibly I didn't know *anyone* well enough to try to describe what had happened at Sofonisba's grave marker. I didn't understand it myself. But I felt in my bones that what I'd seen was true.

Laura said, "You're an archaeologist, right? So...why tombstones?"

Why are you a Fellow—was what her tone conveyed—*and not me?* If I wanted her friendship, I'd have to tread carefully.

I said, keeping my own tone light, "My Ph.D.'s in archaeology, with a concentration in epigraphy."

"Epigraphy," Laura said. "What is it, exactly?"

I gave her the classic definition, a response I'd had to provide so often that it emerged half-sung. "Epigraphers read, identify, and interpret inscriptions carved into resistant materials."

"Such as?"

"Stone, metal, rock, wax, ceramics, precious metals, frescos. Even paintings."

"So, like, the Rosetta Stone?"

"Exactly."

Laura took a swallow of her *corretto*. "Still, how are tombstones archaeology? They're above ground."

I could hear, beneath her belligerence, a kind of plea. A wish to be seen as equal? I said, "Excavation is just a means to an end. The goal is to understand people and cultures from the objects they leave behind. Grave markers pinpoint time and place, and give us information about customs and belief systems—and even individual people."

I reached behind me for my bag and pulled out my drawing materials.

"Are those pastels?" Laura asked. "And a sketchbook! Wow, so...you have a *lot* of talents."

Envy wasn't something I'd encountered much of; for a second, it put me off-balance. Probably better not to mention that all archeologists draw. It would just rub salt in the wound of Laura's Spouse Equivalence—or should that be Spouse Ambivalence?

"Not really," I said, deflectingly. "I'm not any good." Flipping past the page of bright scribbles, I said, "Say you look at Sofonisba's life as a site diagram." I began to draw.

"What interests me is the year right after she was widowed. I call it the Lost Year." My pencil tapped a spot between Level 3 and Level 2. "In December of 1579 Sofonisba sets sail from Palermo, intending to return to her childhood home in Cremona, two hundred kilometers north of here. She never arrives. In December of 1580 she surfaces in Genoa, with a second husband—the ship's captain. Where was she in between? What was she doing? That's what I'm here to find out."

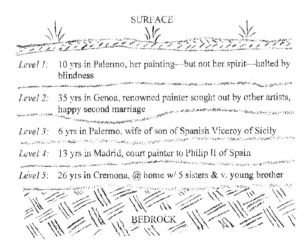

SURFACE

Level 1: 10 yrs in Palermo, her painting—but not her spirit—halted by blindness

Level 2: 35 yrs in Genoa, renowned painter sought out by other artists, happy second marriage

Level 3: 6 yrs in Palermo, wife of son of Spanish Viceroy of Sicily

Level 4: 13 yrs in Madrid, court painter to Philip II of Spain

Level 5: 26 yrs in Cremona, @ home w/ 5 sisters & v. young brother

BEDROCK

Through the café's open door came the steady hum of traffic, voices calling, an occasional cheerfully impatient car horn. Laura said, "Last week, in the Palazzo Reale. One of the paintings—I think it might've been by your lady. Two girls playing chess. Does that sound familiar?"

"Sofonisba's sisters," I breathed.

"I remember it because the guide said there was another painting on the reverse side. Uncovered recently. Visitors don't get to see it."

The Palazzo Reale was one of three museums in Genoa that had paintings by Sofonisba, among them *The Chess Game*. But there'd been no mention of a double-sided painting in anything I'd read before coming to Italy. Excited—here was something I could do while my luggage was AWOL—I scribbled "Sisters—reverse—Palazzo Reale" beneath the diagram of Sofonisba's life.

Laura watched me, looking pleased. She seemed to feel, at least for the moment, that we were peers.

"Kate? Can I ask you something?"

"Sure," I said. Nerving myself to describe vampire burials—the dead person's head cut off and placed in his crotch, so that when excavated, a skull nestles between two femurs—I drained my *corretto*.

"It's just...I'm so fucking isolated here."

Who isn't? I thought—then reproached myself. I knew all too well how it felt to be the trailing spouse. Maybe I'd been more graceful about it than Laura seemed to be; but so what? It was still hard. Hard to give up what you might have been, so that someone else could be that very thing.

"Yeah," I said, sympathetically, "it must be tough."

But Laura seemed to change her mind about whatever she'd been going to ask me. She finished her *corretto* and stood up. "Gotta go relieve the baby sitter. Hollis is buried in some archive, as usual." She gestured at the drawing pad open on the table between us. The belligerence returned to her voice. "Awesome topic. Neglected woman of genius. *And* a mystery."

I took the bus back to Soccorso. The shops had reopened at the end of the *Pausa*, and I found the one that Anna Maria, still telegraphing that puzzling dislike, had recommended. The salesclerk glided up to me, shiny blond hair, shiny lipsticked smile. *"Che cosa desidera, Signora?"* What are you looking for?

"Something like this," I said in Italian, and touched my dingy sweater. "And pants. And also"—what was the word for underwear?—"something for underneath." A shopping spree I couldn't afford: Janet would have said it was just what the doctor ordered. Recklessly I added, "Oh, and a dress—two dresses. Not too fancy. Grey, or black."

The woman regarded my sweater doubtfully. *"Sì, Signora. Mi segua."* She led me to the back of the shop. My velvet-curtained booth smelled of roses from a potpourri basket hanging on one pink-striped wall. Pink light flowed from sconces in the corners. Piano music rippled pinkly somewhere overhead.

In the triple mirror my freshly washed hair sprang out in dark-blond spirals with an exuberance not echoed in my face. I had once had a sort of slapdash beauty. A shifting, uncalculated appeal that—according to the far too numerous partners of my youth—was the momentary sum of my smile, the tilt of my head, my glance. Daniel had loved my changeable eyes. They went from blue to slate to green depending on the light, or what I wore, or even my mood (green when I was excited, sexually or otherwise).

Beauty? scoffed Ceiling-Katherine from one of the sconces. *You're forty-nine years old. That ship has sailed.*

Turning my back to the mirror, I shucked off sweater, jeans, underwear, and let them fall to the floor. The velvet-covered chair looked too good for them. I stood naked in a room with a triple mirror for the first time in…how long? How long since I'd experienced my body as something to enjoy rather than something useful? I kept my back to the mirror, afraid of what I'd see.

"Prego, Signora!" A manicured hand poked between the velvet curtains. It held two wisps of hot-pink silk. I took them.

"Signora?" I said. "These are too small."

No answer. She'd gone.

Still with my back to the mirror, I pulled on the bikini panties, fastened the bra. How had the clerk known my size? The silk felt weightless against my skin—a distant cousin to the white cotton underwear at my feet.

"*Prego, Signora!*" The hand reappeared, holding out a pair of black corduroy jeans. I took them with a quick "*Grazie.*" They were followed by a turquoise sweater.

"Signora?" I said. "This is too bright."

No answer. I put on the black cords, which fit perfectly. I waited several minutes, but the saleswoman didn't return. I pulled the turquoise sweater on, just to see. It was cloud-soft. Slowly I turned to face the mirror.

Not three Kates, but three Caterinas looked back at me. Three long-necked, long-limbed women-of-a-certain-age. Alive, interesting women. Women who could surprise you. The sweater's V-neck showed the rise of my breasts, and its color turned my eyes blue-green.

I hesitated outside the Centro's great iron gates. It was the hour of *aperi-tivi*. My ears picked up the munching sound of feet on gravel as Fellows converged on the courtyard. Heartened by the embrace of one of my two new dresses—a long-sleeved sheath of sea-green wool crepe that managed to be both stately and sexy—I fell in behind the preacher-voiced American composer. His name, Joshua Brayden, appeared in the Spouse Equivalents column beside the French semiotician's in the Centro's "Who's Here This Fall" leaflet—but so, puzzlingly, did that of the man in the black over-coat, Dmitri Antipov. There was no one listed in the leaflet who could have been Signora Catfish, which left me wondering how to address her at dinner.

"I didn't come to Italy to learn how to compose," the American was saying to the diminutive Thai sculptor. His words echoed down the loggia as if intended for a much larger audience. "I *know* how to compose. I came here to learn how to live."

Behind me a woman's voice said, "*Buonasera, Signora.* Perhaps you wish to play hockey?"

I turned. It was Signora Catfish, wearing the conspiratorial air I re-membered from the night before. Hockey? I paused for a second so we could walk side by side. Signora ~~Catfish~~ smelled bracingly of nicotine.

"*Buonasera, Signora,*" I said.

"You know, Caterina—may I call you Caterina? And please, call me Natalia. You know, these dinners are not very diverting. *Allora*, why not, what you Americans delight to call, play hockey? I know a secret place."

Oh…hooky! I laughed out loud. Tempting not to have to face a table-ful of Fellows. I said, "why not?"

Five minutes later we were sitting on a bench at the edge of a garden. Lemon trees, espaliered pear trees heavy with fruit, broccoli, Brussels sprouts, parsley, basil, dill. The garden was surrounded by a whitewashed stone wall with a gate painted blue, through which we'd entered. Signora Catfish (No, must stop thinking of her as that…Natalia) had reached over the top to unfasten it with a practiced hand, then latched it after us. This must, I thought, be the kitchen garden. A place probably forbidden to Fellows; but I was pretty sure that wouldn't discourage my companion.

Natalia lit a cigarette. A plume of smoke drifted past me. In front of us a hummingbird hovered, so close I could see its crimson throat, then spun away.

Natalia gazed after it. "They love the end of the day," she said.

The sun had slipped behind a laurel hedge on the far side of the garden, leaving in its wake a deepening stain. My favorite time of day was approaching: not sunset, but the burning blue sky just after. Inside me something unclenched. I felt a sense of—not lightness, exactly—more like ease. Like sitting on my deck back home with Janet, sipping tea and talking about life.

Natalia leaned over and pinched a stalk of lavender and smelled it, then held the purple blossom under my nose. Obediently, I breathed in. The fragrance traveled through my body like laughter.

"So, Caterina. I have been thinking about your project. You see, I am from Cremona."

Caterina. The name, like the dress I smoothed over my bare knees, made me feel different, more defined. Surer.

"The town where Sofonisba Auguissola grew up," I said.

This was interesting. I looked more closely at my companion, who was twirling the stalk of lavender between her palms. Her fingernails were bitten to the quick. A shrink who smoked *and* bit her nails? My heart warmed to her.

"So you see, Caterina, I was in favor of your project from the start."

"*You* were? What do you mean, Signora…Natalia?"

Her gold tooth winked in the shadow of her smile. "I am on the Centro's Board of Directors. And the Selection Committee, *certo*."

That was why I hadn't found her name in "Who's Here This Fall." So I owed the Centro's largesse—room and board, a stipend, the wine-dark sea—at least partly to Natalia? I sat silent, taking this in.

"Ah, Anguissola!" Natalia bounced a bit on our bench in her enthusiasm. "She was very like the Wife of Bath. Great vigor, a long life, much travel. Only two husbands, however."

I suppressed a giggle. All roads, I was beginning to see, led to the Wife of Bath.

"And you, Caterina? What is your plan?"

For a second I thought Natalia meant my plan for husband-hunting. "Today I went to the Cimitero Staglieno to see Sofonisba's grave marker," I said. "Three museums in Genoa have her paintings. And I'll go to the Archivio di Stato to check for records of birth, death, marriage, domiciles—" I broke off, realizing that Natalia already knew all this, since she'd read my proposal. That she'd known it before she met me. I didn't understand why, but this made me uneasy.

The birds had begun their tender sundown sounds. Stubbing out her cigarette, Natalia made a list of things I would need. A protector to go along on my inquiries around Liguria ("everything bright throws a shadow of danger"); a tutor to improve my Italian ("a lover makes the best tutor"); a partner to go dancing with. All these requirements seemed to be male, I noted—the one thing I was definitely not interested in. When I said so, my companion paid no attention.

"I will find for you these necessaries," she said. "Even in hard times one should pursue happiness."

Her bossy enthusiasm reminded me of Janet, who always thought she knew what was best for me, and seldom hesitated to say it. She touched my elbow. "*Allora*, Caterina, may I ask a favor?"

"Of course."

Natalia leaned closer, her voice a whisper. "Perhaps I should not burden you—but there is no one else I can ask. And time grows short."

Stay free, warned Ceiling-Katherine from the top of the garden wall. *Concentrate on work.*

"If I can. What is it?"

A rattling noise sounded somewhere behind us. The gate we'd entered through, being opened?

Natalia jumped up. "*O Dio*! I am late. I must leave you, *cara*." But I noticed she didn't consult her watch. "You can find yourself back to the courtyard, yes?" She spoke over her shoulder, trotting toward the far side of the garden.

"Wait," I said. "What was it you—"

"I will telephone. We will arrange a day for you to come to me in Genoa."

She plunged between the branches of a laurel hedge and disappeared. There must have been a second gate hidden behind the hedge, because I heard a click.

Seconds later the Slavicist from Edinburgh sat down beside me. How had he found me so fast?

"Ah, Professor Hagesfeld," he said. His Sean Connery voice made my name shimmer. "So this is where you've got to! Puir Anna Maria is in the way of sendin' out a sairch party."

3

"I meant what I said, and I said what I meant: An elephant's faithful, one hundred per cent," I recited to Amber. I held out the green velvet elephant. "Thank you for lending me this."

Amber threw down her jump rope to grab the elephant. She gave me a shy smile, then turned and ran to where Laura stood at the far end of the loggia.

It was my fourth day at the Centro. I was on my way to the village to catch a train for Genoa. My plan was to spend the morning at the Palazzo Reale among Sofonisba's paintings, then have lunch at Natalia's apartment. I was wildly curious to see the double-sided painting Laura had told me about. Picking up Amber's jump rope from the dewy grass, rolling the handles between my palms, I remembered Rachel at about Amber's age. Her navy-blue kindergarten uniform; her hair braided and looped behind her ears ("like the *other* girls, Mom"): her high voice fluting Albanian jump rope rhymes. That was in 1981, when we were spending the academic year in Yugoslavia. Daniel, still able to travel then, had had a Fulbright professorship at the University of Pristina, in Kosovo.

Sparrows were trolling the flowerbed alongside the loggia, releasing the odor of chrysanthemums into the still morning air. "Lucia didn't show today," Laura said when I came up to her. "Never hire a babysitter who's got a boyfriend. Thank God school starts tomorrow." Despite the morning chill, she wore denim shorts and a red silk vest; between them gleamed several inches of tensed, tanned stomach. "I've barely written a word since we got here. Unlike Hollis. *He's* been scribble scribble scribbling."

Amber stood with her arms clasped around her mother's hips. In one hand Laura held a book; the other hovered, not quite touching her daughter's hair. I could almost feel its tickle across my palm.

"I could babysit this weekend," I said. "We could go for a walk."

Laura hesitated. Amber turned her face up to her mother. "Please, mom?"

I held out the jump rope.

Taking it from me, Laura made up her mind. "That would be awesome. Thank you, Kate."

Amber clapped her hands in delight. The sparrows rose from the flowerbed in a single motion and soared over the Centro's tiled roof.

Laura said, "As long as you don't go on the Passeggiata. A cliffwalk without guardrails! What are the Italians thinking?"

To my delight, I found the Palazzo Reale without asking for directions more than twice. But it wasn't open. Worse, a large sign said *CLOSED FOR RENOVATIONS UNTIL JANUARY 2nd*. My heart sank. The sign had an emergency phone number at the bottom. I found a pen in my purse, but nothing to write on except the business card from the Builder of Airports. I scribbled the museum's phone number on the back. But would Anna Maria, with her unexplained dislike for me, be willing to testify that an American researcher constituted an emergency? Meanwhile, I faced an empty morning.

What's your plan? Ceiling-Katherine demanded.

Nearly three hours till I was due at Natalia's. I decided to walk instead of taking the bus, see what I could see of Sofonisba's city. I got out my map. The Palazzo Reale was in the part of Genoa called Le Strade Nuove, the new streets; Natalia's apartment was on the far the edge of the Centro Storico, the medieval quarter. I checked the position of the sun, then headed southwest.

The city's color and noise and motion were a shock after the Centro's peace. An hour, and I took refuge at a fruit and vegetable stand, letting the crowds eddy around me. The white-aproned proprietor said, *"Buon-giorno, Signora. Che cosa desidera?"* On his shoulder sat a striped owl. The greengrocer held a pineapple up to his nose and sniffed theatrically, gestured toward shining heaps of grapes. The owl flapped its wings and re-settled itself.

"Do not fear," the man said. "She don't travel."

The owl lifted one leg and flexed its talons, then sank them into the greengrocer's shoulder. *"Tranquillo!"* he said. He put a hand into his apron pocket and brought out something between thumb and forefinger. I saw it wriggle. He held it up to the owl, whose beak snapped once, a small, decisive click.

"Allora! Che cosa desidera, Signora?"

What *was* I looking for? Oh…so many things. Things no one could give me. Things that were lost.

I bought a paper cone of clementines. The greengrocer reached into his apron pocket—the other pocket, I noted with relief—and produced a bright-red apple-shaped lollipop. Its stick was a twig holding two green paper leaves. I bought it for Amber, and walked on.

A piazza thronged with pigeons. In the center, a marble fountain towered above me in wedding-cake tiers. I sat down on the stone lip to rest. Some of the water went up a level, some down, the streams cancelling one other. The fountain's ambivalence was strangely comforting. After several minutes I got to my feet, refreshed, and crossed the piazza. I recognized Via Canneto il Lungo from the directions Natalia had given me. I started down it. The street curved. Ahead was an underpass, and at the far end, a wedge of sunlight, a knot of people. I walked under the low arch. Exhalations of ancient stone, cindery and bitter—then, suddenly, the stench of urine. The smell stopped me in my tracks.

Coming home from the hospital, the last time I'd taken Daniel to the ER. When I untied the plastic bag the nurse had given me, the smell almost knocked me down. Holding my breath, pulling things out of the bag and putting them in the washer, I found everything—faded blue workshirt, khakis, boxers printed with tiny black keys—in pieces. They'd had to cut the clothes off him.

I was standing, shaking, in the center of the underpass. I reached out to steady myself. The stones were cold and slimy. I pulled my hand away and ran.

Natalia had said that in the medieval quarter you had an almost visceral sense of being pulled into the past. Trudging upward along Vico degli Indoratori, I saw what she meant. The smells of earth and rotting wood, tinged with an occasional briny breath from the unseen sea. Buildings dark with ancient grime, molecules of the past embedded in their walls. The upper floors had balconies where ranks of white laundry floated like guardian angels. A beautiful Romanesque church made me think of Sofonisba. This street would have looked much the same in her day. She would have walked down it many times in the thirty-five years she lived in Genoa.

It was chilly here, the sun just a rumor overhead. I stopped to put on Laura's sweater, which was tied around my waist. Two boys ran by, jostling me as they passed. A *poliziotto* ran after them, shouting, "*Zingari*!" Gypsies. A catchall term, I'd come to understand, for beggars, thieves, and unwanted foreigners. Other walkers passed me, hand in hand: a woman towing a small child; a teenage girl towed by her boyfriend; a middle-aged couple who stopped to look at the graffiti splashed along one stuccoed wall. I felt my aloneness, neither towed nor towing. I wished I had time to study the graffiti. Like most archaeologists, I'm intrigued by it. Cave paintings, petroglyphs, runes—what are they but the graffiti of yesterday?

The shops—jewelry, ceramics, drugstore (Farmacia Cristoforo Colombo: the man was everywhere), fish store—were pulling their grills down for the *Pausa*. I was late. Walking faster, I began to have the feeling of being followed—a kind of tickle at the edge of my awareness—familiar from long-ago days in Yugoslavia, where Westerners were routinely tailed by the UDBA, Tito's secret police. Now I put it down to being in a foreign country for the first time since then. Still, I moved to the middle of the

the street. Vico degli Indoratori became Via San Luca. Not a name I re-membered from Natalia's directions—but I was patient. The Italian con-ception of space can be as elastic as the Italian conception of time. Sure enough, after several minutes a sign apppeared on the wall to my right, above a stone staircase: Salita Sant'Andrea. I counted as I walked, fif-ty-five steps to the top—a quick, jeweled glimpse of the sea—then turned left. Outside Number 7 was a little girl in denim overalls standing on her head, and next to her a toddler, laughing as he tried to do the same.

I stopped to catch my breath. "*Ciao, bambini*," I said.

The little girl turned right side up and grabbed the boy's hand and yanked him to his feet. She looked about Amber's age—five or six—with a mass of tangled pale-blond hair. She peered up at me, her eyes the star-tling blue of Windex. They seemed to hold an unchildlike awareness of secrets to be kept. A look I'd often seen on Rachel's face as she watched her father's slow disintegration. A look that used to make my heart hurt. I smiled; the little girl didn't smile back.

Surprised at the pang of disappointment I felt—why was I so suscepti-ble to little girls lately?—I stepped up to the double doors and pushed the button marked "N. Fabbri, #33." To a fuzzy "*Pronto?*" I answered, "*Sono Caterina.*" The buzzer sounded. With a backward glance at the watchful children, I pulled open the door and went inside. In the foyer the ancient brass birdcage of an elevator had a bench pulled across it. I climbed the steps to the fourth floor.

"*Ciao, cara!*" Natalia flung open the door to Number 33. "*Benvenuta!*" Welcome.

I bent to receive the Italians' customary brush of cheeks. We bumped noses—I'd forgotten there would be a second brush on the other cheek.

"I'm so sorry I'm late."

"*Non fa niente.* Do not worry yourself. I am happy to see you."

I handed her the clementines. Never arrive empty-handed, my grand-mother used to say. Natalia led me down a hall lined with floor-to-ceil-ing shelves full of books and photographs. Shining wood floors in a her-ringbone pattern. A bloom of light at the far end. There was the sound of a piano, something meandering and sad. I glimpsed a child's room, red and blue and yellow; a study with books and papers piled on every surface. The layout reminded me of our apartment in Yugoslavia, in Pristina's old quarter. The music broke off. I could hear someone weeping—not crying, weeping.

"You are hungry?" Natalia threw over her shoulder.

"Very!"

We turned before we reached the bloom of light and entered a small kitchen. A woman stood with her back to the door. There was a rhythmic sound of chopping. The windows had dense vines growing all around them that turned the entering sunlight green. It was like being in an aquarium. Natalia shut the glass door behind her.

At the sound, the woman whirled around. One hand held a knife, poised to strike.

"*Ti presento* Caterina," Natalia said calmly. "Caterina, this is Vida."

"*Piacere,*" I said, extending my hand.

Vida ignored it, her eyes—strange, square-cut eyes the same startling blue as those of the little girl in the street—fixed on my face. She wore jeans and a baggy sweatshirt, and her dirty dark-red hair was scraped back in a bun. All this did nothing to hide her beauty. "I like better to speak English," she said. She didn't smile.

"Of course." I let my own smile melt away.

"Vida comes recently to Italy," Natalia said, apparently feeling that this explained everything. "Now, let us see what we can feed you."

Vida turned back to her chopping. The counter where she stood held lemons, tomatoes, olives, sprigs of rosemary, basil leaves, garlic. A plump slab of veal gleamed.

"Pasta," Natalia decided. "*Aglio e olio.*"

Twenty minutes later, Vida had switched from chopping to pounding, and I was sitting at a table by the window, winding linguini around my fork and shoveling it into my mouth. The smell of rosemary drifted through the kitchen. I was hungrier than I'd realized, and the plain sauce of garlic and oil was surprisingly good. The tomato slices sprinkled with basil and salt. The glass of chilled white wine. Natalia sat with me, sipping and smoking, telling me a story about the fourth husband of the Wife of

Bath. By this time I was wondering, why Chaucer? Why not Dante or Boccaccio? When I said this, Natalia looked at me severely. "We Italians have no one like Chaucer. *Eccolo*! That is why Italy has today such problems." Now and then Vida turned to take something out of the fridge; otherwise, she kept her back to us. But she was listening to our conversation. I could see it in the set of her shoulders, the angle of her head. Something about her felt familiar, yet I knew I'd never seen her before.

"This glass," I said to Natalia when I'd drained the last of my wine. "I'd love to have some like it. Where did you get it?" It was a narrow tumbler with a white line circling it halfway up. Above the line was the word "*Ottimista*"; below it, "*Pessimista*."

"Ah. My late husband stole these glasses from a bar in the Porto Antico. *Purtroppo*, it exists no longer. At one time we had a dozen glasses—Stefano liked very much to drink at this bar—but now there are only two."

Out of nowhere, as I held up the glass, a blue bird lighted on the rim. I kept on holding it up, afraid to move, while the parakeet cocked its head and regarded me out of one shiny black eye.

"Gianpaolo!" Natalia exclaimed. "*Vieni qua!*" She set down her cigarette on the edge of my plate and held out her index finger. With a swirl of wings, the bird hopped on. "I am sorry," Natalia said. "Did he fright you?" I shook my head. "We call him Gianpaolo, after the Pope. He makes free of the place, as you see. Because we haven't to cage him. Cages…upset Vida."

At the sound of her name, Vida turned. "I take," she said. She made a noise somewhere between a chirp and a gurgle, and the bird flew to her shoulder. Without another word, she left the room. I could see the veal she'd been pounding, now cardboard-thin and flecked with rosemary.

"Vida insists to cook," Natalia said, with a shrug. "It is her therapy. Me, no. You know that when a baby girl is born, her ovaries contain all the eggs she will have in her lifetime? So it is, I believe, with cooking. *Allora*, I have long ago prepared all the meals that are in me." She rose. "You have eaten enough? Do you wish an espresso?" I shook my head. "Then come and meet the others."

Entering the living room, at the very end of the hallway, was like emerging from a Genovese alley into an airy, light-filled piazza. It was high-ceilinged and lined with waist-high shelves crowded with books and family photographs and sculptures in wood or terracotta. Above them hung paintings full of vibrant color. A piano stood in one corner. Vida sat stiffly upright on a worn leather sofa, flanked by the two children I'd seen earlier outside the building. A woman in a flowered dress, about my age but with a face deeply lined, sat in an armchair on the other side of the fireplace. She regarded me with the soft gaze of the nearsighted. A teen-aged girl with long dark hair sat on the floor, leaning against the woman's knee; her black T-shirt said *Thank You USA*.

Natalia said each one's name in turn. Vida. The children—Lule (the solemn little girl) and Ardi. The woman my age—Bardha. The girl leaning against her knee—Genta. I wondered which of them had been weeping.

"This is Signora Hagesfeld, a visitor from America."

"Kate," I said, feeling the weight of five pairs of eyes.

Outside, a car backfired. The women jumped. Natalia said gently, "*Tranquillo. Non vi preoccupate.*"

There was a silence. Then Genta turned and said something to the woman behind her in a language I hadn't heard in two decades.

My heart began to beat heavily. I remembered the forbidden Voice of America broadcasts at breakfast, with their slow, magisterial Special English: *Unrest...in the city of...Pristina. Armed troops...sent...to Kosovo.* I remembered the carry-on kept ready under our bed—passports, American dollars, candy bars, cigarettes—in case of evacuation.

The children, who'd sat impressively still during the introductions, began to elbow each other and giggle. Vida said something that sounded stern but only made them laugh harder. Then everyone was talking in Albanian and laughing and gesturing. Confusion seized me. I couldn't reconcile the room where I sat—radiating warmth and safety—with that violent long-ago spring in Yugoslavia.

"Come with me a moment," Natalia said to me.

I followed her to the French doors. We stepped onto a balcony, and she pulled the doors shut behind us. Across the street, pastel apartment buildings huddled together below purple-shadowed hills. Natalia turned and stood with her back against the balustrade. I took a deep breath. The air held the bracing smell of the sea.

"Why didn't you tell me?" I demanded.

"That the people I wanted you to meet were from Kosovo? Because I feared you would refuse." Natalia pulled a pack of cigarettes out of one sweater sleeve and a pack of matches out of the other. Her hands shook as she extracted a cigarette and lit it. "I wish to ask a favor."

"What favor?" Wariness made me curt. So, I thought, it's no coincidence—Natalia's apartment being full of people from an obscure place where I once lived.

"First," Natalia said, the word riding an aromatic cloud of smoke that drifted past my shoulder, "may I tell you about my little group?"

I shrugged.

"These women are political refugees, brought here by *Missione Arcobaleno*. The Rainbow Campaign. Three years ago the Serbs claim Kosovo for Serbs only, as it was long ago, in the sixth century. Just as your husband's book says, they use archaeology to support their nationalism. To justify their theft. *Quindi*, they begin ethnic—how do you call it?—ethnic cleaning—"

"Cleansing," I said.

"—cleansing, *si` si`*." Natalia touched my arm, her cigarette perilously close to Laura's sweater. "All Albanians were forced to flee. The Serbs—you must know this—are most warlike, and their soldiers do not hesitate to rape and torture women. Even young girls. Even children."

"I've read about it, of course. Milosevic. Bosnia."

"*Esatto*! Kosovo two years ago—before NATO bombed to hell Milosevic—was like Bosnia."

Genoa, Natalia continued, had for many centuries received foreigners gladly; here they were not regarded with suspicion, as in the great inland cities like Milan or the backward villages of the south. When Albania couldn't support the increasing numbers of Kosovar refugees, they crossed the Adriatic to Italy. Here they were aided by an organization, *Missione Arcobaleno,* that Natalia worked for. As Natalia talked, her hand found my arm, my elbow, my shoulder. Italians in conversation, I read somewhere, touch each other an average of 100 times an hour. Even knowing this, Natalia's touch felt personal.

"Now *Missione Arcobaleno*, like all organizations sponsored by our government, has descended into corruption. It has failed these women! *Allora,* I join a group called Caritas, a private organization. To help refugees, to find for them housing and temporary visas and work."

Natalia paused for a couple of fierce drags on her cigarette. From beyond the closed French doors came a burst of laughter. Kosovo, when Daniel and I lived there, had been an autonomous republic within Yugoslavia. I remembered with a pang how lively our Kosovar friends had been—the great majority of Kosovars then were Albanian—how warm and welcoming. All that was gone now? The thought lodged painfully in my chest. These women and I might have passed each other on the street two decades ago; they probably knew people Daniel and I had known back then. I took a breath.

"So…you work with this organization, Caritas?"

"*Si*, I worked with them."

Worked.

"What do you do now?"

"Caritas must stay within the law. I can go beyond. And that is how I ask for your help."

"Me? What can I do?"

"It is simple. Come here to my apartment once or twice a week, and speak English to these women."

"Why English? Isn't Italian what they need?"

"*Boh*! My country now is saying it has not room for refugees. Their visas, when they expire, are not renewed. Caritas can no longer help them. *Allora*, these refugees must be in hiding. The women you have met, they try now for entry to Norway or England—or America. These women"— her voice softened—"you can see for yourself how brave they are."

I turned to look through the glass doors. The room's warmth and color beckoned, and I felt my own longing to be there. Natalia's apartment offered a shelter very different from that of the Centro. Her apartment didn't shut the world out; it brought the world in. My eyes fell on Lule.

She saw me looking and looked back, her face assuming that watchful, unchildlike wariness. Again I had a flash of Rachel.

Natalia's eyes followed my gaze. "America would be wonderful for Lule. A great chance." She put a hand on my arm. "You must understand, *cara*, that I am trusting you with this knowledge. I could go to prison."

"Why *do* you trust me?"

"Because you have suffered." Her grip, surprisingly strong, held me fast. "Pain can make you close yourself. Or pain can make you generous."

Generous. The syllables lingered in my ear like a word in a language I no longer knew. Being a caregiver means that, day after day, generosity is pre-empted. You're unable to give because you already owe, always, more than you have.

My heart went out to these women whose voices made me remember that spring twenty years ago in Kosovo, the final year of the dig at Vlashnje. Remember Daniel as he once was. But I was here to find my own life, a life after (a life without) Daniel. I withdrew my hand from Natalia's. Surely there was someone else who could help. The world is full of little girls, I told myself, you can't save all of them.

"I'm sorry. I'm afraid I don't have time, Signora."

Natalia flicked her cigarette into a geranium pot and said, as if I hadn't spoken, "Let us go inside. We will talk again soon."

4

It was pirates, the messenger tells her.

Pirates? Do they imagine she is that stupid? Fabrizio's every voyage has been an invitation to his enemies at Court.

Il corpo? *she says. My husband's body?*

She studies the weeping birch in the center of the courtyard behind the dusty, chamois-clad messenger. Morning sunlight turns it into a hive of shadow-sharpened leaves.

My lord's body was… One booted foot scuffs the cobblestones.

She switches to Spanish. Where is the body?

My lord's body was… consigned to the sea. The ship lay off the coast of Amalfi, my lady, almost to Naples. A voyage back here to Palermo, it would have taken—

Sì`, certo, she whispers. Then, more loudly: It would have taken too long.

Beyond the messenger the branches of the birch waver dangerously, green, gold, greengold. Fabrizio had that tree brought from the slopes of Etna for her in the first year of their marriage. She will not show this young man tears. She turns with a harsh rustle of skirts. Across the great hall, the marble stairs with their gilded balustrade are a world away. With unseemly haste, she begins to run.

———

Slowly my head cleared. I felt the way you do on waking from an un-planned nap: the present swirling and reforming like bits in a kaleido-scope. Smells of dust and varnish; light leaking through velvet drapes; sound of a distant door closing. I was standing in the Palazzo Bianco in front of one of Sofonisba's portraits. It was Sunday afternoon, exactly a week since I'd arrived in Italy.

A man in his early forties looked out from the gilded frame. He wore a gold brocade cloak draped over his shoulders. One hand rested on the hilt of his sword; the other curved across his midriff. The cloak made a triangle of the man's body. At its apex his head rose from a scratchy-look-ing ruff, sporting a black velvet cap with a plume. Scholars agreed that this was Fabrizio de Moncada, second-born son of the Spanish Viceroy of Sicily.

Sofonisba seemed to have treated her husband as she did all her sit-ters. He gazed directly at the viewer—her trademark—his lips parted. His face was clear and open. Reproductions I'd seen didn't do this painting justice. Its presence, its vividness, the sense that its subject was about to step down out of the frame and say the words trembling on his lips. *I moti dell'anima*—I could see it, the thing Sofonisba had said she aimed for. The movements of the soul. And yet… There was something that didn't fit. The face so eloquent; the body just a tent of sumptuous cloth. What was the painter saying, and did she know she was saying it?

Except for a miniature self-portrait in the Boston Museum of Fine Arts, this was the first painting of Sofonisba's that I'd seen in person. It made me eager to see others—three more here in the Palazzo Bianco, two in the Palazzo Spinola, the double-sided one in the Palazzo Reale if I could manage it.

Two men entered the gallery at the far end, speaking a rapid sew-ing-machine Italian. My arms came up to shield Fabrizio de Moncada. To keep him mine. *Whoa,* I could hear Rachel saying, *Get a grip, Mom!* I looked around. The two men, pensioners in soft brimmed caps, began to circle the gallery arm in arm. Otherwise, the room was empty.

Something came over me. I wanted to touch this painting. I *needed* to touch it. I stretched out my hand and put my fingertips to Fabrizio's cheek.

An alarm sounded, clanging through the gallery. Within seconds, a uniformed guard arrived. She strode up to me, frowning.

"*Cosa fa, Signora?*" She pointed to a sign above the gallery entrance. *SIETE PREGATI DI NON TOCCARE.*

"I *didn't* touch it," I lied.

The two men approached, still arm-in-arm, like Tweedledum and Tweedledee. One of them said, in a lisping Genovese accent, "*Non è vero!* We saw the Signora put her hand on the painting." His companion nodded.

"It is not permitted," the guard said. "You must come with me, Signora. You, too, Signori."

The museum director, another fierce-faced middle-aged woman, didn't believe me, either. My being at the Centro, my being a *Dottoressa*—these were not things I could produce evidence of. In fact, not having thought to bring my passport on an excursion like this, I had no ID whatsoever. Under the righteous gaze of the Tweedles I was escorted down the stairs and out onto Via Garibaldi. I was not welcome to return.

On the train back to Soccorso I found a window seat on the upper level and watched the city give way to the blue sweep of the Mediterranean. What was happening to me? I was ashamed: I'd been compelled to touch Fabrizio's portrait even though I knew that skin oils corrode painted surfaces. The painting had pulled me toward it, the way the view from the top of a tall building whispers, *Jump!* Like the pottery shard on my first long-ago dig, it held the print of its maker. Touching it connected her and me. And something else that was strange: the weeping birch had been physically present in the cemetery the other day, not today. It linked today's vision with the first one; it made me feel I was on the track of something. A trail leading deeper into Sofonisba's reality. Unorthodox, yes; but compelling. Daniel and I had often talked about the Archaeologist's Quandary—imagination vs. objectivity—with Daniel claiming I was too readily distracted by the people that objects conjured up. Distressed and exhilarated, I sat staring at flocks of bright sailboats until a tunnel blotted out the sea.

———

The last week in September—my second week at the Centro—was filled with frustration. My ability to do the work I'd come to Italy for felt more and more in doubt.

On Monday morning I went to the Archivio di Stato in Genoa to see the documents and letters the internet listed for Sofonisba. But—*"Mi dispiace, Signora"*—without a letter from my university or a *raccomandazione* from a well-known Italian scholar, access to documents was *impossibile.* The ultraconservative Archivio accepted only originals, no faxes or emails; the originals were with my luggage. Anna Maria couldn't pull strings—so she said. She hadn't been able to get me into the closed Palazzo Reale, either. I had trouble believing there wasn't a cousin somewhere she could call on, if only she'd liked me. What happened to the sympathy vote? I protested silently. Recent widowhood? Caregiverhood?

They both have a termination date, was Ceiling-Katherine's guess.

I spent Tuesday at the Palazzo Spinola, the only museum still open to me, communing with two self-portraits by Sofonisba. Light fell like grace on the faces, the throats, the hands with their strong, curving fingers. One showed a black-clad, serious young woman. She held an open book with Latin inscribed across its pages: "Sofonisba Anguissola, Virgin, made this, 1554." In the other much larger painting, dated 1559, a confident Sofonisba stood arrayed in the style of the Spanish court, in gold-embroidered velvet and pearls. I studied the wide brown eyes, heart-shaped mouth, firm chin. The way she held herself made me think of a cat. In repose, but alert; a hunter at heart.

Self-portraits show their maker from both the outside and the inside. I stood in front of each painting for a long time, hoping. Jonesing, Rae would have said, for a vision. But there was nothing.

One museum closed; another forbidden; the bland refusal at the Archivio di Stato. After my trip to the Palazzo Spinola, each morning stretched before me like a long, golden yawn. The other Fellows dispersed to the city's libraries, where they sat surrounded by leather-bound volumes smelling of mice. I read paperback crime novels left behind by previous Fellows. I spent hours in the Villa Baiardo's basement, known as the Crypt, the only place in the Centro with internet access, emailing Rachel and Janet. I listened to Ceiling-Katherine's catechism: *Will you ever work, really work, again? How do you plan to support yourself?* Finally I discovered the Centro library's collection of books on Italian history and culture, and I set about builing a detailed picture of Sofonisba's daily life. What people wore, at the end of Renaissance; what they ate; how they amused themselves. What their houses were like, their furniture, their gardens. Now and then Laura came and dragged me out into the sunshine for lunch.

Evenings offered some distraction from my growing despair. After dinner in the lantern-lit courtyard I stayed down at the Villa Baiardo. Twice I played pool with Hollis and Dmitri Antipov (hampered by the black overcoat he never seemed to remove), while Angus Dance—the ascetic-looking Slavicist from Edinburgh—lurked around the edges of the game. One evening Joshua Brayden put on a CD in the *salotto* and gave us all tango lessons. Laura was his demonstation partner, breathless and rosy, alight at being the center of attention while "Begin the Beguine" floated on the night air. Thuanthong Vipavakit spent the evenings in a corner, his radish-top of hair bobbing in the lamplight. At the end of each night Chantal Joubert ascended the curving staircase to the second floor between Dmitri and Joshua, the three of them bumbling upward arm-in-arm-in-arm.

On the next-to-last day in September I sat in the Villa Baiardo's *salotto*, struggling with an editorial in the *Corriere della Sera* about Italy's illegal refugees. The doors to the terrace stood open, flooding the room with sunlight and the unceasing murmur of the sea. Since Natalia's request, the issue of political refugees seemed to show up everywhere, like pregnant women when you've just found out you're expecting. The editorial made me wonder, not for the first time, whether I'd done right in saying no to Natalia. What I'd seen in her apartment had haunted me in the week since—Bardha's mild face inscribed with lines of suffering: Vida's fierceness grounded in fear; Lule's unchildlike vigilance.

"*Signora!*" Anna Maria, standing in the doorway, gave me a rare smile. "*Che fortuna!* Massimo has just now told me that your baggage arrives. He will carry it up to the Villa Francesca. After two weeks without them you will be joyed to have your things, I am sure." She paused. "But something goes wrong? You look to have quite problems."

I said, "No problems. Thank you for looking after the luggage."

Anna Maria's smile dimmed as her eyes traveled over me, reclining on a sofa in sunlight in the middle of the morning. She said, "You are fortunate, Signora. They find never the baggage of Signor Vipavakit. And the materials for his installation are lost, as well. *Poverino!*"

No longer qualifying, myself, for the title of Poor Thing, I folded the paper and left. In the courtyard Hollis and Laura sat in green-painted chairs with books on their laps. They didn't see me. Their chairs were side by side, and they held hands as they read. It was as if a crack in time—a hairline fissure I hadn't known was there—had suddenly opened. As if I'd been dropped into my own past. They could have been me and Daniel, sitting with heads bent and hands touching in the dappled light. Me and Daniel in that last warm, wine-y autumn before his diagnosis.

I went up the hill to the Villa Francesca. There were my two suitcases sitting just outside the French doors. The old red one I'd had since college; Daniel's black leather duffel. I felt almost as glad to see them as if they'd been Rachel or Janet. I fell to my knees and opened them and started pulling out things that smelled of home.

"By now you will have guessed, *cara*," Natalia said, "which is the lover and which the husband."

Here she was, dropping into the chair on my right and calling me *dear*, as if I'd never refused her a favor. Across from us Chantal Joubert, resplendent in chartreuse silk, sat between the lugubrious Dmitri, who for once had shed his overcoat, and preacher-voiced Joshua, at the head of the table. Both men were talking to her at once. She leaned left, then right, then left again.

I'd been dreading seeing Natalia, but she didn't look at all reproachful. I said, "*Buonasera, Signora.*"

"Ah, you must not be formal! *Così* I will fear you are annoyed with me."

The season's first evening meal indoors was an event. In the Villa Baiardo's dining room, candlelight scalloped the frescoed doors, the long table with its silver and china and flocks of shining crystal. Through the glass doors that gave onto the terrace, the Mediterranean was too dark to be visible, but the glimmer of lights on a passing freighter told me it was there. Anna Maria had asked everyone via email to "don elegant dress." The men wore suits and ties. The women looked ready for the red carpet. Natalia wore a purple satin gown with a huge collar that fanned out behind her head, like the Wicked Queen's in "Snow White." Amber, allowed to stay up for the occasion, resembled a large pink artichoke in layers of ruffled organdy.

Reuniting with my things after almost two weeks had made me high. My heart had lifted as I stacked my research materials and letters of intro- duction on the desk in the study. They made me feel legitimate enough to lay siege to the Palazzo Reale again, though at the moment I had no idea how to do that. I fingered the card from the Builder of Airports with the museum's phone number scribbled on the back. Reading the name Gene O'Casey, I saw again the beard, curly and silver-flecked; the sweatered slope of belly beneath the bomber jacket. I put the card back face down: it was the museum's phone number I wanted, nothing else. In the bedroom I hung my wren wear at the back of the closet. When it was time to get ready for dinner, I put on the second of the two dresses I'd bought in the village shop—a sleeveless black velvet sheath that followed my body exactly. Diesel! Rae would've said. Around the hem was a lavish band of black ostrich feathers. They tickled my bare knees, frivolous and delicious. Long, glimmering earrings that Janet had given me as a going-away pres- ent; mascara; lipstick. Checking my reflection in the mirror before I left, I'd noticed that my eyes were green.

We finished our *aperitivi*. Antipasto arrived. Each course seemed to require its own wine, and any glass emptied was immediately refilled. As I listened to the conversation going on around me, I realized I'd begun to like living among friendly strangers. Back home I'd been increasingly un- able to join in friends' conversations because my life, hostage to degenera- tive illness, was so unlike theirs. It was as if I'd been catapulted forward a generation into a different life stage, the victim of a timequake. Eventually the problem was solved by what Rachel (sounding so like her father) called the Great Peeling Off. Friends and colleagues disappeared from our lives; Daniel and I were no longer invited to parties.

The people around the table in the Villa Baiardo accepted me as I was now. Here I didn't have to smile away the past or explain why its shadow never left me. Laura, sitting next to the Russian, caught my eye and winked. I winked back. Angus Dance, on her other side, seemed to think I'd winked at him. I looked away and downed the last of my wine. A waiter replaced it. The room had begun to tilt—as if we really were on a cruise, as Natalia had said that first night. Anchors aweigh, I thought, and reached for my glass.

"*Allora*, tell me!" Natalia laid a hand on my arm. "What is happening? How goes your work? Have you found a tutor?" The questions were accompanied by a series of bounces, releasing the scent of mothballs.

"No, I—"

"Good! I will send to you my nephew. At the moment he is at a loose end. *Allora,* Nico will teach; you will learn; both will be happy. Now here comes, what is it? Ah, *che bello*! Gelosia alla Valdostana. You will enjoy."

Relieved that Natalia hadn't brought up the matter of the Kosovar women, and ashamed of my relief, I addressed myself to the palm-sized envelope of golden-brown pasta. It was filled with prosciutto, cheese, spinach, mushrooms, all melted together with unfamiliar, beguiling spices. Natalia devoured hers and waved to the waiter for seconds.

"Kate!" Amber appeared at my elbow. "Do you like my dress? It has an official waist." Hands on hips, she stuck out her stomach, circled by a pink sash. "My mom says I'm invincible. Plus, my name is the color I am. How cool is that?"

"Very cool," I said.

"Amber!" Laura came around the table and put her hands on Amber's shoulders. "Come and sit down and don't bother Kate. You'll see her on Friday."

A bit of maternal jealousy? "It's no bother," I said.

Laura smiled, but she grasped Amber's hand and led her away.

"You have made a friend," Natalia observed. "How have you managed it so soon?"

"Sheer charm," I said. "Plus, I babysit."

Hollis and Joshua, seated at the either end of the long table, began a volley of Bushisms.

I know how hard it is for you to put food on your family...

They misunderestimated me...

This foreign policy stuff is a little frustrating...

"This, from a man who had to apply for a passport after becoming President!"

"Eighty percent of Americans don't have a passport. No wonder the rest of the world thinks we're cultural ignoramuses."

On my left Thuanthong ate steadily, his shoulders hunched as if to take up the smallest possible amount of space. On my right Natalia was deep in conversation with Hollis. Left to myself, I looked around the room. This was the first time I'd been in here, apart from Anna Maria's quick tour the day after I arrived. The frescoes dated from the eighteenth century. Too late to be contemporary with Sofonisba; and, anyway, she hadn't painted frescoes. Still, I felt mysteriously drawn to them. Blurred by three centuries of sea air and sunlight, their aquamarine and rose and saffron seemed to float along the candlelit walls. They showed gods and goddesses seated on nearly invisible thrones or reclining under skeletal trees. Not showed, exactly—more like hinted at. It took an imaginative eye to fill in the details.

I looked away to find Angus Dance's imaginative eye on *me*. I shifted my gaze to the table's centerpiece, autumn roses in a silver bucket.

Natalia leaned close to me. A corner of her purple satin collar grazed my cheek. "Merkin," she muttered.

"Sorry?"

"The beard of Signor Dance." She nodded in the direction of the Slavicist. "So stingy, this beard." I studied the red-blond tuft on his chin. "So not believable. Ah! Perhaps you do not know what is a merkin?"

Lifting my wineglass, I shook my head.

"In Chaucer's time the pubic hair of women was much admired. The more the better. Quite opposite to today! *Allora*, many women wore there a little wig. *I capelli finti.*"

False pubic hair. Taking a fresh look at Angus Dance's chin, I choked on my wine. I had to snatch my napkin off my lap and hold it across my mouth. A black feather from my dress floated down onto my plate.

"It is good to laugh," Natalia said. "Nevertheless, be watchful of this man."

"What do you mean?"

But here came dessert. Tiramisu, which Natalia greeted with scorn ("*Per i turisti!*") but ate with gusto. "*Allora,*" she said between mouthfuls, "I understand you would like to visit the Palazzo Reale. Perhaps I can help. If you wish."

"How did you know that?"

She ignored my question. "I know well the museum's *direttrice.* If you like, I will telephone to her."

I hesitated. How could I accept Natalia's offer when I'd refused to help the Kosovar women? But the chance was—I needed to start thinking this way, learn to seize opportunities—too good to pass up. "Yes," I said. "Thank you."

"*Niente.* I am happy to help." And without a hint of tit for tat, Natalia changed the subject. Nodding across the table, she said, "Which?"

Which what? Oh—which of her two men was Chantal married to. I shook my head.

"The American, *certo.* Who else would put up with it?"

Hollis said something to her, and she turned towards him. Dizzied by the steady stream of wine, I half-listened to Joshua regaling the table with news from the States. *The Senate passed an airline bailout package... Bush addressed a joint session of Congress, demanding the surrender of Bin Laden...*

"Does he think *Congress* is hiding him?" I said to Natalia. "Or that Bin Laden watches American TV?"

Isaac Stern died...

"*Ah, che peccato!*" Natalia said. What a shame.

The room seemed to be waltzing. I'm drunk, I thought.

A man, an Arab, on the Amtrak train from Boston to New York, was caught carrying a knife and taken off the train at Providence—

My heart lurched.

"Providence?" I said, but Joshua's monologue rolled on.

I grabbed the nearest glass of wine and drained it. "Providence?" I asked Natalia, who nodded.

"You have drunk all my *vin santo*," she said. "Perhaps you would like more?"

I woke in darkness. My head seemed to contain a balloon being inflated further and further, pushing against my skull. My mouth was lined with flannel, and my eyelids scratched when I blinked. I inched into a sitting position. Beside me came a soft thump, then a sigh. I yanked the sheet up under my chin. The movement made the body next to mine stir and move closer.

It came back to me in a rush. Crunching across the gravel toward the Villa Baiardo's gate to calls of *"Buona notte!...'Notte!"* Walking up the hill to the Villa Francesca, drunker than I'd ever been in my life, lurching and stumbling, leaning on Angus Dance.

My head began to throb, a steady, pounding rhythm that shook my whole body. What did I use to do, all those wakings next to near-strangers, in the reckless years before Daniel?

I prodded the body next to mine. An arm arced up and embraced my knees. I lifted it off.

"You have to go," I said, as loud as my head could stand.

"Only just...arrived," Angus Dance mumbled. "You're a...wonderful...lover."

"Wake up!" I shook his shoulder. "You have to leave now."

"I say. Would you mind turning on a light?"

"Yes, I would." The last thing I wanted was to look at him. The less I saw—it was coming back to me now, the too-often-repeated ritual from the one-night stands of my youth—the easier it would be to forget this.

I could feel Angus Dance straining to see me. Leaning over the edge of the bed, I groped on the floor for possible clothing. My fingers encountered soft wool. I grabbed Laura's sweater.

"I say! This is jolly sudden." The plummy Sean Connery accent—was that what had persuaded me to sleep with him? I remembered our two bodies sliding and grappling, that luscious voice in my ear—

"Please." I swung my legs over the side of the bed and pulled on Laura's sweater and belted it tight. Pleading, I recalled, the damsel-in-distress routine, often used to work. "I feel awful. I need to be by myself right now."

Groaning, Angus Dance got out of bed and began to put on his clothes, making a big deal out of finding them in the dark. Grumbling ("a rum do"…"treated like a tosser"), he let me herd him out of the bedroom and through the *salotto*. Sighing, groaning—but not, thank Goddess, arguing. There'd been a few fierce and even scary ejection scenes in my younger days. At the French doors Dance stopped short—so short that I walked into him—and put his hands on my shoulders. For the sake of peace—of getting rid of him—I let him fasten his lips to mine and thrust his tongue between them. It was like being kissed by a plunger.

I'll be ashamed of myself in the morning, I thought. Not for the sex; for this. This…*submission*.

"Right, then," he said, releasing me. "We'll talk tomorrow. You're knackered, that's all."

I reached around him to open the door. With an air of having figured things out, he stepped backwards onto the patio. "Cheerio! Sweet dreams."

I shut the door between us and shot the bolt. I stood there, feeling his thin, sticky gruel seeping out of me, and watched until he reached the gate. Until I heard it click shut.

I just made it to the toilet before throwing up. Afterward, mixed with the smell of vomit was a strange odor, acrid and industrial, like burning electrical wire. I stood in the shower for a long time, rinsing the smell—it must have been some kind of cologne Dance wore—out of my hair. I scrubbed myself dry with a towel so scratchy it felt like penance.

Back in the bedroom, I put on the T-shirt of Daniel's that I used for a nightgown, and got into bed. The shower had sobered me up enough to feel stupid. Stupider even than the old pre-Daniel Kate, because at this age I should've known better than to have unprotected sex with a near stranger.

Why, *why*, even drunk, had I slept with that man? Oh, for the same reason I used to—the same old pre-Daniel reason. Because I was alone; because I couldn't admit that I was alone. I reached for Hollis's book.

> *my love is building a building*
> *around you, a frail slippery*
> *house, a strong fragile house*

The words on the page wavered and blurred. I will not cry, I told myself. Will not.

I heaved the book onto the floor and turned off the lamp. There was that smell again, as if I'd stuck my head under the hood of a car. I got up, pulled off sheets and pillowcase and threw them on the floor, pitched Dance's pillow after them.

5

The next morning was blessedly gloomy. I called Rachel the minute I woke.

"I'm fine, Mom. Do you know what time it is here?"

Just hearing my daughter's voice muted the drumbeat of my incredible headache. I could see her sitting up in bed, her eyes dark with sleep, her cockatiel's crest of bright brown hair. *A strong fragile house.*

"Oh, God. Fruffle, I'm sorry. I didn't think." Fruffle—the way she used to say "ruffle"—had always been our nickname for Rae.

She was silent. Five thousand miles crackled between us. *A frail slippery house.* "I just wanted to know you're safe," I said.

"Okay, but we've been over this, Mom. Safe isn't the only thing in life. It isn't even the most important—"

"You're sure you're all right?"

For the second time Rae assured me she was fine—the Arab on the Amtrak train had been about to peel an apple—then sang a chorus of "Waking Up Is Hard to Do."

"Listen," I said before she could hang up, "I can come home—"

"You'd come back *now*? Because you had an inkling of trouble here? Mom! Don't you know better than to inkle?"

"—tomorrow, or the day after. As soon as I can get a flight."

"Mother!" Rachel only called me by my full title when she was annoyed with me, a reverse echo of the way I used to cry, Rachel Louisa Rosen-Hagesfeld! Her voice was chilly with disapproval. "I *knew* you'd wimp out. Don't you get it? This is your *chance*—"

There was a burst of crackling so loud I had to hold the phone away from my ear. Then silence.

"Fruffle? Are you there?"

The connection was broken. When I redialed, it went straight to voicemail. Of course: Rae had said her piece. She'd think it was silly that I'd called back just to say goodbye, go back to sleep, love you. My daughter's unwavering practicality—the quality that had made her the youngest counselor at the Providence Community Action Partnership—had always been her shield. It was how she made peace with things that, at the age of twenty-four, shouldn't even have been on her radar. Driving home from Daniel's funeral, I'd tried to tell her how sad I was that she'd grown up in a family with suffering at its center. That she'd seen too soon how fragile and finite life is. But she'd said, *Better too soon than too late, Mom.*

That was the last real conversation we'd had.

Stretching to hang up the phone, I slid further down the bed's treacherous satin comforter and was dumped on the floor. I sat there for a while, leaning back against the bed and pondering, in my blurred and aching mind, the ways in which I'd failed my daughter. Thinking, I mustn't let her down now.

The beating on the door brought me from the bathroom at a run, visions of harm to Rae crowding my aching head. Outside the French doors to the patio stood a man I'd never seen before. He wore a black leather jacket; a motorcycle helmet hid his hair. He had an old-young face, with deep grooves on either side of a downturned, full-lipped mouth.

I hesitated, tightening the belt on Laura's sweater, which was all I had on (I'd been about to get into the shower for the second time since Angus Dance left), thankful for its length. Unsmiling, looking straight at me, the man knocked again, the same *DUM-da-da-DUM-DUM.*

Without thinking, I knocked back, the ritual response, *DUM-DUM*. The man laughed. I couldn't hear him through the glass, but his whole face lifted.

What the hell, I thought. He can't be a burglar. But how did he get past the villa's locked gate?

I turned the bolt and opened the door a crack. "Yes?"

"*Sono qui per insegnarle,*" the man said.

Here to teach me?

It was too early in the morning for this. Wrong morning altogether. My head throbbed and I squinted against swords of sunlight that pierced the morning gloom.

"Please wait," I said, and closed the door.

In the bedroom I threw on clothes, ran a hand through my hair, failed to locate my shoes. When I returned, half-expecting to find no one, the man was sitting cross-legged on the grass with his back to the door. He'd taken off his helmet, and his shaved head, as perfectly shaped as an egg, was thrown back. He seemed to be communing with the fig tree over-head. I watched for a minute, impressed with his concentration, hoping a fig wouldn't hurtle down and bonk him in the eye.

I opened the door. "*Buongiorno!*"

He turned, scrambling to his feet, and crossed the patio. His face was red with embarrassment, and I could guess why. He'd failed to maintain the *bella figura*, an amalgam of dignity and cool that Italian men prize above all else.

"Come in," I said.

He followed me into the kitchenette. I motioned to him to sit down at the counter. He did, stowing skateboard and helmet on the floor beside him. He shrugged off his jacket and let it fall over the back of his chair—He thinks he's invited to breakfast? I thought—revealing a red T-shirt that said *In Bocca al Lupo!* In the mouth at the wolf.

"Who are you?"

"*Sono* Nicolo` Fabbri." Mercifully, he switched to English. "I am your teacher. No, *scusi*, your tutor."

"My tutor? Oh—Natalia sent you?"

"My aunt, *si`*." He smiled, as if I was already turning out to be a clever pupil. Again there was that quick lifting of his expression, making him look a decade younger. He could almost be one of my students. The swift transformation of his face touched me in some way I didn't understand.

"How did you get inside the gate?"

"There is another entrance *Zia* Natalia told me about, through the ruined part of the villa. A *galleria*—a passage—through the rubble."

Skirting the front half of the building every day, I'd never gone inside. Anna Maria had called it unsafe, and warned me to keep away.

While we spoke, I struggled with the *macchinetta*, a metal espresso pot which had a tendency to explode if its two halves weren't screwed together exactly right. Nicolo` Fabbri got up and with a quick "*Permesso?*" took it from me. Standing so close, I caught the smell of male sweat and sun-warmed skin. He unscrewed the *macchinetta* and put it back together.

"*Ecco qua!*"

A simple thing. But it had been so long since anyone had done simple things for me. Turning around, I busied myself with croissants, butter, sour cherry jam. A ripe pear, which I cut into spears and arranged on a red tin plate. By the time I brought all this to the counter, the moment of sadness had passed.

I poured two cups of espresso and sat down across from Nicolo` Fabbri. He was studying a pot of yellow geraniums that sat at the end of the counter, one finger stroking a leaf. "*Buon appetito!*" he said, and dug in.

The warmth of the cup between my palms, the bitterness of the coffee, comforted me. My pounding head stilled; flashes of the night before receded. We talked—mostly Nicolo` Fabbri talked, because somehow the conversation had shifted to Italian. Pear juice ran down our chins. I found myself gesturing, stretching for words, making them up—amid a good deal of laughter. Talking with someone *simpatico* in a language not my own made me forget everything else and just stay afloat in the moment.

At last we pushed aside our empty plates and sat back. Nicolo` Fabbri slid the pot of geraniums along the counter until it sat in a shaft of sunshine. "Plants eat light," he said. "*Che figo!*" How cool is that?

I said, "Signor Fabbri—"

"Nico."

"Caterina, then." Saying it, I felt ... new. "Would you tell me, please, what you charge for lessons."

"*Italiano!*"

I repeated my question, and after he'd corrected the verb I used, he said, "Forty euros. Today is Tuesday. Let us say, Tuesdays and Fridays. We will spend the afternoon, each time going to a different place. Nearby, at first. Nervi. Genoa. Then Camogli. Portofino. This way, you will experience the beauty of my country. And between our meetings, you will read the newspaper. This way, you will experience the craziness of my country."

A bossy family, these Fabbris. I hadn't said I'd hire him.

The Archivio di Stato—which I planned to revisit, now that I had my documents—would yield the names of places in Genoa where Sofonisba had lived. Places, I told Nico, that might be very hard to locate now. Could Nico help?

"*Sì, certo.*"

"Great," I said, in English. Then, reclaiming my right to choose for myself, "You're hired."

We shook hands across the crumb-strewn counter. After we'd exchanged e-mail addresses and phone numbers, Nico said, "I'll see you on Friday. We'll make a plan—many plans."

I wasn't born a planner. Neither was Daniel. Like Dickens's Micawber, he was eternally confident that something would turn up. We'd been married three years when he began to have first odd, then troublesome, then incapacitating symptoms. Dishes broke; fingers got cut; bruises bloomed. Then falls, blackouts, a couple of fender-benders. Then all the downward notches. Cane; forearm crutches; walker; wheelchair. MS, the most unpredictable of illnesses, careened into the future, dragging us with it. You might think optimism, in these circumstances, would be impossible. But Daniel clung to it, like a prisoner under arrest who denies everything. Managing the day-to-day, preparing for what came next—these were left to me. By necessity, I became a foresighted, expect-the-worst, keep-your-head-down kind of person. I gave up fieldwork. Instead, I became Daniel's arms and legs while he could still travel to the dig at Vlashnje; his living crutch when his legs failed; his fingers when he could no longer type. When someone in trouble is carefree, there are always people in the wings who make that possible. Daniel's unwavering optimism had cost me dearly—and Rae, too.

Now here came Nico, a man with a plan. Young enough to be safe. Sure to have an age-appropriate girlfriend or two already. A man whose presence in my life would be a kind of vaccination protecting me from other, more troubling involvements like last night's.

My face ached from the effort of speaking a foreign language. I got a pencil and paper and, pushing aside the two plates with their crumbs and pear cores, made a list of the new words I'd learned.

On the Via Aurelia, the narrow highway separating the Villa Francesca from the Villa Baiardo, the hum of traffic filled my ears. Every car that shot past seemed to have a dog hanging out a window, tasting the fizzy fragrant air. I started walking toward the Passeggiata, the cliff walk overlooking the Mediterranean. My head, the espressos with Nico having worn off, was throbbing, pierced with shards of the night before. The smell of mingled sweat; grinding and pushing; coming. Coming? Ugh.

I needed something to distract me. At the news of her husband's death, Sofonisba would have gone to the sea. Somehow I was sure of this. For comfort? For where his body was? My string bag full of drawing materials swung from my shoulder. As I walked I thought of the courageous women in the nineteenth century who went on digs to Egypt and Persia and Mesopotamia. Amelia Edwards, Jane Dieulafoy, and my favorite, Gertrude Bell. Ladies of the Field, their male contemporaries called them. It was learning about them in high school that had made me decide to become an archaeologist. The detective work of reconstructing how someone had lived from a mere splinter of bone or shard of pottery fascinated me. But even more, I'd longed for a life of adventure and improvisation, like theirs.

A life of exhilarating, satisfying risk. It felt, as my grandmother used to say, like what I'd been put on earth to do.

Rachel would have admired the person I was then.

The cinder path began to slant downhill, gave way to steps between steep walls. The light narrowed. I passed old women weighed down with shopping, a young couple wrapped around each other in a doorway. Then, abruptly, I emerged into a vast openness. Ahead was the great blue bowl of the sky. Below me, leaping and collapsing into a labyrinth of rocks, was the sea. The rocks merged into a jetty. A lone fisherman in yellow oilskins stood at the end, where the water turned green with stripes of blue and bluer.

The Passeggiata was broad and paved with brick. It had been built in the mid-nineteenth century, I knew from Anna Maria, as a place for wealthy Genovesi to see and be seen. I stood at the Soccorso end; at the other end, a mile of winding cliff to the east, was the village of Nervi, on the outskirts of Genoa. The entire length of the Passeggiata was cut into the rock face of the cliff, high above the sea. I took a deep breath. The vegetable smell of seaweed; the salt smell of the ocean.

I sat down on a bench and began to lay out pencil, pastels, drawing pad. Suddenly I had the feeling of being watched. A prickling. A spider-web wafting across the back of my neck. But when I looked around, I saw three grandmothers on a neighboring bench, nodding and trading aphorisms. I turned back to the sea. The faultiest preservative—far behind the desert, ice, or wetlands. Salt and marine organisms and currents—everything about the ocean conspires at decay. Underwater remains survive only if covered with silt. And even silt shifts, exposing what it once protected. Oh, remains!—I thought—it's always remains. *Relict.* And for a second it seemed to me that archaeology was a species of grief.

I grabbed a blue-green stick of pastel. My heart beat faster, my breath came in sips. Strange how fear and excitement feel the same. I remembered Gertrude Bell's motto, copied out by a sixteen-year-old Kate and still taped above my desk at home. *Few such moments of exhilaration as that which stands at the threshold of wild travel.* My view was unobstructed, thanks to the Italian disdain for railings. Nothing but ocean from here to Africa. The color: blue to blue-green to green, surprising bronze and olive.

The texture: crushed silk. The rocks, like human bones preserved in ash. My hand began to move across the paper.

Nothing but water from here to Naples. Then, further north where the coast turns, Livorno. Then Genoa.

She stands on a promontory with her drawing board under one arm and watches the water lick the rocks. Is that what I shall do, in the end? she wonders. Return home, to Genoa and thence to Cremona? But Papa is dead, and all my sisters gone. Home is not home, now.

Her heart knocks painfully against its cage of bone. Fabrizio was home.

This cove is…was…their special place. Too distant from the harbor to interest the commerce-minded Palermitani, it was the first place Fabrizio brought her when they arrived in Sicily. How grateful she felt then, to be done with the long voyage. To be released from the strictures and scrutiny of life at the Spanish Court. Here they stood, she and her new husband, the Mediterranean opening out before them. Grazie, my lord, *she said,* for all of this. *Fabrizio reached for her hand. His grip was firm and warm. With her free hand she removed the pins from her heavy Spanish ruff with its starch and wires, pulled it off, and hurled it into the sea.*

Now she has nothing to throw into the beckoning water, unless it be her drawing board. Or herself. Against her husband's murderers she is powerless to take revenge. But there is nothing to prevent her from joining Fabrizio in the element that holds him now. She has thought of little else since the messenger came. Three long days and longer nights in which she has scarcely eaten or slept and—worse, far worse—has not been able to paint.

An egret circles and lands on the farthest rock. Bending its long neck, it eyes the water. The creamy curved shape against the rocks makes her dig into the drawstring bag at her waist for a piece of red chalk. In the studio she could do nothing. But here, in the open air, at the edge of the sea that holds Fabrizio… Though she cannot paint, she may be able, still, to draw. Drawing is diffident, approaching its subject at a slant the way one might a wild hare. In hard times drawing has always been her comfort. The board Fabrizio made for her from Umbrian poplar already has a sheet of rag paper affixed to it.

Without taking her eyes off the egret, she bends to lay the board on the ground. She spreads her skirts and sits down beside it. There is no one here to see her, after all.

Her fingers refuse the chalk. She presses down until the paper's grain abrades her knuckles, but her hand will not move. The egret arches its wings and rises effortlessly into the sky. She watches it merge with the clouds on the horizon. The water beckons. Come, it murmurs, lapping the rocks. Come closer.

She gets to her feet, drawing board and chalk falling to the ground. She descends the rocky slope, half-walking, half-falling, until she stands at the water's edge. Above her head gulls scroll through the air, uttering their gaunt cries.

Closer.

The water is cold and smells of fish. She cups her hands and tastes it. Salty, rusty—like blood. Understanding hits her like a fist on the breastbone. She will never see Fabrizio again. Not even his corpse. Nothing remains of him in this world. Nothing.

Except—the waves whisper—under the sea. His grave a carapace of sand. His shroud an octopus.

She takes a step forward. Another. Water drags at her hem. Water pours in over the tops of her boots. Her skirts become heavier and heavier, clinging to her legs as if to pull her down.

"I say, hold on! Hallo?"

I was trotting up the steps away from the Passeggiata. Glancing back over my shoulder, I saw Angus Dance.

No! I thought. I tried to hold onto my vision, to the feeling of having traveled and not quite returned. The sense, at once disturbing and thrilling, that with this third occurrence I had drawn even closer to Sofonisba.

"Hallo! Katherine!"

My sneakers slapped the uneven stones, my bag banged against my ribs. As I entered the narrow passage that led to the Via Aurelia, Dance caught up with me. His hand gripped my elbow so that I had to stop. He was so tall that even though I was standing on the step above his, our eyes were level. His, set deep in their bony sockets, gave him a resemblance to Rasputin.

"Angus," he said, as if reminding me.

My face grew hot at the implication that I'd been to bed with someone whose name I didn't remember. Though before Daniel ended a decade of sexual restlessness (oh…*reck*lessness), that had more than once been the case. The high walls, the steep steps, made me feel as if I were at the bottom of a well. Caught. Cornered.

"Fine afternoon for a stroll, what?" Dance stood so close I could feel his humid breath on my face, smell the strange hot-metal smell of his cologne. Flashes of the night before crowded the edges of my mind. I shifted my bag so that it came between us.

Dance said, "I was hoping to run into you." He gave me a wintry smile that made the red-gold tuft on his chin wag.

Merkin! I thought. It broke the spell. This man had no claim on me. Sketchy, Rae would've called him; maybe even, scumbag. A douchebag; a sleazeball; a tool; a—

Heartened by the flood of Raespeak, I said, "Don't let me keep you, Mr. Dance. You must want to finish your walk before sunset."

Dance's hands took refuge in the pockets of his tweed jacket. "Angus. No worries! I'll be happy to escort you back to the Centro."

"Thanks, but I'm not going there." My tone matched his, cheerful, practical.

I turned and started up the steps toward the Via Aurelia. I could hear him trotting after me, forced by the narrowness of the passage to stay one step behind. After a few seconds he said, "Look—Katherine. I feel I should warn you."

"Warn me?"

"A place like the Centro—there are invisible currents. An undertow, you might say." He warmed to his metaphor. "Hidden shoals. One must be careful whom one befriends."

I stopped and turned to face him. Behind his head, the sun was descending between high walls like a coin dropping into a slot. "What do you mean?"

"Our fellow guests at the Centro may not be what they seem."

"Why tell me something like that? I'll decide for myself who's genuine and who's not."

"Very well. I simply meant to--"

"I can look after myself, Mr. Dance."

"Yes, well. Rath*er*. Do call me Angus. I say, where are you headed? We can walk there together, chat a bit. After all, we did share a lovely night—"

"No!" I said. Then, for fear my vehemence might be mistaken for continuing interest, I said, "Look, Mr. Dance. I was drunk. I made a mistake. We have to spend the next two-and-a-half months living in the same place, eating every dinner together. We're adults. Colleagues. Let's leave it at that."

"Bloody hell!"

I spun around and walked on. The steps ended. The path split in two when it met the Via Aurelia. I turned in the direction away from the Centro.

"Katherine—"

"It's *Kate*." Then, more gently (*We're adults*), "I have shopping to do. Goodbye, Mr. Dance," I said, over my shoulder.

"*A presto!*" he called after me, mangling the Italian so that it came out "Opera's toe." See you soon.

Not if I see you first. The schoolyard reply echoed in my head as I trudged along the Via Aurelia, rush-hour traffic roaring past. The feeling of being followed had disappeared, but my thoughts returned to that year in Pristina.

KOSOVO, YUGOSLAVIA, 1981.

Holding out my *letërnjoftimi* with its plastic-coated photograph, I approached the University of Pristina's gates. Inside the kiosk sat the woman who was always there, middle-aged, hair pasted flat to her temples by a hairnet. She shook her head. She pointed behind her to a banner made from bedsheets, spelling out an Albanian word I didn't know.

Strike, the woman said, in English tinged with scorn.

Students clustered around a platform on the other side of the gates, coatless despite the April cold. On the platform stood Daniel. Beside him his favorite student, Sara of the black, black hair, swiftly handed out fliers. Her ponytail sprang out and curled back onto her shoulder like some glossy animal. I could hear distant sirens.

Please, I said to the woman, *ja lutem*. That's my husband up there.

Strike, she repeated, shaking her head vigorously. On the wall behind her someone had chalked a swastika alongside a drawing of the Yugoslavian flag, with an "equals" sign between them.

The sirens drew closer. Below the platform, standing apart from the others, I saw a black-coated man with the look of the secret police. He was gazing up at Daniel. His bald head and curved neck made me think of a vulture.

Back at the Villa Francesca to change for dinner, I wondered whether Angus Dance had been following me. I imagined him creeping along the Via Aurelia a careful distance behind me, sidling down the steps to the Passeggiata, watching from behind a rock while I drew. I shivered. *Why* would he follow me? Could stalking be some weird Scottish seduction technique? And his cryptic warning about my fellow Fellows—was that a ploy to make me feel in need of his protection? Or was he genuinely concerned?

I sat down on the bed to pull on the pesky pantyhose that dinner-dressing required.

Just because he's a Slavicist doesn't make him a spy, Ceiling-Katherine said.

The strike at the University had begun with a student finding a cockroach in his soup. He tossed his tray onto the refectory floor. The whole student body began protesting living conditions; eventually they would be joined by the entire city of Pristina, then the province of Kosovo. Though no one knew it then, that April day marked the beginning of the dissolution of Yugoslavia. The tray heard round the world, Daniel would later call it.

There was still a half-hour before I had to go down to the Villa Baiardo. It was three o'clock in the morning in Rhode Island; but Janet, who worked shifts as an ER doc, might well be awake. "Call my cell if you need me," she'd said before I left. "Call anytime, I never really sleep anymore."

She answered on the first ring. "Katy! Are you okay?"

"Did I wake you?" I said.

"No, no. I'm at the hospital. I'm on break. What's up?"

Telling her, I felt ashamed. There she was, pulling bullets out of people and restarting stalled hearts, and my problem was whether or not I could manage a few months in a villa on the Mediterranean. I didn't mention the flashes of Sofonisba's life; Janet wouldn't have understood.

"Let's think a minute," Janet said. "You were afraid for Rachel, you got drunk, you slept with someone you don't like. Since 9/11 a *lot* of folks are having sex with people they shouldn't. Terror sex."

"I don't want to go back to who I was before Daniel. Sleeping with everything that moves."

"Yeah. It wasn't pretty. But, Katy, that was a long time ago. Another era. Another you."

I was silent.

"You're working, right?"

"Yeah." I wasn't lying—just drawing a small advance on the truth.

"But not enough to keep you out of trouble." A pause; a deep breath. "Look, Katy. For the past twenty years you had a readymade purpose. You had a life to save, over and over. But Daniel's gone. Remember how Grandma Eva used to ask us, What were you put on earth to do? That's what you need to find out."

The very thing I'd thought just hours ago. I wondered, not for the first time, whether a connection as long and strong as mine with Janet makes you able to read each other's minds. Forty-nine years of bestfriendship *and* cousinship. Born within days of each other. We liked to imagine the two couples—my mother and Janet's father were very competitive siblings—madly copulating in a race to see who could procreate first.

Janet said, "You need to be your own center. Not an empty vessel waiting to be filled by other people. Something else Grandma Eva said: our weaknesses are our strengths gone crazy." Her voice held the muted exasperation of a doctor whose patient doesn't follow advice.

"It's not that easy. You don't understand. You've never been in my—"

"Katy. Listen, I've got something to tell you."

"What?"

"I'm going to Africa."

"You're going *where*?"

"I'm leaving for Tanzania at the end of the week."

"For how long?"

"Not sure. A month. Two months, tops. A group from med school asked me to join them. The project's strictly off-the-grid. So no government meddling."

"Illegal, you mean? Janet, for heaven's sake—"

"We're setting up a clinic. In Mwanza."

"A clinic? An *illegal* clinic."

"A clinic for children."

Children. The sudden flare of envy caught me by surprise. Had some of our parents' competitiveness filtered down to our generation? I didn't examine my envy of Janet. I didn't think, *I could help a child, too*—I didn't go that far. I just saw in my mind Lule's face, her tangle of fair fuzzy hair.

"If you could see these kids. One of the docs made a video. Babies, toddlers, kids who should be sitting at desks in first grade somewhere. Skinny and sick, with huge eyes—and *smiling*, Katy. Smiles that bend your heart."

"Don't do it," I blurted. "Please, Jan. That part of the world is dangerous, especially now. Don't you watch the news?"

"Uh-oh. They're paging me. Bye, sweetie. Hang in there! You know what to do—you just have to do it."

"Wait! Jan! I *can't* do it. I'm not the person you think I am."

"Oh, yeah, sweetie," Janet said. "You are."

BOOM!

The explosion seemed to happen inside me. I sat straight up in bed, my heart racketing against my ribs. *Terrorists!* was my first thought. Something whined around the window, rattled the glass in its frame. Then a flash, filling the room with light. And...

BOOM!

A storm, I realized. Not bombs. Just Mother Nature.

Silence. Then a ticking—a quiet click...click...click, like the cooling of a furnace. Then another round of pounding noise. I reached for the bedside lamp, turned the switch. The room stayed dark.

I got out of bed and went to the window. When I pulled back the shutters a grin of lightning slashed the sky. The tops of the umbrella pines swaggered in the wind. Standing at the window, hands to my ears, what I thought between bursts of shelling was: No wonder the Romans believed in cruel, arbitrary, often violent gods. They're here.

Finally the rain came. It began with drops as fierce as hailstones, ricocheting off the window glass, racketing on the roof. Then sheets of water came at my window sideways. I could no longer make out the pines or the path beneath them. The world had been commandeered by rain. I unbolted the window and swung it open. Water flung itself at me, soaking my hair, pouring over my face and neck, plastering Daniel's T-shirt to my chest.

Enveloped in wild, wet darkness, I thought about what Janet had said. I needed a fulltime job; so, yes, I needed to discover something about Sofonisba interesting enough to publish. But work—I thought wistfully, listening to the rain slacken—didn't fill me with the aliveness I'd heard in Janet's voice when she talked about her bootleg clinic. It didn't restore to me the sense of adventure I'd once had. I remembered Rae's reproaches on the phone that morning. What if, next time we talked, I could tell her I was helping political refugees here in Italy? Rae worked with immigrants at PCAP. She took risks for her clients, found ways around the law. She was a fighter, like her father.

Suppose—just suppose—I said yes to Natalia Fabbri's request? Wouldn't it be possible to combine helping the Kosovar women with pursuing my research project? True, there was Angus Dance's warning. But teaching English wasn't a crime. And a little risk, as the Ladies of the Field knew so well, kept your spirit alive.

I'll do it, I thought. I'll go and speak English a few hours a week with the women from Kosovo. Immediately a great peace seemed to pour into the room.

The rain had stopped. I closed the window. Pulling my soaked T-shirt over my head, I flung it on the floor. I dried my rain-clean face and body with the sheet, then wrapped myself in the silken warmth of the comforter. My eyes closed. I could sleep, I thought. Must sleep. The gods command me to sleep. My wet hair clung to my neck. I lifted it away and stretched it out on the pillow. My breathing slowed. At least this time, I thought drowsily, I woke up in the middle of the night for a reason. Not imaginary sounds or voices.

OCTOBER

C'è qualcosa che non va?

6

The little girl—Lule—answered my knock, then turned and ran down the hall. I closed the door behind me and followed. Passing the kitchen, I heard the sound of chopping. The mingled smells of olive oil and garlic drew me in. Meaning to ask where Natalia was, I stepped across the threshold.

Vida whirled around. A cleaver, raised above her head, splashed drops of red onto her gray sweatshirt.

I jumped back. It took a second to find my voice. "Sorry. I didn't mean to startle you."

Vida backed up against the counter. The cleaver fell to her side, where more blood dripped onto the tiled floor. "Excuse," she muttered.

I said, "My fault. I shouldn't've…crept up on you."

Vida leaned against the counter, rubbing her forehead. Those remarkable square-cut eyes glittered. "Crept," she repeated to herself. She turned away and went back to her chopping.

I understand this woman, I thought. I understand her fierceness. It's what you forge, finally—if you can—when grief and loss are endless. Anger is your corset, your carapace, your protective capsule. Not knowing how to say any of this, doubting whether it would be a good idea to try, I left.

"*Cara*!" Natalia greeted me, just outside the living room. She stood on tiptoe, and I managed the double cheek-brushing almost gracefully. She stayed close to me, in that way Italians have. Her breath was a heartening blast of caffeine and nicotine. "Nervous?"

I shook my head.

"*Va tutto bene*," she said. "Don't worry. Everyone looks very forward to you."

Vida called the two children and sent them outside to play, then went ahead of us into the living room.

The room had the same inviting receptiveness I'd felt the first time. A breeze drifted in from the flower-filled balcony, though I could hear the radiators chiming. Of course, I thought, any government prohibition on heating would be lost on Natalia. She saw me looking at the open door and whispered, "Otherwise, they feel trapped." Afternoon light set schools of dust motes swimming through the room. The three women occupied the same places they had when we met: Vida on the sofa; Bardha in the armchair on the other side of the fireplace; Genta on the floor leaning against Bardha's knee. Bardha and Genta seemed to be arguing—I caught the word for "No" in Albanian. They broke off when they saw me.

On the train into the city I'd made up my mind to follow Nico's example: "lessons" would simply mean being together. Talking and laughing—sharing experiences. We would strive to be light-hearted. I'd made Natalia promise not to tell the women that I'd lived in Kosovo, or about Daniel's illness.

Taking one of two narrow needlepoint chairs opposite the sofa while Natalia perched on the other, I said, "What were you talking about? Please go on. Only, in English, please!"

Silence. Vida folded her arms. Looking down at Genta, Bardha shook her head.

Genta turned to me. "I tell to you a story, okay? I know a girl, she was raped by Serbs—"

"Genta!" Bardha said. She laid a hand on her niece's shoulder.

Genta shrugged away. She looked hard at me, as if to say, *You want to talk? Then talk about* this. "Even though her mother put cow dung over her to make ugly. Skorpios was walking everywhere in those days. Black scarves tied on their heads."

"Skorpios?" I was out of my depth already. So much for lightheartedness. Natalia said, "Scorpions. Serbian paramilitaries."

"Six of them, they push…this girl…down and rape her." Genta's voice rose. "Everywhere, they bite her. Her breasts. Her belly. Her…down there. When she went home to her village, her fiancé, he drooped her. Drooped?"

"Dropped," I said.

"—dropped her. She is no longer suit…suitable for marriage. She is dirty—the castle of the enemy. Her grandmother tell her, Better dead and under the ground. Since that day she never see her family more. Tell me, Signora! Should she not leave her country, her people, and find what she can find?"

Genta looked at me, fierce and trembling. She waited—everyone in the room waited—to see what I would say. Behind her, Bardha, her lined face full of tenderness, reached out to stroke her long dark hair. Vida sat, arms crossed, legs crossed, like someone in an invisible straitjacket, and stared at me, her eyes telegraphing the purest scorn. I recognized it because it was what I'd so often felt myself in the years after Daniel's diagnosis—at dinner parties or hiking with friends or shopping for groceries—whenever I went among the ones whom tragedy hadn't touched.

I looked at Natalia. *You're the shrink. Say something.* Her arms gripped the arms of her chair. She waited. The papal parakeet, Gianpaolo, began to scold from his perch atop one of the paintings.

Should I say what I'd guessed?

Later I would learn that all three women had been victims of rape ("three—out of the forty-five thousand who have suffered it," Natalia said grimly, "what you Americans call a drip in the bucket"), and that was why, when their visas ran out, they'd stayed in Italy. The stigma of rape— the shame it brought on a woman's family—meant they could never go home. At the moment, though, I didn't know any of that; I had only instinct to guide me. At the moment, there was Genta.

I plunged. "I think that"—I swallowed the word *you*—"every woman has the right to, to fight for herself. For her happiness."

Genta didn't look at me, but her shoulders relaxed. She wrapped her arms around her knees and leaned back against Bardha. She's only sixteen, I thought. I remembered how mortified Rachel had been at that age by the public revelation of anything personal. Time for a distraction.

I looked over at Natalia, but she was watching Gianpaolo polish his beak on the picture frame.

"So," I said, wincing at the cheerfulness in my voice, "what have you done since we met last?" One of the questions I thought of as Nico's conversation-goosers. "Did anyone see anything interesting?"

Vida snorted. Genta sat with downcast eyes. It was Bardha who came to my rescue: she'd taken the children to the Aquarium in the Porto Antico the day before. The others remained silent while Bardha sketched fish shapes in the air and I guessed at their English names. Their colors, which Bardha, leaning forward in her flowered dress and frowning, intent, wanted to know. Great vocabulary builder, Nico would've said. Shark, jellyfish, dolphin. Chartreuse, orange, scarlet. Glide, circle, dive.

Natalia walked me down the hall when the lesson ended, one arm around my shoulders, which she had to stretch to reach.

"You will come to us on Mondays and Thursdays, *d'accordo?*" she said when we got to the door. "Come at one and launch with us."

"Lunch."

"You see? You are a natural."

"Why didn't you say anything? To Genta?"

"It was not my place, *cara*. We have therapy sessions on other days. Today was a language lesson. Also, it is good simply to share experience. In this way, we are no longer 'me' and 'them.' We are *us*."

Us, I thought wistfully.

"You have met my nephew, I hear. *Bene!* You will be some days teacher, some days pupil. It is the ideal way to live."

"Nico is a good teacher. I'm just winging it—"

"Till Thursday, then. *Arrivederci!*"

Kisses on both cheeks, interrupted by noses; then Natalia turned and went back down the hall to the living room. I stood looking after her. My reluctance to leave the apartment was physical, like an ache. I wanted its shelter for myself.

The door opened, knocking me backwards, and Lule burst in. When I started past her, she grabbed my hand. "*Signora, vieni!*" She spoke Italian as well as any Genovese child; I remembered that she'd been in Italy a year and a half. Charmed that she seemed to have shed her reserve and decided to accept me, I let her pull me back down the hall into the kitchen.

After a glance over her shoulder, Vida went on with her work. The kitchen smelled like the sea. On the table was a drawing in pencil on a paper bag cut open and laid flat.

"See?" Lule said in Italian. "Big fish—oh!—chasing little fish—oh! Big fish wants to *eat*. Little fish swims between the rocks. Now big fish can't catch him, because—see?—he can't fit. He's blue and red, and little fish is yellow. My crayons are all ruined, Ardi chewed them. So I made it with no color."

"English, Lule!" Vida said.

Admiring the drawing with suitably extravagant adjectives, I made a mental note to bring my pastels next time. This child, who reminded me so much of Rae at her age that my arms ached to hold her, should have color. Everyone in this apartment should have color, all the color they could get.

Lule said, "Fish die. All animals and people die. Do you know that?"

"*Si`, cara*," I said. I'd had more or less this conversation with Rachel when she was five—old enough to see that there was something wrong with her father.

Lule looked up at me, her forehead wrinkling with concern, as if to say, I hate to break this to you. "So…*you* will die."

"*Si`, certo.*"

"Well, doesn't that worry you?"

"Lule!" Vida said, in English. "Don't to bother the Signora with nonsense."

It's not nonsense, it's utter sense, I wanted to say. I put out a hand and stroked Lule's cotton-candy hair. "It won't be for a long time, *cara*," I said. "So, no, I don't worry about it."

"Come see my mama's fish."

Lule darted over to the sink. I went and stood on Vida's other side. Ignoring us, she gripped a large fish by its tail and brought down the cleaver. The severed head fell to one side, rocking on the cutting board. A cold eye stared up at me. Vida laid down the cleaver and picked up what looked like a steel toothbrush with spikes instead of bristles. She ran it along the fish from the tail forward, over and over. Fish scales shot upward, flakes of brightness flying everywhere. They stuck to Vida's hands and sweatshirt and caught in her tangled dark-red hair. A few found their way onto my sweater. Vida flipped the fish over and worked on the other side.

"My mama is strong," Lule told me. She crowded up against her mother's flank to see better.

Vida picked up a knife and slit the belly. I saw a gleaming mass of organs, blue-green and purple and gray. A smell like rotten eggs rose up. Vida wiped her forehead with the back of one hand. "The liver, see?" she said to Lule. "The intestines." She stepped back. "Now you."

How *can* she? I thought. What kind of mother would expose her child to this, expect her to participate in slaughter?

I laid a protective hand on Lule's shoulder. She shrugged it off and took her mother's place. Her chin just cleared the countertop. Standing on tiptoe, she reached into the carnage strewn across the cutting board. I could hear her breathing. Slowly, with two fingers, she pried loose the shivery white ladder of the spine.

Vida clapped her hands. Her smile was the first one I'd seen her give. "*Brava*! That's my girl."

By mid-October my life in Italy had acquired a rhythm. Mondays and Thursdays at Natalia's, where I was—officially, at least—the teacher; Tuesdays and Fridays with Nico, where I was the pupil. My comfort with Italian was growing: I could catch the current of thought and glide on its updraft. Our afternoons left me refreshed, as if I'd not only been somewhere else, but been some*one* else. With Nico, in Italian, I was Caterina.

"*Allora,*" Nico said, at our fifth meeting, "what have you done that's interesting since we met last?"

"*Niente di particolare,*" I answered. Nothing special. I'd never told him that I visited his aunt twice a week, or what I did there. Natalia had asked me not to. Apparently Nico had no idea she was harboring illegal refugees. Thinking about this gave me a pleasant sense of conspiracy; Natalia's *us* echoed in my head.

"—don't you think?"

"What? Sorry."

"*Italiano!*" Nico wore a hurt look, deepening the downward grooves on either side of his mouth. The fact that I'd answered in English showed him how little attention I'd been paying.

Sensitive, I thought, sighing. Emo, as Rae would say.

"*Scusa,* Nico."

This afternoon, he repeated, would be a good time to explore Nervi. "Tuesday is market day. You can practice your vegetables. We'll walk back along the Passeggiata just at sunset."

Many new vocabulary words later—words that, being a hopeless cook, I would only ever use in restaurants—we descended a winding path toward the Passeggiata. This end was different from the Soccorso approach. Green, shady, preserving the wetness of the night before. We moved along a curving avenue lined with laurel and giant aloes, their sword-shaped leaves the size of my arm. We stopped at a tree I didn't know.

"What's that?" I asked.

"Mimosa." Nico crouched and balanced on his haunches. There were several seconds of scolding, like a dozen tiny typewriters, from birds hidden in the foliage. "Come closer."

I went and stood beside him. His shaved head, inches below my chin, had the pleasing roughness and roundness of a tennis ball. Dime-sized circles dotted his shirt from last night's rain. I could smell the frank odor of male sweat.

Concentrate, Ceiling-Katherine admonished from an overhanging eucalyptus.

"Watch." Nico breathed on his fingers to warm them, then touched the tip of one frondlike leaf. Slowly it furled, until it was a green reed. One by one, the other three fronds did the same. Then the whole four-fingered stem drooped until it pointed straight down.

"That's amazing," I said.

"Thigmonasty."

"What?"

"Thigmonasty." Nico switched to English, for clarity. "Movement caused by touch. Only certain plants can do. Now see!"

I looked again at the mimosa. The fronds had unfurled.

"So plants feel it when you touch them?" I said.

"Some scientists think so. Professor Mancuso, in Florence, *per esempio.*" Nico grabbed a gray-green bush growing beneath the mimosa and squeezed it. He held his hand under my nose. I breathed in a ravishing scent.

"The perfume a flower gives off when it's crushed," Nico said, "may be a cry of pain. Plants communicate, Caterina. They have a vocabulary of three thousand chemicals. At the International Laboratory of Plant Neurobiology in Florence—" he broke off, looking abashed. "*Scusa.* It is not so interesting."

"No, it's fascinating. How do you know all this?"

"*Sono botanico.*" Then, in English, "I am a botanist. I have a master's degree from the University of Siena."

Then what are you doing tutoring? I wanted to ask. But I didn't know him well enough; and anyway, it wasn't my business.

We walked on toward the sound of the sea. The rich smell of damp earth rose around us. A crumbling stone wall replaced the shrubbery on our right. Nico pointed to some star-shaped succulents growing out of the wall. "Agave. They flower only once, just before dying."

"Sad," I said.

"No. *E` normale.* They have seeded their offspring. They must make way for them."

"What's that?" I pointed to a tree at the top of the wall. Leafless and hung with bright-orange globes, it had a manufactured gaudiness.

"*Cachi*. Persimmons," Nico answered, sounding surprised. "Did we not saw them in the market?" I suppressed a giggle: he often sounded like a child on his forays into English. "You haven't to see them in America?"

"Not in New England." Even if the climate had allowed it, this fruit looked like everything the Puritans would've shunned.

"Then you must try."

Nico shrugged off his jacket and began climbing the wall, rocks clattering down behind him. *Be careful*, I started to call out—then thought, I'm not his mother. He isn't *that* much younger than me. He scrambled upward, finding invisible handholds and footholds, and swung himself onto the top of the wall, a good ten feet above my head. He reached up, tugged, turned around to look down at me.

"Catch!"

A bright-orange ball hurtled toward me. I put up a hand in time for it to slap into my palm, surprised at how squishy it felt. Nico crouched on the edge of the wall, gathered himself, and jumped. He hit the ground. He rolled over and was still.

I ran to where he lay. "Nico!" He didn't move. I touched his shoulder. "Nico!" I shook him.

He opened his eyes and sat up. "*Eccomi!*"

For a second, I was furious. What a child he was! He'd scared me, but I didn't want to admit it. I said, "*Bravo!*" and was rewarded by that slow lifting of his face. He held out a hand for me to grasp, and pulled himself up. He stood there a moment, in that Italian way, so close his breath warmed my cheek. Then he took the persimmon from me. It wore a star-shaped cap of green leaves. He pierced the cap with his thumbnail and peeled it away, then squeezed until orange jelly emerged through the hole.

"*Eccolo!*"

I bit into it, expecting something syrup-sweet. Instead, it was like a mouthful of laundry detergent. I swallowed, almost gagging. I handed the fruit back to Nico, who took a bite and immediately spat it out. He wiped his mouth on his sleeve and looked at me, crestfallen.

"Too early," he said. "I knew that, but..." He made a face. "I am *ottimista*. In November we'll come back."

He retrieved his jacket from the path, where he'd thrown it. We walked on, the sound of the sea becoming louder. Our silence was companionable. Every now and then I felt Nico look at me. I didn't meet these looks, for fear of encouraging him. (*Him?* said Ceiling-Katherine from the top of the laurel hedge. *Or you?*) So I didn't know if the glances were admiring, or assessing, or just some tic.

And I don't *want* to know, I thought. But somehow this Kate-thought, in Caterina's head, didn't feel convincing.

We emerged onto the brick pavement of the Passeggiata. Sea-spray stung my face, soaked into my sweater, drenched my hair. Huge waves rose one after another, hurled themselves against the rocks, swarmed over them and crashed upward onto the pavement. Nico stood still, so I did, too. The bitterness of the persimmon clung to my tongue. I opened my mouth and drank sea-spray.

"Isn't it great?" Nico shouted. I could see he would have been happy standing here for hours, observing. He had a rare kind of patience, I was beginning to realize. It was what made him a good tutor.

Seagulls filled the air overhead with querulous cries. "It's good hunting for them," Nico said into my ear.

I looked down at the rocks, their hollows full of boiling foam; at the waves rearing up, curling back, then plunging. The sky above all this was calm and blue. Far out at the horizon, the sun had begun gliding down into dreamy remnants of cloud.

"Why are there waves like this, when the storm is over?" I asked.

"It's called swell. After the storm has passed and the wind ceases, there remain waves generated far out to sea. They can continue for days. It takes a long time for the sea to forget."

"So," I said, meaning to tease him, "you're a meteorologist as well as a botanist?"

I felt him recoil. "We should get back," he said, turning, and began to walk.

I'd hit a nerve. Something to do with his being under-employed? Too late, I remembered the *bella figura*. Though my Italian was steadily improving, I still wasn't sure when I might be coming across as brusque. It wasn't just a matter of learning the language; it was learning a grace and warmth that weren't native to my non-Caterina world.

We continued along the cliff walk toward Soccorso, Nico moving faster than before. Seeing me shiver, he pulled off his motorcycle jacket and draped it over my shoulders; but our camaraderie had evaporated. He sped up until there was a distance of three or four steps between us.

A rogue wave leapt over the edge of the pavement and curled around my ankles. The water was unexpectedly warm, and tickled. I laughed. Nico looked back over his shoulder, frowning.

"We've stayed out longer than we should have," he said. "We must hurry."

Squelching along behind him, my soaked shoes sucking at the pavement, I kept both hands on the collar of Nico's jacket to keep it from sliding off. Just before the end of the Passeggiata the coast curved right, toward the sea. Patches of vegetation held sparks of yellow—tiny flowers. I won't ask their name, I thought. Out at sea, where fiery rags of cloud clung to the horizon, a freighter crawled toward some port further east. Which one? I wondered. I wouldn't ask that, either. Even though, as Ceiling-Katherine pointed out from atop the cliff to my left, *It's his* job *to talk to you. That's what you're paying him for.*

We finished the ascent from the Passeggiata in silence. I handed Nico his jacket, along with the usual envelope—thick, embossed Centro stationery—containing the usual twenty-euro bills.

"*Grazie,*" he said. Eyes averted, he stuffed the envelope into the pocket of his jacket, which he slung over one shoulder. Cold; businesslike. "On Thursday we will go to Camogli. *D'accordo?*"

"*D'accordo.*"

A quick *Ciao!* and off he went, in the direction away from the Centro.

Definitely emo. Twenty-five years of marriage, preceded by more lovers than I cared to count, and I still didn't understand men. ("Katy," Janet liked to remind me, "women have more genetic material in common with female mice than they do with human males.") I imagined, trudging along in the twilight toward the Centro, that Caterina would have thought of something to say to Nico. Caterina would have known how to lighten a bad mood instead of falling into it. But I was Kate now, a relapse that regularly occurred at the handing over of the euro-filled envelope.

The next day, Wednesday, held neither tutoring nor being tutored. I decided to go into Genoa and try the Archivio di Stato again. Why wait until Nico consented to go with me? My Italian was now good enough to argue in, and my decision to help the Kosovar women had made me feel I could make things happen. The thought of handling paper Sofonisba herself had touched had me fizzy-stomached all the way in on the train.

At the Archivio I laid out my Dean's letter with its impressive Rhode Island School of Design crest, my passport, my letter of acceptance from the Centro, a one-page Italian statement of my research purposes, and the *autorizzazione* from the Ministry of Culture that Anna Maria had provided for each of the Fellows. The Chief Archivist puffed out his thin cheeks. His breath smelled of spearmint. After a long minute he said, "*Benvenuta, Dottoressa* Hagesfeld!" and swept my documents together and stood up. "But you should have telephoned ahead. Perhaps the material you seek is not accessible." He gave me a severe look. "An archive is not a library, you know. Come. We'll copy your documents and register you."

It took a good half-hour, including a lecture from the Chief Archivist that duplicated the one I gave my students every year, on how to work with primary sources. Finally I settled into a spindly chair with a cardboard file-box on the table in front of me. On its spine was written *Sofonisba Anguissola, 1532(?)-1625* and a list of the materials it contained. Looking at it, I shivered. Or maybe it was the dry chill of the room, with its arched ceiling and endless shelves of boxes and dimmed light. I'd had to check my windbreaker along with my purse. The only other patron, a thin, graying man at the table next to mine, had a yellow muffler wound around his neck. The walls of the Archivio di Stato must have been fortress-thick: all sight, sound, even thought, of the city outside had vanished. Windowless, the room held a church hush. A church *smell*: paper and beeswax and old wood.

Sofonisba's materials were separated into labeled paper folders. I picked the one marked "*Documenti Legali.*" A sheaf of *Fides Vitae*—notarized affidavits of residence—came first. The white gloves doled out to visitors made it hard to handle the stiff parchment. Sixteenth-century handwriting is ornate and tiny. It was slow going. Using the eraserless stub of pencil and the scrap paper which were all I'd been allowed to bring inside the room, I made a list of the seven *contrade*—neighborhoods—where Sofonisba and her husband had lived during their years in Genoa. The records gave no exact addresses. Still, when I had time I would go there—they were all in the Maddalena district, which had changed very little since the sixteenth century—and see what I could see.

I looked through various other legal documents, most having to do with the yearly collection of Sofonisba's pension or the return of her dowry from her first marriage. No birth or death certificates, since they weren't issued in Italy before the 1800's. I looked for a ship's manifest. Sofonisba had sailed from Palermo to Genoa on a ship called *La Patrona*, a voyage that had changed the course of her life. I wanted to know what kind of ship. But there was nothing. Damn! I thought. I must have spoken out loud, because the man at the next table muttered, without looking up, "*Silenzio!*" Discouraged, I almost closed the folder without looking at the rest of the documents. Sofonisba's biographer must have combed through this material already, along with the curators who'd written catalogue essays for exhibitions of her work. But still. *Often what you find is not what you were looking for*, my favorite professor used to tell her students. *Be awake to new discoveries*. I read through the rest of the folder.

My discovery was what *wasn't* there. The *Documenti Legali* included no record of a second marriage. I was puzzled. Why had Sofonisba's biographer and other scholars all assumed a second marriage had taken place?

I'd saved the *Corrispondenza* folder for last—documents Sofonisba herself had surely touched. The letters in this folder, on rag paper, fought gloved fingers even more than parchment. And they were more difficult to read, since they were written in a less formal hand. My chair was pewhard—clearly the Archivio di Stato did not want visitors to linger—and my lunchless stomach rumbled. Still, it was a thrill to see Sofonisba's actual handwriting. She knew how to make a goose quill behave: her writing sloped decorously, with long graceful tails on the f's and g's. The best letter was her response to the Duke of Tuscany's warning against an unsuitable second marriage. Reading it, I laughed out loud, disturbing the liturgical hush and earning a reproach from my fellow visitor.

> *I received a letter from Your Most Serene Highness that comforted me greatly in my current troubles, as I saw with what benevolence Your Most Serene Highness remembers me in a matter so important….But since marriages are made first in heaven and only then on earth, your letter reached me too late.*

Scholars' assumption of a second marriage seemed to hinge on this one letter. On this one sentence. And the sentence was equivocal. *Marriages are made first in heaven and only then on earth*: not a statement that Sofonisba had married, just an observation (one that blew the patriarchal tradition of her time sky-high). *Your letter reached me too late*: noncommittal as to what the royal letter had arrived too late for. I knew from my previous research that the Duke of Tuscany, who governed Genoa at the time, would have had to consent to any remarriage, as would Philip II of Spain, from whom Sofonisba received a pension. It would also have required the approval of her brother, as head of the family. Had Sofonisba really managed to marry without the required permissions? This letter, sent from a convent in Pisa, was dated 24 December; Sofonisba had left Palermo in early December. It seemed unlikely that she could have found and married a second husband in less than a month. Was her letter to the Duke a strategic lie later made good? Or had she—this possibility made my breath catch—never remarried? Lived—for thirty-five years, in the midst of Genovese society, and in the eyes of the international art world—a lie?

The mystery of the Lost Year had deepened. It's often a good sign in archaeology—getting in deeper. A sign that you're on the right track even though you now see less clearly than you did before. Excitement traveled through me like a shot of *grappa*. I wanted to tell someone. I wanted to leap up, grab the man at the next table by his frayed lapels and cry, *Listen to this!*

I wanted to tell Daniel.

With one white-gloved finger I traced the letter's signature.

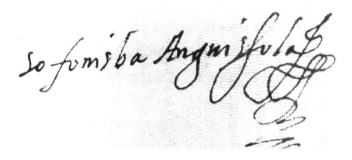

Swinging through the swift curves and figure-skater loops made me dizzy with desire. I wanted this signature. I wanted to have it and keep it. There was, of course, no photocopying permitted in the Archivio di Stato. No cameras. I seized my stub of pencil and a scrap of permitted paper and began to draw.

Her brother's visit makes a welcome distraction for her household after two long months of mourning. The servants come quickly when he summons them, smile whenever he appears. In the courtyard the outdoor dogs swarm around him, their muscular tails thumping his shins. He is charming, Asdrubale. In childhood it was his talent, as painting was hers, and music, Lucia's. And he has grown up handsome, with their mother's erect posture, their father's bright, black, calculating eyes.

A week into Asdrubale's visit the two of them sit wrapped in woolen cloaks on the bench outside her studio. The crickets' steady, metallic song is magnified by the night air. The smell of horse dung drifts from the garofano *beds, covered with straw against the winter rains.*

Let us agree it's settled, allora, *Asdrubale says in a low voice. He spreads his legs wide and locks his hands behind his head. A ship leaves for Genoa in four weeks. By then I'll have set in motion the return of your dowry. He huffs, to show his righteousness. How your husband,* pace all'anima sua, *could have left on such a voyage without making a will, I'll never understand.*

She glances sideways at this bearded stranger with his deep voice and assured gestures. Starlight sharpens his profile. What have you done with the chubby, cheerful boy of eight? she wonders. The one whose round-eyed, round-cheeked laughter I sketched over and over? The one who wept when my ship left for Spain two decades ago?

Her brother says, more gently, What other course is open to you, Sofi? You cannot stay here, under Spanish rule. Your husband's murderers… He stops, perhaps afraid of upsetting her.

But she knows that if Fabrizio's ship had been attacked by pirates, he would not have been the only one killed. His enemies at Court—men who were his rivals, men who were his lovers—must have ordered his death. And might not stop there.

I must consider, she says. Thinking, I must ask Fabrizio what he— O Dio! *Will I never accustom myself to his absence?*

Asdrubale has his own reasons for urging her return to Cremona. Still, he makes a good point. Since every woman must be under the protection of some male or other, she has but two choices. Return to the Spanish court, as King Philip has suggested—become again the ornamental lady painter every monarch seems to need these days. Or return to her childhood home, where feckless Asdrubale has replaced poor dead Papa as head of a diminished household.

Asdrubale sits cracking his knuckles. She can feel the effort he makes to hold back speech.

When she thinks of life at Court—of the hours when she wasn't in the studio, painting—what she remembers is endless afternoons of needlework with the other ladies-in-waiting. The percussive sound (punto! punto!) *of sixteen needles punching through linen—like a roomful of tiny clocks ticking away her life. The high, starched ruff that punished every yawn. No conversation more interesting than whether there might be fresh cherries for dessert.*

Her home in Cremona, on the other hand, will not be the home she remembers. Minerva and Lucia dead; Elena long since immured in the convent in Pisa; Europa and Anna married and raising families. (Her sisters had a way, just when Papa thought the family would begin to profit from their lovingly nurtured gifts, of either dying or going off to lives of their own.) The slate-roofed house across from Chiesa di San Giorgio will no longer hold the sound of Lucia's spinetta, *notes dropping like pearls—*

Sofi! Asdrubale leans forward. The family needs you. We have sorely missed you.

For two decades? It's hard to believe they remember her, much less miss her. Asdrubale—boh! He needs her pension to maintain the family home—as she has done for the past quarter-century—and pay for his caprices. The smell of horse dung seems oddly appropriate.

She pulls her cloak about her. In truth, she cannot see a way forward. Since Fabrizio's death it's as if she were sealed inside a pouch of heavy velvet, all life's pleasures—sight sound smell taste touch—muted. She cannot paint because she cannot see. And if she cannot paint, what does anything matter?

Perhaps she should have continued walking into the sea that day a month ago, when the waves called to her. She isn't sure, even now, why she turned back.

Va bene, *she says at last, from inside her velvet pouch. I will go with you to Cremona. But it's as if a caul of chainmail had settled over her heart.*

Asdrubale leaps up, snaps his fingers. Bravissima! *he cries.*

7

With my weekdays so full, weekends felt empty. On the third Saturday in October, when I'd been at the Centro a month, I decided to go for a hike. The path that ran alongside the Villa Francesca ended at an olive grove further uphill. I'd been wanting to see what lay beyond that, where the land continued its long ascent from the sea to the mountains. Lunch went into my string bag: a baguette, olives, a tomato, a wedge of dill-flecked cheese Nico and I had found at the market in Nervi. Before setting out, I went down to the Villa Baiardo to see if Anna Maria had a map. It was a glorious day, bright and warm but with the coolness of autumn tucked inside—like fried ice cream, Rae would've said. Above the Via Aurelia a white moon was etched against the blue sky: a ghost moon.

The mountains were the Apennines, Anna Maria told me. There was no map of the *entroterra*, the stretch before the mountains began. (*Entroterra*, when I looked it up afterwards, meant "hinterland," a word that conjured up visions of bandits and travel on horseback.) Do not go alone, Anna Maria warned. "Bad people can be there. People who harm you. *Zingari*." But I wanted to be by myself, so that I could really feel the place. I'd read, before coming to Italy, how being sandwiched between the mountains and the sea defined the region of Liguria. Any archaeologist knows that terrain influences a people's history, their culture, even their temperament.

At the edge of the olive grove I stumbled into a sagging fence of rusted iron hidden by long grass. Caught in the palings, I had to pull myself free. I felt a searing pain. When I rolled up the leg of my jeans, there was a long bleeding gash on my right shin. Laura's sweater—she'd urged me to keep it, even after my luggage showed up—was tied around my waist. Feeling in the pockets, I found some Kleenex and packed them against the wound. At the bottom of one pocket was an elastic ponytail band. I pulled it up over my hiking boot and let it snap around the wad of tissue, then eased the leg of my jeans down. Perfect. A solution worthy of the Ladies of the Field. Thank Goddess I'd had a tetanus shot before leaving Providence.

I clambered over the fence. The olive grove held the scent of wood-smoke, and orange nets hanging from the trees sagged with fallen olives. I had to try one. It was nut-hard and bitter. I spit it out and began to make my way between the gray, gnarled trees. Once I left the grove, the ascent grew steeper. The trail led through terrain that was not exactly woods, not exactly wild. Trees I recognized—pine and oak, chestnut, here and there the white gleam of birch—mingled with others I didn't know. Under-growth suggested that this area had once been cultivated: I passed laurel, juniper, rhododendron. The ground became rocker, steeper. Birds called from the thickening trees.

While I walked I thought about my discovery in the Archivio di Stato the previous Wednesday. Had Sofonisba faked a second marriage? In six-teenth-century Italy all decent women lived under male protection. Their time, their money, their very bodies belonged to that male. I could imag-ine the Sofonisba I was beginning to know inventing a way to escape her brother's control without falling into some other man's. Would she have kept up the pretence for a lifetime? I remembered a self-portrait repro-duced in her biography. Sofonisba in her late seventies, at the height of her fame. White ruff, black gown, net cap over thin gray hair; but the eyes in the lined face held the same banked fire as those of the young artist who'd signed herself "Virgo" half a century before. Sofonisba, I realized, resem-bled the Ladies of the Field. Her spirit; her strength and determination. Was that what had enabled her to make the leap out of widowhood, to return from grief to life?

Archaeologists tend to find what they're looking for. Therefore—every student is warned—choose your quest carefully. Had I gone astray with mine? Sofonisba was supposed to be my ticket out of academic limbo. She was becoming more and more a *person* to me, when I needed her to remain an object of investigation. Still, when I thought about the visions I'd had—more like visitations than visions—I realized that all four of them had been triggered by objects Sofonisba had left behind. I remembered my compulsion to touch the portrait of Fabrizio de Moncada. Archaeology begins with objects. Archaeologists *touch*. First, the most primitive sense; then imagination takes over, forming a bridge between the present and the past. Reconstructing the life of people before us through the objects they left behind. Okay, then. The Visitations—I told myself—were just a heightened version of archaeological reconstruction.

I'd been climbing for half an hour when I came to a steep outcropping. The cliff face, punctuated by tough-looking plants, seemed to rise straight up. The scent of wild thyme filled my nostrils. I stopped—I was tired, and my wounded leg throbbed. Time for lunch. As I was looking around for somewhere to sit, I heard voices.

"…ridiculous!"

"Not if you think about it."

My heart speeded up, keeping time with the pulse in my injured leg. *Hiking alone!* Ceiling-Katherine said from the cliff that blocked my escape.

"Think! That's all you ever do. How about deeds, not words?"

American voices. Not *zingari*, then. A woman and…a high-pitched man? The second voice didn't quite sound male.

There was a shout of "Deeds? Fuck deeds!" A crashing and snapping of branches. Pine and hemlock parted to reveal Laura.

Relief flooded through me. "Hi," I breathed.

Laura stood wiping the sweat from her face with the sleeve of her red windbreaker. Her cheeks were flushed, her eyes bright. No one else emerged from the trees. She saw me looking and said, "I was…uh…practicing. I'm giving a poetry reading next week at the University of Genoa."

That was no poem, I wanted to say. You were talking to yourself, in two different voices. But I, a woman lectured by a fragment of herself that hung out on ceilings, was hardly in a position to criticize.

"I'm glad to see you," I said. In the month we'd been at the Centro, we'd embarked on a precarious friendship. I'd babysat several times for Amber, who liked me, and that endeared me to Laura. But the difference in our positions at the Centro seemed to rankle.

I gestured to the cliff behind me. "We can't go any farther."

I sat down on the ground, where the exposed roots of a chestnut tree made a sort of armchair. When my right leg folded under me, I yelped.

Laura said, "What's the matter? Are you hurt?"

"It's nothing. Listen, I was about to have lunch. There's plenty."

Laura sat down in the root-armchair next to mine. I got busy pulling things out of my bag. The food, in separate paper wrappings; a bottle of water; a couple of paper towels; a knife. I tore the baguette in two, sliced the tomato and cut the cheese in half, divided the olives—then assembled everything on two smoothed-out paper wrappers. I handed one to Laura. "Here you go."

We ate in silence, the sun through the pines sending slender streams of light onto our makeshift picnic. A lone bee made lazy figure eights above the food. High in the sky a silver jet appeared, and I watched it stitch its way across the blue. My leg was hurting more.

Suddenly Laura laughed. She held up a twist of waxed paper containing a mixture of pepper and salt, which I'd packed for the tomato. "You're so...planful." She leaned back against the trunk of the chestnut tree. Again I noticed how odd she looked: disheveled, almost feverish. "It feels great to eat food prepared by someone else. You're so lucky to be here on your own. Not have to look after anyone."

Lucky? Had Laura not noticed that my husband had had to *die*, for this to happen? And how about the long, sad lead-up to that death? But I'd never mentioned Daniel's illness to Laura. I'd seen too many strangers' reactions. What did he die of? they'd ask, inevitably (humanly) interested in what could kill someone not yet old. Multiple sclerosis, I'd say. Was he sick for a long time? Yes—twenty years. And at that phrase, *twenty years*, I'd see my questioner's face change. I'd watch disbelief roll over it like a cloud crossing the sun. It was too long *twenty years* no one suffered like that nowadays, it was epic *twenty years* like something out of Homer. Mythological—as in, imaginary. As in, made up.

"Amber's lovely," I ventured. "So curious and smart. You and Hollis must be very proud of her."

"You don't understand." Laura's voice wavered. "You're a Fellow, not a"—she spat the word out—"*spouse*. You don't know what it's like to have to follow your husband around, go where he needs you to go, do what he needs you to do."

Oh, don't I?

"…you don't know how it feels. To always be second. Like a servant or a satellite or, or…riding around in somebody's sidecar."

Sidecar? Beats a wheelchair.

"It *blows*," Laura said. "It just fucking blows." She dabbed at her eyes with a paper towel.

I didn't want to think mean thoughts, to compete in suffering. It never helped. I reached over and touched Laura's arm. "It *is* hard," I said. "I know that."

She looked at me gratefully, about to speak, when there was a rustling in the underbrush on the other side of the clearing. We both sat up. The rustling deepened; the bushes swayed back and forth. Laura's hand seized mine. I thought of the animals Anna Maria had said inhabited the *entro-terra*: hedgehogs, weasels, deer. Wild boar. If a wild boar charges, she'd said, stand still till it's almost on you, then jump sideways. Boar can only run straight ahead.

But it was just a trio of rooks, bursting through the trees like a bolt of blackness. Surprisingly large, they settled at the edge of the clearing. Laura let go of my hand. She blew her nose and smoothed her hair.

"We should go," I said. I began to get to my feet. Pain clamped around my shin. I drew in a sharp breath, tried again. I fell back, landing on my elbows in the leaves and pine needles.

"What is it?" Laura asked. Her expression shifted from self-pity to alarm.

"It's nothing. Just…I hurt myself, earlier."

"Here," Laura said. "Lean on me."

As she put her face next to mine, I smelled liquor on her breath. Ah, I thought, That explains the rosy face, the glittering eyes. The tears.

Laura helped me stand, one hand on the tree trunk for support. Then she knelt down and shoveled the remains of our picnic into my bag, which she slung over her shoulder. She put a hand under my elbow, and the two of us stepped forward clumsily. The rooks rose, ploughing the air, and disappeared into the trees. Their derisive calls followed us as we began walking back toward the Centro. Laura was silent all the way, holding tight to my arm, taking my weight whenever I stumbled. When we reached the Villa Francesca's gate and stopped, she kept holding onto me.

"Thanks. This was really nice of you," I said. Gently I unlinked our arms.

Laura said, "You need to take care of that leg right away. You have disinfectant? Bandaids?"

"Yes," I lied.

"Okay, then." For a second Laura stood there, swaying slightly. Then she leaned towards me. "Listen. Don't say anything to Hollis, okay? I'm… I don't usually drink in the daytime. Ever, really."

"Of course," I said. Thinking, What about that afternoon in the café near the Cimitero Staglieno?

Relief lit Laura's face. For the first time that afternoon, she smiled. "It'll be our secret. *Ciao*, then. See you at dinner."

Grandma Eva used to say, *Those whom you minister to will climb into your heart*. Laura had ministered to me—and I to her, in a way. And now we shared a secret.

By the third English lesson at Natalia's—I thought of these sessions as The Conversations—I'd begun to feel more ease. That first experience had taught me to stick, with flutey cheerfulness, to a Nico-type agenda. *What did you do on the weekend? What did you see? What's your favorite color? What do you like to watch on TV? Any questions?*

At the end of the session, as usual, the three women chorused, "Thank you very many, Signora!" Natalia beckoned to Vida, then to me. "We must tend your wound."

"My what?"

"You have been limping since you arrived. Come."

Bossy; bossy.

In the bathroom Vida took off my clumsy bandage, clucked at the long red gash edged with purple, dabbed disinfectant from a bottle. The hands that had whacked a fish's head off the week before were inquiring and gentle on my leg.

"Thank you," I said. "This is really kind of you."

"Nothing," she said, without looking up.

Feeling at a loss, as always, in the face of Vida's reserve, I was silent. She spoke a lot in the group—she seemed avid to practice her English—but never said anything personal. The scant facts I knew about her had all come from Natalia: she was a nurse-midwife; a Serb who'd married an Albanian Kosovar; a widow. Vida's reticence aroused my interest, of course. After all, archaeology is the art of persuading a sliver of pottery or a splinter of bone to give up its secrets. To speak. Janet would have warned me not to confuse art with life. I could hear her saying, *Vida is a person, not a pot.*

My shin was wrapped in gauze and neatly taped. It did feel better. As I was brushing cheeks with Natalia at the door, Vida reappeared with a thimble-sized glass of *grappa*. She stood in the dim foyer, her strange square-cut eyes never leaving my face, and watched me drink. Ignoring my thanks, she said, "You must be less busier. Rest, and not use." Something in her tone caught my ear. Not sympathy. Something more abstract and larger, summoned by the act of nursing. I recognized a momentary victory in the unending battle to remain yourself in the grip of tragedy. If I could find a way to tell her so, maybe we could—

At that moment Lule came running down the hall, all skinny arms and legs. I'd been surprised to learn that she was seven—two years older than Amber. But then, she hadn't had Amber's good food, unbroken sleep, freedom from fear. My mind's eye stood the two girls next to each other: caramel-colored Amber with her black aureole of hair, Lule with her pale skin and hair like spun sugar. They were a negative and its print. They were Rose Red and Snow White in the fairy tale.

I'd brought my pastels and given them to Lule before the lesson started. Now she held up a drawing. "*Guarda, mamma!* Look what I made for the *Signora!*"

"English, Lule."

Lule crouched and spread the drawing out on the floor between her mother and me, smoothing each corner in turn. She sat back on her heels and looked up at us expectantly.

A yellow house with jagged windows, its roof erupting in streamers of red. Beside it a figure in green with a hat like an upside-down bowl, and one arm ending in a long black snout. The sky was filled with boiling purple clouds. At the bottom Lule had printed her name in tall, leaning letters.

When I glanced up, Vida's face wore an expression of such naked grief that I had to turn away.

How can she let Lule dwell on these terrible things? I wondered. Why not encourage her to forget? *A joy shared is a joy doubled; a sorrow shared is a sorrow halved*, Grandma Eva used to say. I hadn't wanted Rae to shoulder half my grief. I was supposed to be the parent who was *all right*. I made sure Rae never saw me cry.

In front of Brignole Station the *tassista*—Natalia had insisted on calling a taxi—pocketed my generous tip and said, "*Buona fortuna, Signora.*" Inside, I found the platform for the next train to Soccorso, stuck my ticket into the metal box on the wall and heard the chomp. If a conductor checked, I'd be legal.

Legal? Ceiling-Katherine said from the platform roof. *And involved with illegal aliens?*

Sitting down on a bench to wait for my train, I let myself remember Kosovo, region of contrasts: palm trees and snow; Albanians and Serbs; marble sidewalks and the poorest poor in all of Tito's empire. I remembered the affection I'd felt for Daniel's Albanian students, shepherding them around the dig at Vlashnje, talking by lanternlight long into the night, arguing and laughing. I remembered our brief honeymoon at

Drina Gorge, a weekend stolen from the dig. Glacier-fed water mirrored mountains with snow already on the peaks. We brought a borrowed tent and pitched it on a bluff overlooking the river and made love—

Illegal aliens, in a country where YOU are an alien? pursued Ceiling-Katherine.

The Israeli neuropsychiatrist I'd consulted after Daniel died had called Ceiling-Katherine a defense mechanism. Dissociation. "It will disappear," she said, "when your part-selves coalesce." When, I wondered now, would that be?

In the meantime, I'd come to look forward to the Conversations. I liked feeling part of something larger than myself; I liked the chance to *act*. Helping these women was something I needed to do, not for them, but for me. I remembered the three boxes Daniel used to keep on his desk at the University, labeled "OUT," "IN," and "IN DEEPER."

Illegal or not, I was IN.

My train halted with a screech and a grinding of wheels. Everyone rushed to the platform's edge. In the tide of exiters fighting their way out, I stumbled and almost fell. When I looked up, the man behind me veered away and headed for the exit—but not before I'd had a glimpse of his face.

It was Angus Dance.

8

In the last week of October the Centro buzzed with preparations for the opening of an installation by Thuanthong. Anna Maria rented a disused mausoleum in Staglieno Cemetery and prepared a glossy bilingual brochure. She got me to correct the English text. It must impress, she explained, many different readers: donors who supported the Centro, city officials, the art critic from the *Corriere della Sera*. In fact, I saw as I corrected the tense of various verbs, it *was* impressive. Like me, Thuanthong had arrived in Genoa without luggage; his had never been found. *Un segno*, the brochure said—he'd taken this as a sign. Forced to abandon what he'd planned, he resolved to make an installation using only materials gathered on the grounds of the Centro. Anna Maria recruited Dmitri—who seemed to spend most of his time on one of the sofas in the *salotto* with his black overcoat wrapped around him like a shroud—and the ever-helpful Hollis to assist with the installing. The fuss being made seemed to distress Thuanthong, who trundled around the Centro with his head bent and his shoulders hunched, his radish-top of hair the most exuberant thing about him.

Every day, as ordered by Nico, I spent an hour wrestling with Italian newspapers. The *Corriere della Sera* continued its series on political refugees. The U. N. bombardment of Milosevic's headquarters a year earlier, though it ended hostilities, had not solved the problem of *people.*

The end of war, as always, had not meant the end of suffering caused by war. I read about this side by side with continuing coverage of the aftermath of 9/11 in my own country. ("You do not anger that we are Muslim?" Genta asked me. I hadn't even thought about it.) The daily body count, tthe invasion of Afghanistan—these things seemed remote. The suffering of my own countrymen felt less real to me than what I heard from Bardha and Genta and Vida. As the women's reserve lifted, their talk grew darker. I could no longer succeed in diverting our discussions into bland conversational channels—and I found I did not want to. Inside me, as the women spoke, something seemed to expand. The same sort of enlargement I felt during the Visitations, as if my mind were a furled leaf unfolding. Whenever the Conversations carried me out of my depth, I reminded myself where my real usefulness lay. I listened. I corrected the women's English.

"I'm so excited we're going to Portofino," I said. "Everyone says how beautiful it is."

Nico and I were walking along the Via Aurelia toward the train station in Soccorso.

"We aren't going to Portofino," he said, in his bossy Fabbri way. "I have changed our plan."

I was disappointed but thought better of saying so. Nico's face wore an expression I hadn't seen before, a divot of anxiety between his eyebrows. I saw him look at my running shoes, which he'd ordered me to wear for this excursion. Apparently they met with his approval. I also wore a cashmere-lined black leather jacket I'd bought in the village shop—beautifully cut, buttery, a garment Rae would've called diesel—along with my best-fitting jeans and my now-favorite turquoise sweater. I couldn't tell whether Nico noticed these, too.

He grabbed my hand and we squeezed between stopped automobiles, ducking under a red-and-white-striped barrier with a sign reading "VI-ETATO." Forbidden. When I pointed it out, Nico grinned. "Just a suggestion. Dipende."

Dipende—one of his favorite words. Forbidden? *Dipende.* Dangerous? *Dipende.*

Bypassing the station entrance, we hoisted ourselves up onto the east-bound platform just in time. A sleek white Intercity train roared past without stopping.

"Where are we going?" I asked.

Nico pulled two train tickets out of the pocket of his motorcycle jacket and offered them to the bite of the *obliteratrice* on the platform wall. "You'll see."

I made a grab for the tickets. He held them high over his head. I jumped for them. He thrust them down the front of his jeans. "Come and get 'em!"

What's gotten into him? I wondered. His playfulness had never crossed the line into *double entendre* before.

I turned away, laughing. "*Boh!*" I said, plopping down on a bench. "*Che cazzo?*" The week before, we'd spent a lesson on *le parolacce*—bad words. Where English uses 'fuck,' Italian uses 'dick.' *Cazzo* lies at the heart of all Italian curses, except for those involving the hearer's mother. And, like 'fuck,' you can throw *cazzo* into your sentence almost anywhere. I could see it was going to be useful.

Our train came, a Regionale. So we weren't going to, say, Livorno. I wondered, as I had before, why Nico was so available for daytime excursions. Why didn't someone so intelligent and educated have a real job? I didn't feel I knew Natalia well enough to ask her, and I certainly wasn't about to ask Nico.

Settled in a window seat—Nico's choice for me—I watched the terraced houses of Soccorso dwindle and disappear.

"This track runs along the coast," Nico said, "from Genoa all the way to La Spezia. *Certo*, in the nineteenth century it was believed that travelers deserve beauty."

The worn plush seat was comfortable but narrow. I could feel warmth radiating from Nico's hip to mine. His smell of plain soap and sweat and leather seemed to curl around me. A sign above the scratched, cloudy window informed me that it was dangerous to lean out. Nico saw me reading it and said, "*Dipende*! The government means, 'If you want to lean out, just know what you risk. It is not our business to come between you and your destiny'."

I laughed. I remembered Yugoslavian trains with their curt injunction, Don't Lean!

I'd get used to the Italian way, Nico told me. There was no room for *i pignoli*—rules-spouting sticklers. I thought it wasn't so much the Italian way as the Fabbri way. A way that, I had to admit, appealed to me. The more I saw of this family, the more I felt as if I'd fallen under some kind of spell.

The train gathered speed. At the front of the car, two young men with two large puppets, Raggedy Andy lookalikes, carried on a conversation in falsetto voices. Nico began to expound on the history of Genoa. Its epithet since the early Renaissance had been *La Superba*, as Venice was *La Serenissima*, and Rome *La Citta` Eterna*. So we weren't going farther than Genoa? I felt a stab of disappointment. I'd hoped for somewhere unfamiliar.

"We will walk, but not far," Nico told me. "Your leg will be fine."

"My leg *is* fine," I said. Then, feeling him draw back, I added, "Thank you for thinking of it," and was rewarded with the swift upward tilt of his features.

A sensitive man. I felt a whisper of weariness at the thought.

The train's steady rocking, the rhythmic sound of wheels on the track, the high-backed seats, made me think of museum field trips to New York with my students. Though this train was nothing like Amtrak. One of the two old men across from us took a cigar out of his breast pocket and lit it. The aroma, not unpleasant, spread through the car. "In the interests of fairness," Nico explained, "Italian trains are divided down the middle into Smoking and Nonsmoking." The scenery flowing past was nothing like what we would have been seeing from Amtrak's much cleaner windows. When I started to describe New England's October foliage to Nico, he interrupted me with "*Ah, si`*—I remember. When I went to America for the first time, the colors hurt my eyes."

"You've been to the States? When? What did you do there?"

"It was a long time ago."

His tone was dismissive: end of story. I thought, No, you don't, and looked at him inquiringly. "And?"

The train stopped. More people came into our car: a man carrying a brass floor lamp on his shoulder, another with a small girl on his. I looked out at the platform splashed with late-morning sunlight and remembered my first trip into the city to visit Natalia. Was it really only a month ago? I didn't feel like the same person. Nico gazed past me as if he, too, saw some past self sitting on the green-painted bench. The train jerked, stumbled, began to move.

"And?" I repeated.

"Italy is a small country. There is not enough work for everyone—especially those who've been to university. A few doctors, engineers, scientists"—I remembered he was a botanist—"can find jobs in their fields. The rest have two choices. Be under-employed, bored, and depressed, for a lifetime. Or leave. It is very hard to leave."

I nodded. I'd begun to see what Italians felt for their country.

Nico went on, gathering speed as he saw I understood. He'd been accepted into the Ph.D. program at the University of Maine, and hoped, as many did, to stay on in the States after he finished the degree. "I made it through one year. Then I came home for the summer, and I couldn't make myself go back. The homesickness—it was terrible." *Nostalgia* is the Italian word for homesickness, as if home contained everything one could possibly miss. "So now I work as a tutor some days, and other days I work with remains."

"Remains?"

"Skeletons, fossils, taxidermied animals. Insects and butterflies under glass. We sell to museums all over the world. Laboratories. A few crazy individuals."

This didn't sound particularly rewarding.

"You sell them?"

"I make them. Or rather, I make them into objects that can be sold." He shrugged. "Perhaps it is my fate. *Fabbri* means 'blacksmiths.' My ancestors were artisans, not scientists."

This sounded like European fatalism to me, and I said so. "Don't you miss botany?" I asked.

Nico frowned. "*Americani* never understand that others' hearts are not like yours."

But I remembered the way his face had lit with passion as we bent over the mimosa leaf on the Passeggiata. As if the unaccustomed self-revelation had exhausted him, Nico leaned back, relaxing so that our shoulders touched. The rest of the ride passed in silence.

Outside Brignole Station we set out in the opposite direction from Natalia's apartment, winding downhill through cobblestoned alleys to the Porto Antico. I trotted along beside Nico. Now and then a shop window offered our reflections, the turned-up collars of our jackets giving us a commanding yet jaunty aspect.

In the harbor was an old sailing ship, weathered wood with three sailless masts and three decks. Its gloom was relieved by gold paint on the stern and the bow, to which clung a nearly nude white Neptune. The approach, up a gangplank, had a short line this late in the season. Several tourists bristling with backpacks, cameras out and pointing; a trio of nuns in the medieval habits I'd grown used to seeing; the man with the child on his shoulders who'd been on our train. Nico paid for our tickets. When I held out some money, he frowned. "I'm your employer," I said, "you're working right now." He shook his head and stalked off toward the entrance.

We went inside behind the nuns. Graffiti crowded the walls. I slowed to look. "Guðrun & Einar," "Ennio ♥ Rina," "Dan + Stacey 4-evah!" But these were outnumbered by drawings of sea creatures—fish, seahorses, sea anemones, an octopus with a leering eye. I thought of the grim, angry graffiti on the I-95 underpass in Providence, which I walked through every day on my way to class. Here, joy reigned.

I said as much to Nico. He sighed. "*Boh!* It's a nuisance. They come, they whitewash, it starts all over again." He pulled a baseball cap out of his pocket and put it on. "Did you bring a hat, Caterina? The afternoon sun will be strong up there." He nudged me toward a flight of steps.

No, I said, didn't he see? Graffiti were the spoor left by the past. "These could be as valuable to future archaeologists as the cave paintings at Altamira or Lascaux are to us. Through graffiti, people *speak*."

Nico looked at me. In the shade cast by the brim of his cap his brown eyes shone. But not, I saw, with understanding—more a kind of affectionate amusement. "How passionate you are, Caterina."

Aggravated, I turned and climbed the steps to the main deck. The sea breeze fingered my hair and I breathed in its rich, freighted smell, slyly reminiscent of sex. I walked over to the railing. Below me stretched the sea, all the way to Corsica, netted with tiny jewels of light. Its medley of blues and greens changed from second to second, never repeating. You'd have to stand here forever, I thought, to be able to say you'd truly seen it. As always, the ocean made me think of Sofonisba. Strange, when she'd never painted a single seascape—not that survived, anyway.

Beside me, Nico said, "*Azzurro*. Azure. The color of your eyes at this moment. But on the train, Caterina, they were gray."

His gaze made me feel both gratified and embarrassed, reluctant and eager: a teenage stew of contradictions.

"Your eyes change, *dipende*."

Trying to retrieve my role as student, I said, "How old is this ship?"

"It dates to 1672. Didn't you read the sign? It's a Spanish galleon—a replica, but they say it is faithful."

A century too late, and too large a vessel for the Mediterranean. Nevertheless, standing there in the noon sun with gulls calling overhead, I felt something. Some connection.

"Don't you like it?" Nico's face had fallen into its grooves of sadness. "I thought it would be good for your research. Didn't your lady come to Genoa from Palermo? To sail would be the only way."

"It's a great idea," I said. "Thank you, Nico."

His face lifted. "Come and see the rest."

We walked the length of the deck. Slabs of sunlight were flung across our path every few yards from gun portals overlooking the sea. Up ahead sailed the three nuns, arms linked like a chain of paper dolls, skirts billowing. In the stern we came to an iron grate blocking off the last few feet of the ship.

"The brig," I said, surprising myself. How did I know that?

On the stairs to the second deck we had to detour around a couple in jeans and backpacks kissing vigorously. Along each side of this deck were another dozen guns, with empty barrels set between them.

"What were these for?" Nico wondered.

"Vinegar," I said. "To put out fires."

The ship's sole cabin was tucked in the stern beneath the highest, smallest deck. Nico put his hand on a thick wooden pole that came up through a hole in the floor outside the cabin door. "What does this do, I wonder?"

"It's the whipstaff," I said absently. "It works the rudder."

I was puzzling over a placard that said this was the captain's cabin. Where did the passengers sleep? Where would Sofonisba have spent the six or so nights of her voyage?

"You know these things, Caterina? You have researched ships, no?"

"No." Confusion swept over me. "I just...*know*."

Nico gave me an odd look. He seemed about to say more, but a balding tourist in a Hawaiian shirt came up and asked us to take a picture of him and his much younger girlfriend. Resenting the interruption—I wanted to stay in the seventeenth century—I left the picture-taking to Nico and went off to climb a ladder beside the cabin door. I emerged onto the third deck, tiny and very high. The poop deck, I somehow knew. A sweet, tarry smell rose up from the sun-heated boards. The silence felt wrong. Life on board wouldn't have gone a moment without sound and motion. I gazed down the length of the ship to where two enormous iron anchors reposed on coils of rope. I imagined how it would have been if we were about to get underway: the sailors' voices, the creak of the ship's timbers, the shudder beneath my feet—

The dawn air is like being wrapped in cobwebs. From the bow of the ship she watches fog amble along the shore, the sky fill with bruise-colored clouds. The consolation of sunrise will be withheld. Men swarm over the deck, shouting calls and responses, heaving casks and olive jars and plump sacks of Sicilian wheat across the planks and wrestling them down the ladder into the hold. The ship strains at the great ropes on either side of the bow. She sways to keep her balance.

Sofi, vieni! *her brother says into her ear. It is not fitting for a woman to be on deck.*

Fitting! She shakes her head to ward off his warning and looks down over the rail. The water ripples like the pelt of some great animal. She rubs her eyes. The third sea voyage of my life, she thinks: in forty-seven years, only three. No doubt Asdru thinks three a lot, for a woman. Genoa to Barcelona; Barcelona to Palermo; and now this voyage, Palermo to Genoa, closes the circle. My life: a snake with its tail in its mouth.

The sky begins to shake out drops of rain, spare at first, then thickening. She pulls the hood of her cloak up over her head. Rain blurs the shoreline. She imagines it falling on the cobblestoned streets, the campanile of the Chiesa dei Genovesi, the weeping birch in her courtyard—

O Dio! Caught up in the exhilaration of departure, its unquestioning assumption of a future, for a moment she forgot. Three months since the sea took Fabrizio. She thinks, In three days this ship will carry me over the place where he—

The velvet pouch. Stay inside the velvet pouch.

She keeps her eyes on the last of the cargo being shepherded down the hatch. Slatted crates of lemons, limes, blood oranges send momentary flashes of color into the gray dawn. Lomellini ships are well-provisioned, Asdrubale told her. No scurvy will weaken their sailors; no weevils—Asdru is fond of his food— bedevil their biscuits.

Asdrubale puts a hand on her shoulder. You'll be ill, Sofi. Look—your cloak is wet through. Margherita waits in your cabin.

He conducted a careful investigation before leaving Cremona. The Lo- mellini are a distinguished Genovese family whose ships have plied the Mediterranean for generations. Only at the last moment did Asdrubale discover that, on the return journey, La Patrona *would be captained by an illegitimate son with a reputation as* una testa calda. *A young hothead, known to have actually given chase to a pirate ship that attempted to attack him off the coast of Corsica.*

One of the mariners appears beside her, young and shiny-faced, with a shock of red hair and constellations of freckles. His rain-soaked doublet smells like wet dog. She recognizes him: the page who handed her aboard from the skiff earlier. He lifts something on a pole over her head. An ombrellino, *she sees, looking up—a rough, ochre-colored version of the circular canopy held over the priest in processions.*

What in the name of God—? Asdrubale exclaims.

Signor Lomellini sends this for my lady, the mariner says. Mumbles, really—he is shy and speaks the soft, susurrating Genovese dialect. He glances back at the sterncastle, at a figure looking down over the ship, which she supposes must be their hotheaded captain.

Asdrubale reaches up to touch the ombrellino's *fabric. Sailcloth, he says. Coated with oil so water cannot penetrate. Ingenious!*

His captain's invention, the page intimates. He thrusts the pole at Asdrubale and turns and lopes back along the deck.

Her brother holds up the ombrellino, *so absorbed in marveling at it that he forgets about her. She should be grateful to the unknown captain for his thoughtfulness; but she doesn't care. Wet, dry, it's all the same to her. She leans out over the rail. A lone cormorant plummets into the water. She watches the black sickle shape vanish and reappear and vanish again.*

There's a break in the noise and commotion. For an instant, everything stops. She can hear the cries of gulls, the slap of the sea against the ship's side. Then behind her a voice shouts, Salpate l'ancora! *The cry is taken up and repeated, a chain of echoes traveling forward along the deck.*

L'ancora!...L'ancora!

On either side of her the ropes holding the anchors begin to thud against the ship. They thunder up onto the deck, thick as a man's thigh, followed by the great iron anchors. A cheer goes up. She seizes the rail. There's a slow, reverberating shudder, the deck quaking as if it will open beneath her feet, and La Patrona *gives herself to the sea.*

A hand on my arm. "Caterina? Where have you gone?"

Surfacing, I was embarrassed to find Nico's eyes on me. I hadn't had a Visitation in front of anyone before.

"*Va tutto bene?*"

I blinked, nodded, tried to arrange my face in a semblance of normal. "Sorry. Must be the sun."

Nico loosened his grip on my arm and led me to the shady side of the poopdeck. Two women brushed past us and started down the ladder, discussing in nasal New Jersey accents whether the hotel maids would replace the towels—the same thing they would have been talking about on the boardwalk in Atlantic City. I looked at Nico, wanting to share my amusement. He didn't seem to have noticed. He took off his cap and thrust it into his pocket and leaned against the railing with his back to the sea, looking at me. Behind his head the coast curved: purple cliffs, bright water, burning blue sky. I felt a brief rush of happiness, like a zipper un-zipping. Nico's hands came up and cupped my shoulders. His expression was a mixture of concern and tenderness and lust and the discovery of all these. We stood like that for a long moment. Then he spoke.

"Your eyes—they've changed again. They're green."

"It's the light," I lied, just before ~~he kissed me~~
~~I kissed him~~
we kissed.

9

"We walk…walked…many days, through the mountains. It was very hard. Winter. Well, you know. You know how it is."

Bardha was recounting her journey out of Kosovo. It was almost the end of October and this was the eighth Conversation. Between this meeting and our first one lay a very long month. We were a group now.

"The Signora *doesn't* know," Vida said. She sat next to Bardha on the sofa in her usual sweats, arms and ankles crossed—well-defended.

Today Natalia wasn't here. An emergency, Bardha had said when I arrived. The room's sunlit peace was only slightly diminished by her absence. I felt the usual yearning—as if reminded, as the other women must be, of a home I'd lost. The two children were always sent out to play, because of the turn the women's talk often took. But today Ardi sat in front of the fireplace on the worn oriental carpet with a pile of torn-off paper towels, which he was laying out around him in a circle. His upper lip gleamed with mucus and his cheeks were fever-red. He looked up at me, eyes the velvety gold of pansies, and said something in Albanian.

"Sunflower," Genta translated. Her English had made the fastest progress. She was young and supple and, despite everything, optimistic; and she'd studied English in her village school before a NATO bomb leveled it.

"We were many, on the journey to Montenegro," Bardha continued in her soft, halting voice. "Every day more people join. We pass villages much destroyed. So many bodies. Every day we see them, it is normal."

Bardha had been a children's book illustrator; she described the journey with a painter's eye. I could see the long procession, most on foot, over roads ribbed with ice. The dead sprawled in ditches in the snow. The coppery smell of blood; the charred bodies; the pink cloud rising from a blown-up church where dozens of people had taken refuge. Women in headscarves carrying bundled babies. People with children on their backs or shoulders or strapped to their chests; people pushing old women in wheelbarrows. A boy with both arms in casts sitting atop a horse-drawn cart on a stack of clothing and blankets. A pregnant woman on a donkey led by her mother. Walking, walking. Low hills behind them, mountains in front.

How many of those people had been students at the University of Pristina in 1981? People we'd known; people who'd invited us to their homes or taken us out to one of Pristina's clandestine beer houses.

Vida interrupted. "You do not tell the journey's beginning. How the Serbs come to your village and shoot all men and boys—"

"Stop," Bardha said. "It is not necessary."

"It is necessary. The Signora must know these things. How they shoot your husband. Your father. How they laugh and say to the women which they rape, 'You miss your husbands? Look! We replace them.'"

Bardha closed her eyes. Genta, sitting as always on the floor at Bardha's feet, reached up a hand and clasped her aunt's. "Tell your own story," she said to Vida. "Not ours."

Vida took over the narrative, but it wasn't her story she told. She pointed to Ardi, still solemnly deploying paper towels across the sunlit blues and reds of the rug. His mother had walked for a hundred kilometers alongside Vida through the forest, following the snow-encrusted railroad track from Kosovo to Montenegro. She had to nurse her baby as she walked, stumbling on the slippery ties; you could see the half-moons of healed bite marks on her breasts. At the border she was pulled out of line by three Skorpios. "She was very beautiful," Vida said, "they choose always the beautiful ones. It is how she got pregnant in first place." The woman just had time to thrust her baby at Vida before she was dragged off behind the smoking skeleton of a tractor. She didn't come back.

I wanted desperately to believe that Ardi's long-lashed golden eyes came from his mother.

Bardha had recovered enough to go on with her story. "In Montenegro, on the coast, there were Albanians which take people across the Adriatic to Italy."

"Not ferries," I said. "Small boats?" I'd seen Montenegro's Adriatic coast when Daniel and I took his students on a field trip to the ruins at Haj-Nehaj. I pictured something like the rescue operation at Dunkirk at the beginning of World War II: heroic civilians risking their lives in the stormy blackness.

"*Scafisti*!" Vida spit out the word, casting a contemptuous glance at me." It wasn't a word I knew. I looked at Genta, who translated, "Smugglers."

I flinched. How ignorant I felt. How ignorant I *was*.

Bardha and Genta—aunt and niece, the only ones in their family who'd survived—waited for weeks in a refugee camp in Montenegro, until a cousin in Oslo sent the two thousand American dollars demanded by the *scafisti*. As Bardha spoke, I saw the rows of olive tarps sagging with rain; the frozen ground; the figures pressed against the barbed wire and gazing out. I felt the frigid Balkan night held off only by the canvas above your head, while you shivered in a sleeping bag made from an old quilt, wearing every piece of clothing you owned.

"And some you didn't," Vida added. She watched me for a reaction. "Some which you stole."

"When you're cold," Genta put in, "everything hurts more." Leaning back against Bardha's knees in her bright red T-shirt, she looked too young to be hearing all this, much less to have lived it.

The *scafisti* took Bardha and Genta across on a moonless night, running no lights, in a rough winter sea. The boat was a large *gommone*, a popular sporting craft—a glorified rubber raft with an outboard motor—made to hold a dozen people. Bardha and Genta counted thirty men, women, and children on the nine-hour voyage. They would land, they'd been told, in Puglia. But before they could see any sign of shore, the boat stopped. In blackness punctuated only by the *scafisti*'s kerosene lanterns, the terrified passengers had to clamber over the side and drop into the water. They did not know until they were in it that it was shallow enough for the adults to stand. "Go that way!" one of the *scafisti* shouted, pointing with his rifle. The motor roared to life. The boat shot away.

Bardha and Genta and the others waited on the beach till dawn for a promised truck that never came. The Guardia found them. They were interned among six hundred refugees in a former children's summer camp in San Foca. Vida and Lule and Ardi were in the same cabin. It was at this internment center that the three women met Natalia, who was then working for Caritas.

"We were lucky," Bardha said.

Genta, rubbing her forehead with two fingers, nodded.

"All survived. Many which go with *scafisti* did not. They..." Bardha touched Genta's shoulder and said something in Albanian.

"Drown," Genta supplied.

Vida said, "If Guardia boats chase them, *scafisti* throw the smallest child into the sea. To distract."

"It was a few scary. But we were lucky," Bardha repeated. "We land safe. Also, Natalia finds us." She reached down and lifted Genta's hair and began to braid it. I had a quick flash of doing the same with Rae's. How comforting the age-old motions were, the lemony fragrance of the hair as it slid between your fingers.

"Also"—Genta looked up at me—"the Signora."

Vida said, "What can Americans understand of all this? You, who have had no war in your own country. On your land. On your body."

A cloud seemed to pass over at her words. The room lost its enfolding peace. *Che cazzo*! I thought. Why is this woman angry with *me*? But of course I knew why. It was the same anger I used to feel toward women with healthy, unappreciated husbands. Vida's anger bound us together. I wanted to show her that I understood.

"The Revolutionary War," I said. "The Civil War."

"*You* were not entrapped in these."

"The World Trade Center." Even to my own ears, my voice sounded feeble. "Nearly three thousand people died."

"Were *you* there?"

I felt my face grow hot. I fought the thought that prowled the edges of my mind. What it felt like to be helpless *twenty years*—to be continually erased *twenty years*—to be swept up in something utterly beyond your control. If I could tell Vida about Daniel *twenty years* would she accept me then?

I reached for my own anger, in need of its protective insulation. Where the hell is Natalia? I thought, glaring at the empty chair beside me as if that would make her materialize. I'm not trained for this.

Vida, taking my silence as an admission of defeat, stood up.

"Americans! Innocent…ignorant. The only Americans which *know* are black people and Indians. The Indians has a saying—maybe you have heard? 'A nation is not conquered until the women's hearts lie on the ground.'"

Out on the street I gulped mouthfuls of cool, sea-smelling air, glad to leave the apartment that till this afternoon had seemed so welcoming. I remembered a fragment of rhyme that Grandma Eva used to recite whenever Janet and I complained about something. *I cried because I had no shoes/Until I saw a man who had no feet.* Vida was right. What had happened to me wasn't in the same universe as what the three women had endured. What they'd lost.

I fled along the shortcut Nico had shown me. Down the *spina di pesce*—the shallow "fish spine" steps—of Via San Luca, into one of the narrow alleys I'd learned to call *carruggi*, which exist only in Genoa. The sky above still held some blue, but the high-walled *carruggi* drank up all the daylight. I found the street that led to Brignole Station, with its shops and outdoor stands and pairs of white-haired women all in black with wishbone legs. The *Pausa* had ended. I stopped to examine fillets lounging in pans of water in a fish shop window, eavesdropped on some children playing marbles on its steps. I thought: Sofonisba could have done these things in this very spot. The shop I stood in front of had most likely sold fish for centuries.

At the end of the street, in the yellow beam from a shop window, stood Natalia. I opened my mouth to call out, then stopped. She was talking to a man in a broad-brimmed straw hat. A street musician: behind him I could see a small organ, keyboard and pipes, on wheels. Natalia seemed agitated, her hands flying, even for an Italian. While I watched, she grabbed the man's arm and stood looking up into his face. He shook her off. Turning, he picked up the handle of his organ cart and strode toward me, wheels galumphing over the cobblestones. He brushed past—I had a quick impression of ruddiness, a blond mustache, shadowed by his straw hat—and disappeared down one of the *carruggi* to my left.

Would Natalia have acknowledged me if I hadn't called out? She stood staring after Straw Hat, her shoulders slumped. "*Ciao, cara,*" she said, when I caught up to her. We brushed cheeks. I could feel her trembling. For the first time since we'd met, she spoke to me in Italian. "Forgive me for not being there this afternoon. I had urgent matters to attend to."

"*C'è qualcosa che non va?*" I asked, as Nico had taught me. Is something wrong?

"No, no. But forgive me, I must hurry. You will come again on Thursday?"

"Of course." Despite Vida's behavior, it hadn't occurred to me to quit. Feeling part of something larger than myself the way Rae's work made her feel brought me closer to her. These women offered me the chance to earn my daughter's respect.

"*Bene.* There is something I wish to ask you. Ah...that reminds me. This morning I succeeded at last in reaching my friend Carla Agostini. You have an appointment with her a week from tomorrow. *Arrivederci, cara.*"

"Wait! Who's Carla Agostini?"

"The *Direttrice* of the Palazzo Reale."

Another cushiony collision of cheeks, and Natalia hurried off in the direction Straw Hat had gone. Looking after her, I realized this was the first time I'd seen her flustered. It was distressing. But didn't Natalia have the right (she bit her nails; she smoked) to fall apart once in a while like anybody else?

Church bells began to ring, pealing all around me from nearby streets. Five o'clock. I broke into a run. I'd promised to babysit Amber at 7:00.

I just made it onto the 5:13. I leaned back in my seat, happily contemplating next week's visit to the Palazzo Reale and the chance—I hoped—to see the mysterious double-sided painting. The train hissed and coughed but didn't move. I glanced at my watch. Laura was counting on me, and tonight was important for her: she'd be reading her poetry at Genoa's best bookstore. My eyes searched the platorm, reflexively, for Angus Dance. He'd been distant and coolly formal since the afternoon on the Passeggiata almost a month ago; but often at dinner I caught his sideways glance.

I sighed. Too loudly: the man next to me shook out his newspaper and held it up between us. He smelled of male cologne and mints. *FLOOD RECEDES IN PIEMONTE,* I translated. *...CRACKDOWN ON ILLEGAL IMMIGRATION...Prosecution of Accessories.*

Accessories! Ceiling-Katherine cawed from the car's domed roof. *That would be you.* Her (its?) comments were becoming rarer but more abusive.

"Buzz off," I said. Talking back to an imaginary governess: was that progress, or the opposite?

My neighbor edged closer to the window, rattling his paper.

At last the train began to move. Looking out at the sunset-stained horizon above the sea, I thought of the train ride back from my afternoon on the ship with Nico two days before.

"*Sei contenta, cara?*" he'd asked me as we ambled eastward.

"*Si`. Molto.*"

Are you happy?

Yes. Very.

And there was that quick little zipper of happiness. I tried to remember when, in my Providence life, I'd felt it. Not for a long time; not since Daniel's illness had begun to accelerate, shortly after our year in Kosovo. A different life. A different me? Gertrude Bell, in a letter home from the desert excavations near Teheran: "Are we the same people, I wonder, when all our surroundings, associations, and acquaintances are changed?" Maybe even now I couldn't have been happy in English; but I was happy in Italian.

"*E` vero,*" I murmured. My neighbor sighed heavily behind his paper.

———

"Mom? Mom, it's me."

The sound of my daughter's voice: how much I missed her! I'd been on my way out the door, but I sat down on the too-big bed, sliding on the satin coverlet. Her voice sounded happy.

"What's up, Fruffle?" It was after midnight in Rhode Island.

"Listen, Mom, it's still just an idea, and I know it could wait, you'll be home in seven weeks…"

I felt a grin spread across my face. Rae was counting the weeks till she saw me?

"Rae! What?"

"The thing is. With Cousin Janet about to leave for Africa, I got to thinking how *I* could be doing more. Janet's got a rockin' spirit, you know? She just goes right after things. So I've decided—I think I've decided—I want to go to law school. I want to be the one to help my Abbies." Rae's nickname for her clients: *Ab* was Hmong for 'precious.' "Not send them somewhere else, and then wait and wait for them to be seen, and then their lame random lawyer's not up for taking risks."

My daughter's praise of my cousin-and-best-friend should have made me happy. Instead I felt a pang of jealousy. I longed to tell Rae about working with the Kosovar women—*Your mother can go right after things, too*—but this wasn't the moment.

"I think law school's…a great idea," I said. "You'd be good at the law. You're practical and logical and persuasive. But what about…" I stopped, not wanting to squelch Rae's enthusiasm.

"The cost? That's what student loans are for."

"But you've already got—"

"Mom. Don't wig! Could you just, for once, not try to get your ducks lined up? Anyway, Jeez, these're *my* ducks."

It brought me up short—my daughter's certainty that, even from five thousand miles away, even with Daniel gone, I'd be trying to overprotect her.

"Mom? You there?"

"I'm here." Desperately trying to collect my thoughts. "Look, I think it's a great idea. I really do. I just want you to be sure—"

"Mother. I've got this! You don't need to worry about me. Even though"—a deep sigh threaded through the transatlantic hum between us—"that *is* how you roll."

"So—"

"Sew buttons! Remember how Daddy used to say that? *Daddy* would've—" Her voice broke.

I looked out the window. Dusk had given way to darkness.

"Fruffle," I said. "Don't. Daddy wouldn't want you to be sad."

I didn't know what more to say—I felt close to tears, and I'd promised myself on the day of Daniel's memorial service that I would not cry in front of Rae again, ever—so I waited.

Rae made a sound—a little puff. She was blowing her cares away, as I'd taught her to do when she was small. We'd purse our lips and pretend we were blowing the seed head off a dandelion. Then we'd crane our necks to watch all the tiny winged worries float away.

"Okay," Rae said finally. Her voice had regained its usual matter-of-factness. "Gotta split. Catch you on the flip side."

After we hung up, I was filled with regret. For a few minutes my daughter had sounded like the old Rae; I'd felt tendrils of our old closeness. Then, as if we were still inside the Black Balloon, I'd muffed it.

The bedside clock said 7:05. I'd promised to be at Laura's by 7:00. Better, anyway, to call Rae back tomorrow, when I was calm. When I could be sure of shielding her from my own grief. I grabbed my jacket from the floor where I'd flung it in my haste to get to the phone, and went outside.

Rachel didn't see—and how, with her grief still so fresh, could I tell her?—that her adored father's refusal to deal with the realities of his illness meant that I had had to. How much—I wondered for the thousandth time, as I wrestled with the keys to the Villa Francesca's gate—how much of the attention and love and care that should have gone to Rae had been siphoned off by MS? Stifled by the Black Balloon? Coming home from work after picking Rae up at school. My key stuttering in the lock, reluctance made physical. That breath-held moment—*What will we find?* Daddy askew in his wheelchair, unable to right himself, raising his good hand to hide tears of fury. Daddy sprawled headfirst down the steps to the basement. Daddy on the floor, blood pooling under his temple.

I forced the big iron key all the way in. The villa gate clicked open.

Was that a sound from Amber's room?

When I went down the hall to check, she was sound asleep, her dark hair spilling across the pillow in glow of the night light. I pulled the covers over her feet where she'd kicked them loose, the way Rachel used to do.

In the Carmichaels' living room a chilly breeze came through the open window, carrying night noises from the Villa Baiardo's *salotto* two stories below. My watch said midnight. Laura and Hollis were due back any minute. But just in case, I went to check the drawer in the table by the front door that held Amber's asthma inhaler and the doctor's emergency phone number. Two passports were in there, too. I couldn't resist opening them. Hollis had one passport; Laura and Amber shared the other. It was sweet, a triple-decker: Laura holding Amber on her lap, Amber holding the green velvet elephant on hers.

I went back to the Agatha Christie book I'd brought with me. My bookmark fell out: the yellow card from the Builder of Airports with the phone number of the Palazzo Reale scribbled on the other side. Why was the world suddenly full of interested men? Was I emitting some available-widow pheromone? It seemed that I could have Nico if I wanted him. The question was, did I? I watched a bat skim past the open window. Any involvement with Nico would be time-limited. That, and the difference in our ages, and the likelihood of his having a girlfriend somewhere in the wings—these were all safeguards against getting in too deep. It would be sex, not love; but that didn't mean it would be without affection. Sex, Janet had been urging for years, kept a woman's spirit alive. ("You need something in your life besides sorrow and duty. Even it if isn't exactly happiness.") Multiple sclerosis causes impotence. Impotence causes shame; shame causes the sick person to turn away, time after heart-dulling time—

"Mommy! *Mom!*"

Amber's voice was shrill with fear. I jumped up, sending Agatha Christie to the floor, and ran to get the inhaler. But it was just a nightmare. I smoothed Amber's hair and patted the sweat from her face with a soft towel. Then I told her a story while her eyelids fluttered closed, the way I used to do with Rae.

The Crypt, the only part of the Centro wired for internet, had walls of rough-hewn stone that shone with moisture. They made me think of the catacombs, damp with the sweat of martyrs. There were four rows of tables with a pair of computers on each one. I sat down at the front of the empty room. On the wall next to my computer was a ragged patch of rust that looked, under the quavering fluorescent lights, like dried blood.

I sent my usual Sunday emails to Rachel and Janet, then settled down to work, reminding myself that the fulltime job my dean had dangled—desperately needed now that I was the sole support of me—required publication. My time in Italy had to yield something of interest to scholars, an actual discovery of some kind. So far I had just the picture of Sofonisba's life that was accumulating Visitation by Visitation. Too intuitive, too tied to my individual imagination to be scholarly—but I trusted that it would lead to something concrete. Today was earmarked for researching sixteenth-century ships. I was curious to know how closely they resembled the seventeenth-century replica in the Porto Antico. Why had being on *that* ship triggered a Visitation?

Behind me someone sneezed. Turning, I saw Angus Dance.

He was perched on the last table, swinging his legs. A smile lifted the reddish tuft on his chin. "Do you Americans not say 'Bless you'?"

Deciding to treat this as a rhetorical question, I turned back to my computer.

"Creepy place, this," Dance continued, apparently happy to address my back. "Not as creepy as some, though. The Capuchin Crypt in Rome, for instance. Or… you must know the Skull Tower at Niš? You made so many trips to Yugoslavia. You and your huisband."

The Yugoslavian government had given Fulbrighters a tour of the tower, built by the Turks from the skulls of a thousand Serbian soldiers. I ignored Dance and kept my eyes on my computer screen. According to the internet, no paintings or engravings of ships that plied the Mediterranean in the late sixteenth century survived; but I did find a website for Genoa's Naval Museum. I'd visit it and see if someone there could help.

Dance was nothing if not persistent. "A monument to the defeat of the Sairbian rebels in 1809." His voice, bouncing off the stone walls, sounded like Sean Connery narrating a PBS documentary. "Puir buggers. Supposed to be a warning, but it just made the Sairbs more detairmined. Within six years the Tairks were gone."

I'd managed to avoid being alone with Dance since the afternoon on the Passeggiata. A quick glance at my Inbox: no instant replies from Rachel or Janet. I scribbled the address of the Museo del Mare on a scrap of paper and logged out. I headed for the exit, hips bumping the long tables, not looking in Dance's direction.

"But you know all this. The Skull Tower's not that far from where your huisband—Daniel...Rosen, wasn't it?—had his excavation."

"Can't talk right now, sorry." I pushed open the Crypt's heavy door.

"Vlashnje, wasn't it? How did your huisband come to be interested in Yugoslavia?"

Sunlight embraced me as I emerged from the stairway. I trotted down the loggia to the espresso bar. Thankfully, someone else was there, sitting at a table behind a newspaper. I sank into the other chair. My companion lowered his paper. Hollis: at this moment he was a godsend.

A figure paused at the bar's entrance, half-obscured by the vines that twined around the stone columns.

"Morning, Angus," Hollis said.

"*Buongiorno*," Dance replied. In his fractured Italian it came out "bone journey."

I'm with someone, I telegraphed without looking in Dance's direction, *I have a protector. Go away.*

Which, finally, he did.

I got a cappuccino from the bar and sat down again. Lifting the cup, my hand shook. The encounter with Dance had upset me more than I liked to admit. All this time, when I thought he'd stopped following me, had he been waiting? Watching? I hated hearing Daniel's name in his mouth. How did Dance know so much about him, anyway?

Hollis was silent, gazing out at the sunny courtyard. The fountain in the center had been turned off until spring. Its marble Neptune lounged disconsolately, surrounded by bored-looking nymphs.

"Have you been to the Capuchin Crypt?" I asked him, for something to say.

"Yeah. Chandeliers made from human spinal disks—stuff like that. Why? Are you planning a trip to Rome? There're better things to see there, if you've never been."

"No trip. I just wondered…why do people go to see something like that? Normal people, who aren't archaeologists?"

"It takes a certain kind of sensibility, I think. The Marquis de Sade loved the place."

I laughed out loud. Hollis leaned back in his chair, looking pleased. His perpetual worried expression softened, and the gap between his teeth made him look like a boy.

"I've been wanted to thank you for being a friend to Laura," he said. "She's had a rough year. Lost a baby. Didn't get her own fellowship to the Centro." He paused, then added, as if to ward off judgment (but whose?), "She's a good poet and a *great* mother. She takes really good care of Amber."

He bent down to pull something out of his book-bag. "I was going to give you this at dinner. But since you're here." He handed me the copy of *Murder on the Orient Express* that I'd been reading while I babysat the night before.

"*Your* book!" I said, just remembering it.

Hollis raised an eyebrow. "My book?"

"I never gave it back to you. e. e. cummings."

His face fell. Too late, I realized he'd assumed I meant his own book, his latest collection of poems. Which I hadn't read, or even thought to ask for.

"That's okay." he said. He looked depressed; even his afro seemed to droop. "Keep it as long as you like. Look, I've got to go relieve Laura. See you around?"

Damn, I thought. The one thing every poet wants, and I blew it.

I got up, wishing I could ask Hollis to walk me back to the Villa Francesca. But how could I explain? He'd think I was crazy, feeling stalked by another Fellow. Or he'd think I had some kind of *femme fatale* complex.

Or that you're some kind of slut, Ceiling-Katherine said from the top of a vine-covered column.

We emerged from the loggia into the noonday sun and went our separate ways. While I stood on the edge of the Via Aurelia waiting for a gap in the traffic, Ceiling-Katherine observed, *He rescued you from Sean Connery.*

Che cazzo! I answered as I dove into the stream of cars. I rescued myself.

"We have broke your lamp, *cara*."

My ear against Nico's belly picked up the faint gurgling of his stomach. My lips grazed the hair that spiralled from his groin to his chest.

He reached over and righted the lamp. Its milk-glass shade had cracked in two. The pieces lay on the tabletop like an egg just hatched.

"*Guasto*," I said, with mock sadness.

"No. *Rotto. Guasto* is for larger things. Things with motors."

"I see. So the Centro's elevator is *guasto*?"

"*L'ascensore*? No. *L'ascensore non funziona.*"

How like Italian to have different kinds of brokenness. It seemed Nico and I were having a lesson, after all. I suppressed a giggle and said, "Ah, I see! So, a car would be... *La macchina non funziona?*"

"No. *La macchina non va.* It does not go. *C'è qualcosa che non va.* Something is wrong—" His young-old face broke into a grin as he realized I was teasing him. "It's not nice to make fun of your lover."

My lover. Not a one-afternoon stand, then? You knew it wasn't, I reproached myself. You wouldn't have had a package of condoms in the drawer of the nightstand otherwise. I waited for a wave of the old pre-Daniel remorse that used to set in about now, in the cooling aftermath. Instead, I felt happy. How long had it been? Except for the unfortunate night with Angus Dance—and (I smiled to myself) *this* erased *that*.

Afternoon sun painted our bodies with light. Nico's arms, his shoulders, were so smooth. So young. I touched his neck, the skin springy against my fingers in a way mine would never be again. Turgor—that was the word Nico had taught me for plants that answered your touch. Young plants. From hints he'd dropped I figured Nico's age to be about thirty-three. Nine years older than Rae. For an instant I wondered how my body seemed to him (older? *old*?). Then I let the thought go. My eyes followed the light into the trees outside.

"The *Pausa*," Nico said. "They say it's to remind us of the *Grande Pausa*. When life ends."

Even the umbrella pines outside my window seemed to fold into themselves. Late afternoon: our lesson time. When Nico arrived, I'd handed him the bills in their envelope, as usual. He'd dropped it on the floor, shaking his head and growling "*Mai più*"—never again—and grabbed my shoulders. Kissing me, he'd walked me backwards into the bedroom.

I felt Nico's hand smooth my hair, his fingers catch in its tangled ends.

"*Sei contenta?*"

"*Sì*. Very." Then I realized he meant, had I come. It's always been my policy not to lie about orgasm. But in this case there was the *bella figura* to consider.

I put out a hand to rub Nico's shaved head, satisfyingly rough against my palm. "You have nice ears," I said, discovering this. "Spoon-shaped. And so flat to your head."

"That is good, *cara*, because I have a big head. My motorcycle helmets have to be custom made. Big stuck-out ears, they would— Why are you laughing?"

"Because." I pointed. "Speaking of big, stuck-out parts—" I'd forgotten how quickly a young man's desire can return.

"It is your fault, *cara*. You see? You wake up my *uccello*."

"Your bird? Is that what you call it?"

Nico, busy turning me upside-down, had no time now for vocabulary practice. So bossy, these Fabbris.

This time was slower, more intentional. This time, our bodies recognized each other. I felt mine greet his with an abandon that usually came, if at all, only after several encounters. This time—

"*Tesoro*," Nico said softly, when we lay back against the pillows.

Hauling myself, with great effort, into the world of words, I murmured into his neck, "I love to come."

"I can see that."

"It's so...so *joyful*. It's the most pleasure there is," I said—then felt my face grow hot with embarrassment at how girlish I sounded. But maybe he didn't hear it that way? We'd been speaking English this whole time, his courtesy to me.

"You're blushing." Nico trailed a finger along my collarbone and down into the space between my breasts. "When you come, you blush *here*."

He was whistling as he left. Standing at my open French doors, I watched him cross the grass. Ahead of him a small, fleeing shadow—rabbit? fox?— vanished into the indigo reaches of the cypress hedge. The post-sunset sky looked like something you could drink. Deep, burning blue; sour-sweet rose. Delicious. Like my body, radioactive with well-being inside the staid embrace of Laura's sweater.

("This changes everything," I'd said as Nico was pulling on his clothes in the twilight bedroom.

"*Dipende.*"

"It does. It has to."

"Don't be so American." A note of impatience in his voice. "Okay, yes, it's true. But only because everything changes everything. *E` normale!*")

I went into the bedroom to dress for dinner. The rumpled sheets, the comforter flung on the floor, the yeasty smell of joined bodies greeted me. I scooped up two fistfuls of sheets and buried my face in them.

———

KOSOVO, 1975.

A hot, still August day, the last day of our brief honeymoon at Drina Gorge. Our rowboat rocked between wooded banks, the sole movement besides the glitter of gnats, the red wing of a bird deep in the trees. We could hear the far-off barking of an axe, and the water pulsed with fish. Daniel propped his rod on the gunwale. The sky began to fill with clouds—dove-colored, mauve, steel-gray. Looks like rain, Daniel said.

Later, the smell of woodsmoke from our campfire. Catfish bones and orange rinds on a paper plate. Sex drying on our skin, crusty and essential as salt. The first drops of rain tapped out a slow waltz on the tent above our heads. Though we didn't know it, we had just made Rachel.

NOVEMBER

In bocca al lupo!

10

On the first of November—*Ognissanti*, the Feast of All Saints—Italians rejoice. On the next day—*Il Giorno dei Morti*, the Day of the Dead—they mourn. On that day, Anna Maria took the Fellows to the opening of Thuanthong's installation. In the Centro jitney, which she drove with rib-rattling panache along the SS-1, she had me give an impromptu lecture on cemeteries. I fell back on my opening talk for the first day of class, "Grave Markers through the Ages." Weaving and swerving, the jitney climbed the hills above Genoa to the gates of Staglieno Cemetery, where it lurched into a parking space marked *"VIETATO."* Still stunned from last night's festive dinner, which had featured *cannonau*, a blood-red wine from Sardinia, we climbed out. The cemetery was crowded and noisy, the afternoon sun hotter than seemed right for November. We ambled among marble monuments toward the mausoleum the Centro had rented for Thuanthong's installation. Church bells tolled, amplifying our headaches. Children chased each other between the graves, two of them running into Dmitri and knocking him flat.

The mausoleum looked like a house in a fairytale, tattooed with age, vines surrounding an oval door. Thuanthong stood to the right. A young man in a security uniform stood to the left, letting people in. Apparently you had to enter one at a time while others waited outside, like going to confession. People emerging from the exhibition walked over to Thuanthong and shook his hand. His hair had been tamed into two blue-black eaves, and he seemed half a foot taller. It took me a second to realize that he was standing up straight for the first time since I'd met him. I got in line behind a gaggle of schoolchildren. While I waited I amused myself by trying to decipher their quick, fluted Italian, full of *–ino*'s and *-etta*'s.

Inside, the cavelike space was lit by a single floodlight on the wall by the door. You stepped onto a pavement of cut stumps fitted next to each other, raw end up—putting you off-balance. The fragrance of fresh-cut wood flooded your brain. In the far corner a leafless tree stood upright, extending a large branch overhead across the log pavement. From the branch hung a helmet like a medieval warrior's, woven out of acorns. When you got to the center of the uneven log pavement, you stopped beneath the helmet. You fitted your head into it. Now your shadow fell starkly across the wall opposite. You stood, wobbling, and watched the shadow-play of branches/helmet/you against a white-washed rectangle on the wall opposite. A sign beside it said:

> *The way to truth is to rethink our place in the world.*
> *Then, after a period of loss, balance will be achieved.*

Teetering on the cut logs, the helmet's acorns catching in my hair, I saw my shadow-self waver. I could feel my heart beating in my throat. *After a period of loss.* Something fell inside me.

The spell was broken by the larger-than-life voice of Joshua ("He puts the 'bray' in Brayden," Laura liked to say) outside the mausoleum door. "Bach's Organ Works?" he boomed, reading a concert poster I'd seen on my way in. "So does mine!"

I turned and fled.

Outside I grasped Thuanthong's bird-boned hand and congratulated him. Beyond him a table held plastic cups of *vin santo* and platters of sliced pomegranate and finger-shaped cookies called Bones of the Dead. The other Fellows had helped themselves and were sitting in a row on a low stone wall across from the installation entrance. I watched Angus

Dance take Anna Maria's arm and lead her around the side of the mausoleum, where they disappeared.

I never saw the reclusive Dmitri except at dinner, and then it was always under Dance's eye. Here, with Dance out of sight, was my chance. I took my wine and cookies over to where the Russian in his black overcoat lolled along a stretch of wall.

"*Ciao,*" I said, sitting down beside him.

He raised a languid eyebrow in response, then went back to watching Chantal, who sat with Joshua at the other end of the row of Fellows.

I took a sip of caramel-sweet *vin santo.* "What do you think of Angus's Russian?" I asked. "He must be glad for the chance to speak it with you."

Dmitri shrugged. "With me, *nyet.* Never."

Aha, I thought. Maybe Dance isn't a Slavicist at all. But then what is he? In the six weeks I'd been in Italy, Angus Dance had followed me three times: to the Passeggiata, to Genoa, to the Crypt. Why? I couldn't see anything to do about my suspicions, except be wary. Which I was already.

Dmitri uncoiled and stood up. "Excuse." He gave me a nod and slouched off in the direction of his lover.

"Thank Goddess for this!" Laura flopped down beside me and clicked her cup of wine against mine. Her yellow T-shirt said *Somewhere in Texas a Village Is Missing Its Idiot.* "I can use a little hair of the dog. What *was* that stuff we were drinking last night? It's got an afterlife that's, like, nuclear."

We watched the new taller Thuanthong shake hand after hand, bowing and beaming. Behind him the sun was descending into the cypress trees. Their shadows inched toward us across the grass.

"I believe this is yours." Laura dangled a small rectangle of yellow cardboard in front of me. The Builder of Airports, my bookmark. "Another conquest?"

"What do you mean, another?" Did she know I'd slept with Angus Dance? Did everyone in the hermetic, gossip-fueled world of the Centro know? I took the card and stuck it in my jeans pocket.

Laura moved closer, her face lit by a mixture of curiosity and envy and something that looked like wistfulness. I was struck all over again by her likeness to my younger self. Curly dark-blond hair worn long; blue eyes—Laura's a true blue—at the same level, our height being more or less equal. The two decades that separated us muted the resemblance enough that no one at the Centro had remarked on it. It was in any case just an outward alikeness. Twenty years of living alongside MS had tempered an unthinking, self-centered, judgmental young woman into the (I devoutly hoped) very different one who sat opposite Laura now.

"Where did you find this?" I asked, although I knew. I must have left it behind last time I babysat.

"It was under the sofa," Laura said. "Of course I never vacuum. And certainly not under the furniture. But Hollis does."

"Hollis found it?"

I looked down the row of Fellows to where he sat talking with Joshua Brayden, his afro an aureole in the lowering sun.

Laura laid a hand on my arm. "You know, you can tell me anything. Anything. Here we are, the two of us, marooned in a sea of men." She seemed to have forgotten the other women at the Centro. "We need each other. And besides, we're friends. Aren't we?"

"It's just someone I met at the airport, back when I first got here. No one special."

"But there *is* someone?"

I couldn't resist. I hadn't talked to Janet much about Nico—she approved heartily of my having a fling but insisted on referring to him as Supertutor or Signor Too-Good-to-Be-True—and of course I couldn't mention him to Rae. "Yes," I said.

"Who? It can't be anyone at the Centro. Where did you meet him?"

Since the afternoon in the *entroterra* our bond had become stronger. I told Laura about Nico, down-playing so as not to excite envy: how young he was, how new we were, how temporary our affair must inevitably be.

Laura said, "Good for you!" and downed the rest of her *vin santo*. "Don't worry—I won't tell anyone. It'll be our secret." She set her empty cup on the ledge between us and gazed at the encroaching shadows of the cypresses, twisting her wedding ring. "You should have someone. Everyone should have someone."

"Hollis—"

"Don't talk to me about Hollis. You don't know him. You don't know what he puts me through. Hollis likes to have his cake and renounce it, too."

"*Signori, Signore!*" Anna Maria called. "We depart!"

One by one the other Fellows began to leave the wall where we were sitting. Laura, still staring into the distance, said, "If only I had something real to do here. Something of my own."

The look on her face—wistfulness laid over quietly simmering anger—made me remember what it was like to be in her position. Made me think of my own position now—a version of no-good-deed-goes-unpunished in which having made Daniel the center of my life, far from being rewarded, had left me scrambling to support myself. Was that what lay ahead for Laura?

"I know," I said. "It's hard."

Laura got up, brushing loose bits of mortar from her skirt. "It's almost time for Amber's snack. Lucia never remembers to give her milk, not juice." She paused, bestowed on me a small but genuine smile, then started off across the gravel.

I sat a few moments longer, watching the Fellows gather around Anna Maria. The shadows of the cypresses licked at my feet; the sun's deceptive warmth had gone.

After Thuanthong's opening, life at the Centro settled back into its usual stately pace, while winter tightened its grip on Liguria. An uneventful week later, I went into Genoa for the appointment Natalia had set up for me with the director of the Palazzo Reale. When I rounded the corner onto Via Garibaldi I saw a slender young man on a *moto* pull up at the museum entrance. He lifted the visor of his helmet and took it off, revealing a woman of thirty or so—younger than she'd sounded on the phone—petite, with a cap of tight brown curls like a Renaissance cherub. We shook hands, and Carla Agostini asked after Natalia. "Come," she said, "we have only a short time."

Entering the shuttered museum from the street was like being plunged into twilight. A long flight of marble steps, and we emerged into a reception hall lined with mirrors that gave back our reflections as we passed. Lecturing, Carla Agostini led me through chamber after chamber, her staccato Italian echoing the hammer-tap of her boots on the shining floors. We cruised through a carnival of crystal chandeliers and gilt-framed mirrors and wedding-cake moldings. We came to rest, finally, in a gallery that was also a bedroom, with a double bed lavishly draped and canopied. Carla Agostini saw my surprise. All the rooms in the Palazzo Reale, she explained, had been, for most of its three-and-a-half centuries, rooms people lived in.

"This building is a palimpsest—one era written on top of another. Like the city of Genoa itself. Like the human mind, as Freud used to say."

She walked over to the far corner and pushed against the wall. An invisible door opened. She touched a switch, and the room beyond sprang to life. A throng of velvet-covered chairs; piles of empty frames; paintings in linen shrouds stacked against the walls. Seeing them, I felt the old fizzy tingling that used to precede a find. Carla Agostini bent down and lifted one. She struggled to get her arms around it, but when I tried to help, she shook her head. "The insurance forbids." She wrangled the bulky package over to a chair and propped it up. Dust rose from the linen wrapping as she pulled it off.

Two girls in embroidered dresses with high lace-trimmed collars, their hair in coronets of tight braids. Clearly sisters, they sit on either side of a chess board. The older girl, about to move one of the pieces, looks out at the viewer with a crafty expression. The younger one holds up a hand in warning, or perhaps in protest. A third girl watches, laughing. I already knew this painting from reproductions. I was wild to see the other side.

Carla Agostini, "I am forbidden to show it, you understand." Then she grabbed the top and bottom of the ornate frame and walked the painting around and set it down again, face to the chair back. We stood gazing at the reverse side.

It was like coming to a place that you've never been to before but that somehow you know—a place you might have seen in a dream. The cottage with its white-washed walls and climbing roses. The lion-colored meadow where it stood. The trees that sheltered it, with fruit glowing among their leaves. The sunlit suggestion of other dwellings further down the slope.

"Do you know what place this is?" I asked.

"I believe it may be a village west of here, near the border with France. Most of it is in ruins now. Bussana Vecchia. Other representations—in the sixteenth century it was called simply Bussana—exist from about the same period. The experts are uncertain whether this one was painted by Anguissola herself."

"Why? When it's on the back of a painting that *is* by her?"

"Because she didn't sign it. A technicality, perhaps—but when it comes to provenance, an important one. Also, there exist no other landscapes by Anguissola. As far as we know, she was strictly a portrait painter."

"What do *you* think, Signora Agostini?"

"As you see, this is a landscape after the manner of the Dutch and Flemish painters of Sofonisba's era. Anguissola knew a number of artists from the Netherlands—they visited her here in Genoa. That's why I believe it was she who made this painting."

The longer I stood there, the more the mystery of the Lost Year deepened. *Always the beautiful answer who asks a more beautiful question.* I would have to go and see this place, even if it was in ruins.

I pulled my camera out of the pocket of my Caterina jacket. It was a digital camera that Rae had given me as a going-away present. She'd shown me how to use it, made me practice till she was satisfied.

Carla Agostini put a hand on my arm. "*Mi dispiace, Signora.* Photographs are forbidden."

"*Prego!*" I said. "I'm only in Italy till mid-December. The museum will still be closed when I leave."

"I cannot allow it." She ran a hand through her cherub curls, then gave me a cherubic grin. "You know, you look a bit pale, Signora. Perhaps you do not feel well? Please, wait here. I'll go and get some water."

She can tell which of them is following her by the smell. Mint (against nausea) means Asdrubale; ginger (for sore throat), Margherita. Both wish her to

remain shut up day and night in the windowless cell of the ship's only cabin.
But this voyage will take, God willing, six days.

By the second day curiosity (the greatest gift for a portrait painter, Michel-
angelo used to say) led her to gather her bothersome skirts in one hand and
venture out. She has walked the ship's deck from stern to bow, passing the fire
pit where the cook prepares food, the rope hammocks in which the mariners
sleep, the hatch with its odor of bilge rising up in ambush. She's watched the
ship's cooper shape glowing hot iron into hoops for his barrels, her fingers tin-
gling with the need to work, to make something.

This morning, the start of the third day, La Patrona *is approaching the coast*
of Amalfi, where Fabrizio's ship was attacked. She thought to stay inside until
they passed Naples. But riding the ship's motion blind, closed off from the sea,
makes her think of Fabrizio's lightless eyes. The beating of her heart, loud in the
cabin's silence, makes her think of his stilled one. And so, at noon, she emerges.
The helmsman's post is just outside the door. She persuades him to let her ply the
whipstaff that works the ship's rudder. He shows her how to grip the heavy pole
in two spots worn smooth by use. She feels the great ship move under her hands.
She hears, beneath La Patrona, *the deep organ notes of the sea.*

By late afternoon Naples is behind them. She climbs up to the topmost
deck, the small one that forms the roof of her cabin, where the sky feels closer
than the sea. The ship's pilot, a short, compact Genovese with cheeks netted
with smallpox scars, lowers a brass disk three handspans wide. He lays down
the rag he's been polishing it with.

May I be of assistance, my lady?

What's that? She gestures toward the object he holds.

A mariner's astrolabe, my lady.

Show me, she says.

As he moves to put the disk into her hands, the captain appears, stepping
onto the deck as if the ladder were a grand staircase. They met formally on the
first morning, after La Patrona *got underway, but not since.*

Signor Lomellini, she says. Buonasera.

Buonasera, *Signora.*

Curtsey; bow. A motion from Lomellini, and the pilot hands him the as-
trolabe and disappears down the ladder.

Below, on the main deck, the mariners chant a rhythmic Genovese song as they haul on the ropes that work the great triangular sails. The ship swings into its turn. She and Orazio Lomellini stand facing each other. Sunlight, stark up here, polishes his black springy curls and full spade beard and illumines his air of mingled brashness and competence. His eyes—like black opals, she thinks—hold hers.

She will not be the first to look away.

We sail to windward now, Lomellini says, gesturing toward the sails. You are interested in navigation, Signora?

Sì`, certo.

He moves to stand beside her and holds up the astrolabe by the ring at the top. This allows us to calculate our latitude, he says. It must be at eye level and perpendicular to the sea.

Explaining celestial navigation, he chooses his words with care, giving them the Genovese pronunciation, soft and liquefying, as if the sound of the sea has crept into his speech. He shows her how to sight the sun through two holes in the astrolabe's moveable vane. Then he has her tell the sun's altitude from the scale engraved around the rim. She is as intrigued by the man as by the instrument. Unlike most of his sex, he does not appear to consider women in the same category as children and slaves. She finds herself reading his hands—wide, deft, decisive rather than impulsive—as she might those of a sitter.

Is it accurate always? she asks, for something to say.

Dipende. *In fair weather, with calm seas, reasonably so. Lacking those conditions, we rely instead on dead reckoning.*

Dead reckoning? She would like to ask what it is, this other, ominous-sounding method. But his gaze gives her a feeling of exposure. As if the velvet pouch had fallen away. She says only, Thank you, Signore. It is an interesting device. I am most grateful.

He tucks the astrolabe under one arm. Might I ask a favor in return?

She looks at him, feeling an unaccustomed quiver of apprehension.

Would you be kind enough to make a drawing of me, Signora, whilst we're en route? It is another three days before we dock at Genoa.

At the word 'drawing' she's already stiffened and begun to turn away. She shakes her head. I regret, Signore, that that will not be possible.

She gathers her skirts and moves toward the ladder, wishing yet again for the male freedom of doublet and hose. Turning to descend, she sees him see her wish, and blushes.

Figurati! she huffs to Margherita on entering their cabin. Imagine! The temerity of asking me to draw his portrait.

The airless room smells of mint. Margherita says, Signor Asdrubale has gone to search for you, my lady.

In any case, I can make no one's portrait. I've no materials.

Margherita busies herself setting out the evening meal on the plank table between their two beds. Trembling light from the one candle allowed onboard a wooden ship makes the room contract. She says, I stowed drawing materials in the bottom of your trunk before we left Palermo, my lady.

You should not have done that. I did not request it.

She stares unseeing at the salted meat and sea biscuit and cheese. Can you imagine? she says again. And he would have us use my cabin for the purpose.

But, my lady, did you not know? This is his *cabin. Signor Lomellini has given it up to us for the duration of the voyage.*

11

"This will be our last meeting," Natalia said.

It was the twelfth of November, a Monday. The women sat in the places they'd occupied for the past seven weeks. Vida on the sofa; Bardha in the chair on the other side of the fireplace; Genta on the floor leaning back against Bardha's legs, her dark hair in a long braid that curved like a question mark. Natalia and I occupied two chairs opposite the sofa.

Surprise flicked through me in a kind of cramp. I hadn't known today was our last day together. Natalia hadn't told me.

"Where will you go?" I asked the three women.

Vida frowned and raked a hand through her dirty dark-red hair. Bardha said that she and Genta, taking Ardi with them, would go to Oslo. A cousin had arranged to sponsor them. Once out of Italy, they'd be legal. I wondered how they'd manage to leave the country when their visas had expired—then realized that Natalia would have found a way.

"Here in Italy we are ghosts," Bardha said. "We must be invisible."

"Norway!" Genta made a face. "Cold and snow and dried fish."

I looked around the room with a sharpening sense of loss. The French doors stood open, as usual. Indecisive autumn sunlight crept across the oriental rug and fingered Natalia's books and paintings. On the balcony an eruption of orange and yellow had occurred since my Thursday visit. Plants flower, Nico had told me, because they're going to die soon.

This apartment had welcomed me. Here I'd felt part of something.

"Today," Bardha said, "we wish to speak of shame."

Vida snorted but said nothing.

The women hadn't announced a topic at any of the earlier Conversations. Why today?

Reading my thoughts, Bardha added, "Because certain things must not be un... unsayed. And now is the last time we are together."

I hesitated. Natalia was here; but when I got out of my depth, would she come to the rescue? I said, "Of course. Please go on."

There was a silence. Gianpaolo chirped. A flurry of car horns spiralled up from the street below, and a shudder ran through the three women. "*Tranquillo!*" Natalia said. I studied a primitive sculpture on the bookcase beside me—a woman carrying a baby, but oddly: holding it at her waist, horizontal and stiff, its arms bent upwards, its hands curved into claws. I'd puzzled over the figure many times during lulls in the Conversations. Now I realized: This baby is dead.

At last Bardha said, "For me, it is this. I am not the woman I was... before. Things which I do—did—change me. I make a wall in my mind against these things. I think now, this wall, it must fall down. I ask, am I a good person still? I have lost much. Have I lost to be human?"

Oh my God, I thought. By shame, I'd assumed Bardha meant the shame of what had been done to her. To all of them. The deaths of those they loved. The stigma of rape so great that its victims could never return to their families. But no: the women wanted to talk about *their* transgressions.

Bardha sat up straighter, ankles locked below her flowing flowered skirt, hands clutching each other. She opened her mouth to speak, when Genta said, "One morning, a week before the war, we are walking to school, like always. A Serb, a strong boy of two classes ahead, he take—grab?—my best friend. And he beats him in front of my eyes. Rinor falls in the street. The rest of us—" She broke off, her voice trembling. Her aunt reached down to touch her shoulder. Genta put a hand on top of hers and held on. "The rest of us, we run."

There was a silence. *I would've run, too*, I wanted to say, to comfort Genta. But was it true? I'd stayed with Daniel to the end.

Looking past me with her soft, near-sighted gaze, Bardha said, "In the camp, in Montenegro, I steal. I steal an egg."

"An egg?" I said. "Surely that's not—"

"The old man I take from, he is sick. Thin like skeleton, and cold. Well, all of us, we are cold." She paused. "Two days later, he dies."

We were all silent. Bardha watched me, gauging my reaction. But how could I be shocked? Didn't I know from experience how desperate circumstances can make you do desperate things? How trying to hang onto who you used to be can make you into someone else altogether?

I said, "You did it to survive. Surely many people would've—"

"The best of us did not survive!" Bardha buried her face in her hands.

Genta had twisted around and was staring up at her aunt. She pulled Bardha's hands away and murmured something in Albanian.

I forced myself to say, "English, please."

"This egg," Genta said to Bardha. "I remember. You gave to me, yes? When we were so hungry, that week when supplies never come." Bardha nodded. "I still remember how it tastes. Slip…slippery and wonderful."

Vida's strange square-cut eyes were fixed not on Bardha or Genta but on me. All this time she'd said nothing.

Genta told about when she and her brother were hiding in the cellar of their house, during the bombing of Kosovo by the UN forces. This was before Bardha found her. A neighbor lay screaming in the street all day, and no one helped him. It was too dangerous to go outside. His son, Genta's friend Rinor, lay dead beside him. "I did not help Rinor, that time before. And I do not help his father now. I want to save my own self."

Genta hugged her drawn-up knees and stared at the floor. How terrible to have these moments stuck like fish hooks in your heart. She was sixteen, for God's sake. Natalia had told me, back when the Conversations started, that the only way through trauma was to remember, relive, re-see. I didn't believe this. I wanted to get up and put my arms around Genta and hold her as I would have held Rachel. *Shhh*, I wanted to whisper into her hair, *It's okay, don't think about it. Dandelion puffs!*

Natalia said to Genta, "If one does not save oneself, one cannot save others, *cara*."

"The most bad thing," Bardha began. "Fucking terrible thing."

Her lined face flooded with color. The week before, taking a leaf from Nico's book, I'd given the women a lesson on cursing in English.

"It is when the Skorpios come and say, Go back to Albania. Make everyone go out onto the road, and burn our houses. Make the women start to walk. All of us crying. Leaving the men. Boys, even. As young as fourteen. My neighbor's boy, who carry my baskets for me on market day. My sister's son." She swallowed. "My husband. We walk slow, the women, so slow, and we hear the guns over and over.

"In that moment I become a killer. Because it is the first time in my life when I want to kill."

Vida said, "I did."

Silence. I said, "Did what?"

"Killed someone. And I am not sorry to it. Fucking never."

This time I *was* shocked. Yet not, somehow, surprised. I waited—we all waited—for Vida to go on.

Vida leaned forward, her hands balled into fists. "She was a brave woman, the mother of Ardi," she said. "Such babies were not welcome in Kosovo—children of rape, children of Serbs. Scum-babies. At the clinic where I am—was—working, many mothers abandon their infants. Some snap their necks when they are born."

My horror must have shown in my face, because Vida cast me a look of scorn from those Windex-blue eyes. "He died," she said. "One of the men who killed Ardi's mother. He died screaming."

I flinched, which I saw her register.

"Tell me, Signora," she said softly, "do you know what is the smell of human flesh burning?"

"Vida!" Bardha said.

Vida sat back. Her eyes left mine and fastened on Gianpaolo, perched on a lampshade across the room. The bird raised each clawlike leg in turn and stretched each wing voluptuously.

The others watched me, waiting for me to return Vida's anger. But I didn't—I couldn't—because I understood it. In fact, I envied Vida. She had someone to blame—plenty of someone's. Plenty of fury to keep herself from melting away. And she had courage: she'd taken action, even if brutal, even if wrong. She'd *done something.* I remembered her hands gentle on my injured leg; I thought of her generosity in taking on the orphaned Ardi.

Natalia sat without speaking, arms resting on the arms of her chair in a Lincolnesque pose. I looked at her. She gave an almost imperceptible shake of her head. I knew it meant: This is conversation class, not group therapy.

At last Bardha said, "I think that now we must look to the future. Not the past. The lifes— Lifes?" She looked at me.

"Lives."

"The lives which we had before, they took. We cannot let them take also the future. We who have lost so much, now we know how precious this world is."

Vida shot her an incredulous look. "Forgive? Turn the cheek to other side? This is…fucking…bullshit."

"Vida, come on!" Genta sounded almost like a normal teenager. She let go of her knees and sat up straight. "My aunt doesn't mean that. And I don't, too."

"Not forgive. Never! And not forget," Bardha agreed. "But go…go…" She leaned down to say something in Albanian to Genta.

"Forward."

"…go forward. It is oh-kay, as Natalia has told us. Even after terrible things happens. It is no dishonor to again love life."

Genta, clearly quoting Natalia, said, "The hole is always there. But when time passes, we weave it into the cloth of us."

Natalia leaned her chin on one hand and looked at Bardha and Genta. I recognized the expression on her face. She was proud.

Vida got up and stalked out of the room.

After the chorus of "Thank you very many!," after the cheek-brushing that turned into fierce final hugs, after Bardha had gone to the kitchen and returned with an armful of lilies that she thrust into my hands, after

Genta had sat down at the piano and banged out a lively marching tune, Natalia followed me down the hall. In the doorway she waited, holding the flowers, while I shrugged into my jacket and pulled on my beret.

"By God," she said, "if women had but written stories."

By now I recognized the Wife of Bath when I heard her. I looked down at Natalia's face, framed in bright silvery spikes of hair. I was always surprised by how small she was.

"By God, if women had but written stories,/They would have written of men more wickedness/Than all the race of Adam could redress." She shook her head. "Ah, well. One is born not to suffer but to negotiate with suffering."

"Will I see you again?" I said. "At the Centro? Or we could—"

"Have you a moment now?"

"Of course." There was an hour till my train.

"Come with me."

Natalia led me back down the hall into her study, where she closed the door behind us. It was the first time I'd been in here. The room was full of a deep, long-held quiet. Like the rest of the apartment it spoke eloquently of its owner, a woman who inhabited the center of her own life. The last of the afternoon light fell in long bars across walls lined with bookshelves. Piles of books, leaning perilously, stood on the floor, the desk, the broad windowsill. Manila folders covered the sofa. Natalia swept them to one side and said, "This place and I are falling apart together. Please. Sit."

I laid my armload of flowers on the sofa between us. "I meant to thank you for arranging my visit to the Palazzo Reale. Signora Agostini was very helpful. Very *simpatica*."

"*Sì, sì. Simpaticissima*." Natalia's hands held each other, twisting gently, in her lap. Her nails looked more bitten than ever. "I am happy to help. Now there is a favor that I—that we—need. It is a great one, and there is some risk. You must promise you will not agree unless you truly wish it." Her bright brown eyes held mine. She waited.

"I promise."

"My city has been always a refuge. Even in medieval times. Her natural harbor. The great mountain range that shields her. The *carruggi* in which it is so easy to lose oneself." Natalia shook her head as if to clear it. "But no longer."

"Why not?"

I knew about the new laws, yes? That even immigrants who'd been granted political asylum were being deported once their visas expired? Bardha and Genta and Ardi could go to Norway, one of the few European countries still willing to accept Kosovar refugees, "now that the glamour of war is over. Now that the world has moved on to fresher tragedies." But for Lule and Vida, anywhere in Europe was too risky.

"Why?" I asked.

Because Vida was Serbian. The minute this became known—"and it *will* become known, the refugee community is small and full of bitter anger"—she and Lule would be in grave danger. Bardha and Genta accepted Vida because her dead husband had been a member of the Kosovo Liberation Army, known for killing Serbs. Other Kosovar refugees might not give her time to explain this. And because of her husband, any Serbian refugees she met would be even more eager to kill her than Kosovars were.

My heart began to slam slowly and painfully. Lule. What would happen to Lule? I felt a flash of anger at Vida, as if her nationality were a choice, an act of faulty mothering.

Natalia leaned toward me and touched my arm. Reading my mind, she said, "Lule would be left quite alone in a strange country."

"Isn't there anything you can do?"

"Lule and Vida would be safe—at least, safer—in America. But since your country's tragedy very few visa applications from political refugees are accepted. And the process takes years. Vida cannot enter the United States as a foreigner. There is not time. She needs an American passport."

"How can *I*…"

But I saw how. It was *my* passport Natalia wanted. Of course: Vida and I were close enough in age, in height, even (if, say, Vida bleached her hair) in coloring. It could, just possibly, be done.

Natalia saw me understand. She said, "Once Lule and Vida are safely in New York, your passport would be returned to you here. The needed stamps—for the brief trip home you will appear to have made, a family emergency—my associates can provide. You will then leave Italy as planned, a month from now, at the end of your fellowship."

"Couldn't your…associates—"

"No. A false passport, no matter how good, will not pass your country's security now, after your tragedy of September."

"What about Lule?"

"My associates believe that for her they can make a credible passport. A child's will not be so scrutinized. Especially if her mother's is genuine."

I sat, absorbing all this. Natalia sat watching me absorb it. She felt in her skirt pocket for cigarettes and matches. Fingers trembling, she lit one. Its aromatic scent wrapped around us.

"But Lule and Vida would be illegal aliens in the U.S., just as they are in Italy."

"Someone who is already in your country—even illegally!—can request political asylum. Asylum is far easier to obtain than permission to *enter* as a political refugee. Especially now."

That sounded like the U. S. government, all right. Break the law in order to become legal. But wasn't Natalia's solution—her very Italian solution—the same thing? Better to ask forgiveness than permission.

"In any case, they must leave soon. It is no longer safe for them here with me. The authorities are getting too close."

The last of the light had gone. In the dimness I could hear the ticking of an old-fashioned pendulum clock perched on one of the piles of books. *Authorities*, it tapped out. *Associates*. I remembered Angus Dance's warning, weeks ago, when he followed me onto the Passeggiata.

"Natalia…"

The sensible thing was to refuse, of course. But I was tired of sensible. I thought of Vida's courage, her clarity. Did I have it in me, after twenty years of sensible, to take action, as she had, and damn the moral ambiguity? Or had the Ladies of the Field long since abandoned me?

"Do not answer now, *cara*. Think over it. But there is some urgency." Natalia took a long drag on her cigarette. "Vida has not been kind to you. I apologize for her. She—"

"No need," I said. "I understand. I've been there."

"Ah, *si*`. And you have done so much for these women. They feel safe because you have took them on your heart. You have got them to talk in blue streaks, and this will heal them. Now it remains this one thing of more."

She was tired, I saw, her English beginning to unravel. I gathered my flowers and stood up. Natalia rose, too, moving slowly. We brushed cheeks.

"Just what you feel, do. Will you see yourself out?"

My hand on the doorknob, I hesitated. "Nico doesn't know about this?"

Natalia shook her head. "No. And please do not tell. The fewer which know, the better." She gave me a sudden gold-flecked grin. "You are happy, you and he, *vero?*"

I nodded.

"You are good for him. A man shall pay his debt."

"The Wife of Bath?" I said.

Natalia nodded. "And he is good for you, also. Even though he is what you Americans call a raw diamond."

"A rough diamond."

"Pursuit makes a woman come alive. Let him pursue. Be the flame, not the moth."

"The Wife of Bath?"

"Casanova."

Leaving, I almost tripped over Lule, who was sprawled on the floor in the kitchen doorway, drawing. Beyond her Vida stood with her back turned, her hair a tangled skein of brightness in the light over the sink, Gianpaolo a spot of blue on one shoulder. "Lule!" she said, without turning around.

Lule looked up and frowned. She began with slow, resigned movements to slot the pastels back into their cardboard tray.

"No—keep them," I said. "Fair exchange for the drawing you gave me."

Was that a flicker of interest from Vida? But she didn't turn around.

Lule's face cleared. "*Grazie!*"

I added, "Just keep them away from Ardi, okay? He's too young," and was rewarded with a grin.

Lule went back to her work. I stood looking down at her, my fingers tingling with the desire to smooth her wild, pale hair. I would miss her. Her hand moved with sure strokes across the paper. Long anguished splashes of blue-green; a swirl of bitter yellow.

"That looks interesting," I said. "What is it?"

"I don't know yet."

Mid-November mornings saw fog lying milk-white along the Centro paths. Liguria, Anna Maria informed us, never got cold enough to snow. It was fog that signaled the end of autumn. Fog and rain: "*i segni d'inverno.*"

"Signs of hell?" Joshua said, alarmed.

Everyone laughed except Dmitri, who sat at the far end of the table, sunk in Slavic gloom.

"No, of winter, you idiot," Hollis said. "*Inverno*, not *inferno*."

Chantal and Joshua had just returned from a trip to Sardinia with four kinds of honey—Sardinia's hardworking bees were famous—and Anna Maria had declared a festive brunch. I was happy to have the distraction: since Natalia's request—six days ago, now—I hadn't been able to think of anything else. The Fellows sat at the long table in the Centro's dining room, passing each other pots of lavender and eucalyptus and wildflower and thistle honey. All except—

"Where is Angus?" Chantal asked.

"He has gone," Anna Maria said.

"Gone?" My heart lifted.

"To London. For business. He returns this evening."

Too bad. It would've been nice not to see him ever again. If I agreed to lend my passport, how much of a danger would he be? I sat eating and listening to the talk of the other Fellows. It comforted me to feel how invisible my worries were to them. Like the early years when we kept Daniel's diagnosis a secret, so that we could escape from it into the unawareness of others.

"Hello? Earth to Kate." Laura touched my arm. She lowered her voice to a whisper. "What's the matter? You seem so out of it. What's wrong?"

For an instant I thought, I could tell her. How good it would feel to share my problem—to halve it. But it was too dangerous. I said, "Nothing's wrong. I don't know—winter, maybe."

Laura frowned, unconvinced. I helped myself to a couple of Sardinian *papassini* from the tray she held out, then took it from her and passed it to Thuanthong on my left.

"These are great, aren't they?" Made with almonds and raisins and of course honey, the *papassini* were ravishingly good. "Beautiful!"

He nodded, chewing his *papassino* as if it were broccoli.

Across the table, Joshua boomed, "Your *piece* is beautiful. Right, Thong?"

Thuanthong looked pained. "You cannot *make* beauty—only invite," he said. "If desire, it will find you."

"Death," Dmitri said, "is the mother of beauty." He'd been so sad while Chantal was away that Laura had christened him the Prince of Lugubria. Late last night he'd started running a bath, then forgotten about it. This morning a section of the game room ceiling had been found on the ping-pong table, and Dmitri had been found asleep beneath it in his overcoat, his arms around an empty vodka bottle and a large box of chocolates.

Joshua gave up on Thuanthong—bullying just bounced off the little sculptor's serenity—and started on me. "What about you, Katherine? How's your work going?"

Beside me, Laura stiffened. I could read her thoughts as if her body were telegraphing them. *How come no one ever asks about* my *work?* It was the fault line in our friendship—this inequity. If only, I thought for the hundredth time, we could be *even*. Or if Laura could at least see us that way.

Anna Maria watched me from the foot of the table, her ear caught by Joshua's question. Here was a perfect chance to talk up my work—the kind of opportunity I needed to seize, if I were to become the fulltime academic I needed to be. My camera was in my jacket pocket; I thought of showing

my fellow Fellows the painting of Bussana Vecchia. I'd taken several photos—Carla Agostini had left me alone with the painting for a good five
minutes. But if I showed them, it might get her in trouble. I could imagine
Anna Maria reporting it to the higher-ups at the Palazzo Reale.

"My work's going well," I mumbled through a mouthful of thistle
honey.

"What did you think of Bush's address to the U. N.?" Hollis asked,
neatly redirecting Joshua's attention.

The talk turned to events in the States—the newly declared War on
Terror; the twenty-five-million-dollar reward for Osama bin Laden—
then descended into Bush-beating. Spectator citizenship, Daniel used to
call this.

"—the haves and the have mores—" (Hollis)

"—when we talk about war, we're really talking about peace—" (Joshua)

"—I do not need to explain things, that's the interesting thing about
being President—" (Hollis)

"In France" (Chantal, sounding bored) "politicians do not say such
things."

I listened, feeling outside the conversation, as if I were watching a play.
I kept seeing the faces of the Kosovar women, as real to me as the people
around the table. This was how it had been since Natalia had made her
request. My mind a stew of doubt, hope, guilt, desire. A see-saw of *now/
then, here/there, Caterina/Kate.* I needed to choose one side or the other,
and soon.

That afternoon I went to the bookshelf above my desk and took down my
passport. I sank into the chair and swiveled back and forth, studying my
photograph. Because passports don't state hair-color or eye-color or height
or weight, Vida only had to fit the date of birth and the photo. Her hair
was dark red, her eyes that Windex blue. But hair was easily lightened;
and in the photo my eyes echoed the intense blue of my shirt. And though
Vida was at least a decade younger me, she didn't look it. Suffering: the
Fountain of Age.

The passport gave me no reason to refuse Natalia's request. But there *are* reasons, I thought. Plenty of them.

There was the near certainty that I'd been set up. Natalia had served on the Selection Committee for this autumn's Fellows. She'd seen the photos submitted with our applications; she'd known from my biographical statement that I'd lived in Kosovo. And Natalia herself was a rogue character. Quitting a government-sponsored humanitarian organization to work for an unlicensed one, then quitting that. Generally recognizing—like her nephew—no rules. A true wild card: not the ideal partner in crime.

And it *would* be a crime. Yesterday's *Corriere della Sera* had run an article about the arrest of a British expatriate in nearby Recco who'd been caught helping illegal refugees. He faced a fine and possibly prison. And that was just the Italian side of things. I'd done some research on the internet. The penalty for passport fraud in the U. S. was ten to twenty-five years in jail. Here the shadow of Angus Dance fell over my thoughts. I'd begun to wonder if he might be at the Centro undercover, some sort of EU policeman. Or an Interpol agent—though all I knew about Interpol came from James Bond movies.

Church bells began to ring. Their sound flooded in through the open window, clear and silver and insistent. Why take a huge risk to help two people I barely knew? Janet had asked me. But that was just it: I *did* know them. I knew Vida from the inside out. I knew Lule like my own daughter. I knew their pain, their loss, their generosity, their courage. Others' hearts are not like yours, Nico liked to say. Maybe not. But maybe my heart could be like theirs.

"Your *friend* got you into this? Would a bona fide psychiatrist ask you to break the law? And Signor Too-Good-to-Be-True—is he in on it?"

"Nico. He doesn't know anything about this."

"You think."

"Jan!"

"Okay, okay. Now, listen, Katy—"

Fuzz, crackling, louder crackling. A crash. A child wailing. It was evening in Tanzania, but Janet was still at the clinic. Of course I shouldn't have told her about the Kosovar women, or about Natalia's request. But I'd needed a sounding board, the way Daniel used to be.

"What? I can't hear you."

"—and now your feelings are involved. Look, Katy, I understand. All those years when Daniel was sick, you didn't have much choice but to do whatever he needed. You had to be his Katydid. Now how about some Katydidn't?"

"Like Grandma Eva used to say: People first; then principles. Emotion isn't a *bad* thing. You said so yourself."

"Katy. You're opening up, and that's great. But *Rachel* is who you should be opening up to—not strangers. Rachel's the one who needs you. Whenever I call her I hear how she misses Daniel. Have the two of you ever sat down and cried together?"

"I don't do tears," I said stiffly, "not in front of people. They never help. They would've interrupted Daniel's dying. And they'd make his death worse for Rae now."

Janet sighed. "You need to use your head as well as your heart. You need a *wise* heart. Breaking the law, in a foreign country—"

Another wave of trans-Mediterranean static crested, then retreated.

"—a huge risk to help two people you barely know. You've got, what?, a month left in Italy. Concentrate on your work, and let people who know what they're doing take care of your refugees."

"If you could just see Lule! She's a *child*, Jan. She's had nothing in her life so far but suffering." I thought better of mentioning Vida. Janet would never have understood her.

"You have a child of your own, who's suffered plenty."

"*You're* in a foreign country, helping other people's children. How legal is your clinic?"

"That's different. No one else will suffer from my bad decisions."

"That's right," I said meanly. "Because you don't have children. What do you know about what my child needs?"

I heard a sharp intake of breath. More static, ending in a string of painful chirps. Then silence.

"Jan? Jan!"

By the time dinner ended, my anger at Janet—at her unshakeable conviction that she knew better than I did how I should live my life—had subsided. My mind had returned to wrestling with Natalia's request. What should I do? What could I do? What, in my heart, did I want to do?

"Katherine! I say! Hold up a second, won't you?"

The moon was round and bright as a searchlight in the night sky. Still, a flashlight was useful for the rocky path uphill to the Villa Francesca. I turned and shone it on my pursuer's face.

Angus Dance put up a hand to shield his eyes from the light. His lips curved in a frugal smile. "I wonder if I might have a word?"

We stood facing each other, close enough for a whiff of brimstone cologne to reach me. I took a step back.

"What?" I said. I'd been feeling so good, so freed, my body still alight from an afternoon in bed with Nico. Now this.

Dance said, "I thought I should warn you—"

"Oh, stop! I don't need any warnings. Certainly not yours."

I turned away. Dance reached out and gripped my arm. The beam from my flashlight caromed among the branches of the umbrella pines. "Katherine! It's bloody crucial that you"—I jerked my arm out of his grasp—"that you pairceive the situation clearly."

"What situation?"

"Natalia Fabbri is under obsairvation. She's being watched. And anyone who associates with her is being watched."

"I don't believe you. Watched by who?"

"I'm not at liberty to say."

"Well, when you are, get back to me. Till then, *arrivederci*."

Dance's flashlight bobbed as he folded his arms. His voice took on a tinge of exasperation. "Look, Katherine. I know you think I'm naff. All mouth and no trousers. But don't you see? I shouldn't be telling you this at all. I'm taking a bloody great risk."

"Why?"

"Because you…are…a pairson of value."

I couldn't see his face, with the moon behind him; but his voice had softened. Was he trying, in his stiff Scottish way, to say he *cared* for me? This thought caused the strangest change in the night around me, which narrowed and darkened, as if the moon had disappeared. I had to reclaim myself.

"You don't even know me," I said. "What we had was just…Freudian hydraulics."

I felt him flinch. "In your situation, your husband would surely—"

"Leave Daniel out of this! What do you even know about him? Who are you, anyway? What are you doing here?"

"You haven't a bleeding clue, have ye? Your new friend is under investigation. Do I have to spell it out? No bloody good for a foreigner to be involved with. Especially in times like these."

"You *said* observation. Now it's investigation?"

Dance turned and began to walk back downhill toward the Villa Baiardo.

"*Buona notte,*" he called over his shoulder, in his terrible accent. It came out "Boner not."

Fury swept through me. Anger at this man for trying to intimidate me; anger at myself for being afraid. I waited, breathing the cold night air and listening to the soft night sounds, while his figure receded. Moonlight pursued the pale egg of his head.

Standing there on the path, I made up my mind.

KOSOVO, 1981.

Martial law was declared in early April. One gray afternoon Daniel was approached by his favorite student, Sara of the glossy, leaping hair. The one he'd seen, back in September, was going to take to the dirt; the one he'd nurtured and watched grow. They sat over glasses of tea in the student cafeteria. Was there any way *Zotëri Profesor* Rosen could help her get a letter to her family in Israel?

Daniel thought of the diplomatic pouch at the American Embassy in Belgrade, which Fulbright professors were allowed to use. One or another of the Fulbrighters made a weekly mail run from Pristina. Mail had to be submitted open, for the censors. Ah—but not the flimsy blue aerograms that folded up to serve as their own envelopes. Those could be sent sealed.

Okay, *po*! Sara nodded, her cheeks pink with joy. Daniel brought her a blank aerogram the next day.

12

The next day I handed my passport, sealed inside an envelope, to Natalia. We were sitting in her living room in front of the fire, while rain drummed on the balcony. Natalia balanced the envelope on one palm. *"Grazie, cara! Grazie mille!"* Her face in the firelight made me think of Sofonisba's portraits. Looking at her, I realized she'd been sure I would agree. The realization gave me a chill, and yet—

What a difference handing over my passport made! I was no longer merely an observer of others' suffering. As I'd expected, the guilt I'd felt like an undertow all during the Conversations vanished. But there was another feeling—one I hadn't expected, or even known was possible. It was this: I was no longer merely someone who had suffered. My pain—and Daniel's—had been transformed. Because of those twenty years, I was able to understand Vida; because I understood her, I was able to help her and Lule. I hadn't known it was possible to redeem suffering. Had Rachel made the same discovery? I wanted to call her right then and there and say, *Fruffle! I get it!*

Instead, I sat and sipped the *grappa* Natalia had insisted I take "to guard off a chill." The liquor laid a trail of fire from my lips to my stomach. Through my head floated the beautiful Italian word for well-being: *benessere.*

I said, "What about Lule?"

"Lule's passport will be made by the best man in Genoa, as soon as he has yours to match. It will be accepted, *cara*, do not worry. It will pass mustard."

"Muster," I corrected automatically.

Natalia smiled.

I rolled my empty *grappa* glass between my palms. *Ottimista*; *Pessimista*. How apt, I thought: I'm feeling both at once. Exhilarated; afraid. At peace; anxious as hell.

Natalia had already told me that, for safety's sake, this must be our last meeting. I would not get another chance. I said, "Can I ask you something?"

Was her nod the slightest bit wary? But she said, "*Dimmi, cara*."

Haltingly, I explained about Angus Dance following me. About his warnings. Natalia listened, her bright black eyes never leaving mine. When I'd finished, she tossed her head.

"Angus Dance is no more a scholar than I am a ballerina."

"What is he, then?"

"MI6."

"MI6! But…why is the British secret service interested in *you*?" So I'd been right: Dance *was* undercover.

"Genoa is a—how do you call it?—a *conduttura* for political refugees. They flow from Kosovo through Italy to England."

"A pipeline. Illegal?"

"*Si`, certo*. The British wish to stop the widening stream of refugees, without looking bad in the eyes of the European Union. *Boh!* They have always been *xenofobici*. Terrified of being overrun by people whose languages have too many consonants."

"Natalia, why do you do this, when it's so dangerous?'

Natalia rubbed her forehead. Her thoughts seemed to travel great psychic distances to arrive at this rain-curtained, fire-lit room. At last she said, "If a law upholds suffering, how can that law be just? If we uphold an unjust law, how can we be free?"

In the fireplace a log snapped; flames shot up. Natalia rose. "Come. We will tell Vida."

I was about to refuse. I didn't think I could bear it if Vida responded to my generosity with her usual contempt. But Natalia was already walking down the hall, and I found I wanted to see Vida's face when she realized that she and Lule were saved. I followed. As we approached the kitchen there was the sound of pummeling, the clean smell of cinnamon and cloves. Vida whirled around when we entered, holding a large ball of dough in front of her like a shield.

Natalia said, "*Tutto va bene.*" She walked over to Vida and gently took away the dough and set it on the counter. "Look, *carissima*! You and Lule will go to America." She held out the passport.

Vida slapped floury hands on the backside of her sweatpants. She glanced at me. Then she took the passport and opened it.

When she looked up, her face was utterly still. "And Lule?"

Natalia said, "We will make for Lule a convincing passport."

Vida's face grew pink. I realized I'd never seen her look happy before. Her arms opened wide. She clutched at Natalia, whose head barely reached her shoulder, as if only Natalia's diminutive form could keep her from falling. They stood in a crooked embrace. Blinking (were those tears? *Vida*?), Vida looked over Natalia's head. Our eyes met. Vida said nothing; but the look that passed between us spoke. My eyes said *Torture, shame, death*. Vida's said *Twenty years*.

In that look we exchanged losses. Then we turned away, without affection, but not without respect.

Natalia disentangled herself. She linked arms with me and we walked like that, bumpily, down the long hall. In the doorway she stood so close that I could smell her hair, its mingled odors of nicotine and sweat. Her hands grasped mine.

"I am mine own woman, well at ease," she said.

"The Wife of Bath?" I ventured.

"*Si`*. When we can say that along with her, then we are free. Remember, *cara*— you must not come here again. It is too much risk."

My eyes stung. I leaned down and brushed my cheeks against her soft, papery ones. "Thank you, Natalia. *Grazie mille.*"

"It is for *me* to thank—"

She broke off. A tinkly music had begun to sound. Hurdy-gurdy music. It seemed to be coming from the bottom of the stairs three stories down. Natalia let go of me and began to withdraw behind her apartment door. "Please, *cara*. Go now!"

On the stairs I brushed past a man ascending. It wasn't until I saw the organ parked in the foyer that I recognized Straw Hat.

OUT. IN. IN DEEPER.

Vida's look still warmed me as I walked down the *spina di pesce*, slippery with rain, for the last time. This was what I'd wanted, I realized—acceptance, respect, a kind of blessing, Vida's blessing—almost as much as I wanted Lule and Vida to be safe. Maybe, after all, I thought, there's no such thing as altruism. Gusts of wet wind propelled me along the *carruggi*. Seeing the mysterious organ grinder—more, seeing Natalia's reaction to him—had shaken me. Natalia's lack of surprise when I handed over my passport had shaken me. Her revelation about Angus Dance had shaken me. And then there were *his* warnings about *her*. I felt as if I no longer knew who anyone was. I would have to be watchful—in every direction.

It was still morning and still raining when I got to the Palazzo Bianco. I hadn't been back since getting thrown out for touching Sofonisba's portrait of her first husband. I bought a ticket, then pulled the hood of my windbreaker around my face as I went past the office. My plan for the day: a stop here, to see the exhibit of everyday objects from the Renaissance that Carla Agostini had told me about; then lunch at a nearby *focacceria*; and finally, on my way back to the train station, a detour to the *contrada* where Sofonisba and her second husband had made their permanent home.

Emerging from the stairs onto the third floor of the Palazzo Bianco was like being plunged inside a treasure chest. I turned and turned again, dizzy with the gallery's sheer thingy abundance. A guard—mercifully, not the same one as on my last visit—materialized in the far doorway. Do not touch, I warned myself. I wandered, hands clasped behind my back, among porcelain and crystal, silver, ceramics, furniture and maps and books. By now I'd learned to recognize, even before the warning tingle that heralded a Visitation, a kind of magnetic force. I followed it to a mannequin in the far corner of the gallery. A black velvet gown embroidered in gold, with a bodice that came to a point and a gathered skirt flowing from waist to toes. I took a step forward. A prickling traveled up my spine. The fabric seemed to emit a fragrance, smoky and a bit like pine trees. Something I'd never smelled before but somehow knew. I moved closer.

The guard coughed.

I turned away. A glass case near the mannequin held undergarments. Stockings of russet silk. A corset. A petticoat. A *camicia* of sheer white linen designed to be worn with its lace peeking out at neck and wrists. Another case displayed a pearl fillet for binding the hair, a pair of wooden platform shoes with bands of jeweled leather.

The velvet-gowned mannequin drew me back. I went and stood in front of it without moving. I waited.

One drawing—that's all she has promised. Out of gratitude for this cramped cabin, lit by a single candle and smelling of tar and camphor. Her hand hovers over the supplies Margherita brought her: charcoal, red and black chalk, a roll of fine linen paper. No drawing board. But Orazio Lomellini, with what she's beginning to see as his customary inventiveness, has had La Patrona's *cooper provide the smooth oak lid of a wine cask.*

He watches with that dark opaline gaze as she picks it up, smoothing the paper held to it by spots of wax, afraid to look down at the chalked lines she set there yesterday. He sits on one bunk, she on the other, as far apart as the space allows. Even so, their knees nearly touch. His proximity evokes in her a sensation she doesn't recognize, a kind of trill deep inside her. Perhaps it's because she's never worked so close to a subject before? But the real question is—

Signora. Will you meet me on the topmost deck at midnight? I will show you how to use the astrolabe with the stars.

Please look at the wasps' nest, as you did yesterday. Not at me.

She indicates the palm-sized vessel, hard as stucco and striated in varying shades of white (which she coveted the moment she saw it) that sits on the shelf by her head.

The real question is how she is able to draw now, when for three months she couldn't make her hand move across the paper. She looks down. Yes: there are the underpinnings of the face opposite hers. Her surprise at the magic of this is as sharp as the very first time, when at five years old she saw her father's face emerge from lines made by her stick of charcoal. Something has happened to her on this voyage. Yesterday she found herself noticing, with a throb of recognition stronger than pleasure, the changing colors of the sunset sky.

Orazio Lomellini says, Also, there is something I wish to discuss with you, Signora.

Va bene, *she thinks. And I, with you.*

But for now, she is drawing. Drawing!

Tell me a fact about yourself, she commands. Something from your childhood.

It's the best way to make la persona dentro—*the person within—inhabit a sitter's features. Yesterday she had Lomellini speak of his native Liguria. The heart-stopping blue of the Mediterranean; the great aquiline chain of the Apennines; the* entroterra *between them, in which one could lose oneself.*

When I was a small boy—Lomellini says—I had a pet monkey who stole grapes from our neighbor's garden. I taught him to do it. His name was Antonello.

Her eyes flick back and forth between his face and her paper as she draws. The familiar rhythm, hypnotic as a clock's pendulum yet altogether outside time. Be careful not to lose the modeling, especially around the lips. Note where the light strikes temples, cheekbones, bridge of nose. Remember Michelangelo's counsel: Trifles make perfection possible—and perfection is no trifle. Neck. Shoulders. Imagine (with, again, that strange trill low in her abdomen) the play of muscle and bone beneath the heavy doublet. She feels a blush heat her face. But why? She has always pictured her sitters unclothed. How else get the body right?

Tell me another fact, she says. Reminding herself: The body expresses the spirit whose envelope it is.

He says, Sometimes one must do the wrong thing in order to know one is alive.

That is not a fact, Signor Lomellini.

Boh! *Now she's broken her own rule: never address a sitter by name, so that* la persona dentro *will not retreat behind appearances. In this way she kept, amidst the strictures of the Spanish court, a painter's lifeline to the child in the Infanta, the woman in the Queen.*

It can well be a fact, Signora Anguissola. Dipende!

Of all mediums, drawing is the most intimate, exposing the nerve ends of both artist and sitter. This man suits this medium. He is fearlessly and wholly present.

If it were I, drawing you, he says, I would set down bright eyes, a full oval face with glowing skin, hair coiled on a graceful neck—

Please keep your eyes on the wasps' nest, Signore.

—humor, warmheartedness, energy, decisiveness—

I cannot continue if you persist in—

—and to these qualities I could add diplomacy. But I do not think I want that, from you.

She throws down her chalk. We have but one sitting after this, Signore. Prego! *Unless you hold your pose, I shall not finish by the time we dock at—*

At the door, a shower of commanding knocks. Before she can give permission, it opens.

Sofí! Asdrubale says. You have been at your task for more than an hour. Is everything in order?

Her brother would claim concern at her being closeted alone with a man. Does he think she doesn't know it's her fortune rather than her honor that he wishes to preserve? Poor Asdru! The only one of Papa's children born without an imagination.

We were just finishing, Signore, Lomellini says. He gets to his feet.

Mezzanotte, he murmurs as he brushes past her. Midnight.

It is not long thought that counts— Michelangelo used to say—it is deep thought. A moment of consideration; then act. Yesterday's sun balanced on the horizon like a great glowing cinder before it slid into the water.

Her heart lifts. She thinks, Orazio Lomellini is ready for my plan.

She wonders whether Margherita has packed, among her mourning garments, the black velvet gown with the gold embroidery.

I managed to leave the Palazzo Bianco without being stopped. Still dazed by my encounter with Sofonisba, I caught a bus headed in the right direction just as it pulled away. Its doors stayed folded back so passengers who couldn't fit into the packed interior could stand on the steps. I hauled myself up onto the lowest one and grabbed the handrail. My umbrella, still open, leapt out of my grasp. I watched it bounce into the gushing gutter. Impossible to reach the ticket-punching machine from my perch. I'd just have to be illegal. Plead ignorant *americana*.

Then, with a prick of fear, I remembered: I don't have a passport to prove that.

Clinging to the bus as it lumbered along Via Garibaldi, I breathed in the rain-amplified smells of car exhaust and earth and old drains. Water falling out of the sky, unasked for, in long slanting strings of silver: it seemed like such a generosity. I tried to work out a strategy for times like this. At first I thought that if I was stopped for any reason—on a bus or a train, on the street—I'd express surprise at not finding my passport in my shoulderbag, say it must have been stolen. Then I realized: if I said that, my passport would be annulled. Vida wouldn't be able to use it. And if I said nothing? No—once it was known that I couldn't produce a passport, the outcome would be the same. Okay, I thought. I have no strategy. I'll just have to be incredibly careful. I must not get stopped.

Meanwhile, best to get off the bus. At a red light I jumped down. Safe on the sidewalk, I yanked up the hood of my windbreaker. Rain dripped from its edges onto my cold hands. By now I was used to Genoa's warren of intersecting alleys, its arches long and dark enough to qualify as tunnels. The six *contrade* I'd visited so far hadn't offered any revelations. I'd found the neighborhoods of three churches. Nico and I had *moto*ed through the Porta Nuova, sixteenth-century Genoa's version of Greenwich Village, and cruised the neighborhood of the De Franchi family, who'd rented apartments to Genovesi with cash-flow problems. The sixth *contrada*, Piazza dei Nobili Salvago, had disappeared. Now I thought: Seventh time lucky?

I started walking, the wind at my back, in what felt like the direction of the Carruggio dell'Oro. The street where for centuries goldsmiths had worked; the street where Sofonisba had finally settled. It appeared just where my map placed it, a staircase rather than a street. Jumping aside as a *moto* splashed past, I started walking up between grime-encrusted walls with shuttered doors. When I got to the top, I found myself in front of a lingerie boutique.

What had I been thinking? By what magic would I have known the exact door that, four hundred years ago, had sheltered Sofonisba? Defeated, I stood gazing up at the smooth nude limbs of the mannequins. Rain plastered my hair to my cheeks and crawled under the collar of my windbreaker. The glow of the shop window beckoned. I grasped a bronze handle in the shape of the Venus de Milo and went in. When the saleswoman, sleek and smiling and *dry*, approached me, I pointed to a nightgown in the center of the window. Sapphire-blue chiffon so sheer the mannequin's nipples showed through, its calf-length hem a swirl of silver-threaded pleats. *Be the flame, not the moth.*

Brignole Station in the rain was a mass of jellied lights and gleaming stone. The tide of commuters swept me inside. Their voices bounced off the walls, an indistinct crowd-sound broken here and there by cries of *"Ragazzi!"* or *"Ciao, bella!"* Out of habit I looked all around. (Daniel, that year in Kosovo: "They don't have to watch us all the time. They just have to make us *think* they do.") No sign of Angus Dance. I hated to admit it, but he frightened me now. Before today I'd done nothing wrong—I could always have claimed that I believed I was teaching English to legal immigrants. Handing over my passport was a different matter. Handing over my passport, I'd crossed the line. I was tense and cold and wet; my damp jeans chafed; my stomach growled. I should have been miserable. Instead, here came that quick little zipper of happiness. *Benessere.* Lule and Vida would be safe.

I waited for Ceiling-Katherine's sardonic comment. None came. Come to think of it, I hadn't heard from her in…how long was it? Not since the morning Angus Dance had accosted me in the Crypt. More than than three weeks ago. The Israeli neuropsychiatrist had said that Ceiling-Katherine would disappear when my part-selves coalesced. Did this mean I was now whole? I tucked my package under my arm and quickened my step toward the platform for my train. Around me skirled the sound of Italian. End-of-the-day chatter. Ordinary happiness

Fitting back into myself, I felt the gradually deepening embrace of the present. Late afternoon sun flashed off a pair of wineglasses on the nightstand, fingered a bra tossed over the mirror, inched across the floor over jeans and Nico's micro-briefs.

"*Sei sveglia, piccola?*"

"How did you know?"

"When you're waking up, you flutter your toes."

Piccola, he called me: baby. *Dolcezza*: sweetheart. *Amore mio*: my love. Maybe Natalia had been right about lovers making the best tutors. Here we were, just three weeks into our affair, and my vocabulary had increased exponentially.

Nico's breath sparkled on my neck. His lips found the ticklish spot where it curved into my shoulder. I turned over and straddled him. His hands traced the stretch marks along my stomach. "Snail tracks." I caught his hands in mine and set my palms against his broader ones, my fingers along his. I watched the slow tide of pleasure lift his features.

"How old are you, Nico?"

"Ah, *piccola*. What does it matter?"

I squeezed his fingers, bent them back. "Tell me!"

"Older than you think. Younger than I'd like."

"Why aren't you with someone your age? Or younger?" Someone my daughter's age. "You must get hit on all the time."

"Hit? Who would hit me?"

"No, no. Hit *on*. As in, flirted with."

"Ah. *Sì*, it happens. But…how to say? I don't want to…bond onto… someone I don't know."

"And I'm someone you do know?"

He gave me an evil grin. "*Dipende!* Have you forgotten, *dolcezza*? When we met, you were wearing only a sweater."

"So what you're saying is, you broke your rule."

"Rules!" Nico's expression turned serious. "Listen, *piccola*. There is something I must tell you. I should have told you before now. But I did not want to lose you."

My heart began to beat, slow and heavy. He knows, I thought. He's found out about the refugees, he knows that my passport—

"My *fidanzata*, she comes home early for Christmas."

Relief, followed immediately by a stitch of pain. I started to climb off him. He grasped my waist and squeezed. He knew I liked that. I knew he felt the shiver of femaleness that went through me whenever he did it.

"December seventh. But it is two weeks away, *dolcezza*. Two weeks that we have still each other."

A *fidanzata* is an entity halfway between girlfriend and fiancée. A *fidanzata* takes precedence over other women, but she can't expect chastity as well. Of course I'd known someone like Nico couldn't be wandering around unattached. And it wasn't as if I wanted him to attach to me. Still, he should have told me sooner—or not at all. I reached for anger to hold me together; but, as always, lovemaking had chased it out of reach. Those few wonderful hours when I didn't want to hold together—when it was my pleasure to come completely apart. Each time, as the rollercoaster of orgasm slowed, I could feel my heart unclench.

"Look at me, *cara*," Nico said. "I want your eyes."

Reluctantly, I looked down at him.

He said, "It is this way. Cupid's arrows are like pollen, falling always, everywhere. But invisible. When they strike—when you are so lucky—you do not argue. You obey. There is only a small space of time in which two people can take pleasure in each other. You and me, we have it now."

A chill rippled over me. The room was cold now that the sun had gone. Getting up to close the window, I stopped, imagining Nico's view of my no longer firm backside. But finiteness—knowing something will end—gives you confidence. Even more than the bleak freedom of a one-night stand. *Che cazzo!* I thought, and walked lightly across the room.

Before Nico left, we drank from a single long-necked bottle of *limoncello* and shared a chunk of bread and a pomegranate, sitting at the kitchen counter. This was our custom, and I was too proud to let Nico's revelation change things. He'd brought me some branches full of red-orange leaves, still wet from the week's rain. Now he pulled off a leaf and spread it on the counter between us. Different environments, he said, favored the evolution of different kinds of leaves. Plants in drought-prone Italy tended to have blunt, broad peasant leaves with many veins.

The pomegranate seeds burst between my teeth, salty and sweet at once. I drank more *limoncello*. Why do men take refuge in facts when they've hurt us? Why do we let them?

"*Acer monspessulanum*. See, *piccola?* The many veins"—his index finger traced them—"carry water to the chloroplasts, for photosynthesis. The more water a leaf absorbs, the better it can feed itself." He shot me a devilish look. "This leaf, it is *avida*. Like you."

Greedy. I made a face.

"Plants are intelligent, like we are. Maybe more so. They must find everything they need, they must protect themselves from diseases and from predators—all without being able to move. Imagine, *amore*! Plants are always thinking to themselves: *Dipende*."

Most lovers exchange childhoods. Most lovers tell each other their deepest fears, their wildest hopes. Nico and I had discussions like this. Just as well, I told myself; because I wouldn't be able to talk to Nico in that other way. I wouldn't know how to tell him about Daniel, about degeneration and dying and death, about caregiving and how it shapes you, the way a plant's environment shapes a plant. I wouldn't be able *twenty years* to watch Nico's face fall, heavy with sadness *twenty years* but doubtful too *twenty years* and ashamed of his disbelief.

"…and that is why plants dominate. Plants are 99% of the biomass on earth. *Dolcezza*, are you listening?"

"*Si`, certo.*" I scoured my brain for remnants of what Nico had been saying. "Ninety percent! That's amazing."

"Ninety-nine." He gave me a tutorial frown.

"Ninety-nine."

Nico sat gazing at the leaf with devotion. I envied him. Whenever he talked to me about plants I thought, How could he bear to give that up? Grandma Eva would've taken him to task. Nico knew what he'd been put on earth to do, and he wasn't doing it.

We had wandered a safe distance from the *fidanzata*. Nico handed me the leaf. I held it in my palm, smoothing its fibrous skin with my thumb. It was almost dry now, its rich color already fading. "So you can read a leaf," I said, "like a person." Or a pottery shard.

Nico shook his head. "Every leaf from a tree is like every other leaf from that tree. Any plant can lose up to 90% of its body without being killed. With persons, each is different. *Cuore d'altri non e` simile al tuo.*"

"The heart of others is not like yours. So you say."

"It is Montale who said it, and he was right. You know Montale?"

"No."

Nico clicked his tongue, the way his aunt liked to do. "Eugenio Montale is Liguria's greatest poet. You must know him, or you do not know Liguria. I will bring you next time a book of his poems."

13

For the first time in my life I saw myself as a criminal. Passportless, I felt uneasy whenever I left the Villa Francesca. The watchfulness learned in Tito's Yugoslavia—monitoring my peripheral vision, looking behind my reflection in shop windows, glancing over my shoulder as I went around a corner—was my only strategy. I thought, This is how Bardha and Genta felt *all the time*. How Vida still feels. I caught myself slinking around with my shoulders hunched and my head down, the way Thuanthong used to do. Laura, sensing that something was up, kept offering me chances to confide in her; but of course I couldn't.

Lule and Vida's departure was set for December fourth. This allowed, according to Natalia's plan, a week and a half for the making of Lule's passport and other preparations, and still left ten days for the return of mine before I needed it myself. (The Centro would close for the holidays on December fifteenth.) To get through the time between now and then, I thought of Rae. I clung to the conviction that, when I could finally tell her what I'd done, she'd be proud of me.

Meanwhile, as November crawled to a close, life at the Centro went on as before—except that Dmitri Antipov disappeared. No explanation was offered. There was one less place set for dinner, and that was that. No one seemed to have any facts, though it was generally agreed that the Russian must have finally done something too egregious to overlook. ("Don't kid yourself, Kate," Laura said. "The Centro may treat us like an overindulgent mother. But if anyone steps out of line…" She drew a finger across her throat.) Dmitri's disappearance made me reconsider Anna Maria's role at the Centro. Her job wasn't just the care and feeding of Fellows; she had to protect the Centro and the prestigious foundation that supported it. Wouldn't that mean knowing everything that went on? I remembered seeing her go off with Angus Dance at Thuanthong's opening. If Dance was at the Centro undercover, wouldn't Anna Maria have to be in on it? I began to feel watched whenever I went down to the Villa Baiardo: in the Crypt; at dinner; over pool-playing and tangoing and *digestivi*. Only within the walls of the Villa Francesca did I feel free.

On the last Tuesday in November Nico arrived late for our lesson. He entered without an embrace and flung his motorcycle helmet in the direction of the sofa. "*Che diavolo succede?*" he shouted. What the hell is going on?

I stared at him. I'd never seen him this angry before.

He held up my passport. "*Zia* Natalia asked me to return this to you. She claims it fell out of your pocket last time you were at her apartment. That is *merda*."

My heart lurched. Nico grabbed my palm and slapped the passport on it and closed my fingers around it. His face—its downward lines deepened by anger—his neck, even his ears were flushed with emotion.

"My aunt is *pazza* ever since my cousin died. *Pazzissima!* She thinks she can do whatever she wants, because she has suffered. She believes that she alone can understand the suffering of others."

My mind went into overdrive, pedaling gerbil-like to nowhere. Natalia had had my passport for a week. Why return it now? What had happened? Was there another, better plan? But wait—

"Your cousin? Natalia's daughter?"

"*Sì, certo*. That's not the point—"

"When did she die?"

"*Boh!* A long time ago. Seventeen—no, eighteen years. Listen to me—"

"How old was she?"

"Fourteen."

I had a quick flash of the bedroom—light and color and the floor scattered with toys—where Lule and Vida slept. Natalia had lost a daughter. This one fact explained so much.

"*Poverina!*" I said.

Nico stepped toward me. He put his hands on my shoulders. "Caterina! My aunt has a way of getting people to do what she wants. She makes them think it's *their* idea. Get yourself out of whatever this is, I beg you. And stay out." His hands cupped my shoulders, pressing down. Their weight trapped me.

My one clear thought was that I mustn't let Nico see how upset I was. He was smart, and he was already suspicious. One wrong move on my part, and he'd figure out what was going on. I didn't know what he might do—surely he wouldn't turn his aunt in to the authorities?—but I couldn't risk it. Feeling like a mother bird who leads the hawk away from her nest, I turned towards the bedroom. "Don't worry, *piccolo*," I said, over my shoulder. "I won't be seeing your aunt again."

We went to bed, pulling garments off each other, feeling the electric surprise of flesh against flesh. But this time, the forgetfulness that our lovemaking had always brought eluded me. My brain ticked away. What would become of Lule and Vida now? When I tried to stay in the moment, my busy mind kept *noticing* things. How desire remodelled Nico's face above me, making his lips bunch together and his eyes grow smaller. How the winter sun pierced the shutters at a new, sharper angle. How the slap of our sweat-slicked bellies bisected the quiet of the *Pausa*. Afterwards, the cooling of my skin felt lonely. Nico put his arms behind his head and gazed at the ceiling. We lay there for several minutes in a silence that wasn't shared. Then I got up to go to the bathroom.

When I came back, I straddled Nico. His hands on my waist began to guide my body into his favorite position.

"Wait." I pulled free and lowered myself to lie on top of him. His pubic hair tickled my midriff.

Kate would never have taken advantage of the stirring there. Caterina could. Caterina did. But something besides sex was needed to distract

Nico from the business of my passport. To persuade him that it was so unimportant I'd already forgotten about it. "Do something for me?"

"Anything, *amore*."

"Take me to Bussana Vecchia."

"Too far, I have told you this. We would need a car."

Accepting the *fidanzata* ought to have earned me a favor or two. I dug my chin into Nico's chest and said, remindingly, "You have your priorities, *amore*, and I have mine. Take me. Yes or no?"

"*Rompicazzo!*" Dick-buster. But he was laughing.

"*Sì o no?*"

"Okay, okay! First I finish the giraffe skeleton at work. Then we will go. But only if you spend the night with me."

"At Bussana Vecchia?"

"At Bussana Vecchia. Now come here, before I come without you."

Later, over *limoncello*, we made a list of places that, according to Nico, I had to see before I left Italy. Before, though neither of us said this, the *fidanzata* returned. Portofino; the prehistoric caves at Balzi Rossi; the Cinque Terre. "We could stay overnight," Nico added. "If we go well together at Bussana Vecchia." It was an echo of the list we'd made on our first meeting, sitting at this same kitchen counter. But I wondered, with a shiver of premonition, whether any of these excursions would happen.

At the French doors to the patio, Nico said, "*Zia* Natalia made me promise to use the hidden entrance today. You didn't know I came in that way, did you?"

"I don't even know what you're talking about."

"Watch for me out your window when I leave." He gripped my elbows with both hands. "*Dolcezza—*"

To fend off what he was about to say, I read his T-shirt out loud. It was the red one, the one he'd worn the day we met. "*In Bocca al Lupo!*" I said. In the mouth at the wolf—the Italian equivalent, I remembered, of saying "Break a leg!" as a way of wishing someone luck.

"You'll need more than luck if you have anything to do with whatever *Zia* Natalia is hatching. She will stop at nothing. Maybe, with Giulia gone, she hasn't anything to lose. But you do."

So he hadn't believed my show of indifference. Of course not: he was smarter than that.

He looked at me, his face more serious than I'd ever seen it. Older than I'd ever seen it. The happiness that had played across it while we sat at the counter making our list had vanished. "Do you know what the response is, when someone says *In bocca al lupo*?"

I shook my head.

"*Che crepi il lupo!*"

"*Che crepi il lupo*," I repeated, a dutiful student's echo. May the wolf croak!

"Tell her no, *piccola*. Promise me."

What could I do? I promised.

Nico let go of my elbows. He turned and walked over to the sofa and picked up his motorcycle helmet. Without another word, he went out through the French doors. But instead of crossing the lawn to the villa gate, he turned left and vanished.

I went into the bedroom to watch from the window. A ladder of stars climbed the sky above the umbrella pines. One by one the overhead lamps flicked on, throwing down steppingstones of light. After a few minutes Nico appeared, much further down the path. I realized he must have gone through the ruined half of the Villa Francesca—that it must form some sort of hidden walkway or tunnel. I leaned out, ready to call *Ciao, bello!*—then stopped. Beneath me, almost hidden among the cypresses, stood a motionless figure. Nico bent his head to put on his helmet. I could see the back of his neck, tender, exposed. My heart flickered. *Don't turn around, Nico* mio. *Don't call goodbye.* He straightened and began walking quickly, through one circle of light after another, until he was out of sight.

Angus Dance never heard Nico's rubber-soled steps behind him. All his attention was up ahead, his eyes fixed on the villa gate.

Relief made me tremble all over. Good luck! I thought. *In bocca al lupo.* Lurk all you like.

There was nothing, now, for Dance to find out. My chance to take a risk had vanished. My chance to show Rae a mother different from the one she knew—a mother she could respect. My chance to help Lule and

Vida find safety. Feeling robbed, I slammed the window shut and went to dress for dinner.

Laura kept looking at me all through the meal. When it ended I didn't follow the others into the *salotto* for dancing, as proposed by Joshua. Realizing my despair must show on my face, I went out into the entry hall and got my jacket from the closet. Laura caught me at the front door.

"Kate! What's wrong? You look awful."

I pushed open the door. Cold night air sweetened with some late-flowering shrub flowed over us. "Nothing." Hearing how abrupt I sounded, I turned back. "I'm just tired. I'm…not sleeping well."

Laura leapt right over my lame explanation. "Did you and your guy break up?" A look of disgust crossed her face. "God. Why is our first thought always *men*? Did something happen with your daughter, is that it?"

"No, honestly. Nothing happened. You're sweet to be concerned, but—"

"We're *friends*, Kate. For godsake! Listen, when you're ready to talk, I'm here. Anything you need, just ask. Anything. Ask me, okay?"

I nodded. A quick hug from Laura, and I fled into the night.

"Hey, Mom. It's me."

The bedside clock said 6:00 a. m. Midnight in Rhode Island. I struggled through cobwebs of sleep. This was the second time in three weeks that Rae had been the one to call. Remorsefully, I realized that, in all that time, we'd emailed but we hadn't spoken.

"Fruffle! What is it? Is something wrong?"

"No, no. Chill, *mamacita*. I just called to say Happy Thanksgiving. Six days late," Rae added pointedly.

Thanksgiving! I'd forgotten all about it. Lending Natalia my passport had driven everything else out of my head. Penitent, I said, "Same to you, Fruffle. What did you do to celebrate?"

"Went to Mac's mom's place." Mac was Rachel's on-again-off-again boyfriend. "Mac's brother and his wife and kids were there. His brother was really off the hook—he's such a douche. The entire day was bunk... Uh, mom." Rae's voice softened. "Cousin Janet called me today. She's worried about you."

You're worried about me, I thought. My watchful daughter, for whom wariness had been the default mode since childhood.

"She said, talk some sense into you. Sense about what?"

"Nothing. I mean, you know Janet. She always thinks she knows what everybody else should do."

"She called from *Africa*, Mom. She said to tell you, Where your treasure lies. It kind of weirded me out."

I had an instant of pure fury. Janet herself was on an unsanctioned mission in a dangerous part of the world. My Ladies-of-the-Field cousin got to take risks, but *I* shouldn't? And it was low of her to enlist my daughter in her effort to run my life.

"What did she mean? What treasure? What's going down?"

"Nothing, Fruffle. Janet thinks..." I forced conviction into my voice. "She thinks...I'm...working too hard. Running around trying to see everything my Paintress"—Rae's name for Sofonisba—"might have done. Everywhere she might've gone."

"You sound kind of faded. You're not, like, sick or anything?"

"I'm fine, sweetie, I promise."

I pulled the comforter up around my shoulders against the dawn chill. I told Rae about looking for the places where Sofonisba had lived. The past *in* the present, as so often in Italy. I chattered on about living in this layered reality. This palimpsest. How it changed your view of yourself and your own importance—

"I miss..." Rae's voice quavered. "I missed Daddy, on Thanksgiving."

The chill in the room seemed to deepen. I veered away from the abyss that opened at Rae's words. "Listen, Fruffle—"

"I missed how he used to joke and laugh and...you know...make us have adventures. How he did what he wanted, regardless. He wasn't easy. But I never doubted how he felt about us."

"Listen, Fruffle, I have to go—"

"I don't see how you can just…just cavort around Italy for months without ever thinking of him."

I could hear the longing beneath Rae's reproachfulness, and my heart ached for her. She wanted to talk about her father—wanted *me* to talk about him. I knew I should; but I couldn't. I'd made it through the first year without breaking down. If I let myself unfreeze now—

"Mom?"

"I'm not cavorting, I'm working. You should be, too. And, hey, three more weeks and I'll be home."

"You never want to talk about him. You cut me off whenever I— Oh, fuck it!"

A click. I sat holding onto the receiver, listening to the silence where my daughter's voice had been. I knew I should call her back. But I couldn't find the words to comfort her. My heart ached for my girl; but I didn't know how to reach her.

Razor-thin light was beginning to outline the shuttered window. I laid the receiver in its cradle. *Where your treasure lies*, Grandma Eva the Bible-quoting atheist used to say, *there will your heart be also*.

He has actually brought it. She sees the linen-wrapped shape tucked under one arm, as he extends the other to guide her up the last few steps of the ladder. Above them the midnight sky is brilliant with stars, a boundless field with a hundred seeds of brightness. Light from a quarter-moon like a slice of lemon sketches his features.

The astrolabe! she says.

No, Signora. It is something else. Something better.

She turns her face up to the night air, fresh and cold after the closeness of the cabin. Margherita slept on as she readied herself for this meeting; Asdrubale, too, snoring complacently in his hammock outside the cabin door.

The moon is very bright, she observes.

Half its surface is glass—so astronomers tell us. That is why it gleams.

The topmost deck is small. They stand in silence, close enough to touch, swaying with the ship's motion. Below them the mariners on watch call back and forth. Around them the darkness feels alive. The body opposite, outlined against the night sky, makes her aware of her own.

Lomellini says, I fear this will sound abrupt, Signora. But two more days will see the end of this voyage. Therefore, I speak in haste. But not without thought.

A pause. Wait, she tells herself. Pazienza. *She hears the creaking of the ship's timbers, the wind's sighs in the rigging. Then Lomellini's voice, bold and clear.*

I wish with all my heart to become your husband. Tell me, Signora. Would you consider this?

He has anticipated her plan. How did he know? She does not wish him to see her surprise. She says coolly, What do you offer, Signore?

They both know what she *would bring to such a union. Her social standing. Her wealth.*

To his credit, he does not say, the protection of marriage. He says, I offer the Lomellini name; a place in Genovese society; and time.

Time?

I am a sea captain. You will have plenty of time for your work. I do not seek a wife who twines around me, I the oak, she the ivy.

Her breath catches. She expected to fight for her autonomy—or at least negotiate fiercely. That he would offer this—that he understands this already— means he knows her.

While she is thinking, he surprises her again.

I offer one thing more, Signora. Something no one else will give you. Something you have never had.

Again she waits, drawing her cloak closer against the night chill. A fine, cold mist from the sea strokes her face. His is a dim oval, pale as parchment. People think of black as the absence of color. It is not. White is.

He says, I offer you the opportunity to draw the male body from life. For life.

No woman artist, no matter her stature, is permitted to draw the male from life. Watching her in the close confines of the cabin, he must have seen her struggle to imagine muscle and bone beneath cloth.

Yes, he knows her.

She says, How will we... My brother...

I have a plan.

Of course he does. The ombrellino. *The astrolabe. The pirate ship pursued along the coast of Corsica.*

Will you trust me? he asks.

She nods. Then, mindful of how faint the light is, she says out loud, Si`. Mi fido di te.

His head lifts; his shoulders straighten. She has addressed him as te—*the pronoun used between intimates. He takes a step toward her.*

There is one thing more.

What is that, Signore?

He speaks slowly, choosing his words with care. If perhaps you are thinking... If the difference in our ages suggests... I do not propose a matrimonio non consumato.

She didn't expect this. In the soft brilliance of the night she can hear the ocean breathing. A matrimonio non consumato *is the only kind she has known—or desired.*

I can no longer bear children, she protests. Feeling, as always, relief at the thought; seeing, as always, her sisters and her beloved Queen, whom childbirth stole.

I have a son of seventeen, born out of wedlock, whom I have acknowledged. It is not for childbearing that I would wish to—

Che diavolo, Sofi!

Her brother's head appears at the top of the ladder. The ocean smell gives way to the scent of mint.

What are you doing here? Come away this instant!

I left the Museo del Mare feeling suspended between *then* and *now*— the liminal state I'd come to expect after a Visitation. I had tried, after this one, to retrieve some shred of scholarly perspective by focusing on the factual. "A caravel," one of the museum guards said when I asked what kind of trading vessels plied the Mediterranean in the sixteenth century. "A sweet-handling ship! Shallow draft. Lateen sails." Caravels could go places other ships couldn't—sail close to shore, enter hidden coves. Pretty much what I'd imagined on my tour of the harbor ship with Nico—except for the livestock traveling in canvas slings hoisted up the masts. "Never walk beneath them!" the guard had said, and grinned.

The ship. The astrolabe. And, according to the internet, the ghost scent emitted by the black velvet gown on display in the Palazzo Bianco was myrrh, a perfume popular in Sofonisba's day. The Visitations—eight of them, now—felt more and more real, more and more reliable. I was onto something. It should have thrilled me—this increasing closeness to So-fonisba. I should have felt exhilarated, on a roll, looking forward to Bus-sana Vecchia.

Instead, for the two days since Nico had returned my passport, I'd felt miserably alone and adrift. I had no idea why the passport had been rejected. At first I'd thought maybe, because Nico had found it, Natalia had had to relinquish it to him. But that didn't sound like her. Natalia had hung up on me when I finally found the courage to call and ask. Re-turning the passport must have been her decision. Had there been some problem with the authorities? Or had the forger been unable to make a satisfactory passport for Lule? I didn't dare go to Natalia's apartment and confront her, for fear of making the situation worse. Had Lule and Vida's trip been called off? I wanted desperately to know that they'd still be safe; I wanted to do whatever I could to help. But I was shut out.

On the street I gulped cold ozone-charged air and shook my head to clear it. Pulling up the collar of my jacket and scanning the sky for rain, I heard a voice pipe, "Kate! Kate!"

I turned. No mistaking Hollis's retro afro or his tall, stooped figure—the very opposite of the *bella figura*. Amber, in a school-bus yellow slicker, held his hand. Surprised and pleased, I said, "Hi, you two."

Amber galloped up to me and threw her arms around my waist. In the gray light, her upturned face was the golden-brown of a perfect biscuit.

I smiled down at her. "What are you doing in the city in the middle of a Wednesday?"

"School holiday," Hollis said.

"No, Daddy," Amber said. "Remember? It's our Private Hooky Day."

"Oh, right." Hollis looked uncomfortable. "I forgot."

But I didn't judge him for spiriting Amber off to the city under false pretences. Rae and I had had Mother/Daughter Days all through elementary school; we'd put them on the calender at the beginning of each school year, a day in fall, a day in spring. She'd loved our shared sense of mischief, of purloined pleasure.

"So you've been researching sixteenth-century life at sea?" Hollis said, nodding toward the museum. "Your lady was quite the traveler, as I recall."

I pulled my drawing pad out of my shoulderbag and opened it to the sketch I'd made of the astrolabe.

Amber crowded up against me to see.

"The museum has a Petting Zoo for navigational instruments," I told her. "Like this astrolabe. And there's a compass, a quadrant, a cross staff..." Amber scuffed the pavement, bored. "You can touch them. The guard shows you how to use them. It's really cool." I felt again the weight of the brass astrolabe when I'd held it up to sight along the alidade. Early archaeologists used similar instruments to check sites like Stonehenge for their alignment with the stars.

Hollis examined my drawing. "You're a real worker," he said. "Not like some. Did you hear about Dmitri?"

"What about him? Has he come back?"

"No, no. But Chantal told me what he got thrown out for."

Hollis paused to watch Amber detach herself and wander off to look in the window of a pet boutique next-door to the museum. "Stay close, Sugarbug," he called. He moved to my other side so he could keep an eye on her.

"What *did* Dmitri get thrown out for?" I asked.

"Smuggling."

"Drugs?" That would explain the heavy-lidded indolence, the Slavic shuffle.

"Nope."

"Well, what?"

"Icons."

"*Icons?*"

"Medieval Russian Orthodox icons. There's a huge market for them in the West."

"But how did he… Oh. All those boxes of chocolates."

"Nope." Aglow with his secret, Hollis waited.

"The coat!" I exclaimed.

"Bingo! The lining was sewn with a couple dozen pockets the size of an index card. Perfect for small icons."

"But…wouldn't he have been arrested?"

"He must have been. But Anna Maria would never let the rest of us see that kind of *disgrazia*. I bet Dmitri Antipov isn't the first Centro perp to quietly disappear."

"But…icons. It doesn't seem like that big a deal."

A frown etched Hollis's forehead. "After drugs and weapons, antiquities are the third most profitable item for smugglers. As an archaeologist, you must know that."

There it was, the flip side of helpfulness—that sudden swerve into judgment. But he was right, of course. These days, Indiana Jones would be in jail for looting.

"Smuggling really sets the Italians off. Corruption is supposed to stay strictly intramural. Smuggling of any kind is an insupportable invasion."

Three men in pea-green military uniforms approached and detoured around us. They were young, solemn, their peaked hats adorned with a single vigilant feather.

"Even people?" I wondered out loud before I could stop myself.

Hollis shot me a puzzled look. "People?"

Amber came back to us and tugged at Hollis's sleeve. "I want to see the boats."

"If you mean refugees—"

"Daddy, come on. Is there a gift shop?"

The rain started. Drops caught in Amber's cloud of fine dark hair. Hollis lifted the hood of her slicker up over her head. She batted his hand away. "I want Kate to come with us." Her face, with her chin stuck out in that determined way, reminded me of Lule's. My heart caught. The feeling of failure that had dogged me since Nico returned my passport was bitter in my throat.

"I can't, sweetie," I said. "I've just been there. Now I have to go home."

Her new-penny eyes, shiny with disappointment, met mine. I thought, incongruously: They're the wrong color.

Hollis put a protective arm around his daughter. "We'd better go, Sugarbug," he said. "Don't want you to catch cold."

I watched them walk into the museum, Amber shrugging off Hollis's fatherly arm and stumping along by herself. I thought of Lule, who had no fatherly arm and no father.

What had Hollis been going to say? I wondered as I trotted down the street to the bus stop, wishing I still had my umbrella. *Refugees are a different thing altogether*? Or (stern, uncompromising gaze) *Refugees are no different. The laws are there for a reason. Smuggling is smuggling.* If he knew what I was up to, I wondered, would he—

I pushed my cold hands deeper into my pockets. It didn't matter which way Hollis felt about aiding and abetting the persecuted. I knew how *I* felt. I just hadn't known what more I could do about it.

But looking into Amber's eyes, I'd had an idea.

14

Anything you need, just ask, Laura had said the night before, when she caught me leaving the Villa Baiardo. I believed she meant it. But could I take her up on it? Could I ask her, the mother of a young child, to take a huge risk?

All the way back from the Museo del Mare I considered this question. All afternoon I paced the Villa Francesca, thinking. Ask her. Can't ask her. Ask her.

If my guess was right, and the problem with my passport wasn't the passport itself but the lack of a convincing one for Lule, then Laura and Amber's joint passport could be the solution. The mere presence of a child was likely to deflect suspicion. With her hair lightened, Vida would look as much like Laura as she would have looked like me. More, even—she and Laura were closer in age. Lule's hair could be dyed black, her face and hands bronzed with self-tanner; and in the photograph her eyes were cast down, focused on her elephant. Anyway, the picture had been taken when Amber was about three. A child naturally wouldn't look the same now. It could work.

If my guess about why Natalia had returned my passport was right. And if it wasn't? Then Natalia would refuse Laura's passport, and that would be that.

I thought of Laura's wistful envy, her love of secrets, her longing for something to do here in Italy, something that mattered. Her longing to *act*, which mirrored my own. Was it wrong for me to take advantage of that? Yes. But—I thought finally, pacing, pacing—it was less wrong than failing to help Lule and Vida.

And so I decided. Feeling ruthless, conflicted, a little like a judas, I went into the study and got one of the drawings Lule had given me, and one of Amber's. Then I put on my jacket and started down the hill to the Villa Baiardo.

Laura emerged from her kitchen with a pot of chamomile tea and two cups, which she arranged on the table in front of the sofa, on either side of a pot of red begonias. She switched on a lamp to fight off the twilight, and sat down beside me. "This stuff is hard to find here," she said. "Italians only drink tea when they're sick."

We sipped. The tea tasted like puréed hamster shavings, but it was something warm on a cold day.

"So," Laura said. "What's up?"

I laid Amber's drawing on the sofa between us, and Lule's drawing beside it. Laura bent her head to look.

Amber's drawing showed a house—blue windows, red door—cherishingly fenced and watched over by pink and blue flowers. A benign sun hovered above it. Lule's drawing was the one she'd made the day I'd given her my pastels. I watched Laura take in the house with its roof on fire, the soldier, the black snout of his gun. I thought of the most recent drawing Lule had shown me—a midsummer garden. My heart had lifted. Oh, I'd thought, she's making progress. She's healing. Then "That's blood," Lule had said, pointing to the windblown roses. "And what's that?" I'd indicated a pink shape like a peony. "That's his head."

"The little girl who made the drawing is seven," I said. "Her name is Lule. She's a refugee from Kosovo." I told Laura the whole story, from the day I first met the Kosovar women right through to the afternoon two days before, when Nico returned my passport. What a relief it was—to have one other person in the world know what I was struggling with. Night fell while I spoke, pooling in the corners of the room beyond the lamplight. After I'd finished, Laura gazed at the drawing for a few moments in silence. When she looked up, there were tears in her eyes. Hope shot through me, fire and ice.

"I want to help," Laura said. "What can I do?"

I took a deep breath. "I think *your* passport would work. Yours and Amber's."

Laura got up and went into the kitchen, returning with a bottle of wine and two glasses. Her hands shook as she filled them. We drank. Laura's eyes flicked back and forth between the drawings. Her expression was a volatile mix of fear, curiosity, self-importance, concern. I could barely breathe for fear of tipping her in one direction or the other. At last she stacked the two drawings together with Amber's on top, and sank back into her corner of the sofa.

"What if they're caught—this woman and her daughter? If the passport they're using... If the real owner *gave* it to them... That's got to be a serious crime?"

I admitted that it was. "Punishable by prison. Minimum ten years."

"Ten years! That's how long Hollis and I have been married." Laura wrapped both arms around herself and stared out the window into the darkness. "If I agree to do this, I couldn't tell him. Hollis doesn't believe in taking the law into your own hands. He says, if Machiavelli was right—if the end justifies the means—then anyone can do anything they want. He says, consider what you're unleashing on the world."

So that was what Hollis had been going to tell me earlier, outside the Museo del Mare. Fortunate man! Life had not yet forced him to choose between two evils.

"Laws are made by men," I said.

Laura shuffled the drawings and picked up Lule's. Her hands smoothed it over and over; her face had the painful openness of someone desperately divided. Weighing the defeat of patriarchy against the risk of falling into its clutches? Weighing her own welfare and her child's against that of two people unknown to her?

Year-long minutes ticked by. I stayed silent. There might not be a limit to Natalia's manipulativeness, but there was a limit to mine.

Laura set Lule's drawing down next to Amber's. "In ten years Amber will be sixteen," she said, almost to herself.

I thought, Would I have agreed to lend my own passport, if Rachel had been on it? Remorse seized me. I reached out a hand and laid it on Laura's. "I'm sorry," I said. "I shouldn't have asked you. I'll find some other way."

Laura's eyes were still on the drawings, her head bent over them. I couldn't see her expression. The sound of church bells came dimly through the windows. Hollis and Amber would be home soon. I let go of Laura's hand and stood up. "I'm so sorry—"

"Steal it," Laura said.

"What?"

"Steal my passport." Laura raised her head. She spoke slowly, her voice low but clear. "I don't want to know when. Or how. Then if there's trouble, I can truthfully say I had nothing to do with it."

Now, right now, I had to be absolutely honest; I'd never be able to live with myself otherwise. "There'd still be some risk to you, if things go wrong," I said. "Suppose they don't believe you? If Vida and Lule are caught, of course I'll confess. But you might still be seen as an accessory to fraud."

"I need to do this, Kate. Not for this little girl, or for you, or even for me." Laura looked at me steadily. "For Amber. Safety isn't everything. I want Amber to grow up to be a woman with spirit. I need to show her how. I haven't been doing that. I need to start."

Laura's words were a series of punches that left me breathless. I thought, She wants the same thing from her daughter that I want from mine. All through the years of Daniel's illness, Rae had never seen me as strong. Now she would.

"Thank you," I said. Inadequate words for the joy rolling through me.

Laura frowned, still thinking. "I won't check that drawer from now till we all leave the Centro. That way I can honestly say I didn't know the passport was missing. The only thing is, will Hollis notice? But why would he check? It'll be okay."

It was brilliant. How I'd manage my part, I didn't know; but I would.

"You're sure?"

Laura picked up her wineglass and emptied it into the begonias. "Co-conspirators," she said. "Women are the best, aren't they? If only more of us knew that." She clinked her empty glass against mine. "To us!"

In the darkness we walked single-file along the ridge. First Laura and Hollis, carrying between them the hamper Anna Maria had packed; then Anna Maria; Thuanthong; Chantal; Joshua; me. Angus Dance, his arms full of blankets and quilts, brought up the rear. Ordinarily I wouldn't have wanted him on my heels. Tonight, with what I planned to do, I was glad to know his whereabouts.

It was the day after Laura and I had spoken. Anna Maria had organized a trip up the mountain to take in the last night of the Leonid meteor shower. The air was clear and cold, the sky freckled with stars. Joshua whistled a marching tune as we tramped along. In the midst of my anxiety about what I planned to do, I felt one of those quick rushes of bliss, as if happiness filtered up from the rock-strewn earth and poured down from the night sky.

"I'd like to try this on rollerblades," Joshua said.

"In your dreams," said Laura, over her shoulder.

Anna Maria stopped. We all stood looking out over the valley. The Villa Francesca, almost hidden by trees, glowed faintly below us. The Villa Baiardo, further down, was invisible. At Anna Maria's command, we spread out across the ground, less rocky here and padded with pine needles. I waited until Dance had chosen a spot; then I spread my folded blanket at the other end of the row, as far away from him as I could get. Next to me, Laura and Hollis shared an old down comforter; then Anna Maria, Thuanthong, Chantal and Joshua, Angus Dance. Eight people, each with his or her secrets. We stretched out on our backs. The sky opened above us, deep and sparkling.

"So how do we do this?" Laura asked.

"Falling meteors are very fast," Anna Maria said. "One must look everywhere—*dappertutto!*—and concentrate."

"Take in the whole field, but be ready to focus when there's movement," Hollis said. "Like playing pinball."

Joshua said, "I'm da bomb at pinball."

"Sh!" Laura said. "Concentrate." I felt Hollis reach for her hand.

The night smelled of earth and pine, and tree frogs sang. Lying there wide-eyed, I went over all the considerations. I had fifteen days left in Italy. If Laura's and my plan were to succeed, it would have to be tonight. We needed an occasion when the attention of everyone at the Centro was engaged. An occasion when Amber was left in the care of the unreliable Lucia, and both Hollis and Laura were so involved with whatever was going on that it made sense for me to be the one to check on Amber. To-night's event was perfect. There wouldn't be another, not in time.

Still, my stomach hurt when I considered how this new plan doubled the risk, putting not just myself in jeopardy, but Laura too. I gazed up-ward, my eyes aching. Am I doing right? I asked the throbbing sky. But I could not imagine getting on a plane two weeks from now and leaving Lule and Vida behind.

Then it happened. The first meteor arced across the sky, swift as a blink. No trail. Just a sudden shimmering dive.

"Oh!" we all said at once. The swoop, the shock, the opening out into a parachute of pleasure. It's like sex, I thought.

Laura breathed, "A falling star! I've never seen one before."

"*Una stella cadente*," Anna Maria said.

Hollis said, so softly only Laura was meant to hear, "Stella. That would be a good name for a girl."

Oh no, I thought. Could Laura be pregnant? But wouldn't our con-versation yesterday have gone differently if she were? She would have told me—we were, in her own word, confidantes.

This shining night was our only chance. "Laura," I whispered. "Want me to check on Amber? I have to pee, anyway."

Hollis heard me. "I'll go," he said to Laura. "You stay here."

"No, no, let me," I said. "You need this for your work. Both of you."

Hollis hesitated. I felt Laura stiffen.

"It's supposed to be the best Leonid shower in decades," I whispered, try-ing not to sound urgent. "The next one this good won't be until 2023." This was true—I'd read it in yesterday's *Corriere della Sera*. "If *I* were a poet—"

"All right. Thanks." Hollis reached across Laura to hand me the key. "Make sure she's covered up, okay? And that her night light's on. And make sure Lucia doesn't have Bruno there."

Whenever I looked up, on the endless journey back to the Centro, I was amazed. Stars crowded the sky right down to the tree-tops, where they trembled like unearthly blossoms. Whenever I turned to see if Angus Dance was following me, there they were. Company as I trudged downhill, following the path my flashlight picked out.

I met no one on my way across the foyer and up the stairs to Hollis and Laura's apartment. Turning the key silently in the lock, I pushed open the door just enough to slip inside. The living room, bright with lamplight, was empty. Its cheerful ordinariness made me stop where I was, the key heavy in my hand. It disturbed me that this second crime was less unthinkable than the first. A slipping-down life, Grandma Eva would have said. It's not too late, I thought. I can just check on Amber and go.

A thud sounded somewhere in the apartment. I crossed the room, quietly, quietly, and peered into the hall. Halfway down was the rosy glow from Amber's night light. At the end, the door to the master bedroom stood open a crack. I heard voices, a giggle, a squeal quickly smothered. Lucia and her Bruno. I went back to the table by the front door, opened the drawer, grabbed a passport. Checking to make sure I had Laura and Amber's, not Hollis's, I saw the ear of Amber's green velvet elephant grazing her chin. That gave me an idea.

But first I slipped the passport into the pocket of my jacket and took out my own and put it in its place. If Hollis glanced inside the drawer he'd see two passports. If he went further and opened them (but, as Laura had said, why would he?), leaving mine would make it clear who had done the stealing. Somehow this helped justify the risk I was imposing on Laura.

Another thud. I slid the drawer closed and crept down the hall. Amber lay with one arm flung over her head. The covers had pulled up, revealing two small caramel-colored feet. I tucked the blanket around them, and she stirred and sighed. Her sleep-soft face made me hesitate—somehow what I was about to do seemed like a worse theft than the passport. But here was a stroke of luck: the stuffed animal Amber's other arm curled around was a brown bear. The green velvet elephant lay in a corner, face down.

A sound, a muted cough. I grabbed the elephant and backed up against the wall by the door, where I wouldn't be seen by someone looking into the room. My heart kicked at my ribs. Had the sound come from the front door, or the master bedroom? I stood motionless, straining to hear over the rasp of my own breathing. Silence now. I'd have to risk it. The longer I stood here, the greater my chance of being caught—by Hollis and Laura returning, or by Romeo and Juliet emerging from the master bedroom.

The living room was empty. With the velvet elephant tucked under one arm, I let myself out. Down the stairs; across the foyer; through the outer door. The night air hit my face, a splash of cold. I set off along the loggia toward the Centro gate. My heart slowed and I was beginning to breathe normally, when a voice called out from across the courtyard. A plummy, Sean Connery voice.

"Katherine? Halloo!"

You have a legitimate reason for being here, I told myself. Keep walking. Look sure. *I am mine own woman, well at ease.* Then I remembered the elephant. I thrust it behind my back and stopped. Dance was still a good distance away, but his eyes would be more adjusted to night vision than mine, after the long hike down from the ridge. Could he see me? No time to make sure.

"Katherine! I say, is everything all right?"

I looked around. A planter, a waste can, a hidden corner. Nothing.

"You've been gone a fair while. We were a wee bit consairned."

Those bushes at the end of the loggia. Could I? Think of it as a foul shot.

Angus Dance struck out across the lawn toward me. I turned my back and took aim. The elephant sank into the shadows. I straightened my shoulders, ran a hand over my hair, composed my face. *Mine own woman.* I turned around.

"Mr. Dance?" I called, in as sweet a voice as I could muster. "How kind of you to worry about me."

———

The next morning, pacing back and forth inside the Villa Francesca, I hesitated. Could I do this thing? It was unlike me, and yet it *was* me. Me before MS, before the Black Balloon left no room to act, only react. The me who used to dream about the Ladies of the Field. It's not too late, I'd think, I could still put Laura's passport back; but then I'd see Vida's face when I brought Natalia my passport, her eyes meeting mine. I'd feel again my great discovery: that pain and grief could be made useful. Tragedy was arbitrary; but it didn't have to be meaningless. Without that understanding, I was lost.

One thing I had to do before I could act. I went into the bedroom and called Laura. The phone rang and rang, drilling into my brain. Finally Laura picked up.

I said, "I need to ask you something."

"I can't talk now. I'm about to go out with Hollis." Her voice lingered warningly on Hollis's name.

"Please. Just tell me yes or no. Are you pregnant?"

A pause, then: "No. But thanks for calling. See you at dinner." Laura hung up.

I dialed Janet's cell. I couldn't tell her what I was planning—she'd be horrified; still, hearing her voice would give me strength. But her cell was, for the first time I could remember, turned off. Fear snapped through my body. Had something happened to her? I went down the hill to the Villa Baiardo, the noon sun shining overhead, to check email in the Crypt. I found this, sent the day before:

From: JMonpereMD@MwanzaClinic.tz
To: Katherine.Hagesfeld@Centro.it
Date: Thurs, Nov 29, 2001
Subject: Last Minute

The driver will be here any second to take me upcountry—two of us are going to the bush villages that are too far from the clinic for people to travel. But I've been thinking about our last unhappy conversation, and I just want to say this. You must take of yourself—you must stay safe, dearest Katy—because I love you, and I am selfish.

Sorry to sound so apocalyptic. I must be what Grandma Eva used to call journey-proud—all swollen up with the prospect of travel.

I'll be out of reach for the next two weeks. No cell phone reception in the bush and of course no internet.

Home for Christmas. See you when we both get back.

Love,

J

P.S. Call Rae! Talk to her!

Aloneness knifed through me. Everything and everyone familiar was out of reach. There was not a soul on earth I could turn to for advice.

Sara's family would wish to write back, she told Daniel, the week after he'd smuggled her letter out through the diplomatic pouch. She wanted desperately to know how they were, especially her little boy. Would Daniel agree to receive letters?

Incoming mail isn't supposed to be censored, Daniel said when I objected.

Supposed to be, I said.

Aerograms are almost impossible to tamper with.

Almost, I said.

Daniel closed his book and looked at me. How can we refuse, Katy? These people have been through so much. Sara's child is two years old.

The risk! I said. If you lose your security clearance, you lose the dig at Vlashnje.

I'll lose the dig anyway, the minute I can't manage without a wheelchair. There have to be *some* things MS can't take away from me. Otherwise, I'm toast.

———

Daniel, Janet, Rae—they all took risks for what they believed in. Why shouldn't I? How could I not? The world is full of little girls—I'd said to myself when Natalia first asked me to teach English to the women from Kosovo—you can't save all of them. But of course that wasn't what mattered. What mattered was that I could save one.

I went that afternoon to Natalia's. When she saw me, she stepped back and shut the door on me. I kept knocking.

"Caterina!" she said through the closed door. "It is not safe. You endanger others besides yourself."

"I need to give you something. Please."

"Were you followed? Did anyone see you?"

"No." I'd taken steps to make sure Angus Dance was otherwise occupied. "No one. I promise."

Natalia swung the door just wide enough to pull me inside, then shut it behind us. Before she could reproach me further, I took the passport from my jacket pocket and held it out.

"*Boh!*" she said, not reaching for it, "We cannot use this."

I opened the passport and turned it so the photo faced her. "I think you can."

Natalia clapped both hands to her chest and stepped back, then leaned against the wall as if to catch her breath. After a second, she took the passport and examined it. At last she looked up at me.

"How did you get this? Did you tell Signora Sweeney about—"

"No, of course not! What do you take me for?" To fraud and theft, add lying.

"Then how?"

"I stole it." That at least was the truth. More or less.

Natalia snapped the passport shut and held it out to me.

"It won't be missed," I said. "I promise you."

"But if it is? If?"

I'd thought about this. I said, "Hollis and Laura keep their passports in the same drawer with Amber's meds. Sometimes I need the meds when I'm babysitting. I'll say I looked at the passport—it's so cute, Amber on Laura's lap, the stuffed elephant on Amber's—and I must've misplaced it. If Lule and Vida have already made it to the States by then, it won't matter. If the loss is discovered before they leave, I'll call you, and you can abort." Abort? I sounded like a character in a spy movie.

"It is risky, *cara*. Twice the risk as before."

"Of course it's risky. But what's the alternative?"

Natalia opened the passport and studied it, frowning. I looked down the hall, hoping for a glimpse of Vida or Lule. No cooking smells; no kitchen sounds.

"It'll work," I said. "You can make it work. You can make Vida and Lule look enough like the photograph to pass. See the date? No child looks the same at three as she does at five."

Natalia's frown faded.

"A passport that's genuine," I persisted. "A *joint* passport. What could be more convincing?"

Decision swept over Natalia's face. She reached up and put an arm around my shoulders. "*Sei meravigliosa!*" You're amazing. She pulled my head down and kissed me—real kisses—on both cheeks. Her breath smelled like bananas.

When she let me go and stepped back, her expression—bright-eyed, greedy—made her look like an aged child.

"Let's go tell Vida," I said.

Natalia shook her head. "She has gone to the market with Lule."

"I can wait till she comes back—may I?" During the train ride, the walk through the city, all I'd thought about was Vida's face when she saw this second passport. The look that had passed between us the last time we'd met.

"It is too dangerous."

Natalia stepped closer to me, the passport tucked under one arm, and reached up to seize my shoulders. "You have done a great thing, *cara*. You have taken two strangers on your heart. We haven't to forget that there is such a thing as post-traumatic stress delight. It is possible to feel, alongside sorrow, joy. Lule and Vida will again have joy. And it will be thanks to you." She seized me in a hug. "Do not tempt fate, I beg you. Go now."

The 3:42 from Brignole station was almost empty. My car held a dozen school children, attended by a pair of the ubiquitous black-clad nuns. They clustered at the front of the car, their high sweet voices like a flock of birds. I looked out at the platform, scanning for Angus Dance, even though I'd arranged for him to overhear me tell Anna Maria I was spending the afternoon in Portofino. I took a seat at the back of the car and, for probably the last time, watched the grimy majesty of Genoa inch past.

My whole body shrilled with nerves. I took refuge in my thoughts, considering the metamorphosis of Vida, which Natalia had begun when I'd given her my passport ten days before and which would now be resumed, with additions. I went over the details of Natalia's plan. Vida's hair bleached and cut—and *clean*; Lule's hair black and her skin caramel. American clothing for both. Natalia would coach them in an American walk: confident, arms swinging. An American face: smiling—liars seldom smile—or when not smiling, a mouth that hung open. (*Too bad about your teeth*, I imagined Natalia telling Vida, and clicking her tongue.) As for American voices, Natalia's strategy was no voice. Vida would be suffering from laryngitis—whispering disguises accents—and Lule would be too shy to speak.

All this, in three days. That made—counting today plus all day Tuesday for traveling—five days in which Hollis mustn't notice that the passport was missing. Assuming all went well, a member of Natalia's renegade organization would collect the passport at JFK and fly straight back with it. He or she would bring it to Natalia, who would find a way to return it to me.

The train shook off the last remnants of the city and trundled eastward. I stared out at the seam of brightness where dark-blue sea met pale-blue sky. A terrible thought occurred to me. Natalia's plan seemed suddenly *too* workable. Her response when I'd offered her Laura's passport seemed, in retrospect, theatrical. Bogus, Rae would've said. Had Natalia been *expecting* me to provide the passport? A chill swept through me. If so, I'd been manipulated even more thoroughly than I'd suspected. But it was too late to change that. And, really, I asked myself, would I want to? Lule and Vida would be saved; that was what mattered. Not how. Anyway, were Natalia's relations with me so different from mine with Laura? Desires (weaknesses) accommodated; participation invited, not coerced.

At Nervi, the last station before Soccorso, the children trooped down the aisle two by two, holding hands and chattering and laughing. Their voices seemed to come from a great distance, though they passed by close enough to touch. They were very young—about Amber's age— and several of them clutched dolls or stuffed animals, reminding me that the green velvet elephant was still in the bushes where I'd thrown it the night before. *Che cazzo!* I'd meant the elephant for Lule, so she could carry it through Security. It would have confirmed the passport's genuineness.

"I say—you're out late. How was Portofino?"

I turned to see Angus Dance in the doorway of the bar, framed by serpentine vines, darkness thickening behind him.

I'd stayed up at the Villa Francesca till after dinner, then gone down to the loggia to retrieve Amber's elephant. Anticipating its clammy damp-ness, I reached into the juniper bushes where I'd thrown it the night be-fore. It wasn't there. I'd batted the bushes, loosing a rain of needles. I'd raked with my bare hands through the damp earth beneath. Nothing.

Now, unable to face the Fellows' after-dinner revelry—afraid that they, Hollis especially, would sense my nervousness—I sat at one of the bar's tile-topped tables, nursing a Campari soda. Without asking permis-sion, Angus Dance sat down in the chair across from me.

"You look knackered. Anything I can help with?"

He seemed more like Rasputin than ever in a collarless shirt of un-bleached linen. A wave of his hot-metal cologne came toward me. I felt as if the night filtering in through the open door had deepened.

"I'm fine," I said. "Long day sight-seeing, that's all. You know. Two weeks till we leave. Got to get it all in."

I was talking too much. Never apologize; never explain. Act as if there's nothing *to* explain. I downed my bright-red drink, waved to the young blonde barista for another.

"I rather think there's too much in Italy for one visit, in any case." Dance's eyes rested on my hands, covered with fine red scratches like a message in cuneiform, the nails rimmed with dirt. "Have you had, er, a fruitful stay? Wairkwise?"

"Work's gone well. Some very useful research." Let him make what he could of that. "A lot left to do, of course."

"Rath*er*." His joyless laugh sent a shiver through me.

The barista, whose downy beginnings of a beard gave him a face like a peach, brought my second Campari. Dance ordered an espresso with a twist of lemon. He watched me drink with a thoughtful expression. Remembering my second night in Italy, when alcohol had allowed him to get lucky? The thought made me set down my glass hard. It rang on the ceramic tabletop. Then, as Dance and I watched, it separated without a sound into two halves, leaving a pool of what looked like blood.

The peach-faced barista hurried over with a rag. He was as dismayed as if he'd broken the glass himself. The ensuing bustle (*"Signora! Si e` fatta male? Mi scusi!"*) gave me time to compose myself. Dance was after something, I realized. Had he seen me scrabbling in the bushes?

By the time the barista left us, I'd downed half my refill. Angus Dance waited till he was out of earshot, then leaned toward me.

"Your friend. Signora Fabbri."

"Yes?"

Dance's hand cupped his merkin of a beard. "Interest has been withdrawn." He waited. I looked at him without speaking. "I thought you might like to know."

I wanted to believe him. If what he said was true, Lule and Vida were safe. I said, "There shouldn't have been any interest in the first place. She's a well-known psychiatrist and a member of the Centro's Board of Directors."

"Yes, well. Frightfully respectable, that. The pairfect cover." Two fingers traveled upward through the merkin. I had to smother a nervous giggle.

"Cover?"

Dance leaned forward. I saw him decide something. He said, "Sairtain professions lend themselves to my line of wairk. Take your late huisband, for example."

"What? What do you mean?"

"A profession that provides a topnotch excuse for poking about in odd corners of the world. A great many trips to a Communist country. And of course the Fulbright program—but you must know this—is run by the CIA."

"You mean… You're not saying you think Daniel was a *spy*?"

I began to laugh, a peal rising up into the dim rafters of the bar, a geyser of laughter I couldn't stem. All the day's tension draining out of me. Oh, Daniel! I thought. If only you were here to hear this.

Dance waited with grim patience until I'd subsided. "Come now, Katherine. Let's level with each other. We were already watching Natalia Fabbri, trying to discover her netwairk. Refugees were fluiding into Britain, but how did they get there? Brown and Yale are prime recruiting grounds for the CIA. Even we puir insular Brits know that. So when our intelligence suggested that one of the Americans at the Centro this autumn might be a bairdwatcher, that meant either you or Joshua."

"A birdwatcher?"

"An agent," Dance said impatiently. "A spy, if you will."

I wiped my eyes on my napkin. A stray bubble of laughter escaped, like a hiccup.

"Both of you had plenty of window-dressing, so we couldn't tell which—"

"Window-dressing?" I felt like I'd been dropped into another dialect. Another world-view.

"Credentials. Well, yours *wair* a bit weak. And then our source said Signora Fabbri had insisted you be offered a fellowship. So naturally one concluded…" He paused, watching me.

Strains of music drifted into the bar from across the courtyard. The Fellows must be tangoing tonight, I thought. Sinatra launched into "Begin the Beguine," a frequent favorite.

This was the first time Dance had said outright what he was after Natalia for. And *telling* me he was a spycatcher? He could only be revealing these things as a way of trapping me into admissions of my own. Any hope that he really had given up his pursuit of Natalia evaporated. I suddenly felt tired—so tired. I wanted to stand up and leave, but I wasn't sure I could.

Dance leaned back in his chair, spreading his legs so wide he made the table wobble, and put his arms behind his head. "Well, as the saying goes, horses for courses. It's all been something of a tempest in a teapot, what? It needn't come between us any longer."

Us. How obtuse I'd been!

"You slept with me to check me out as possible CIA?"

Dance actually winced. "What do you take me for?"

"Either way, there is no *us*," I said. "I thought we'd established that."

Dance ran his tongue over his upper teeth, then said coldly, "Of course, once I…got to know you, I realized. Your huisband may have been CIA, but *you* couldn't be. You don't have the requisite—shall we say?—spirit of adventure."

If you only knew, I thought, annoyed. Then realized that annoyed was just what he wanted me to be. If he could get under my skin, I might give something away.

"You haven't a bloody clue, have ye?' he went on. "You academics see law enforcers as pitiless robots pairsecuting the desairving. You forget that laws are designed to protect. Smugglers of refugees often turn out to be human traffickers. And refugees aren't necessarily the salt of the airth. Look at all the Nazis who were given safe harbor in your country after Wairld War II."

I said nothing. Dance watched me. Even if he guessed that I'd gone to Natalia's apartment today, he couldn't—I realized, with the last of my dwindling wits—know why. He couldn't know for certain that I was involved in Natalia's activities; it was only because of what passed for intuition in the chilly reaches of his brain that he was sitting here. He's fishing, I told myself. Don't give him anything.

The music from the *salotto* grew louder. Sinatra segued from tender tropical nights to wasted chances.

Impossible to think fast enough, in the state I was in, to parry Dance's thrusts. I rose, pushing myself up, palms on the table-top.

"Of course you knew," I said, leaning toward him, "that my husband had chronic progressive multiple sclerosis? That for the last twenty years of his life he was more and more disabled? *Drastically* disabled?"

At last, at last, Angus Dance was silent. His face went pink with surprise. I watched him fight for control of his expression, one hand plucking at his beard. By now Sinatra's crooning had turned to warning. Don't begin the beguine in the first place, he pleaded.

"Didn't your researchers, or whatever you call them, tell you that? You know"—I gave my best imitation of his chilly smile—"you're right. I really am knackered. *Buona notte*," I said, with the last ounce of firmness in me. I turned and fled.

DECEMBER

Che crepi il lupo!

15

Nico drove with one hand caressing the steering wheel, radiating *bella figura*. His other arm lay along the seat back, his hand cupping my shoulder. He was happy, because he thought this trip to Bussana Vecchia was a healthy quest that had replaced his aunt's schemes. It was a sparkling, cold day—fitting for the first of December. The westbound A-10 poured under our wheels; it ran through mountains all the way. Terraced vineyards and steep forests flowed past my window. Every few miles we plunged into the fluorescent gloom of a tunnel. I hid my anxiety as best I could. The sense of failure, of being a helpless observer, had lifted; in it its place was fear. Thirty-six hours had passed without Hollis discovering the theft of the passport. Would he continue in ignorance? I'd be away from the Centro for two days, leaving Laura to carry our secret alone. Would she hold firm? At least this trip meant two whole days without looking over my shoulder for Angus Dance. He wouldn't have laid his cards on the table unless he thought we were engaged in a fight. If he'd once harbored conflicting feelings towards me, he didn't now. Now, we were enemies.

Nico told a joke. Two Sicilian shepherds sit on a hillside having a conversation over bread and cheese. Calogero says to Salvatore, Which would you rather be—beautiful, or stupid? Salvatore thinks for several minutes, then says: Stupid. Because beauty doesn't last.

Laughter traveled through me like a drum-roll. It almost made me forget my fears, and I thought, Why not really forget them? There's nothing more I can do. Why not, for a day and a night, be carefree Caterina? The sapphire-blue nightgown I'd bought in Genoa was in my duffel. And we would find something in Bussana Vecchia, I was sure of it—some trace of Sofonisba.

"Read to me," Nico said, when we'd sobered. He nodded toward the book he'd dropped in my lap as we shot away from the Centro, *The Collected Poems of Eugenio Montale.*

I shook my head. One week, and the *fidanzata* would return; two weeks, and I'd be gone. I didn't say, I'd rather be with you, look at you, talk to you. I said, "I want to watch where we're going. This is a part of Liguria I haven't seen."

That sparked a lecture, as I'd known it would. Our route lay along the Riviera di Ponente, "the coast of the setting sun." Bussana Vecchia, a hundred and fifty kilometers west of Genoa, was tucked into the *entroterra* between sea and mountains. Like all Italians, Nico was unable to speak without gesturing, which meant both hands left the steering wheel. Kate would have been tense with fear; Caterina leaned back. "Bussana Vecchia is in ruins, from the earthquake of 1887," he continued. "Those who live there now, they are…I forget the word. People which live illegal in a place which is forbidden."

"Squatters."

"*Davvero*? Okay, these squatters, they continue an old, old tradition of artists in this place."

"How old?"

"Perhaps it begins in the *quattrocento*. Perhaps a bit later. The village itself is a medieval fortress since many centuries."

The *quattrocento*: the fifteenth century. So artists would have colonized Bussana well before Sofonisba went there in 1579. *If* she went there, I corrected myself, anxious not to jinx things.

"Whose car is this?" I asked, to change the subject. It was an old Kharmann-Ghia, a bright-orange convertible with leather seats and a mahogany dashboard.

"My aunt's. She takes no care of it. She doesn't drive anymore, since the accident— *Madonna!*" Nico stuck his arm out the window and shook it, palm up, at a blue Fiat that had cut in front of us. "*Stupido! Cretino!*" He grabbed the steering wheel again. I breathed, deeply.

"Accident?"

"My cousin, Giulia. She was killed when this car crashed into a bus. That's why the front end is newer than the rest. *Zia* Natalia, she was driving."

"Oh my God." This new information colored and complicated everything I knew about Natalia.

Nico said, his voice hard, "God had nothing to do with it." He changed lanes and swept past the blue Fiat.

After a half-hour of silence I said, "I see it!"

"No, *dolcezza*—that is Bussana Nuova. After the earthquake the town was rebuilt lower down, closer to the sea." A snort expressed disgust for such faint-heartedness. "To reach Bussana Vecchia we must ascend. Hold on!"

Suddenly we were driving up a mountain. Tall hedges beat against my window. We corkscrewed upward. Flung from side to side, I wondered whether grabbing the dashboard would seem like a lack of faith. Nico slammed on the brakes. His arm shot out to catch me a second before I would have hit the windshield. A piercing squeal as the car opposite came to rest inches from our own.

"*Idiota!*" Nico shouted.

"*Idiota tu! Cazzo!*"

Nico's face turned red. I could feel him hold himself back. If I weren't here, I thought, he'd jump out of the car and go for that man's throat.

The man—middle-aged, golf-capped, equally red—thrust both hands out the window and made a violent gesture whose meaning I didn't know but could guess. Nico did the same. Then he backed up. The two cars inched past each other. When we reached the top of the road, Nico got out and slammed the door and stood there, still furious. I knew he thought the near-collision had made him look foolish, eroding the *bella figura*. Climbing shakily out of the car and looking down the hill behind us, I saw the spot where we'd almost crashed. The frail-looking bushes on my side of the car screened a sheer drop to the valley below.

Nico and I sat on the low stone wall of someone's garden. Jade trees, palms, pots filled with cactuses of different shapes. Looking closer, I could make out sculptures half-hidden by vegetation. A bronze woman; a wooden centaur; a regal stone cat wearing a headdress of multi-colored plastic pinwheels. It was late afternoon and turning colder by the minute. I'd worn my windbreaker, not wanting to risk my Caterina jacket on what might be a rough expedition; I was grateful for Laura's sweater underneath it.

We'd been walking for hours up and down the narrow cobblestoned alleys of Bussana Vecchia. Artists had reclaimed the ancient stone buildings, turning them into homes and studios. My archaeologist's heart faltered at the sight of so much valuable evidence destroyed. As we walked, streets turned into steps, then back into streets again. Giant aloes ("*Aloe ferox*," Nico said) crouched in crevices in the walls. Children kicked a soccer ball back and forth. Old men sat gossiping, sending wreaths of smoke up into the cold blue air. In what would have been the center of the village we came to a ruined church. Only the campanile still stood; the rest was roofless, open to the sky. High padlocked iron gates blocked the entrance, and a sign said *VIETATO*. We peered in. A peacock peered back at us, then spread its starry midnight tail. My breath caught. Nico took my hand.

We'd seen a lot of interesting and beautiful things. What we hadn't seen was any trace of Sofonisba.

Now I pulled my camera out of my windbreaker pocket and studied, for the hundredth time, Sofonisba's painting. Or what I believed was Sofonisba's painting. What had I been thinking? Had I imagined that this very scene would pop up in the middle of the ruins, more than four hundred years later? That the old archaeologist's tingle would lead me, like a divining rod, to whatever Sofonisba had left behind?

"It's hopeless," I said. "How can we find what we don't even know we're looking for?"

Nico reached across and took the camera from me and put it in his pocket. "You are tired, *piccola*. And you are hungry," he informed me in his bossy Fabbri way. "It is easy to discourage when your body has not *benessere*." He pulled out a Swiss Army knife and swung around and cut something off a nearby cactus.

"*Eccola!*" He showed me a purple, potato-sized globe studded with glittery blond hairs. Holding it between two fingers, he peeled it. "*Che cazzo*! The spines are sharp." He tossed the skin into the garden. "Watch me, *amore*." He held the fruit at either end like an ear of corn and bit into it, chewed, then spat. "Don't eat the seeds." He handed the lump of purple flesh to me.

It felt slimy between my fingers. Nico looked at me, the downward lines in his face picked out by the sun, which had moved low in the sky. I took a bite. It tasted like watermelon. I finished it off, spitting the seeds onto the ground, and was rewarded by the swift upward lift of Nico's features.

"*Opuntia ficus-indica*," he said happily. "Prickly pear." Suddenly he swiveled around and stood up. "Time to go." He held out a hand to me. Turning, I saw an old woman hobbling toward us across the garden, dressed all in black and brandishing a hoe. Two white geese tumbled before her, squabbling.

"You stole her fruit," I said to Nico as we ran, hand in hand, over the cobblestones. We were both laughing. "You stole from a crippled old woman."

He dragged me headlong up a flight of steps. "Things belong to the people who want them most."

"It's at the church," I said. "That's the logical place. There's something there. Something she left behind."

"Campari on an empty stomach—it has gone to your head, *cara*. There's a reason those gates were locked. These buildings could collapse at any time." Nico looked around the *Trattoria degli Artisti*, the one restaurant open in this season. Its roof, our waiter had told us proudly, dated from the eleventh century. "This place, for instance. It could fall on our heads in the next minute."

"Like life," I said.

"In Bussana Vecchia one goes back in time, *e` vero*. But one is also in the present. The dangerous present."

"Like life."

The food came—dishes our waiter, a short, smiling man with a limp, had recommended—along with two kinds of wine. Anchovy-and-olive salad. A plate of what looked like sparkling maggots. I demurred; Nico insisted. We were in luck, he said. The transparent morsels were immature sardines, legal only a few months a year, and December (why would this be a surprise?) wasn't one of them. They were delicious. Tender, salty, touched with oil and lemon. Dessert, Ligurian sweet milk fritters, turned out to be Nico's childhood favorite. He told me how they were a Sunday treat at the orphanage where he'd spent the year he was five. "My mother got pneumonia. She was sick for a long time. She bribed the nuns to take special care of me by bringing them *i gialli*. How do you say it?"

"Crime novels."

"Ah, *si`*. I remember how the books vanish into their long black skirts, like a magician trick."

"And your father?" My mind was still on the ruined church, or I wouldn't have asked so bluntly.

Nico winced. "I never know—knew—him. Mamma always said he died before they could marry. But *Zia* Natalia told me he disappeared when Mamma got pregnant."

This was more personal information than Nico had imparted in the whole two months we'd known each other. Looking down, I discovered that while he was talking he'd put a hand on mine and I'd covered it with my other one. Now he put his other one on top. A stack of hands.

"We need to go back to the church," I said. "We need to at least try."

"Anyway, it is forbidden."

"Since when did that stop you?"

Nico pulled his hands away. His right was dotted with angry red spots. "What happened?" I said.

"*Boh*! The spines of the prickly pear. I didn't avoided them all."

"Does it hurt?"

"It's nothing." He turned around and called out a word I didn't know. After a few minutes the waiter limped over to our table with a roll of duct tape. Nico wrapped tape around his hand. When he pulled it away, it held half-a-dozen tiny hair-thin spines. "You see? It's nothing."

We emerged from the *trattoria* to a post-sunset sky the color of bruises. Nico murmured something in Italian.

"What?" I said.

"The unraveling of the evening is ours."

"Montale?"

"*Sì*."

The air held the the bittersweet smell of frost. I zipped up my windbreaker. So there could be winter in Italy, after all?

Nico put an arm around me. "It is very cold, no? Do you still want to look at the church?" When I nodded he said resignedly, "*Va bene*," and produced a small flashlight from his jacket pocket. We hurried, arms around each other, to the iron gates of the church. They were higher than I remembered.

"Hold this." Nico thrust the flashlight at me. Its beam picked out the padlock. Nico pulled out his Swiss Army knife, broke off the tweezers and bent them into an L shape, then inserted one end into the lock.

"Have you got a *spilla*?"

"A what?"

"*Una spilla di sicurezza*," Nico whispered impatiently. "To hold up clothes."

A safetypin. I didn't have one, of course. But wait. I pulled a bobbypin out of my hair and handed it to him. In the flashlight's beam his fingers held the tweezer steady while he jiggled the bobbypin in the lock. "*Eccolo!*" A snap; then a screech as Nico pushed open the gates.

Hard to believe we were inside what had once been a church. It felt more like a courtyard surrounded by arches. The stones seemed to exhale dampness and cold. We walked the perimeter, the flashlight picking out rubble and clumps of grass growing up through gaps in the marble floor.

Nothing else. No place for anything to hide, much less to remain preserved for centuries.

Something grazed my cheek. I screamed. Nico pulled me close. Then he laughed.

"What is it?"

"*Pipistrelli.*"

"What?"

"Bats."

Another dark shape shot past. In spite of myself, I let out a shout.

Nico swung the flashlight above our heads. Black lumps clotted the arches. "*Madonna!* They are living here a long time. See those stains on the walls?" The lumps pulsed and twitched. Their motion made me queasy. And what if my scream brought someone to investigate? I tugged on Nico's arm.

"Let's go," I said. "There's nothing here. I give up."

Nico did his best to comfort me, and for a while he succeeded. The bed-and-breakfast he'd reserved for us was warm and welcoming, with a small brown dog asleep on its paws and a cheerful, plump proprietress. Our top-floor room, as Nico pointed out proudly, had both a fireplace and an enormous bathtub.

We sat in candlelight in the warm scented water—Nico behind, and me, with my back to him, between his outstretched legs. Nico's erection nosed my spine. He cupped both my breasts in one hand while the other explored the wavering wet hair between my legs. I thought of his fingers on the padlock outside the church.

"What is the English name for this?"

"Clitoris."

"No—a light name. For fun. We call it *grillo.*"

"Cricket?"

"*Sì, dolcezza.* This"—his fingers approached, then withdrew—"is your cricket."

"Don't stop! Go back."

"I do not need to. It will come to me."

My hips were already lifting. His fingers moved away. My pelvis followed.

"You see? It is thigmonasty."

The bed, when we finally got into it, was high and soft and warm, the feather-filled comforter light as air. The proprietress had pressed on us extra blankets because of the bitter night—a record cold, she said, was expected. But Nico's flesh warmed mine like a giant hot-water bottle. I had thought it would be difficult to sleep all night beside him. I had thought I'd be haunted by images of the *fidanzata*, whose place I was usurping. But I was tired from the day. And my body, that demanding and rewarding animal, was filled with *benessere*.

I turned on my side. Nico wrapped himself around me. I felt myself falling. "Pleasant dreams," I whispered. "*Sogni piacevoli*."

"*Sogni d'oro*," he corrected me.

Golden dreams.

I woke before Nico and slipped out of bed. The cold struck through my nightgown, prickling my flesh and making my nipples tighten. I crossed the room and stood looking out the dormer window as the sky began to lighten. I thought how every romance has its high point—after which it's all downhill to the end—and you recognize the moment when it comes, even though you deny it. Was last night that moment?

I leaned my forehead against the cold glass. This view—what was it? I must be looking out the back of the B & B. Last night I'd noticed that our street was at the very end of the inhabited part of Bussana Vecchia. Now I saw a stretch of abandoned ruins, more crumbling and much more overgrown than those Nico and I had walked through yesterday. A deer emerged from a stand of pines. She stood still for several seconds, and a plume of steam rose from the long grass. She must have been peeing.

The deer turned and ambled away. Farther off, ruins gave way to chaos. Tall grasses silver with frost; a tangle of underbrush and fallen trees. A chill traveled down my spine. It's *out there*! I thought. We've been looking in the wrong place. Whatever it is is in the part of the ruins that's fenced off. The part marked "*VIETATO*."

"It is the first time we have slept all the night together, *dolcezza*." Nico's arms came around me, the sapphire-blue nightgown whispering at his touch. He rested his chin in the curve of my neck. "What are you looking at? Aren't you cold? Come back to bed."

I said, "We have to find a way to get into the forbidden part. If Sofonisba left anything, it would be there. Where no squatters have settled. That's why it hasn't been found."

"What hasn't been found, *cara*?"

I turned, breaking the circle of his arms. "Come on. Let's get dressed."

Over breakfast in the sunny kitchen our proprietress answered my questions while Nico gazed sulkily into his *cappuccino*. He wore a green T-shirt that said, *Chi va piano va sano.* He who goes softly goes sanely. Not advice I was following at the moment. But how could I leave Bussana Vecchia without exploring this one last possibility?

Si`*—our proprietress said—*la citta` fantasma, the ghost town, was cordoned off from the rest. There was a high cyclone fence topped with barbed wire. If we'd walked up from the new town instead of driving, we would have seen it. *Si`*—the area was dangerous. Even today, more than a century later, every now and then you could hear part of a building crumble, like the roar of distant lions. *Si`*—it was illegal to go there.

"It is absolutely forbidden. So when you go, don't leave a trace."

We didn't know how to get in, I told her. Nico heaved a sigh.

Our proprietress was delighted to show us. Everyone who'd been a child in Bussana Vecchia knew the secret entrance. She would take us there. She went off to get a sheepskin coat and boots, "for the snakes."

"*Che cazzo!*" Nico muttered.

"*Dipende*," I said.

We set out along the top of the ridge, the sun at our backs. The tall grass glowed with frost. I shivered in my windbreaker and slapped my arms against my sides to warm up. This area must once have been a stretch

of well-tended chestnut and olive groves. Now we waded through underbrush, climbed over piles of stones. The exhilaration I used to feel at
the beginning of a dig took hold of me. I forgot the moment of forebod-
ing when our proprietress pulled aside the stretch of cyclone fencing that
long-ago children had cut and hinged to make a hidden door. I forgot that
the running shoes Nico and I wore offered no protection against snakes.
I forgot to look over my shoulder, to worry about what I'd say if we were
stopped.

Nico let me lead the way, making no attempt to help me over fallen
trees or hold aside the branches that now and then slapped me in the face.
He skulked along, the very opposite of the *bella figura*.

"We are breaking *probabilmente* three different laws," he grumbled.

"Since when do you care about laws, *piccolo*?"

"I see why you and *Zia* Natalia get along so well. She thinks she is im-
mune. But she is not. You know that she was thrown out of *Missione Arcobaleno* for unprofessional conduct? And that Caritas asked her to leave?"

Of course I hadn't known. I almost told him then. What a relief it
would have been to share my fear. But what if Nico failed to grasp the
women's plight?

"Some laws need to be broken," I said. "You believe that, yourself.
What happened to *Dipende*?"

"*Boh*! *Dipende* depends. Right now, we break the law for no good reason. You believe—a mistake!—that your American passport protects you.
And we do not know even what we look for."

"Yes, we do."

"What?"

Sofonisba and Lomellini would have lived in secret until their marriage was recognized. Or until enough time had passed for people to
assume they'd married. "A habitable spot," I said. "But set apart. A spot
where someone could live in comfort without getting involved socially.
Trees. Of course they can't be the same trees now as then—but couldn't
they be their great-great-grandchildren? Water. Though that could've
disappeared by now, too, or gone underground. A hill or a small rise,
for safe outlook."

Nico looked skeptical. He's forgotten I'm an archaeologist, I thought. That was when it struck me. Yesterday a whole day had passed in which I had not thought of Daniel. It was the first time since he'd died.

"And something that might once have looked like this." I pulled out my camera.

Nico groaned. "Signorina Cappicchioni said she didn't know any spot like that." It was true: our proprietress had studied the photograph of the painting and shaken her head. "And four centuries later? *Impossibile!*"

"You said the lives of plants unfold in a much slower dimension of time." He'd given me a lecture the week before on the evidence that plants move. He'd shown me a time-lapse video he'd made for his master's thesis: a bean plant searching for its beanpole, hurling itself forward over and over, like a fisherman casting his line.

"Could you just look, Nico *mio?* Look for the kind of vegetation that would grow near a hidden water source."

We plowed along, clambering over uprooted trees, crunching through the crust of black earth that sparkled with frost. Saplings parted to let us through, then snapped shut behind us. Sweet cold air and birdcalls and being in search of something vegetable gradually improved Nico's mood. He walked more slowly, muttering species names. The wildness that surrounded us sparked a lecture on the superiority of plants. Did I know that some plants commanded animals? Their chemical signals could summon wasps to eat attacking caterpillars, or persuade a bee to remember a particular plant and come back to pollinate it again. And not only that—plants were indispensable to all life. "If humans become extinct tomorrow, the planet will survive. But if plant life dies, that's the end."

Ahead lay a rise crowned with a copse of olive trees. Through their trunks came a gleam of something light-colored, close to the ground. I grabbed Nico's arm. If what we saw was the remains of a dwelling, it was set apart from any others, just as I'd imagined.

The overgrowth looked even worse than what we'd struggled through so far. Impenetrable; untended for centuries. Nico clicked his tongue in the Fabbri family sound of disapproval. While we stood studying the vegetation for a way in, a white owl flew out from among the higher branches of the olive trees. And there, at last, was the tingle. A needle-fine vibration, pulling me forward.

Nico said, "Let me see that photo again."

I handed him the camera. He looked at the painting, then ahead. "This way," he said, with Fabbri decisiveness.

I followed the path he tramped through the underbrush, catching the low branches he thrust to either side. The ground rose as we went, then leveled off.

There it was. Moss-covered stones, overgrown with vines and shrubs but visible, sketched out a rectangle. I started toward the tallest pile.

Nico put a hand on my arm. "*Pera volpina*," he said.

"What?" I tried to shake him off, eager to explore.

"Fox pear. See?" He was still holding my camera. He pointed to a tree in the foreground of Sofonisba's painting: leathery heart-shaped leaves, glowing globes of fruit. Then he pulled me over to a tree growing near one corner of the ruins. It held no fruit, and only a few dry brown leaves clung to its branches. I would not have known it was the same tree. Nico looked at me, his face lifting, expectant.

"Well, okay," I said. "Great. But—"

"No, *piccola*, you don't understand. *Pera volpina* is a very rare species. If it is in your lady's painting, and it is here, then it is possible that your lady was here."

"If this *is* her painting." I was struck with the utter craziness of my quest: finding a structure recorded nowhere, on the strength of a painting attributed to no one.

"*Pera volpina* re-seeds itself. Even for centuries. You cannot discourage now, *piccola*. Go! See what you can find." Nico handed the camera back to me and went closer to study his tree.

I fought my way through tangled vines, thistles, fallen limbs, to the tallest pile of pale stone. Up close I could see that it was solid, not loose. A piece of wall, intact up to my waist. Stepping toward it, I saw something that made the back of my neck prickle. On the wall's scarred surface, near the ground: a glimpse of color.

———

A woman alone in a carriage would draw unwanted attention. So she wears breeches and a padded doublet, hastily altered by Margherita at midnight; her hair is tucked up inside her black velvet berretto. *She can leave the curtains open to the early morning air and gaze all she pleases at the mud-strewn streets, full of noise and life. Children chase a pig over the cobble-stones; a crier passes, warning of bandits in the* entroterra; *workers chant as they haul stones and earth from several building sites. The Medicis, Orazio told her, have determined to make Livorno a port to rival Genoa. He is with one of them now, negotiating the sale of Sicilian grain and raw silk and wool.*

She's restless on the plump cushions, her body missing the ship's motion. She ponders Orazio's plan, proffered with somewhat disquieting alacrity. Because they disappeared at Livorno—leaving it to Orazio's pilot to bring La Patrona *home to Genoa—it will be assumed they've taken refuge in Pisa. The carriage with its hired* vetturino *on the coach box will in fact convey them as far as Pisa. She will appear to have gone into seclusion there, at the convent where her sister Elena resides. Thus she will be* al riparo di pettegolezzi—*sheltered from gossip. In reality, she and Orazio will hire horses for the five-day journey through the* entroterra *to a village west of Genoa. The* vetturino *will guide them, his fee buying off the bandits along their route.*

Your brother will sleep for many hours, Orazio told her as he handed her into the carriage at dawn. My page brought him a wine of poppy seeds in place of his bedtime grappa. *By the time he wakes,* La Patrona *will be halfway to Genoa.*

She trusts Orazio's plan—has she not had ample evidence of his resource-fulness?—but there are consequences beyond it that she fears. Asdrubale is determined to stop the union he suspects her of contemplating. He made that plain the night before, invoking the supposed wishes of poor dead Papa. Enu-merating impediments. First of all, she hasn't the permission of king, duke, or male relative: who, lacking those, would be willing to perform the ceremo-ny? Secondly, gossips will say it was she—so much older than Orazio—who proposed. And finally, she cannot, on six days' acquaintance, know this man.

And then there is the breath-stopping matter of the marriage itself. Consumato: *she does not even know, not really, what that entails.*

But she does know Orazio. She wants to—she must—believe that. The trust between him and his pilot; the passion in his voice when he speaks of his ship; the ombrellino.

And he knows her.

She picks up the wasp's nest from the seat beside her. Its not-quite-spherical shape fits perfectly between her palms. Its ridges invite her touch. My wedding gift to you, cara, *he said when he put it in her hands. He'd meant to give it to her earlier—it was this, and not the astrolabe, that he brought with him to the deck at midnight—but Asdrubale had interrupted them.*

A vendor passes her window, calling, Oranges! Fresh, firm oranges! Smells reach her: an odor like the ship's bilge that speaks of open sewers nearby; the coppery scent of blood from a butcher's shop; the fragrance of baking bread. She's hungry. They left the ship at dawn, breakfastless. She watches a man pull a cart up to the tavern across the street and unload a barrel of eels.

Did Orazio know, when he proposed marriage, that she was already plotting it? Did he perhaps even maneuver her—delicately, deftly, devotedly—into thinking of it in the first place? Does it matter? For the first time in her nearly five decades of life, she is choosing her own path. Her silk hose whisper as she crosses and recrosses her legs for the sheer pleasure of feeling their freedom.

Forgive me, carissima, *Orazio says. I have taken longer than I anticipated.*

Settling into the cushions beside her, he holds out a linen pouch of hot chestnuts from a street vendor. The smell makes her stomach leap.

It is a long journey, he says. He snaps the shell away from a chestnut and slips off the brown membrane and hands it to her, then peels another.

I shall not mind, she says.

She crams the two warm chestnuts into her mouth at once. They crumble, earthy and sweet. He smiles at her greed, then leans out to call, Avanti!

The vetturino's *whip snaps; the carriage bounds forward. They leave behind them the sea, leapfrog glints of sun on water. For a second she remembers landing as a new bride at the harbor in Palermo, with its strange smell of violets. Then she faces forward. Ahead loom the mountains, steep and green. The sky above is cloudless save for a long skein like carded wool.*

Tell me of our destination, Orazio.

His name still feels strange on her tongue.

It is a remote village whose inhabitants are loyal to the Lomellini family. White-walled houses. Date palms and lemon trees, and winter roses.

He picks up her hand and laces his fingers through hers. There is that trill again, deep inside her. Fear, yes; but also excitement. Curiosity.

We will make one of the houses into a studio, Orazio tells her. And perhaps there you will try something altogether different. Frescoes, perhaps. Perchè no?

The art of buonfresco *is said to be impossible for a woman, she says, more to herself than to him.*

Exactly, he replies.

She laughs. What is the name of this remarkable village? she asks.

Bussana.

By now I'd grown used to being gathered up into Sofonisba's world—achingly vivid and full of invitation—then flung back into my own. This time was different. This time, it felt as if our eras, hers and mine, coincided. They fit, one over the other. Nothing was lost—only hidden.

I reached back to basics, to the principles Daniel and I had taught his students at Vlashnje.

Rule One: Maintain the integrity of the site.

Every time you touch an archaeological site, you destroy. Even the most meticulous excavation inflicts damage. I remembered how Daniel used to inveigh against lone pot-hunters. Like them, I was without the proper tools—Massimo, the Centro's gardener, had lent me a trowel, and I'd brought my toothbrush; but that was all. Still, I was going to have to risk moving things. First I knelt down to photograph the wall, a close-up view followed by one that showed the surrounding vegetation. Then I started pulling away thorn bushes, so excited I barely noticed the pain when I grasped them.

Rule Two: Nothing should be removed from its location unless it is likely to be disturbed or lost before an excavation can take place.

I broke off the stoutest, straightest branch from a fallen tree and stripped away the smaller branches. With my crude pole I began to poke gently among the stones. Lifting them away, holding my breath, praying not to disturb whatever they hid. My hair kept getting between me and the sun. I twisted it into a ponytail and tucked it inside the collar of my windbreaker. When enough stones were cleared away, I took another photo.

The wall looked to be half-buried. The soil around it had shrunk, exposing it, because of the previous night's rare cold. Frost heaves, we call them in New England. The lowest part of the wall would have remained invisible otherwise. My trowel loosened the hard-packed soil, but I couldn't dig deep, for fear of damaging possible artefacts. Holding my fingers straight and tight together, I began to sweep away the crumbling earth. Slow and focused. Archaeologists are earth-whisperers. Blue-green dirt can mean bronze; iridescence can signal glass; earth-encrusted pebbles can turn out to be tiles or coins. The intoxicating smell of turned earth filled my nostrils. It was damp and clung to my skin. My hands already sore, I used my toothbrush to sweep the wall's surface clean.

Yes, there they were. Colors.

I looked closer. Scattered patches of blue, rose, saffron. An embedded look to the pigment—like the faded frescoes in the Centro's dining-room. My heart began to fire with excitement. The sun at my back lit the wall. Hands shaking, I snapped a photo, then another. A shadow fell over me.

"*Amore*! You have found something?"

I stood up, arching my back, rubbing my sore knees. "Look."

Nico crouched in front of the wall. "*Madonna!*" he breathed. I'd never before heard him say the word with reverence. He stretched out a hand toward the flowering of ghost colors.

"Don't!" I exclaimed. "Don't touch anything."

He looked up at me. For a moment I thought I'd insulted him, cast doubt on the *bella figura*. Then his face relaxed. "*Certo,*" he said. "How can I help?" His voice held a note of respect. It was, I realized, the first time I'd heard that from Nico.

I stood looking down at my work. I'd gone as far as I could. Or should.

Rule Three: No artifacts uncovered, regardless of their quality or nature, are of much use to archaeologists unless information about the excavation is recorded in a systematic manner.

In grad school they taught us that the business of archaeologists—including epigraphers—was authenticating, dating, and noting any relevant circumstances. Interpreting was to be left to historians. From the beginning I'd had trouble with this division of labor.

I said, "These are fresco remnants, very old. Whatever this site is"—but in my heart I knew, I *knew* this had to be the cottage in the painting, the place where Sofonisba had taken refuge during the Lost Year—"it's valuable. It should be left to the proper authorities"—I ignored Nico's snort of derision—"to uncover."

I'd already broken the law. (*A state antiquity permit or land-use license is required for any survey, testing, or excavation conducted on state lands.*) The least I could do was document what I'd done. My mind ran over the necessary elements. Site report; feature register; stratigraphy record; photo or sketch with scale sticks... Scale sticks!

"Nico *mio*, would you get down and put your hand next to the wall? Straight up, like this. But don't touch it." Nico squatted so that his hand was level with the patches of color. "Yes, there. Perfect."

"Stinging nettles," Nico observed, looking at the pile of greenery I'd torn away from the wall. "*Urtica dioica.*"

Nettles! Often a sign of previous habitation. I knelt beside Nico and leaned the camera on his shoulder to snap two more photos. Now the size of what I'd uncovered would be clear. But in the field you back up everything. Batteries die; cameras get lost; technology fails.

"Don't move, *piccolo*," I said to Nico. "Keep your hand right there." I pulled paper and pencil out of my windbreaker pocket.

When I'd finished my sketch, we got to our feet and stood for a minute, looking—the two of us fused by the sense of being a living bridge between the present and the past. *A joy shared is a joy doubled.*

Nico said, "*Lontani andremo e serberemo un'eco della tua voce, come si recorda del sole l'erba grigia.*" From far away we'll come, and we will keep an echo of your voice, the way gray grass recalls the sun.

"Montale?"

"*Sì, dolcezza.* Montale."

Nico's face held an expression I'd seen before: wistfulness. Was he thinking of his own abandoned vocation?

"I too have found something." He pulled some greenery out of his jacket pocket. Wild onions, slender as grasses. He pinched off a snail the size of a pearl and set it on the ground. Then he wiped the dirt from an iridescent blister and handed it to me. When I bit into it, its sharpness made my eyes water.

"You see," Nico said, handing me another and biting into one himself, "you are hungry. We must go." He sounded like his bossy Fabbri self again. But he was right. The sun had begun to move down the western sky. We'd been out for hours.

Rule Four: Leave part of each excavation for the future. Archaeologists will come who have more knowledge, better tools, more funding. You excavate for the next generation.

Meanwhile, though, you can't leave the patient open on the operating table. Time to stabilize the site. First I took a couple of photographs from further away, to place the bit I'd uncovered in the context of the rest of the wall. Then I replaced as much of the dirt as I could, backfilling to protect the part of the wall I'd uncovered. If only I had a tarp, I thought—something to shelter it from the winter rains until it can be properly excavated. I unzipped my windbreaker and pulled it off.

"*Piccola*! What are you doing?"

I picked up the stick I'd used to lift stones and broke it in half. "We need two more this length—"

Nico was already pulling another long, straight branch off the same tree. He snapped it in two. Together we pushed the four poles into the damp earth and stretched my windbreaker across them. Now there was a canopy over the part of the wall where I'd worked. But how to keep it there, through wind and rain? Nico grasped the cord that ran through a channel at the bottom of the windbreaker. Grinning at his own ingenuity, he took his Swiss Army knife, cut off the knot at one end, and pulled the cord free. He chopped it into four equal pieces. We tied the windbreaker to the top of each pole.

A breeze came up as we made our way, Nico in the lead, back toward the village. I felt deeply happy. We all leave something behind, I thought—all of us. No one is truly lost. Everything I looked at seemed to shine with this knowledge, every blade of grass, every bramble, every fallen tree.

At last we reached a stretch where we could walk side by side. Nico shrugged off his leather jacket and helped me into it, then put an arm around me. I tucked my sore, cold hands into the pockets. Our joined shadows traveled before us, and the wind whispered in the long grass. I could hear in the distance a muffled clanking.

"Sheep," Nico said. "The shepherd is bringing them home."

———

It was midnight by the time Nico dropped me off at the Centro. Still lit from within by the day's discovery, I walked up the path to the Villa Francesca. What we'd uncovered today was every archaeologist's dream. The find of a lifetime.

At the Villa Francesca's gate my key stuck in the lock. I pushed. My fingers hurt, the skin abraded from digging. Footsteps sounded on the path, louder, closer. Fear rolled through me. I yanked the heavy iron key out of the lock and clenched it in my fist like a dagger.

"Kate! Is that you?"

Hollis's voice. I slumped against the wall in relief. Then, before I could wonder what he was doing at my door at midnight, he emerged into the pool of light above the gate. One hand held up a small blue booklet.

"Kate? What the *hell* is going on?

16

Massimo the Gardener bent to set down a straw basket outside my French doors. He was such a small man and his large ears stuck out so far, it seemed as if you could pick him up by them. When he saw me through the glass he put a hand across his mouth—to signify that he was forbidden to speak to me—and shrugged. I watched him trot back across the lawn, glossy with dew, then went out to retrieve my breakfast. A cold breeze lifted my hair, and I brushed it back from my face.

Last night Anna Maria had appeared to think that isolation would flush me out. I was forbidden to go down to the Villa Baiardo, so as not to infect the other Fellows with my lawlessness. This being Italy, though, there was no question of trying to starve me out. Over espresso and croissants and sour cherry jam and a ripe pear, I began my first day of confinement. My thoughts caromed from the day ahead to the night just past, when Hollis had appeared at the Villa Francesca's gate.

His tall stoop-shouldered form loomed over me in the darkness.

"Why was your passport in our drawer?" he demanded. "What happened to Laura and Amber's?"

My stomach felt as if I'd swallowed a length of rope. I gazed into the darkness behind him. *Remember your story.* "Oh! I must've left it," I said, "when I was babysitting."

"Why were you looking in the drawer in the first place?"

"Amber's asthma medicine is in there. Her inhaler. I always check at the beginning of the evening, to make sure."

"And you just happened to be holding your passport while you checked?"

"I was." I stared him down. The whites of his eyes shone like boiled eggs. "I'd just taken it out of my pocket to put it in my purse. I remember dropping it. I must've picked up Laura's by mistake. I put it in my purse without opening it, naturally."

On the path leading up from the Via Aurelia a light bobbed, advancing toward us. Hollis's back was to the path. He couldn't see it.

"I don't believe you," he said. "Just tell me the truth, Kate. Please."

"That *is* the truth," I said, making my voice sound indignant.

Hollis grabbed my arm. My heart began to slam, slow and hard, against my ribs. He said in a low, choked voice, "Where. Is. The. Passport."

From somewhere in the trees came an owl's throaty call. Behind Hollis the light drew nearer. I could make out a figure with a smaller one attached.

Hollis's grip on my arm tightened. He shone his flashlight on my face. "Let's go get it."

Blinded, I tried to pull away. He pushed me forward till my stomach pressed against the gate. I dug my heels into the gravel. My arm hurt. I thought of the Hollis who'd caught Daniel as he began to fall, all those years ago. The helpful Hollis of the past two-and-a-half-months at the Centro. Surely *that* Hollis would have mercy on me?

"I can't," I said.

"You'd better."

Laura caught up to us then. She stood with an arm around Amber, who shivered in the cold night air. The beam from her flashlight wavered past Hollis. He turned, his flashlight leaving my face.

"Laura! What are you doing here? Go back to the apartment. Amber should be in bed."

He turned back to me, still gripping my arm. I could feel him shaking. "We trusted you. We trusted you with *Amber*. What the hell are you up to?"

I blinked rapidly, half-blinded by the afterimage of light on my retina. Laura said, "Hollis."

Amber had run up to me then and pulled at her father's arm. "I don't want you to hurt Kate!" she'd cried.

It did no good to keep going over last night. Returning to the problematic present, I piled plates and silverware into the basket and set it out on the patio for Massimo. Somehow I had to get through today and tomorrow. At dawn tomorrow Lule and Vida would leave Italy; they would land in New York at the end of the day, and Laura's passport would travel back to me immediately by courier. Hollis had already told Anna Maria about the missing passport by the time he caught me at the Villa Francesca's gate. I had told both of them that I didn't know where Laura's passport was—that I would look for it. Of course they hadn't believed me. Now questions flooded my tired brain. Why had Hollis checked the passports? I was sure from the way Laura had reproached him last night that she hadn't betrayed me. But how long could she keep our secret? And how was I going to keep Hollis *and* Anna Maria at bay for two whole days?

I walked across the grass to the other side of the garden. The stone wall was cold to my touch, and rough. If I stood on a chair I could scale it, then creep down the path to the Via Aurelia. But where would I go? Anna Maria had confiscated my passport, so I couldn't fly home. *Dizgraziata*, she'd called me. Disgraced. She'd warned me that house arrest—villa arrest, I supposed I'd have to call it—would turn into actual arrest if I tried to leave. Anyway, I didn't *want* to leave. Not until I knew the plan had worked. So: two days—now, thirty-six hours—of waiting. This felt like the hardest part of the whole thing so far. Had an autumn in Italy changed me that much? I used to be good at waiting—at standing by. Now I just wanted to do something. But what?

The breeze carried the scent of approaching rain, and I breathed in its loamy freshness. Think. Start braining, Rae would have said. I'd promised to phone Natalia if the loss of Laura's passport was discovered before Lule and Vida left Italy, so that the plan could be aborted. But I found myself unwilling to make that call. Something about my current disgrace didn't ring true. Presumably Angus Dance could put out an APB, or whatever the international equivalent was, for anyone using Laura's passport. But he hadn't, not yet. If he had, Anna Maria wouldn't be keeping me prisoner. She'd have had to turn me over to the *polizia*.

Why hadn't Dance acted?

No one came near me all morning. My confinement was a kind of shunning, and I was surprised by how it threw me off balance. My whole body ached, and my brain felt like blue cheese. I paced the apartment, kitchen to bedroom and back again, my reflection in the *salotto* mirror reproaching me each time I passed. *Boh!* Caterina would never stand for this. Work—that was what I needed. Work would help me keep my bearings in this fog of waiting.

In the study I laid out the makeshift documentation of my find at Bussana Vecchia: my camera with photos of the site; the drawing with Nico's hand; a rough site map drawn from memory. Looking at the material, scant as it was, reminded me why I'd come to Italy in the first place. *The find of a lifetime*—how I wanted that! How I needed it, and the future it would secure for me: a fulltime job; a career. A year or two before, in Assisi, Italian restorers had reassembled a Giotto fresco from 50,000 fragments left behind by a major earthquake. If a twelfth-century fresco could be revived, why not a sixeenth-century one? Sofonisba had begun by being my ticket out of professional limbo. She'd become much more than that. Having drawn close to her over the past two months, didn't I owe it to her to give the world what she'd left it? To be the living bridge between her *then* and my *now*? Because bridges—I reminded myself as I searched for the Ministry of Culture in the ponderous *Provincia di Liguria* phonebook—go both ways. The dead once wanted to reach us as passionately as we now want to reach them.

Perhaps they still do.

Ordinarily the first step would have been to get the government's okay to do a site survey. Then, with some evidence in hand, I could have made the argument for a license to excavate. But as things stood, I'd never be granted such a license. I needed to bring the site to the attention of someone in Italy who would want to pursue the matter. This at least, I thought, is something I can do. An action, to cut through the fog of waiting.

I was wrong. One hour and three minor bureaucrats later, I hung up, disgusted. Bureaucrat No. 1 pointed out that I was neither an Italian citizen nor a practicing archaeologist; nor did I have the Habilitation. (It took several minutes to learn that this was a degree beyond the Ph. D., granted by just a few European universities.) Bureaucrat No. 2 wondered whether I could furnish a *raccomandazione* from an Italian archaeologist possessing the Habilitation? Ah, *peccato*. I *probabilmente* did not realize that the Renaissance art of *buonfresco* was not practiced by women, as it required great strength and stamina. *Certo*, if I insisted, I could apply to the Ministry in Rome. Bureaucrat No. 3 gave me the address. No permissions could be granted until the matter was reviewed. *Grazie. Arrivederci*. Click.

I slammed the receiver down, as frustrated as I'd felt in the darkest days of Daniel. As helpless. A letter! How, under villa arrest, could I even put a letter in the mail? Besides, the site wasn't protected enough to wait for a letter to make its way upstream through Italian bureaucratic channels. I needed someone who could command the Minister's ear. Daniel would have known who the leading Italian archaeologist was—would have already been on the phone to him.

Daniel isn't here, I reminded myself. This problem belongs solely to—

There was a sound of thumping. By the time I got to the French doors Anna Maria had already let herself in. "*Buongiorno, Signora*," she said, striding past me into the *salotto*, shedding her hairy orange coat as she went.

"*Buongiorno*," I answered, wondering how often during the autumn she'd come in when I wasn't here.

Anna Maria sat down uninvited on the sofa. I sat down beside her. She smelled like her office in the Villa Baiardo, of espresso and lemons and dust.

"We both know why I am here, *vero*?" She waited schoolmarmishly for my nod. "*Bene*. You have found the passport?"

"*Mi dispiace*. I've looked everywhere. I don't have the passport."

Anna Maria's face darkened, but she kept her voice reasonable. "I appeal to your better nature, Signora. You have taken what does not belong to you."

Things belong to the people who want them most.

"I am sure you did not mean to commit a crime. Return the passport, and no action will be taken. *Per fortuna,* Signor Carmichael has been persuaded not to press charges."

I'll bet he has, I thought. Persuaded by whom? The *Fondazione's* president, a world away in Rome? And who had persuaded *him*? Angus Dance? The Italian government?

When I didn't reply, Anna Maria moved closer to me on the sofa. "Italy is not your country, Signora. You do not understand the situation into which you insert yourself. Illegal immigration is a plague on the *bel paese.*"

So Anna Maria *was* in cahoots with Angus Dance. How else would she know that illegal immigration was involved? But why hadn't he issued that APB?

Then it came to me. Anna Maria's desire to protect the Centro trumped everything, including any orders she might be under from the Italian government. Angus Dance had no idea why I'd stopped showing up down at the Villa Baiardo. *He didn't know the passport was missing.*

My heart leapt. As long as Dance remained in the dark, Lule and Vida had a chance of escape. I'd been right not to call Natalia and tell her to abort. Hastily I arranged my face to hide my elation.

"…and such people will work for little. They take jobs, even as Italians must emigrate to find work. Such people are stealing Italy from our young men and women. In this fashion"—Anna Maria's eyes narrowed and her voice grew bitter—"such people repay the generosity of my country."

I remembered what Nico had said about having to choose between his homeland and his vocation, how sad he'd sounded.

Encouraged by something in my look, which must have softened as I thought of Nico, Anna Maria continued, "And now you yourself have become a thief."

I denied it.

Anna Maria paid no attention. "In this fashion you repay the generosity of the Centro. You become like those you protect. Surely you do not wish to be one of such people?" She leaned back against the cushions and waited, her chin held aloft on the wings of logic.

While we were talking, the morning had turned gray. Now it began to rain, slow, fat drops sliding down the floor-to-ceiling windows. I felt a qualm at what Anna Maria had said: the Centro *had* been generous to me. But Vida and Lule's safety mattered more. I couldn't afford qualms. I needed to make sure Anna Maria kept Dance in ignorance for—I snatched a glance at my watch—the next thirty-two hours.

"If you do not comply, it will go ill for you. For your career. You will leave the Centro in disgrace. You will never again be allowed to enter Italy."

Anna Maria paused and looked at me. I remembered Dmitri Antipov, so suddenly and completely gone.

"On the other hand, if you cooperate, no one will know what has occurred. Nothing will be made public. You will be able to list the Centro fellowship among your professional honors. You will be able to complete the work you have begun here."

"*Mi dispiace.* I cannot return what I do not have."

Anna Maria stiffened, fury lighting her face. We were at a stalemate, and she knew it. Forcing me to return the passport meant exposing me—and that would bring disgrace to the Centro. She rose and pulled on the orange coat, which made her look as if she were upholstered in rust. Standing in front of me, she leaned down so close I could count the hairs sprouting from a mole on her chin.

"*Attenzione*, Signora!" she said softly. "You are walking the edge of the razor."

She withdrew and stalked across the room. At the door to the patio she turned to face me. "We will see how you feel after another day alone."

Anna Maria's visit left me shaken. She'd struck a nerve. Gertrude Bell's question echoed in my head: "Are we the same people when all our surroundings, associations, and acquaintances are changed?" I considered what, since arriving in Italy, I had become. A perpetrator of fraud. A liar. A thief. I thought of Natalia's lost daughter—of the emptiness that must demand to be filled, over and over, every single day since Giulia's death.

Tragedy changes you, and not just emotionally. Morally. The question that remains is whether you are someone who can go to extremes, cross moral boundaries, *do what is necessary*—and not be corrupted. I sighed. This question could as well be asked of me as of Natalia. We were more alike than I'd realized.

OUT—IN—IN DEEPER. IN DEEPEST.

I thought miserably, I don't want to lose my career before I've even reclaimed it. Wasn't there—couldn't there be—some way to salvage both Vida and Lule's future and my own? I went into the study. I would do what I could, even if it seemed hopeless. I'd begun a letter to the *Ministero per i Beni e le Attività Culturali* and was considering how to address such a personage ("Your Honor"? "Your Excellency"? "Esteemed *Signora*"?) when I heard more knocking. I got up and went into the *salotto*.

There on the patio stood Laura, fingertips against the glass, peering in. I opened the door and pulled her inside. Rain dripped from the hood of her yellow slicker. She took it off and let it drop to the floor. Her eyes were dark with fatigue. When we hugged each other I could smell her sweat.

"Come and sit down," I said.

Laura sank into Anna Maria's corner of the sofa, and I took the other. When I offered espresso or juice or water, she shook her head. Raindrops made a steady percussive sound on the windows behind us.

"I thought nobody was supposed to talk to me," I said. "Does Anna Maria know you're here?"

"She sent me."

This was the end, then? Laura had capitulated? I folded my arms to keep from shaking.

"She thinks I can persuade you to give the passport back. She said, mention Amber. That you're putting Amber at risk." Laura dug into the suitcase-sized handbag by her feet. "Anna Maria told everyone you have influenza. Amber begged to come see you, but of course I said no. She asked me to give you this."

She pulled out Amber's green velvet elephant and handed it to me.

"It's bullshit, of course." Laura's words were tough—brave—but her voice trembled. Her hands curved around her plaid-skirted belly like parentheses. "About Amber's safety. All we have to do is go to the Embassy and report the passport lost. They'll give us another one. End of story."

Relief filled me. We were still on. But—

"Laura," I said gently. "You lied to me the other day, didn't you? You *are* pregnant."

"Four months."

So she'd had a secret of her own for the whole length of our friendship. I felt a rush of remorse at the danger I'd drawn her into. I stood up. "I'm going down to the Villa Baiardo right now and tell Anna Maria everything. They can arrest me if they want. Just not you."

"No! Kate, wait." Laura reached up and put a hand on my arm and pulled. I sat down again.

"If I report the passport lost, that protects me. But if I report it before your woman and her daughter use it, they'll be stopped." Laura looked at me. "Arrested?"

I nodded. "And deported."

"How much longer do they need to keep it? The passport?"

"One more day after today. It'll be returned"—I heard myself sounding calm and sure—"the day after tomorrow."

The rain, growing heavier, surrounded us with its muted drumbeat. Laura sat looking down at her lap. I was still holding Amber's elephant, none the worse for its stay under the bushes. Massimo must have groomed it after he'd retrieved it. I sat stroking its ears. Their worn softness felt like home to me. Something nibbled at the edge of my mind, something about Lule; but when I tried to see it, I lost it.

When Laura looked up there were tears in her eyes. Pregnancy hormones, maybe; but also real tenderness. She took a deep breath. "We can't stop now. Not when we're so close."

We.

"Laura! Why on earth would you take a risk like this, when you're expecting another child?"

Laura's lips curved in a near-smile. "That's why."

"I don't understand."

"This baby will be another girl." One hand caressed the barely perceptible mound of her stomach. "Don't you see? I'll have *two* young women to raise. I want them to grow up brave and strong and fierce."

"Are you sure?"

"Absolutely."

"And you can keep Hollis from reporting it lost? He mustn't know why he can't report it. He wouldn't—"

"I *know*, Kate. I know my husband. Don't worry"—her smile widened into a conspiratorial grin—"if I didn't, he wouldn't still *be* my husband."

She let me make her some tea then—chamomile, the same kind she'd given me the day I'd asked her to be my co-conspirator—and we sat for precious minutes drinking and nibbling biscotti. We talked about ordinary things, children and work and plans for Christmas, like ordinary friends. Then Laura got up to go.

At the door to the garden I said, "There's one more thing. If you're willing."

Laura fingers paused on the zipper of her slicker. "What?"

"Actually, two things. There's no internet access up here. I need to know who's the most respected archaeologist in Italy. And I need to know if there were any frescos in the Renaissance painted by women."

She raised her eyebrows. "Why?"

"It's about my painter. I think I might be onto something." As always, I feared arousing Laura's envy. Remembering her hunger for confidences, I said, "We don't have time now. But when I can, I'll tell you the whole story."

"Okay," Laura said, looking only a little doubtful. "I'll go down to the Crypt after lunch and do some research."

"How will you let me know? No one's supposed to come up here—"

Laura touched her index finger to the corner of her eye, the Italian sign for *wily*. "Leave it to me."

It's true that the Renaissance tradition of *buonfresco* was not hospitable to women. Paint could be applied only while the plaster was fresh—*fresco*.

Once a section of wall was plastered, the artist had to work continuously for twenty or so hours, until crystallization set in and the surface would no longer accept paint. The artist didn't sleep. Meals were eaten on the scaffold, which presumably held a chamberpot as well.

But Laura, bless her, had found a Renaissance woman fresco painter. I took her note out of Massimo's dinner basket. Onorata Rodiana, molested by a retainer of the prince whose palace walls she was decorating, stabbed her would-be rapist and had to flee. Disguised as man, she joined a group of mercenaries, and died with a sword in her hand in 1452. And here was something: Onorata Rodiana was a native of Cremona—the town where Sofonisba, a century later, grew up. Laura's note included, as well, the name of Italy's most respected archaeologist and the words, "Good luck to us!"

Initially what I'd felt when Laura insisted on continuing was relief—it was her choice, her free choice—and joy. Now my mind began to racket around a gerbil wheel of worries. Could I rely on Laura to control Hollis? Was Anna Maria's protectiveness of the Centro strong enough to make her keep Angus Dance at bay? Would Natalia's coaching get Lule and Vida through Security?

Work was the best weapon against gerbil mind. The real test for whether an archaeologist had a vocation or not, Daniel used to say, wasn't heat or cold or dirt or snakes or insects—it was whether you could survive the paperwork. I went into the study. My letter to the Minister of Culture filled a sheet of Centro stationery with an Italian as authoritative as I could manage, channeling Caterina. At the recommendation of Professor Giorgio Mencaroni, Dr. habil., I requested that the Ministry authorize a site survey of the cordoned-off part of Bussana Vecchia, specifically the area indicated on the enclosed map. It was likely that artifacts long hidden had been rendered accessible by the 1887 earthquake. These artifacts were now exposed—temporarily—due to the recent record-breaking frost. The matter was, in the opinion of Professor Mencaroni, of the utmost urgency. Very sincerely indeed, Dottoressa Katherine Hagesfeld, Fellow, Centro Studi Internazionali.

The letter, the rough site map, the drawing with Nico's hand, all went into one of the Centro's embossed envelopes. Enclosing the drawing, I hesitated: it revealed that I had partially excavated the site. I could be accused of violating UNESCO's Cultural Heritage Protection Act and the Valetta Treaty, along with *probabilmente* a dozen different Italian laws. Nothing to be done about that, though. I sealed the envelope and addressed it to Sua Eccellenza Giovanna Melandri, Ministero per i Beni e le Attivta` Culturali, via del Collegio Romano 27, Roma 00186. Then I propped it against the desk lamp so I wouldn't forget it when I packed to leave. If they let me pack. If they let me *leave*.

I sat there for a minute, looking at the envelope and thinking about Sofonisba—not the historical figure, but the woman I had come to know. If there was one woman fresco painter, why not two? If in Cremona, why not in Bussana? Sofonisba had had not only perseverance and talent, but something better: she recognized opportunity, however veiled, when it appeared. She knew how to pounce.

Done right, a fresco can last a thousand years.

Night had fallen while I worked. The rain had ceased. Shadows filled the Villa Francesca, and the radiators chimed softly. In the kitchen the overhead light made me flinch. I rummaged in a drawer for some candles and lit them instead. Sitting down at the counter with Massimo's dinner basket, I poured a glass of wine and raised a toast to Laura. Then my aloneness ambushed me. Over my *trenette con pesto* I saw the candle-lit diningroom of the Villa Baiardo with its windows overlooking the Mediterranean; I heard, beneath the Fellows' chatter, the push-pull sound of the sea. I imagined Joshua Brayden describing for the hundredth time his piece for cavaquinho and pygmies. (The pygmies were to wear nothing but LED necklaces that flashed colors corresponding to the dominant chords.) I imagined Thuangthong's serene, silent nodding. I imagined, with a stab of loss, Laura catching my eye and winking—

"*Piccola!* Are you okay?"

I thought I was hallucinating. "Nico?" I whispered.

"*Eccomi!*"

On a wave of chill night air, the shadows beyond the kitchen deepened and took form. Nico's face in candlelight was, at that moment, the most welcome sight in the world. A rush of affection made me mute.

"You are all right, *amore?*" Nico's question lost itself in my hair. His unshaven cheek grazed my ear as his arms went around me. We stood in each other's embrace for a long minute without moving.

When Nico finally let me go, I went to the cupboard and took out another wineglass. We sat at the counter, on the same sides where we'd sat the day we met, and I poured him some wine and refilled my own glass. Nico drank deeply.

"How did you get in?" I said.

"Your door was unlocked. And I used the secret entrance, *certo*. Did you forgot it?"

"Oh, right. Did anyone see you?"

Nico gave me a look.

"Of course they didn't," I said hastily.

He put a hand over mine. "I heard you were sick. But you are not?"

"How did you hear that?"

"I have my sources." His fingers, firm and warm, tightened around mine.

"Nico," I said. "Would you do me a favor? Would you mail a letter for me?"

"*Dipende.* Not if it has anything to with what *Zia* Natalia is up to."

"It doesn't." I could see he didn't believe me. "It's about what we found at Bussana Vecchia, it's to ask the Ministry—"

"*Non importa.* That doesn't matter now. *Carissima,* there is something I must tell you."

He hesitated, looking grave. Candlelight softened the downward lines of his face and made his shaved head shine. I wanted to touch it. I could almost feel its prickly warmth graze my palm.

He said, "*Zia* Natalia is gone."

"Gone? Gone where?"

"That's just it. She left no message. No note, no voicemail. *Niente.*"

My field of vision contracted; all I could see was two bright spears of candlelight. "There must be someone…" My voice seemed to come from a long way off.

"I've asked her neighbors, her former colleagues at Caritas. Her friend Donata."

My first thought was: the passport. If Natalia was incommunicado, how could she get it back from whoever was going to meet Lule and Vida in New York? How could she return it to me? It was only my second thought, I was ashamed to note, that was for Natalia's safety.

"I have a key to her apartment," Nico said, reading my mind. "There was no sign she'd been forced to leave. Nothing out of place or broken. I could not tell if her clothes were missing, or her luggage. But..."

"But?"

"She'd cleaned her refrigerator. It was empty. Her trash had been emptied." He sighed heavily. "She planned to leave. To disappear. And..."

"And?"

"It's not the first time. My aunt has never been a respecter of rules. *Fatta la legge, trovato l'inganno*—that's her motto."

Every law has its loophole. Like aunt, like nephew, I wanted to say. I reached for my glass and swallowed the rest of my wine.

Nico went on, "Ever since I was small, now and then she would vanish, and the family would know she'd been up to something illegal, and then she would return, and nothing would be said. Except that my mother would shake her head and mutter, *Prima o poi, prima o poi.*"

"Sooner or later?"

"Sooner or later you get caught."

I contemplated the wine's jeweled gleam in the candlelight. Did Natalia have it in her, was she ruthless enough to abandon me? Yes—if doing so was necessary to ensure Lule and Vida's safety. I reached for the bottle and splashed more wine into my glass. A few ruby drops scattered across the counter. Nico watched me. I realized he'd figured out, if not everything, at least that I was involved with Natalia in something illegal. Something dangerous.

"So you see, *piccola*, what if the moment of *Zia* Natalia's capture is now? You must get clear of what she has entangled you in. I am here to help you."

I shook my head. "They've confiscated my passport. I can't go anywhere."

He clapped both hands to his head and groaned. "Ah, that aunt of mine. This time she has gone too far! *Disgraziata!*"

I said, "Don't worry, *piccolo*. Please. I promise, just one more day and everything will be fine." Though now, with Natalia's disappearance, I was sure of no such thing.

"Who has your passport? Where is it?"

"It's locked in the office safe, I think."

He thought for a few seconds; then his face lifted. "*Non c'e` problema!* I know a way we can manage. Pack a small bag. We will go now, tonight."

"I can't leave."

The word *leave* reverberated between us. Nico drained his glass and reached for the bottle of wine. "*Ancora?*" I shook my head.

Nico poured and drank, then leaned forward. The trembling light from the candles gave his eyes a wolfish gleam. "I can guess what *Zia* Natalia is up to," he said. "And I'm not the only one. The *clandestini* she shelters—do you think her neighbors do not notice?"

"But you don't think she's been arrested?"

"For now, no. She has went into hiding before they can catch her." Nico slammed his glass down on the counter. He switched to Italian, staccato syllables that hammered at me. "Don't you understand? My aunt has abandoned you."

He was angrier than I'd ever seen him. His eyes burned with fury. "And I'll tell you something else, Caterina. What *Zia* Natalia is doing— what *you* are doing—is not just illegal. It." His hand slapped the counter. "Is." Slap. "Wrong."

"How do you know Natalia left of her own accord? What if the—the Secret Police or whatever you have here—took her away? Would you even know if they did? Does Italy have the writ of *habeas corpus?*"

As if I hadn't spoken, Nico went on, "These people my aunt hides, they are here because my country"—he emphasized the *my*, shutting me out, making me an interloper, which, I realized, I was—"my country invites them. My country offers them refuge. To repay, they abuse my country's generosity by staying on, outside the law."

"I know how hard the employment situation is for young Italians, for you—"

"Caterina. The problem is not jobs these people take. That is an American idea, typical, ungenerous. The problem is that they are joined by other refugees who were never invited, who are smuggled into Italy. The *clandestini* and the *scafisti*, together they make *un mondo ombra*—a shadow world. A world of lies and theft and violence. A poison which Italia has taken into her body unawares and now cannot get rid of."

"Nico, if you could see these women, if you could hear what they've gone through—"

"*Madonna!* Let them apply for legal refugee status, then. Let them ask rather than take. Rather than steal."

Nico fell silent, but his eyes didn't leave mine. The downward lines in his face deepened. I saw him understand that he'd failed to persuade me. He said heavily, "And you, Caterina, if you help them, you are no better."

There was no more to say after that. Nico got up and strode into the *salotto*.

"Wait," I said, following him. "Please. Let me give you the letter—"

"No. Come with me. I'll show you the secret way out. I think you will need it."

Fraying clouds parted to reveal a bosomy moon. Its light seemed to overflow the night sky. The fragrance of wet grass, amplified by rain-washed air, went to my head like the first drag on a cigarette. Instead of crossing the lawn to the villa gate, Nico turned left. I followed him along the side of the villa, squeezing between overgrown juniper and laurel. Darkness swallowed him. Then a splash of yellow light outlined his body a few feet below me. There was a powerful smell of mildew and ancient stone and rot.

"*Attenzione!*" Nico shone his flashlight on the crumbling stone steps between us, then let its beam stab the blackness ahead. The basement of the villa's other half. "You follow this *sentiero*"—I made out the beginnings of a path through rubble piled high on either side—"until it leads you up and out. *Semplice!* You will find yourself on the path going down to the Via Aurelia."

We stood in the damp, spidery air, him looking up, me looking down. The three feet between us might as well have been three miles. In that moment, seeing what I was about to lose, I understood what I'd had. Quicksilver Nico with his irresistible exuberance, his desire lighting my desire like a flame passing from one candle to another—he'd *opened* me. My body wanted to fling itself toward him, the way a bean plant seeks its beanpole.

After Nico vanished into the black maw of the Villa Francesca's unrestored half, I went inside and packed up Massimo's dinner basket and took it out to the patio. When I set it down there was something on the flagstones beside it. As my fingers released the straw handle, I saw a plump gray shape like a pouch. I jumped back. The rat lay still. Dead, I thought; it must be dead. I didn't stay to investigate. I left the basket and ran.

Inside, I went to the bedroom window. Nico was already out of sight. Looking down at the path where I'd so often watched him leave, I thought how we hadn't made love—too caught up in arguing and anger—which meant that the night in Bussana Vecchia would forever be our final time together. I opened the window and leaned out, feeling the cold slap my cheeks, breathing in the disinfectant scent of pine. One more day—I thought—less than twenty-four hours, and Vida and Lule are safe. Then it hit me. What was the point of a countdown? What was the point of my resistance, of the risk I was taking, the risk Laura was taking? Natalia had clearly, as the saying goes, hung me out to dry. She had her reasons, of that I was sure. What I didn't know was whether the whole project had been abandoned, or just expendable me. Would Lule and Vida still go to the airport at dawn tomorrow? Even if they did—even if they made it to the States—how could Laura's passport be returned to me without Natalia's help?

I had been so proud of my new Caterina-self. So glorying in action, in agency. And all the time I was someone's puppet. Freedom? I'd been as constricted by Natalia's machinations as I'd ever been by MS. More so—because with Natalia I'd been unaware of my captivity.

The night air invading the room seemed to drag darkness in with it. What now? I could follow Natalia's plan, keeping silent and waiting and hoping that somehow Lule and Vida could still escape. Or I could cave in to Anna Maria, salvage my professional reputation, and honor my obligation to Sofonisba—to archaeology. "The find of a lifetime," I said out loud. From high in the umbrella pines an owl sent back a wistful echo. *Lifetime….Lifetime.*

One course of action betrayed my work; the other betrayed two people. Three, if you counted Laura. Both courses of action of action were wrong, and both were right. A dilemma beyond even Grandma Eva's eclectic wisdom. Despair washed over me. I had never, not even in the darkest days of Daniel, felt so forsaken. Daniel had been, to the end, the one person in the world who could make me feel not alone. If only he were here, I thought. Even the way he was those last few months, lying flat in the bed, his left hand—the only part of him he could still move—lifting an inch to greet me. Just *here.*

You don't mean that, Daniel said.

We were standing in the bedroom of the apartment in Pristina, the three feet between us an uncrossable gulf. Outside the windows an unexpected April snow spiraled down in the light from the streetlamps. Martial law had just been declared. The streets were empty except for armed troops.

I do mean it. Kosovo is a police state now. You and Sara are breaking I don't know how many laws.

Sometimes the wrong thing is the right thing. Some mistakes we would always regret not making.

Daniel, for God's sake! Don't you see? Sara picked you because you're so…fucking…*optimistic.* Even MS hasn't made a dent.

Daniel's face went white. I saw him, with tremendous effort, pull himself back from anger. He stepped close to me and took my hands away from my face and held them.

Katy; Katy. I'll be as careful as I can—preternaturally careful—but I'm going to help her. I *need* to help her. If I can't take a risk for something I believe in, MS wins.

I fell onto the bed and lay there, clutching the slippery satin comforter and seeing, at last really seeing, what I had lost.

Not the damaged Daniel, whom death had at last released. Not even the Daniel he had been before MS. No—what I'd lost was the Daniel that, alive, he didn't get to keep on being. The twenty good years he should have had. Ghost decades of a Daniel sated with sun and sex, gazing up through green summer leaves; splashing into the sea; recording the day's dig by lamplight; climbing into our camp bed his warm hands the tickle of his breath *Katy? You awake?*

My wise and foolish, selfish, generous husband. Whose life, if it had had to end, should have gone in a burst of fireworks, spinning out joy and optimism and promises and mistakes. *He wasn't* easy, Rae had said, *but I never doubted how he felt about* us. A great ache spread through me, as if I were black and blue on the inside. I wanted to turn in my dear difficult husband's arms and put my mouth against his neck and tell him, *Something terrible has happened. You died.*

A sound filled the room, soft at first then growing louder—bleak and insistent. Desolate.

The sound of weeping.

17

I almost couldn't bring myself to leave the night's star-strewn clarity. My whole body pulled back. I gripped the string bag slung over my shoulder—an apple, a thermos of coffee, and Amber's elephant, matted and damp with tears—and forced my feet to move. Slowly I felt my way down the steps into the ruined half of the villa. At the bottom I turned on my flashlight. I'd been afraid to leave the Villa Francesca in the usual way, in case anyone was keeping an eye on the gate. For the same reason, I hadn't wanted to show a light until I was hidden from view.

My tears for Daniel had taken me over with the scouring force of Liguria's storms. For a year I'd been afraid that once I started to cry, I'd break apart. Instead, when at last the tears ceased, something inside me seemed to expand. I slept. I woke at three in the morning with my arms around Amber's elephant and my vision clear. I gathered the things I would need, and left.

Beyond the flashlight's beam blackness was absolute. I crept forward along my yellow lifeline. Cobwebs brushed my face. Somewhere water dripped, a slow ticking sound. The smell of dirt—not the fresh-turned earth of a dig, but ancient and tamped down—narrowed the breath in my throat. I tried to guess how far ahead the opening onto the path would be. Assuming this part of the villa was the same size as my apartment, and remembering the spot on the path where I'd seen Nico emerge, I figured about fifty feet. So far I'd traveled maybe ten.

The passage narrowed. Rough stone bit my ankles, gouged my hips. Cave smells crowded close, ancient exhalations like dinosaur breath. The passage turned. More turns, my flashlight bouncing. A scuffling sound up ahead. I froze, listening. Too small to be human. I moved forward. The scuffling sounded closer. I thought of the pouch on the patio. Then I remembered how at Vlashnje we'd always taken a Colman lantern on night trips to the privy, because nocturnal creatures avoid light. Relief swept through me. Rats would not approach as long as I had the flashlight.

And then, abruptly, I didn't have it. Without even a warning flicker, light vanished. Blackness like a stifling blanket. I thumbed the switch back and forth, shaking, the cylinder knocking against a rock. Sweat sprang out on my forehead and pooled under my arms. I took a step forward, stumbled, fell. On my knees, I fought for balance. Images flashed through my mind. Daniel sliding aerograms into the diplomatic pouch; Gertrude Bell in the desert; Vida on the trek to Montenegro, holding out her arms for baby Ardi.

Dandelion puffs. I made myself breathe: in, out, quick, deep. I clutched at cold, slimy rock, pulled myself up. I stretched my arms out in front of me. Just ahead was a dot of light. A firefly? No—my watch. Not enough to see by; but enough to comfort. The world of light and air was behind me, lost, not to be thought of. *This* was the world now: doubt and blackness. My ears filled with the harsh sound of my own breathing. Forward—don't stop—forward. *Forward.* My heart like a fist punching me from the inside. Something soft and warm brushed my outstretched fingers. I jumped back, banged my thigh on a sharp outcropping. My "Shit!" ruptured the silence. I stood still, shivering. A drop of something struck my forehead. *Don't think of bats.* I shuffled forward.

There, just ahead of my watch's gleam. Was darkness bleeding into lesser darkness? My foot struck something hard. I stumbled. My elbows landed on a ledge. A step? More steps, ascending. On hands and knees I crawled upward.

A breeze of indescribable freshness; cold that was alive and stinging. When I stood up and threw back my head, the stars poured into me. Cold and bruised and damp, but feeling as if I'd just downed a glass of champagne, I looked up the path. The lights were always turned off after midnight. I didn't expect to see anyone. My watch said almost four. Who would be that obsessive? Then a shadow shifted in the well of deeper shadows. I swallowed a scream. A cat flowed down the wall and streaked across the path.

Relieved, I was about to turn and start downhill, when a familiar odor reached me, faint but unmistakable. The smell of burning electrical wire. My stomach lurched. *Chill!* I said to myself, in Rae's voice. *Don't wig!* I stood still and waited. The night was suddenly full of sound: wind rifling the trees, an owl's spectral call. After what seemed like several minutes—I didn't dare move my arm to look at my watch—I heard a soft cough. Higher up the path, across from the Villa Francesca's gate, something shifted in the blackness.

My heart was beating so hard I was afraid Angus Dance would hear it. He hadn't seen me. A blessing that my flashlight had failed; its beam emerging from the ruins would have given me away. I couldn't stay here— sooner or later he would notice something, some tiny sound or movement. I would have to risk it. Gamble that he had his back to me, his eyes fixed on the villa gate. Grateful for my rubber soles, I stepped to the edge of the path. I began to creep, shadow to shadow, down the hill toward the Via Aurelia.

The flags atop Aeroporto Cristoforo Colombo snapped with military precision in the cold breeze. Beneath them the contradictory chaos of construction was everywhere, cranes and backhoes and upturned earth and heaps of gravel outlined in light from the sodium fixtures outside the terminal. I thought of the Builder of Airports, of my arrival in Genoa two-and-a-half months ago. How different everything was now. How different *I* was.

I made myself as inconspicuous as I could, standing against the terminal wall by a tanklike machine with tires almost as tall as I was. The air smelled of jet exhaust—the perfume of travel, Daniel used to call it—and earth and cinders. I thrust my cold hands into the pockets of my Caterina jacket. My watch said 4:45. Lule and Vida's flight—the first flight of the day—was scheduled to leave at 6:00. As early as it was, a few people were already entering the terminal. I kept my eyes on the lozenges of light cast by the entry doors. Amber's elephant was tucked under my arm.

After my adrenaline-fueled run along the Via Aurelia—by a miracle Soccorso had an all-night taxi stand outside the train station—now, finally, I had time to think. No one had followed me here. I'd watched out the back of the taxi during the half-hour drive from Soccorso, looked all around as I got out. My plan was to find Lule and Vida, put the elephant into Lule's arms, then disappear. If their passport was questioned, the green velvet elephant, I was sure, would be the clincher. Mother, daughter, *and* elephant—who could doubt that the passport's bearer was its true owner?

If they came.

The pre-dawn chill seemed to reach into my bones. I turned up the collar of my jacket. A young man in a blue airport uniform brought an empty wheelchair out of the terminal and parked it. I shrank back. The young man lit a cigarette and stood tapping his foot. When the breeze carried the smoke in my direction I breathed in its heady fragrance. I waited, watching the fitful orange glow of his cigarette.

It felt weird to be lurking. No doubt what spies spent a lot of their time doing. Angus Dance's daffy idea that Daniel had been CIA came back to me. I uncapped my thermos and took several swigs of steaming coffee. Well, I thought, archaeologists *are* a species of spy. We infiltrate the past and expose its secrets. Gertrude Bell had actually worked with British intelligence in Cairo during World War II. In a letter home she wrote, "Better to journey over earth and sky than to sit upon a column all your days." And I? What had I done with my life so far? It was true, as the bureaucrats at the Ministry of Culture had intimated, that I had no standing in my field. That was the trade I'd made: my work in exchange for Daniel's work; my life for his. But Daniel no longer needed me. I'd sat upon a column long enough.

My watch said 5:00. I capped my thermos and put it in my bag. The young man beside the wheelchair threw down his cigarette and ground it under his heel. A thickening stream of passengers on their way into the terminal eddied around him. I strained to see each one, watching, watching. 5:15. Vida's calling it awfully close, I thought, even if she does want to minimize the time they hang around. The passengers flocking into the terminal chattered and laughed, as lively as if it were high noon. Above them palm trees streamed in the wind. How beautifully they bend, I thought; how gracefully they give. If only people were as wise as trees, I imagined Nico saying.

5:30. They weren't coming. They'd been caught or, with luck, had gone into hiding. Desolation swept over me, followed by fury. Natalia might have abandoned Lule and Vida; I had not. I had chosen people over principles. I'd given up the find of a lifetime. A bitter mealy taste filled my mouth. I sank to the ground and threw up onto a pile of gravel. Straightening, trying to still my retching, I wiped a strand of liquid from my chin and pushed my hair back. Amber's elephant went into my bag. I got to my feet and looked toward the terminal entrance to make sure the last few straggling passengers hadn't noticed me.

It was Lule I saw first, her hair a black aureole in the gassy light. Vida was holding her hand. Relief flooded through me in a stinging rush. But they were walking away from the terminal entrance, not toward it. I didn't stop to think why. I scrambled to my feet and ran.

They didn't hear me approach. I grabbed Vida's shoulder. She whirled around, thrusting Lule behind her. In the same motion, her arm came up and struck me hard across the windpipe. I staggered.

"Mamma! *La Signora!*"

"Sh!"

I wrapped my arms around myself and bent over, gasping. *Breathe.* Blackness came and went across my field of vision. *Breathe.* My fault. I should have remembered: no creeping up.

Slowly I straightened. Vida must have been surprised to see me, but she didn't show it. She didn't say a word, just pulled Lule close. Her hair was now dark-blond, like mine and Laura's, and cut so that it fell just to her shoulders. And clean. Lule smiled up at me. With her bronzed face, its frame of black hair teased into wildness, she made a credible Amber.

I reached into my bag for the elephant and held it out.

Vida shook her head.

"Please," I managed, the word burning my bruised throat. It was so cold that my breath hung in the air between us. "It will be all right." Though of course I knew no such thing.

Vida hesitated, her eyes flicking from the elephant to me and back to the elephant. I saw her decide to trust me. She pounced on the elephant and thrust it at Lule. With Vida's arm around Lule's shoulders, they walked quickly into the terminal.

My plan had been to leave the airport at this point, to minimize the risk my presence created for Lule and Vida. I couldn't make myself do it. I needed to see them leave.

I took a beret out of my pocket and tucked all my hair inside and pulled it down over my forehead. Walking toward the terminal entrance, I saw the still-empty wheelchair. I looked around. The young man was nowhere in sight. *Once a thief*, I thought briskly. No time to brush off the sequins of ash that carpeted the seat. Heart pounding—strange how fear and excitement feel the same—I sat down and began to wheel myself into the airport. Wheelchairs were one thing I knew about. I tooled along, careful not to go too fast. Just as I'd thought, the chair made me less conspicuous, not more. As they had with Daniel, people looked away, their glances—embarrassed for their own good fortune—taking in only the chair, bouncing off the actual person.

Inside the terminal the atmosphere was the usual airport mix of weariness, nervousness, elation. Twenty-five minutes to takeoff, and no sign of a line for a security check. The waiting area was ringed with red metal chairs and, in the corners, shuttered kiosks marked BAR SNACK, *TABACCHERIA*, ITALIAN NAVY GEAR. In the center a staircase led up to an unused gallery. The staircase was walled in so you couldn't see around it. People perched on the red chairs or leaned against red-painted columns or stood in line at long red counters. I wheeled myself into a corner sheltered by a ficus in a huge pot. I watched Vida check in, then find seats near a couple with a pink-jacketed, striving baby. A man rolled a bucket and mop across the floor.

Suddenly, at some imperceptible signal, everyone got up and walked around behind the staircase. I followed, hugging the wall. My eyes swept back and forth over the line of passengers that zigzagged between ropes toward the security guard's podium. Where were they? Oh, there. Behind a pair of blue-jeaned lovers, arms twined around each other, who shuffled sleepily forward. Lule and Vida, dressed in drab, attention-deflecting colors, were hard to keep in view as the line snaked along. Behind them was a woman in a shawl the color of marigolds. My eyes followed that. Vida carried herself stiffly, holding tight to Lule's hand. I reminded myself that everyone in an airport security line is tense, everyone looks vaguely guilty. It was obvious they were foreigners—the Italians were all talking and gesturing. Behind me the snack bar's grill rose with a clatter. Several people left the line to get coffee.

A pair of *poliziotti* passed me, chatting and genial, the butt of the nearer one's gun at the level of my shoulder, so close I could have grabbed it. I kept an anxious eye on them until they strolled into the snack bar, then went back to watching the security line. My eyes found the marigold shawl, a few places from the head of the line. Vida tightened the dun-colored scarf she wore around her throat to uphold her claim to laryngitis. Lule pointed at something, and Vida pulled her arm down. The line moved, and the two of them stepped forward; Vida's hand hovered at Lule's shoulder blades but didn't touch her. Lule moved on her own, her back as straight as her mother's. I thought of all that she—they— had already endured. Vida had been one of the beautiful ones. Unspeakable things must have been done to her. I thought of Lule's unchildlike self-possession, so like Rachel's as she'd watched her father's slow destruction. But Lule was encouraged to remember; Lule tamed the past with her drawings.

And in that moment I saw. It is devastating when you can't protect your child from knowing there are things worse than death. But never to speak of what she's seen? *A sorrow shared is a sorrow halved.* I hadn't understood Grandma Eva's saying, I saw now. I'd worried about loading my own sorrow onto Rae; I hadn't thought I might be relieving her of hers. Not speaking leaves your child all alone with her terrible knowledge. I saw that what Vida had done for *her* daughter, I had not done for mine. Was it too late? Would Rae—

"*Posso aiutarLa, figliuola?*" Can I help you, dearie?

I looked up into the inquiring face of a policeman. Fear throbbed in my bruised throat.

"*Tutto va bene?*" the policeman persisted. He was very tall and had to bend almost in half to bring his face close to mine. "Do you need help? Where is your baggage?"

"*Grazie,*" I said, finding my voice. It hurt to speak. "*Tutto va bene.*" My bags were with with my husband, I added, who... I shrugged shyly.

The policeman nodded. "*Ah! Si`, si`. Il bagno.*" The restroom.

When he'd left to join his colleagues in the snack bar, I scanned the line. My heart was beating hard enough to make my vision waver. Had they already gone through, or, oh God, had they been—

Vida stood erect as the mustached guard took their boarding passes and passport, flipping through the pages. Her arms were folded, and I imagined her hands clenched into fists. It occurred to me that I had no idea what had made her turn away from the terminal at the last minute. What if something about the borrowed passport was wrong? The guard looked up at Vida, then down at Lule, then up at Vida again. I realized I was leaning out of the wheelchair in a noticeably unhandicapped way, and made myself sink back. Vida's hand gripped her daughter's shoulder. She bent down to whisper in her ear. Lule lifted the green velvet elephant and sat it on her head. Laughing, the guard held up his hand, palm outward, making a circle of thumb and forefinger. Then his stamp came down.

I didn't know I'd been holding my breath until it poured out. It seared my throat where Vida had landed her blow. I let go of the wheelchair's arms, their rubber padding slick with sweat. Beyond the guard's podium now, Lule and Vida walked toward a high white partition. The red sign above it read *SALE D'IMBARCO*. Just before they passed out of view, Vida turned to look back. An instant, a half-heartbeat—but I could have sworn she smiled. Then they were gone.

My heart slowed. I spun around and wheeled myself with suitable stateliness back across the bright, noisy terminal and out into the morning. Around the corner of the building, behind a crane, I stopped and stood up. My legs buckled. I had to sit down again. I was trembling. Taking deep breaths of cold dawn air, I pulled off my beret and shook my hair free. Then I levered myself up out of the wheelchair and began to walk toward the Volabus stop, trying to look as if I'd just seen friends off on a holiday, loose-limbed and light.

I had to stay away from the Centro for the day. I couldn't risk being seen re-entering the Villa Francesca. If Angus Dance knew I'd been out in the night, it would arouse suspicion; he might manage to bully Anna Maria into revealing the truth. Once he knew a passport was missing, the game would be up. But if I stayed away, my absence would go unnoticed, assuming Anna Maria kept her promise to leave me in solitary confinement for the day. I calmed myself with calculations. Lule and Vida's plane was scheduled to arrive in New York at 1:30 in the afternoon—7:30 in the evening here. Add another hour and a half—no, two hours—to clear customs (Natalia's "associates," I assumed, would make that go smoothly) and be spirited away into the city. That made it 9:30 here. Everyone at the Centro would be at dinner. I'd return—via the secret passage—under cover of night. Even if I was caught, Lule and Vida would be safe by then.

I leaned back against the Volabus's bony headrest and closed my eyes. Beneath my anxiety about today's outcome stirred a deeper fear. I had failed Rae. Silence isn't protection. Speaking the truth is the only shield there is. Had this knowledge come too late?

The Volabus stopped at Brignole Station. I found a telephone kiosk and bought a phone card at the *tabaccheria* next door. One a. m. in Rhode Island—surely Rae would be home. Wouldn't she have to answer, at this hour? The brusque ringing, on and on, matched the speed of my heart. Finally Rae's voicemail picked up. *You've reached 401/351-1181. Leave your number and I'll reach you back.* What I had to say needed to be said voice-to-voice, if not face-to-face. I mumbled, "Hi, Fruffle" and "I'm sorry. I'm so sorry. Please call me." If Rae called back, the Villa Francesca phone would go to voicemail; I wouldn't get her message until tonight. I tried twice more, but Rae didn't pick up. Bitterly disappointed, I went to find the platform for the train to Santa Margherita.

Thirteen hours till I could return to the Villa Francesca. I would force myself to act like an ordinary tourist. I'd go to Portofino, the romantic fishing village Nico had planned to take me to. At 7:15, waiting on the platform at Brignole, I thought: Now they're in mid-air. At 8:00, boarding a bus in Santa Margherita: Now they've landed in Rome. At 9:00, looking out at Portofino harbor over breakfast: Now their plane is taxiing down the runway and taking off for New York. I couldn't eat the *cornetto* I'd ordered. My bruised throat hurt when I chewed. I had yogurt instead—savoring the bright sourness that makes Italian yogurt feel closer to the cow—and fresh orange juice. Two double espressos infused me with optimism. It seemed as if things really might belong to the people who want them most.

Daniel had sent and received letters for Sara through the diplomatic pouch until early June, when all foreigners were forced to leave Kosovo. He wasn't caught. But the following year two exacerbations of MS in quick succession put him in a wheelchair; he never returned to the dig at Vlashnje. For a year and a half we heard nothing, though Daniel wrote several times to Sara care of the university. Then came a letter postmarked Jerusalem. *You saved my life*, she wrote. *Thank you from my heart, Zotëri Profesor.* Enclosed was a snapshot of a small boy in a yarmulke squinting into the sun. He looked like someone who would take to the dirt.

I spent the morning trying to be distracted by Portofino's pastel houses garlanded with drying laundry, its smells of baking bread and fish and salt air, its seafront under a cloud-paved sky. Maybe because the day was gray, there was hardly anyone in the streets: a boy in a shirt too thin for winter kicked a soccer ball; a bicyclist ambled past; a woman crooned into her cellphone, *"Ah...figurati! Dai!"* At the water's edge I counted the brightly painted boats, mastless for winter, their canvas sails spread flat as coverlets. Farther out to sea the yachts of the wealthy lounged imposingly. I walked along the *piazzetta* until I came to a place that sold flashlight batteries. The soft-voiced, smiling proprietress showed me souvenirs as well, and I found myself debating trip presents as if my return from this trip were assured. A hand-painted ceramic bracelet for Rae; a Pinocchio puppet for Janet. "And for you, Signora?" the woman asked. "You must take away something of Italy, so that you will return." I didn't say that I would never be allowed back into her country. I let her choose for me—a cobwebby moss-green shawl ("Like your eyes, Signora")—and left.

11:30. Their plane was somewhere over the Atlantic.

Ten hours still to get through. I'd had maybe three hours' sleep the night before, and I was feeling it. I stopped to drink an espresso standing up, one foot on the rail along the bar, like the Italians. Then I walked out onto a jetty that stretched into the gray-green sea and turned and walked back. A roller-skater about Lule's age made lavish figure eight's, her younger brother trailing her on his miniature bike. Behind them the village stretched uphill from the sea, houses dwindling into deep woods. My eyelids kept sinking. It would take more than espresso to keep me awake. I decide to hike through those woods to the Abbey of San Fruttuoso. Its namesake—Saint Fruitful—was the patron saint of botanists, according to Nico. He'd planned a hike there, two hours or so over a trail that crossed the Portofino Peninsula. I would do it by myself. There was a ferry back here from the Abbey. By the time my bus from Portofino arrived in Soccorso, Lule and Vida would be safe. I didn't let myself think: Or not.

Hiking alone on an unfamiliar trail wasn't something the old Kate would ever have attempted. The new Kate returned to the café where I'd had breakfast and bought olive-studded cheese focaccia, clementines, and a half-bottle of white wine. "*Una fame da lupo*," the round-faced man behind the counter said admiringly. Hungry as a wolf. He gave me the ferry schedule and directions to the trailhead. Slinging my bag, heavy with my various purchases, over one shoulder, I set out.

Up the steps, a gray-and-white cat flashing across my path; past a church; through the gate meant to keep out wild boar. At first the path uphill wasn't hard: shallow steps paved with brick or stone, hundreds of them, with a high stone wall on one side and on the other a view of terraced hills with vineyards and olive groves. A man pushing a wheelbarrow on treads like a tractor passed me coming down. The noise of a *moto* sounded behind me. I jumped aside to watch it pass, roaring straight up the steps. Now and then an iron-gated opening in the wall hinted at a house. The steps, worn though they were, wouldn't have been here in the sixteenth century. But the trail could have been, I thought. The view was. Hard to imagine Sofonisba hiking, though, in her corset and skirt and overskirt, her high-heeled cork pattens.

After half an hour I came to where the trail split. I took the branch marked "*SAN FRUTTUOSO, 1 ORA*." This trail was dirt, not paved. It led into woods full of the nutty scent of fallen leaves. The terrain reminded me of the *entroterra* above the Villa Francesca, that afternoon when a drunken Laura had appeared out of the shrubbery. I wondered how she was doing. Could she hold firm against Hollis, against Anna Maria, for the next (a glance at my watch) seven hours? The rocky path veered uphill and down, requiring concentration, which calmed me. Now and then the woods disclosed a flash of sky and sea. I thought, This is my last *passeggiata*. My last walk along steep Ligurian cliffs above a sea whose colors change as suddenly as Nico's moods. I swung along between unfamiliar bushes that Nico would've named, dry leaves crunching under my feet. I took deep breaths of sea-scented air. By the time the trail leveled off and the woods dropped away, my watch said two-thirty.

Their plane was somewhere over the Atlantic. Seven hours to go.

The cliff curved. Far below me, at the edge of the wind-roughened sea, San Fruttuoso's bell tower came into view. A tall octagon of pale stone, it kept watch over the abbey cloisters. Around them stood a circle of olive trees tortured by the wind into prayerful shapes. My body felt light and insubstantial from having been in motion so long, as if it might take off like a kite in the chilly breeze. I sat down on a large, flat rock. According to Nico, the abbey was built on the spot where followers of Saint Fruitful had been rescued from shipwreck by three lions. Studying it made me think about crime and punishment—and escape from punishment. Even if Lule and Vida made it to safety, there was still the matter of the missing passport.

Seagulls circling complainingly overhead. Suddenly aware of being hungry and thirsty, I got out my lunch. The focaccia—still warm in its cocoon of tinfoil—was delicious, though it hurt to swallow. The wine tasted of apricots. While I ate, the clouds thinned and disclosed the sun, spreading a wash of gold over everything. When I'd finished I leaned back on my elbows. Yawns welled up, one after another. San Fruttuoso's bell unspooled three notes into the stillness. 3:00. Two hours till the last ferry, which left at sunset. I felt I should stay awake, stay vigilant—as if my open eyes were all that was keeping Lule and Vida's plane in the air. But I was tired, so tired. Surely I'd done all I could? I remembered a lullaby Grandma Eva used to sing to Janet and me.

If you stop one heart from breaking,
Cool one pain,
If you ease one soul from aching,
You've not lived in vain

My watch didn't have an alarm, but I had my internal one. I put the crushed tinfoil and empty bottle back in my bag. I shook out the moss-green shawl and spread it on the ground over a pelt of pine needles. Then I lay down with my hair for a pillow, curled on my side, and faced the sea. So tired. The last thing I saw was the abbey. It sat serenely in the afternoon light, a testament to miracles.

18

No one saw me return to the Villa Francesca. I slipped in through the ruined half of the building, armed this time with a trustworthy flashlight. There was nothing to suggest my absence had been noticed. I'd forgotten to worry about Massimo. Bless him, he must have returned the day's three baskets to the kitchen without mentioning that they hadn't been touched. The first thing I did was check my voicemail. Nothing. I called Rae, my heart high in my throat. No answer. I left the same message as before, then hung up, feeling wretched. Was I too late? Had my daughter given up on me?

I spent a miserable night in the too-big bed, getting up now and then to replace the ice inside a long wool sock I wore tied around my throat. The mark of Vida's blow had blossomed like an iris; it throbbed whenever I swallowed. The phone sat on the pillow next to mine so I'd be sure to hear it. I kept falling into a neon doze. Each time the same question jerked me awake. My eyes roamed the Pope's mistress's bedroom, traveling from the lamp veined along its mended fracture up to the corners empty now of Ceiling-Katherine and back across the bed to the phone. Had Lule and Vida made it, or had they been caught? By the time I heard knocking on my French doors I was sure it was the *polizia*.

What's the etiquette when your jailer appears at your door at dawn?

"*Buongiorno, Signora.*" My voice came out a whisper, and even that hurt. I could barely hear myself over the thudding of my heart. Hesitantly, I asked Anna Maria to come in, to sit down.

She stood there, silent, the glass doors behind her open to a world of fog. I saw her pleasure in making me wait.

At last she said, "You are lucky, Signora Hagesfeld. *Fortunatissima*."

In her eyes I saw how much she despised me. I'd never noticed before how small they were—like black raisins. *Disgraziata*! those eyes said.

"Signora Sweeney's passport has been returned."

So Lule and Vida were safe.

"*Grazie*," I managed. It wasn't Anna Maria that I thanked.

The raisin eyes fastened on my neck, wrapped in the ice-filled sock. "Do not ask for a *raccomandazione* from the Centro, Signora Hagesfeld. Do not list it on your resume. You understand? And I have made sure both the *Ministero per i Beni e le Attivita` Culturale* and the European Association of Archaeologists know that you are unworthy of trust."

It was the lightest retribution I could have expected. Relief swept through me, making my whole body shake. I grabbed the doorframe to keep from falling.

Anna Maria set down the suitcase she was carrying, a small, ancient-looking blue one shaped like a doctor's Gladstone bag. It wobbled and fell over.

"*Boh*! This was left for you outside my office this morning, with the passport. Whoever brought them must have come in the night." She didn't sound as if the intrusion puzzled her. I wondered why not. Did she know, or guess, who the visitor was?

She turned to go. "Your flight departs at 1:30," she said, with her back to me. "We leave at noon. Be ready."

This time Rae didn't let my call go to voicemail.

"Mom! Is everything okay?" It was two in the morning in Rhode Island.

"Fruffle!" My voice emerged hoarse and low, though the pain in my windpipe had subsided to a dull ache. "I'm so sorry I woke you. Listen, I need to talk to you. I mean really talk."

"You sound weird. What's up?"

"I'm coming home early. Can we talk then?"

"When do you get in?"

"Today, actually. Well, it'll be tonight by the time I get there."

I waited for Rae to ask why. But my practical daughter responded to the distress in my voice with practical comfort. "What time? I'll meet your plane."

My heart rose. She sounded almost like the old Rachel. "I don't know. I'm… I don't know the connecting flight from Rome. I'll probably get into Logan around dinnertime."

"I'll figure it out. Whenever you get in, I'll be hangin'. Hey, did you see Janet's email? So rad, you both coming home the same day."

House arrest had meant no going to the Crypt to check email. A wave of relief washed through me: Janet was safe.

Rae said, "Okay, then. I'm gonna grab a few more winks. See you tonight."

"Rae—"

"Don't wig, Mom, okay?"

"Rae, wait!"

"Everything'll be all right. Just come home safe."

There was one thing I couldn't leave for later. "I just… I wanted to tell you…"

Rae waited. The five thousand miles between us made a sound like the ocean rising. I knew I must not, for one more moment, leave my daughter alone with her grief. But all the months of silence clogged my throat. It was as hard to say the next words as it had been, a year ago, to say, *Daddy just died.*

"I miss him."

There was a long pause. Then Rae breathed out—a quick, fierce puff. A million tiny winged seeds flew through the miles of fiber-optic cable.

"Me, too. Oh, Mom. Me, too!"

Three hours to clear out of the Villa Francesca forever. I got busy packing. I set aside my clothes for the plane: turquoise sweater and black cords,

Caterina jacket, moss-green shawl to wrap around my neck to hide the bruise. I cleared the closet and drawers and bathroom shelf. While I worked I thought happily of Rae, of the warmth in her voice at the end of our call. I was folding the last few things and laying them in my suitcase when it hit me.

What if I'd been caught, convicted, jailed? Rae, who'd already lost one parent, would have lost the other. *Fortunatissima*, Anna Maria had called me. She was right. It stopped my breath to think how close I'd come to leaving Rae truly alone. The risk Daniel had taken for Sara had been much less. Why hadn't I seen that till now? I'd acted on instinct, rushing in to follow my heart without stopping to use my head. I thought about the moment when I would Rae what I'd done. She was her father's daughter. She'd be surprised, maybe dismayed, but—I hoped; oh, I hoped—proud.

I'd saved the blue bag Anna Maria had brought for last, almost afraid to look inside. It must have been Nico who left the passport and the bag outside Anna Maria's office; but Nico had been so angry when we parted. I undid the brass hasp. Inside was a box wrapped in speckled paper, about the size of a book. I tore off the paper. In the box, wrapped in tissue, were two glasses with a white line circling them halfway up. Above the line,"*Ottimista*"; below it, "*Pessimista.*"

So Natalia was safe. Of course she was. Like Sofonisba, she knew how to pounce.

I could not honestly say Natalia had pressured me. She'd simply put in my way opportunities she felt would appeal to me. *Our weaknesses are our strengths gone crazy.* So what if I'd been used? Anyway, who was using whom? Couldn't it be said that I had used Natalia—used Vida and Lule—to give me back a sense of purpose? A chance to earn my daughter's respect?

We were alike, Natalia and I. She must have seen this from the beginning.

I returned the two glasses to their nest of tissue. I would treasure them, as she must have known I would. *Ottimista* and *Pessimista*—both at once. I didn't need the glasses to remember that—or any of the other contradictions I'd encountered during my autumn in Italy. Much less the contradictions I'd discovered within myself.

There was something in the bottom of the box, tucked beneath a layer of tissue. A straw broom the size of my palm, decorated with red and yellow plastic flowers and a wooden ladybug. Beneath that was an envelope with my name on it in capitals. I opened it and pulled out a sheet of paper covered with the same square-shouldered writing.

Carissima,

*Zia Natalia has told to me what you did. You are brave
although foolish. I think maybe it is because you have suffer.
Olive growers say this saying: the twisted trees bear the sweetest
fruit.*

*This scacciaguai we give at the feast of Epifania, just after the
New Year. It is to sweep away the guaio of the past and clear a path
forward. Now you will be like the olive tree and change course of
your roots whenever comes an obstacle or a harm.*

*Your trueness to your work makes me see newly. I too leave
Genova. Here is my new address: L.I.N.Z. (International Laboratory
of Plant Neurobiology), via delle Idee, 30, 50019 Firenze. Don't
worry, you have not the last of me. It's coming a big storm of my
emails.*

Zia Natalia makes me copy you this:

*Unto this day it doth myn herte boote
That I have had my world as in my tyme
She says you will understand.
In bocca al lupo, piccola!*

Had Nico written in English as a courtly gesture? Or as a mark of the distance now between us? Still, he wished me luck. You, too, I whispered. And added, as he'd taught me, *Che crepi il lupo!* May the wolf croak!

When I put the letter back, the bristles of the *scacciaguai* pricked my fingers. The Epiphany wasn't until January sixth; Nico must have had it ready to give me before the *fidanzata* returned. My heart gave a painful leap. The swift upward lift of Nico's face, the tennis-ball feel of his head, his perfectly shaped ears—someone else's treasures?

I put the box back in the bag. Shabby as it was, it would be useful as a carry-on. I added the spare underwear and toiletries I should have had with me when I arrived in September. Then I took the bag into the study and put in my notes and computer printouts. The letter to the Minister of Culture made me hesitate—a souvenir of the discovery I would never make, the career I would never have. Anna Maria had made that clear: no one in Italy would listen to me, no one would believe me. As I balanced the envelope on my palm, a thought bounced into my head as if inserted from somewhere outside me.

What if Sofonisba never intended the frescoes to be seen? What if they were the overflowing of an entirely private happiness?

I set the letter to one side. I put *The Long and Adventurous Life* into the blue bag, along with—nefariously, as befitted someone under villa arrest—the copy of e. e. cummings's poetry that belonged to Hollis. As I did so, my bookmark fell out, the card the Builder of Airports had pressed on me when I'd first arrived in Genoa. How long ago that seems, I thought, as I tossed it into the wastebasket. The drawing Lule had given me, with her name staggering along the bottom, I tucked into the bag's inner pocket. Right or wrong, I had had to earn my way back to my daughter by helping someone else's. When Rae saw this drawing, would she understand that? She was her father's daughter; but she was mine, too. It was time she knew it.

In the kitchen I slid the letter to the Ministry of Culture out of its envelope. Skimming it, I had the strangest feeling: as if Sofonisba stood behind my shoulder, reading along with me. The feeling of a presence was so strong that I turned around. Of course there was no one. I held the letter over the sink and flicked the stove-lighter on. For a second I thought of the Ladies of the Field. *They* would have sent this letter; they would have done whatever it took to bring their find to light. I touched the letter to the flame. It caught at once. As it burned, a fragrance pervaded the kitchen, strange but familiar. I thought I recognized the scent of myrrh.

"The doctor said I had a heart break. But as the Signora can see, I am fine like new."

I was on the road to the airport for the second time in two days. On this trip, the driver in the seat in front of me wasn't a *tassista*, but Massimo. His large ears beneath a snug wool cap gave him the silhouette of an upside-down amphora. An iron-faced Anna Maria sat in the backseat beside me, closer than was comfortable. She smelled of garlic. We shot along the Via Aurelia, where the fog was slowly dissipating. I cranked down my window. The wind cooled my face. I breathed in the smell of Italy—sweet and rank, cinders and earth—for the last time.

"—even now I smoke cigars, I drink *vino*," Massimo continued. In fact the interior of the car smelled of both. "Like everybodies. *E` normale!* After all, it is better to be lucky than good."

"Massimo," Anna Maria said, her first word since we'd gotten into the car. "*Prego.* Do not speak to the Signora."

Massimo's right, I thought. If I haven't been good, I *have* been lucky. I did what I needed to do, which I didn't know was what I needed to do until I did it. You have lucky eyes and a high heart, Daniel had said to me when he handed me his trowel that first time.

As if she heard my unrepentant thoughts, Anna Maria sniffed. I turned away and looked out the window. Two lights glimmered up ahead at the side of the road, burning holes in the fog.

"*Guardi, Signora* Hagesfeld," said the irrepressible Massimo. "Look close as we pass."

The lights grew larger, clearer, mist unravelling around them. Their bearers were two old women wrapped in black. They walked slowly but determinedly. They didn't look up as we passed.

Massimo said, half-turning to look at me, "I see these women every day I take this road, without fail."

"Why? Where are they going?" I tried to imagine traversing a whole life—the ups, the downs, the wreckage—with that sure, steady step.

"To the cemetery. Their husbands are buried there, *probabilmente.* Perhaps their children." His tone was matter-of-fact. *Normale.*

Anna Maria clicked her tongue. No fraternizing with the enemy. Massimo fell silent.

Arm in arm, Anna Maria and I picked our way through construction machinery. A cold wind had come up and begun to blow the fog back out to sea. It lay thin and white along the top of the terminal like an old man's hair, a few stray tresses circling the flagpoles. No doubt we looked like any pair of affectionately linked Genovese women, friends or sisters or cousins—only Anna Maria's grip was tight as velcro. We entered the terminal behind two priests, the black skirts of their cassocks swinging. At the counter Anna Maria peeled herself away and stood to one side as I checked in, her raisin eyes not leaving me for a second. Waiting while the clerk telephoned someone—a one-way ticket after 9/11 provoked extra scrutiny—I wondered what cousin had enabled Anna Maria to book a flight on such short notice. A tall, thin man in overalls swirled a mop across the floor, trailed by the smell of vinegar.

When I'd finished, Anna Maria seized my elbow and steered me to a row of red metal chairs in front of the staircase that bisected the terminal. We sat down across from two nuns. The sweeping white wimples that framed their faces made them look ready for takeoff. Was this a religious flight, then? Or were they and the priests (now downing espressos beneath the red BAR SNACK sign) figments of my reproachful imagination? The fragrance of roasting coffee beans made my mouth water and my head pound. I didn't dare ask Anna Maria's permission to get an espresso—or rather, I didn't want to. *Che cazzo!* I was done with asking permission. That was one thing I would take home from this trip, anyway.

Judging by my experience the day before, we had half an hour until the security line formed. It was going to be a long thirty minutes perched beside my unspeaking guardian. I bent to open the blue bag I was using for a carry-on. It fell over. I set it right side up and pulled out *The Long and Adventurous Life.*

I thought of my short and adventurous stay in Italy. Of the people I'd met, whom I'd not been able to say goodbye to. Thuanthong, whose art had braced me when I was afraid. Laura, who'd taken a great risk for two people she'd never met. Amber. Only one person had seen me leave the Centro, standing in the fog by the great iron gates. Too dim to tell who, until Angus Dance stepped into our headlights. *"Avanti!"* Anna Maria had said, and Massimo had swerved and peeled off in a shower of gravel. How maddening it must be for Dance, I thought now. He hadn't caught the American birdwatcher, because there wasn't any. Sent to watch Natalia, he'd seen her growing involvement with me, found out about Daniel's Brown University connection and Yugoslavia—and jumped to conclusions. How would his superiors in MI6 react to an over-imaginative agent who'd slept with his suspect? Would he be *disgraziato*? No, I thought, he'll find a way out. He'll tell his masters that the American woman *was* a spy—she just didn't realize it.

Beside me Anna Maria shifted in her seat. I remembered her calm acceptance of the intruder who'd returned Laura's passport and left the blue bag. Could it be that Anna Maria was somehow in cahoots with Natalia? A double agent? I would never know. In truth, I didn't care.

A sweet-faced young pregnant woman came and sat down across from me, next to the two nuns. Her husband squatted on the floor beside her and stroked her scarlet-coated belly in circles. A loudspeaker coughed importantly, but no words came out. Anna Maria crossed her arms and tucked her hands into the opposite sleeves of her coat, like the nuns. I glanced at her sideways. Now that I thought about it, she reminded me of the nuns in grade school, Sister Mary Cleophas in particular with her long nose and small black eyes. Waiting, she and I, on a bench outside Mother Superior's office to discuss the latest manifestation of my wickedness. At that moment, weirdly, someone started whistling "Ain't Misbehavin'." I looked up to see the cleaner dancing with his mop in the middle of the floor. He caught my eye and waved. Anna Maria clicked her tongue, but she had no authority here, and no one cared.

A knot of men burst through the terminal doors. I heard a stream of Italian, then English with a faint Irish lilt. I turned to look. And there, by one of Daniel's beloved coincidences, was the Builder of Airports. He'd shaved off his beard, but the same bruised-looking bomber jacket swung open over his slope of belly. He stood just inside the doors, flanked by a trio of men in hard hats and yellow padded vests, all talking and gesturing. I must have made some movement, because Anna Maria's hand shot out and gripped my arm. She shook her head. Just as well: when the Builder of Airports turned in our direction, his eyes traveled over me without any sign of recognition.

I wound the moss-green shawl tighter around my neck. My watch said 12:30. How much longer until I could get up and stand in line and shake off my watchdog? I looked down at the book in my hands. From the cover a round-faced, round-eyed Sofonisba looked back at me. I riffled through the pages to find Van Dyck's drawing of her at ninety. I looked from Sofonisba *virgo*—young, untried—to the old woman graceful and upright inside the concealing folds of veil and gown. I thought of the forty-seven-year-old widow midway between the two, whom I had come, so mysteriously, to know. The woman who believed that happiness was a risk worth taking. The woman who knew how to pounce. In the past two-and-a-half months I'd walked where she'd walked, touched what she'd touched, thought—imagined—what she'd thought. But what had I added to the world's understanding of her? What had I actually done?

Now here I was, returning home in disgrace, with no hope of a fulltime teaching job, no possibility of a career in archaeology. Still, if I was honest, I had to ask myself whether that possibility had ever existed. Fostering Daniel's career instead of forging my own: had that really been something forced on me by MS? Wasn't there also the unconscious awareness that I'd never make a real archaeologist? That archaeology wasn't, as Grandma Eva would have said, what I was put on earth (terrible pun) to do? I'd never mastered the unemotional approach to fieldwork that my favorite professor had tried to instill in her students. The restraint to ask only *What is this?* and write up the factual answer and move on. My entanglement with Sofonisba went way beyond that—but, even so, it wasn't where my treasure lay. Or my heart. That was with Lule and Vida, and Bardha and Genta and Ardi. With Janet. With Rae. The living—not the dead.

But if I wasn't an archaeologist, what was I?

A question I couldn't answer—but one that now I could at least see. It wasn't what I'd come to Italy to find, but it was what Italy had given me. *A more beautiful question.* One day, I thought, the answer will appear, looking nothing like what I was expecting. Will I know how to pounce?

Anna Maria nudged me. All around us people were rising, gathering belongings and children, heading for the area behind the staircase. The Builder of Airports high-fived the tallest of the hard-hatted men and joined the stream of passengers. Though he walked right past my row of seats, he didn't see me. Anna Maria got to her feet, pulling me with her. Without a word she relinquished my elbow and stepped away. She must have been surprised when I speeded up to squeeze in line behind the Builder of Airports, beating out a short, stout man haranguing his cell phone. I watched her go and stand in the corner where I'd sat in my wheelchair the day before. Then I faced forward. A security guard settled at the podium under the red *SALE D'IMBARCO* sign, and the line began to move. Herding the blue bag in front of me, I shuffled along. The man behind me shouted bilingual assurances into his cell phone. "*Ti chiamo domani per* sync up! We dialogue!" The optimistic clatter of the terminal, its fluorescent exuberance, the excited chirping of the children—

Always before, Daniel had stood beside me on the threshold of wild travel. This trip, and all my future trips, I would make without him. I missed him differently now. I'd come to Italy in search of a way to live without Daniel, when what I needed was for Daniel to be within me. He would always be part of me; but I was no longer part of him. Now I could remember the well Daniel without betraying the sick one. I could remember him with pleasure as well as sadness.

Up ahead, beyond the security guard's podium and the white partition behind him, I could see a slice of sky. My heart lifted. I couldn't go back to my old life. But that didn't mean I was going back to nothing. Soon I'd see Rachel; we would talk, and we would cry. I'd see Janet, and ask her to forgive me. Right now, though, there was something I wanted to try. I made up my mind. The risks I'd already taken were so much greater than this one.

I put out a hand to touch the shoulder of the man in front of me. The leather of his jacket was cool under my fingers. I started to say, Excuse me; but he was already turning around.

The beginnings of a smile made the skin around his eyes crinkle. He didn't look surprised. So he *had* seen me, before. "Hello! Kate—isn't it? Do you remember me, then?"

"I remember you," I said.

His smile broadened. "Gene O'Casey," he said, and held out his hand.

I hesitated—Anna Maria's scornful gaze burned at the edge of my vision—then I grasped it. The calloused palm was dry and warm, the fingers firm around mine.

I smiled back at him. Words—beautiful, ordinary words—slipped easily off my tongue. "Buy you a cappuccino?"

"Grand, so. But I'm thinking we've not time. And besides"—he jerked his head in the direction of Anna Maria—"what would your handler say?" From nowhere he produced a paper cone of glossy black grapes. "Fancy some of these, instead?"

A large woman in a black kerchief pushed past us. The tide of waiting passengers shifted. The woman was followed by a string of children shoving their way forward. I stumbled into the blue bag, which fell over. Gene O'Casey's hand under my elbow steadied me. He held out the paper cone of grapes. I pulled one, then another, off their stems. The cool globes burst on my tongue, slow and sweet. Gene O'Casey bent down and righted my bag.

"Sure, they still haven't found mine," he said.

ANN HARLEMAN is the author of *Happiness*, which won the Iowa Short Fiction Award, *Bitter Lake, Thoreau's Laundry,* and *The Year She Disappeared.* Among her awards are Guggenheim and Rockefeller fellowships, the Berlin Prize in Literature, the PEN Syndicated Fiction Award, and the O. Henry Award. In an earlier life, Ann was the first woman to earn a Ph.D. in Linguistics from Princeton University, and she has lived and worked in Italy. Having taught for two decades at the Rhode Island School of Design, she is now on the faculty of Brown University. She makes her home within sight of San Francisco Bay.

ELIXIR PRESS TITLES

POETRY

Circassian Girl by Michelle Mitchell-Foust
Imago Mundi by Michelle Mitchell-Foust
Distance From Birth by Tracy Philpot
Original White Animals by Tracy Philpot
Flow Blue by Sarah Kennedy
A Witch's Dictionary by Sarah Kennedy
The Gold Thread by Sarah Kennedy
Rapture by Sarah Kennedy
Monster Zero by Jay Snodgrass
Drag by Duriel E. Harris
Running the Voodoo Down by Jim McGarrah
Assignation at Vanishing Point by Jane Satterfield
Her Familiars by Jane Satterfield
The Jewish Fake Book by Sima Rabinowitz
Recital by Samn Stockwell
Murder Ballads by Jake Adam York
Floating Girl (Angel of War) by Robert Randolph
Puritan Spectacle by Robert Strong
X-testaments by Karen Zealand
Keeping the Tigers Behind Us by Glenn J. Freeman
Bonneville by Jenny Mueller
State Park by Jenny Mueller
Cities of Flesh and the Dead by Diann Blakely
Green Ink Wings by Sherre Myers
Orange Reminds You Of Listening by Kristin Abraham
In What I Have Done & What I Have Failed To Do by Joseph P. Wood
Bray by Paul Gibbons
The Halo Rule by Teresa Leo
Perpetual Care by Katie Cappello
The Raindrop's Gospel: The Trials of St. Jerome and St. Paula by Maurya Simon
Prelude to Air from Water by Sandy Florian
Let Me Open You A Swan by Deborah Bogen
Cargo by Kristin Kelly
Spit by Esther Lee

Rag & Bone by Kathryn Nuerenberger
Kingdom of Throat-stuck Luck by George Kalamaras
Mormon Boy by Seth Brady Tucker
Nostalgia for the Criminal Past by Kathleen Winter
Little Oblivion by Susan Allspaw
Quelled Communiqués by Chloe Joan Lopez
Stupor by David Ray Vance
Curio by John A. Nieves
The Rub by Ariana-Sophia Kartsonis
Visiting Indira Gandhi's Palmist by Kirun Kapur
Freaked by Liz Robbins
Looming by Jennifer Franklin
Flammable Matter by Jacob Victorine
Prayer Book of the Anxious by Josephine Yu
flicker by Lisa Bickmore
Sure Extinction by John Estes
State Park by Jenny Mueller
Selected Proverbs by Michael Cryer
Rise and Fall of the Lesser Sun Gods by Bruce Bond
I will not kick my friends by Kathleen Winter
Barnburner by Erin Hoover
Live from the Mood Board by Candice Reffe

FICTION

How Things Break by Kerala Goodkin
Juju by Judy Moffat
Grass by Sean Aden Lovelace
Hymn of Ash by George Looney
Nine Ten Again by Phil Condon
Memory Sickness by Phong Nguyen
Troglodyte by Tracy DeBrincat
The Loss of All Lost Things by Amina Gautier
The Killer's Dog by Gary Fincke
Everyone Was There by Anthony Varallo
The Wolf Tone by Christy Stillwell